Maxine,

Thoughts are energizing,
Keep them positive.

And keep that great
sence of humor.

Jeanne L. Drouillard

THOUGHTS
CAN BE
MURDER

By

Jeanne L. Drouillard

Argus Enterprises International
North Carolina***New Jersey

Thoughts Can Be Murder © 2009
All rights reserved by
Jeanne L. Drouillard

A-Argus Better Book Publishers, LLC

For information:
A-Argus Better Book Publishers, LLC
Post Office Box 914
Kernersville, North Carolina 27285
www.a-argusbooks.com

ISBN: 978-0-9842596-6-3
ISBN: 0-9842596-6-X

Book Cover designed by Dubya

Printed in the United States of America

DEDICATION

TO THE THINKERS OF THE WORLD

Who Realize That They Are Where They Are Today

Because Of Their Own Thoughts.

JLD

Other Mysteries in the Sammi Evans Series

Thinking Out Loud

Your Thoughts Can Trap You

SPECIAL THANKS TO:

- Vicki Wettach -- whose editing help and insightful critical eye is always   appreciated.

- Maxine McCormack and Vicki Wettach -- who both generously gave me their honest opinions on my theories and ideas. Thanks to the both of you.

- To the gals at Maxima Beauty Salon in Livonia, Michigan -- Peggy Smith, Maryann Furca and Barbara Staszel who always encouraged and delighted me with their enthusiasm and reassurance. I thank you all and so does Sammi Evans.

- Ellen Linville -- Our great steak dinners produced many ideas for me to ponder and utilize. No subject was ever off limits and no theories considered too bizarre. Looking forward to more in the future.

CHAPTER ONE

Samantha Evans Patterson stood in silent shock as she listened to the midday news on TV. *This must be wrong,* she thought; *Oh my God. This has to be a mistake.* She immediately went to the telephone and placed a call to her husband, Detective Dave Patterson.

"Scranton Police Station."

"Is Dave Patterson around? This is his wife."

"No, Ma'am," answered the assistant. "All of the officers are presently in a meeting. Can I have him call you?"

"Yes, please," she said, half in a daze as she put down the receiver.

Again she listened as the TV reporters went over every detail that was presently known. A body had washed up near the Philadelphia shipping docks. The identification wasn't positive yet, but speculation said that it was Terrence Gonzalez, a former policeman who had worked with her husband. He had been convicted of being a mole in the police department, helping in a fraud and money-laundering ring. Terry, as he was called, had been sentenced to four years in prison, but served less than a year as he had given vital information to send known mobster Buzzie Sundrie to jail for murdering a fellow policeman. Terry had only been released slightly less than two months ago.

Remembering Dave saying that Terry had stopped at the police station recently to talk to his former superiors, it was noted that he wanted to go straight. He knew he couldn't be a policeman any longer, and knew the department didn't trust him, but he had been ashamed of what he had done. As a private citizen he hoped to be able to help out in some way.

Sammi, with her unique talent of being able to hear other people's thoughts had spent time around Terry and assured Dave that when he said he was repentant and wanted to do something positive with his life, his thoughts did match his words. He hadn't been given any assignment that she was aware of, so she was surprised that he had been found killed near the docks.

The phone rang, disturbing her thoughts.

"Hi, Sammi, what's up?"

Dave's voice could always calm her down.

"I heard the news about Terry. You already know, right?"

"That's what our meeting was about. We were actually going to start giving him small assignments, after you found out he was sincere. He wasn't on anything official yet, but had heard about something and I think he was trying to find out information. We figured that's what got him killed."

"God, I was so shocked. He just got out of jail."

"And he was pretty lost as to what to do. After you confirmed that he really wanted to do good, we were going to slowly start working with him. Now, he could have been a mole for us and with you around, we could keep a check on him. But somebody got to him fast."

"Did he drown?"

"No, he was shot, execution style, through the back of the head."

"How horrible. This one got to me. I know he was a mole, but ... Are they absolutely sure it's him? I mean, is it a positive I.D.?"

"Afraid so. Hang in there, I'll be home in about an hour. Relax, okay? We'll talk about it later. I've got to go."

* * *

But she couldn't relax. The past year or so had been a whirlwind of arrests and convictions and people were still showing up involved in one way or another. Dave and Sammi worked as a team. He was the detective, but she was the one who could hear people's thoughts and therefore able to pull valuable information from suspects. Strange, but true nevertheless. She could do it since she was a little girl. It was natural to her. She'd simply stand next to someone, concentrate and their thoughts talked to her out loud, like in a real conversation. Her Grandpa Logan could do it, too, but he was the only other one she knew. And he had guided her along helping to keep her gift under control. After he died, she kept everything to herself. It was hard to find anyone she could trust with her secret.

Although she'd known Dave since college, he had dated and married her friend Kelly. The three of them maintained a close friendship and Sammi considered them both best friends. The marriage seemed happy enough at first, but less than five years later, they were both considering splitting up, although they'd hoped to remain friends. But Kelly was at the wrong place at the wrong time and was accidentally killed by a bullet meant for someone else. It took Dave a long time to get over it. After all, he was a policeman and he protected and saved people. But he hadn't been able to save his own wife.

The telephone rang. She had to listen to the sales pitch as her answering machine picked up the call. *Why don't you give us a call if you could use new windows by Downing. We have the sturdiest and yet most flexible windows around. Our sale will be on until the end of this month. Call and save yourself money on new windows.*

She resumed her memories. Throughout his period of mourning, Dave depended on her. They'd always been best friends, but shared a casual platonic-like relationship. For quite a while he dated a lot, mostly in an effort to forget and ease his pain by becoming involved with one after another. Then about two years ago, everything slowly began to change between them. They both took their time, but as their work relationship became more intense, so did their personal life. And six months ago, they'd gotten married. Sammi was happy that she'd married her best friend. And presently only six people in the entire world knew about her special talent, with Dave being the first one she'd told.

When his car pulled into the driveway, she was at the door to meet him. He kissed her and gave her a caring hug upon entering. He always did that.

"Are you feeling better?" he asked.

"I can't quite get over this. How about you?"

"It's strange in a way. We were talking about how angry and disappointed we were with him when we first found out. But he was a talented guy. And we could have used him to get us information. We knew we'd have to watch him, but we've got you, Sammi. You could always tell us if he was playing straight with us."

"I was hoping to get a chance to do that."

"He had called Sergeant Brady last week about something and said he was going to check it out. I didn't get that briefing yet."

"I wonder what he was working on. Did he leave any clues? He did get a light sentence for testifying against Buzzie. Could be someone was angry about that."

"Somehow I don't think so. Our buddy Jim thought it might even be something left over from the kidnappings, but I didn't think he was involved in that."

"Jim thinks so? I never heard anything that suggested those dock crimes and the kidnappings were related, did you?"

"Jim says he's beginning to think everything is related and he may have a point. Anyway, right now, this is another murder to be looked into."

"Is the referee group going to investigate?"

She saw him look over and smile. Jim, Tom and himself referred to themselves as the referees, but would never tell their wives what that meant.

"I don't know yet. Sergeant Brady hasn't said

anything. But I get the feeling he thinks we might be too close to this one. We'll see."

She noticed he was getting restless as she watched him shift his position on the couch for a second time. He plopped his feet onto the ottoman and rested his head on the back of the couch. Walking quietly into the kitchen she came back with two glasses of wine and handed one to Dave as she sat down next to him.

They sat there for a while both lost in their own thoughts sipping their glass of wine. What a complicated world. And what would their part be in the future? They had helped solve many complicated crimes in the past. They worked so well together. Sammi always needed a cover to be able to listen to the thoughts of others. And then she would pass her information on to Dave, who would take appropriate action. With him around, no one questioned how the information was obtained. They assumed it was reliable and moved with it.

Dave grabbed her hand. "What a waste with Terry. He was young and very ambitious, but he was smart. And he was so clever. He had fooled us for a long time until you came along. I imagine he could fool others, too. And we had plans for him."

"How old was he?"

"About thirty-two, I think. And I heard that he'd been engaged. After he got out of prison he had talked about a girl he had known for a while and was thinking of settling down and making some sense out of his life."

She didn't say a word, but felt sad. Everyone deserved a second chance. Then the telephone rang.

Dave answered. "Sarge, what's up?"

"We need you back here right away. Is Sammi available?"

"She's here with me right now. What's the matter?"

"The mayor's coming down with part of his staff. I'm not sure what it's all about, but I'm suspicious. I want to pick up as much as I can. He's having a fit about another murder at the dock and an ex-policeman at that. This publicity is bad for him, but he also wants to know what we're doing about this. I think we need you and Sammi in on this."

"Okay, we're on our way."

* * *

On the way down to the station, Dave shared his thoughts.

"I don't think we're going to be involved in this, but the sarge wants to know the real reason for this visit. I can't help but think this is a strange request."

"How will you get me in there? The mayor might only want officials around."

"I'm going to introduce you as an assistant to the department if I have to. I know the sarge will back me up. He's the one who asked for you to be there."

She nodded. He was glad that she'd be around and pick up what she could.

They beat the mayor and his team into Sergeant Brady's office by about five minutes. But it did give them time to make sure of the reason that Sammi had to be there.

* * *

As soon as the mayor and his three body-guards, along with two other staff members entered Sergeant Brady's office, the dynamics of the room changed considerably. Jim Mucci, and Tom Harrington, Dave's two usual partners were there, too.

The mayor began immediately in a loud and somewhat agitated voice. "This is beginning to look especially bad for the city," he said as he paced the room. "What the hell's going on here?"

As he looked around and noticed Sammi sitting in the corner, he immediately asked, "What's she doing here?"

"I use her as my assistant. She'll take notes and make sure I have all the points of this meeting correct," said the sarge.

The mayor seemed to accept that fact without contradiction. Immediately he moved onto to his main topic.

"Something's got to be done. We barely get one thing under control, sort of at least, and then another one crops up."

Sergeant Brady became vocal, too. He wasn't going to be brow beaten for no reason. "We always have crime in our city. And it's been way down lately, remember that."

"I know that," said the mayor waving his hands around, "but this one makes everything look bad. It's connected with those other ones involving the governor."

"We don't know that for sure yet. That's a guess. I'll have to wait until we can get some proof one way or another before I decide what's going on here."

"Well, let's concentrate on this one," said the mayor. "I'm getting all kind of flack up the line."

"I'm surprised the governor would make any noise about this right now. Remember, we took care of a big problem for him last year, and we're still working overtime getting his computers protected."

"It isn't the governor; I can tell you that. But other state officials are beginning to call me every other day to find out what we're doing on other things and then this comes up. What the hell am I supposed to tell them?"

"Tell them the truth. We're working on it. And we are. Good grief, Ron, we found the body less than twenty-four hours ago. He was shot in the back of the head execution style. That could mean anything. Petty crooks do that. We have no clues that it was tied to anything political."

"But it sure looks like it is."

"I can't help what it looks like cause I have to deal in facts."

"Alright. But as soon as you can, get some information out there to calm down the public. If it's connected to these other crimes, simmer it down so people don't panic. And if it isn't related, let's get the word out fast. Okay?"

The mayor's face turned red in frustration and his physical form showed total exasperation and aggravation. He didn't need bad publicity right now.

And then, as boorishly as he entered, he left without saying goodbye or exhibiting any other semblance of civilized behavior.

* * *

The atmosphere in the room didn't settle down immediately. Even Sergeant Brady was caught up in the moment as the scene slowly began to change from one of chaos and disorder to a more tranquil and reasonable tone. Time seemed suspended during the changeover. But the sarge aggravated the mood as he offered a comment.

"Well, that was one hell fire when he entered and another when he left. What the hell was that all about? I can't believe he blames us at this time. We must be the scapegoat for something else. But I'll be damned if I'm going to allow him to make us look bad. We've all done a terrific job lately and the last year especially we've had phenomenal success. He said so himself at a dinner for us about two months ago. What the hell's wrong with him?"

Most of the officers sat there looking disgusted. Some looked like they had been kicked in the gut. Why were they being made the fall guys? And the crime had been committed less than twenty-four hours ago. Something else was happening with this mayor, and it wasn't anything positive. Whatever his motives, he was losing a big group of supporters and affiliates.

"He sure isn't the mayor we used to know.

He's like a totally different guy and putting out blame ahead of time to make himself look above the fray," said Tom, not pleased with this latest behavior. "Why is he throwing us the crap? My God, give us time to do our jobs."

The sarge saw Dave shake his head. "I don't even understand what this little charade was all about anyway. He didn't say that much. It was like ... find out who did this? Doesn't he think that's what our job is? We investigate and solve murders. That's what we do. Was he trying to throw his weight around for some other reason?"

"He's obviously trying to protect himself, but why make us the bad guys?" asked Jim. "Hell, we've made him look damn good lately."

Sergeant Brady didn't have any answer for that comment.

Tom simply shook his head. He was extremely annoyed. "You know, a while back we would stick together and watch each other's backs when things happened. Now we have to watch for public opinion, cover for each other and fight the mayor at the same time. This is total crap."

As everyone got up to leave, the sarge called back Dave and Sammi.

"Hopefully by tomorrow you can get me some insight into this charade. This is total bull and I need to know more of what's underneath it all."

As they walked out of the room, they could still hear the sarge grumbling and mumbling about this latest episode in the relationship with a mayor who had changed drastically in the last year or so. Gone was the working together attitude that had accomplished so much in the past. Gone

was the philosophy that had helped the public by attacking a problem from the inside first and relaying events as they progressed. And gone was the trust that had almost completely evaporated.

* * *

On the ride home Dave had to ask, "Did you catch any interesting thoughts?"

"I did, at least from the mayor's point of view. You know, we gave that party for Keith Jensen at the governor's mansion a while back. Now remember, he was a guy who was wrongly convicted of a crime, spent over seven years in prison and when he's proven innocent we give him a big party at the governor's mansion and there's lots of good publicity for the governor. He came out looking like a great guy about this thing."

"Well, thanks to the secrecy of you wives," he said, laughing. The wives had taken great pleasure in planning the party with a surprise location which created much needed positive publicity for an innocent guy who'd soon be looking for a job.

"You can't forget this is an election year for the governor, and although he's an honest guy and true to his beliefs, he did play that up to get the best and most positive angle possible."

"Okay, but what does that have to do with Mayor Stillman?"

"A lot. His publicity people are looking for the same type of connection for him. That kid in the blue sweater taking notes, who never said anything is the one who'll get this meeting in the papers tomorrow. It'll be something about the fact

that 'Mayor puts pressure on police department to solve crimes,' or something like that."

"Gees, that should go over big with the sarge."

"I think he almost expects it and he can expect a lot more this year. The mayor is already playing it up for his reelection next year."

"What's your opinion of the mayor?"

"He seems straight enough, but he's so concerned about his reelection that I hope he doesn't go too far and neglect other important things. He's got a few around him that I'm questioning right now."

Dave perked up immediately. "Anyone that was here?"

"Namely, that one bodyguard."

"Which one?"

"The shorter one who sat across from Jim. Something about him isn't right?"

"Did you pick up any thoughts?"

"No, actually, his mind was rather blank, but he had dark colors and a dire mood around him. Whenever I see that it usually means that he has his hands in too many things."

Dave kept quiet as she continued.

"Now someone on his staff is not loyal to him. But I don't know these people by name."

"Which one was that?"

"Well, it was a crowded room, but the taller guy who always seemed to be right behind the mayor, kind of like a shadow."

"Oh, that's Peter Armors," he said almost laughing. "He's always right behind the mayor. People call him "the tracker.""

"Well, I'm not sure how much he knows and

how much the mayor depends on him, but he's trouble. He's not loyal to the mayor. There's someone else out there he gives information to. He's playing both sides of something. I didn't get any names."

"Some of this we'll have to keep to ourselves right now. But I'll have to find out about that bodyguard."

"What do you want to tell the sarge?"

"Mainly about the reelection aspect and what the papers are going to say. I should get him prepared first thing in the morning."

"Shouldn't you call him tonight? What if the morning papers carry this story?"

"Good point, I'll call him as soon as we get home."

* * *

As he pulled into the driveway, Dave shut off the ignition, but didn't make any move to get out of the car. He saw her look over with a questioning gaze.

"I was thinking about when I used to drive you home. These were some of my favorite moments when we'd sit here and talk."

Sammi smiled remembering, and said, "I liked it, too. It seemed we'd always try to prolong the evening."

"We did. But I'm still glad we took it slow. I'm glad we got to know each other."

With that Dave opened his car door and they walked toward the house. Suddenly he kissed her and gave her a hug. Then he said teasingly, "I'm

remembering old times. This was when I really hated to leave, and now, I don't have to."

She laughed. "That's right, now you don't have to leave."

* * *

Dave placed a call to the sarge immediately telling him what to expect tomorrow. He was on the phone more than five minutes.

He told Sammi what they'd talked about. "The isn't too happy that the mayor wants to get publicity at his expense. He's not going to let that continue. He said that if this story appears in the paper like we said, then he'll have an immediate meeting with him. There are other ways for him to get good publicity and he won't let him do it at the expense of the department, especially since it wasn't called for."

"I'm glad. It doesn't seem like a fair thing to do."

"No, and he said that if the mayor continues, then he'll generate his own media releases which the mayor probably won't like."

"A few of those episodes should do it. But I hope it doesn't get to that. The mayor's office and the police department should be working together."

"And with this new information you've picked up about the mayor's group, I'd like to stay in good rapport so that sometime in the future we can clue him in on his own office."

She agreed. Getting drowsy and close to falling asleep, she headed for the bedroom. Dave still had some notes to transcribe and his mind was in full force.

Who killed Terry Gonzalez? What had he gotten himself involved in? He'd recently been let out of prison, a few months at best, so he likely had made some contacts while still in jail. His personality helped him to weave in and out of any group he needed. People liked him and wanted him around. Dave had been particularly hurt when he found out that Terry was the mole. He'd treated him like a younger brother, and although he ended up in jail, he felt that he might be on his way back to the better side of the law. With Sammi around he wanted to work with him again. He could never hate him, although he found it hard to trust him unless his wife was near. He was more affected by his death than he thought he would be, and he wanted to trap his killer. Suddenly he had a strong urge to learn everything he could about his young life and its tragic ending.

* * *

When Dave walked into the station the next day he was met with an outpouring of anger about a newspaper story that wasn't exactly flattering about the department, yet wasn't as detrimental as originally believed. Still Sergeant Brady called a meeting with his people, mainly because of all the grumbling that was coming to his attention, and also because he couldn't let the mayor think that dumping on him would be all that easy in the future.

"I wanted to let you know that I've already put

in a call to the mayor's office and I will squelch today any plan of this mayor using us to get bad publicity off his back. If he doesn't agree, we'll be sending out our own press releases and I need him to be aware of that. We've done a fine job here in the last few years and we need to be congratulated and not used as a scapegoat. And we'll be holding a news conference later today or tomorrow with our own spin on this story. That's all for now."

Everyone broke up, and amidst some of the grumbling still being heard were comments of agreement with the sergeant's remarks.

"Gees, he sure got miffed about that one, didn't he?" said Tom.

"I haven't seen him that hot in a while. But I don't blame him. My God, after all we've done lately, this was bullshit," replied Jim.

At that moment Dave got called back into the sarge's office and he closed the door.

"I wanted to thank you for calling me last night. I'm glad I knew about this before I came in and faced these early morning papers. That damn mayor's got his nerve," he said.

"It's all about publicity for him. He wants to get reelected," offered Dave.

"I know. But we could even work with him on that. But not if he takes this hard line against us. My God, I thought we were supposed to work together. We did in the past. What's happened to him?" he said.

"He could be getting some bad advice." He remembered what Sammi had said about someone on his staff not being loyal. This could be part of the way they would be trying to undermine him.

"What do you mean? He's got his people around him. They're always with him and he's never acted like this before. I liked the fact in the past he'd call me ahead of time to discuss any problems that were surfacing. I thought we had a good working relationship. But if he starts acting like this ..."

He decided to throw out some hints to the sarge.

"He does have a few new people on staff. Possibly they have different ideas on what he should do."

"Who's new? Oh that "tracker" fellow. He's always around him now. How long's he been with him?"

"A little over a year, I think, could be a little longer," he said.

"That's interesting because you know that appreciation dinner that he had given for all of us after we cracked that money laundering case, well, he almost cancelled it and I heard the "tracker" was behind that. I wonder what his problem is."

"I sure don't know, but he does seem different, doesn't he?"

"He's a strange guy. Well, I'll see how my talk goes with the mayor later today. I'm sure going to press him for a change of attitude. And I want to know what the hell to expect in the future."

After hearing the latest information, Dave thought that as usual Sammi was right on target. The tracker wasn't loyal to the mayor and part of the plan might be to cause trouble between the mayor and the police department.

* * *

When Dave got back to his desk, Jim and Tom were already there.

"Report says that Terry had been dead at least a couple of days, but his body was dumped in the water only about eighteen hours before he was found," said Tom.

"Then there's no clues at all."

"No, not yet. But those few brief statements came from the examiner's office, and the complete report should tell us more. I'm curious what kind of bullet."

"Can't believe that would be much help though," said Jim shaking his head in confusion, "unless of course it's an unusual weapon."

Dave's phone rang and it was more business to take care of. He was almost happy these days when routine matters came to his attention. He'd had enough of the high priority excitement for a while. Most of his cases in the recent past had been successful, even if not totally closed yet. He and Sammi had been involved in child abduction cases in Philadelphia a while back and some of the children were found, but not all. Many state agencies were still working with the information they had found. He knew that not everything would have a completely happy ending, and he was happy with the information that they had provided, but he still held out hope for the ones not yet found.

His phone rang again. It was Sammi.

"Hi. What's up?"

"Do we have anything planned for Friday? Jill called and she'd like to meet with me about something."

"No, not from my side. What's going on?"

"Not sure, but I don't think she's talked to Tom about it yet, do sit on this, okay? I'm sure she'll tell him, but I got the feeling she's now making a decision to discuss some worries about someone."

"I understand. Okay, I'd like to relax tonight. You're going to be home, right?"

"Yep, I am. After dinner we can have some quiet time. We haven't had that much lately."

"I know. That's what I was thinking. See ya later."

* * *

Sammi called Jill back to confirm dinner for Friday night. At this point, she couldn't imagine what was on her mind. Jill was a logical and together person. In fact, the only time she'd even heard of her being the least bit uptight was when her husband got shot in the leg a while back, and that would unnerve anyone. And to want to talk to Sammi before she talked to her husband made her realize that Jill was carrying something quite heavy. Anyway, Friday night would answer her questions.

Leaving the bank on Thursday gave Sammi a feeling of accomplishment. The president had been pleased with her work as of late and called her into the office to tell her. And Ben Collier, an

FBI agent that she'd dealt with in the last year, had called her to keep in touch. He worked at the same bank, but in the Philadelphia office.

So she was feeling quite pleased with herself and her life, but when Dave got home from work she felt so much tension from him. The cop's death had affected him quite a bit.

"What's so heavy on your mind?"

"I can't get Terry's killing off my mind. I know he had his problems, but I feel like I lost a younger brother. I honestly thought he was on his way back and now we'll never know. That's so irritating."

"What do you plan to do about it?"

"What? What do you mean?"

"Dave, I know you. Your mind is twisting and turning around all over the place. And no, I'm not listening to your thoughts, but I know how you work. Have you got a plan in place yet?"

Dave took a deep breath and sat down on the couch next to her. She knew she was right, but let it go. He'd tell her when he had his thoughts sorted out. But then, he offered some ideas which showed where he was going.

"I don't know yet. This whole thing is pushing me to something, but I don't know what. It's like something inside of me won't let it go. It's affected everyone in the department, but I'm the one that keeps hashing it out in my mind. I want to take some action, but I don't know what. And I don't even know if the sarge will give me the case."

That's what she thought. He was working on a plan and sooner or later it would come to the surface. But she couldn't imagine what he wanted to accomplish.

"Where do you want to go with this? Do you know?"

"I don't know what I want to do yet, but I'm determined in time to find out what got him killed. We need to know that. But also, I think he was a good guy that went the wrong way for money, you know? He admitted that later and I'd like to learn more about him. Hell, I don't even know anything about his family, nothing at all. He was such a charmer and eased his way in and out of a lot of groups, but no one knew what he was about. That's what we're all finding out. I'd like to learn something about his background."

"That could take you in a lot of directions. Have you talked to the sarge about this?"

"No, not yet. I'm waiting to see what he wants to do first. If I'm not first string on the murder side, maybe he'll let me look into his background. Could find out some interesting stuff there. It's simply a feeling I've got, but now it seems that his life was so mysterious."

She was glad that Dave had learned to trust his feelings. He had good instincts that could be relied upon.

"It's still pretty early yet. I was wondering ... when was the last time you saw Terry?"

"He had stopped in to see the sarge last Thursday. He wasn't there, but we talked for a while. He was so damn likeable, at least I thought so and easy to trust which is why he did so good as a mole. And I'm sure he had the same success on the other side. I sometimes wonder how he got so good at what he did."

"That might be interesting to find out."

"It would and I remember the last thing he said to me. I don't think I could ever forget it. He must have known he was taking a big chance because as he was leaving he said, "If I don't talk to you again, I want you to know that I did care about you, Dave.""

"That seems like a strange thing to say," she said.

"I thought so and I answered—'What? Are you planning on going somewhere?' And he winked and said, 'You never know, Dave, life can be strange'."

Sammi joined Dave's intuitive thoughts.

"I remembered I laughed and said—'Well, you take care of yourself, Terry'. And he said— 'And I hope you have a wonderful life'. Now that was the last thing he said to me and I thought it was a bit strange at the time, but I figured he was in a nostalgic mood and left it at that. We all go there sometime or other."

"And now you wonder if he had a premonition."

"Well, I guess I do."

"If he was doing something dangerous he always knew the possibility was there."

"You know, he called me after I'd been shot and apologized to me. He said he never meant anything bad like that to happen and didn't want anyone hurt. And he was especially specific to apologize for his part in it."

"No kidding. I didn't know that."

"Yep, he called me from jail and his voice

cracked a little. He was quite emotional about my getting hurt."

"It seems like he must have cared for you a lot."

"I think he did. And I think he cared for the other guys, too. And that's what makes me wonder what his life was all about."

That ended the conversation. They both relaxed for the rest of the evening, but Terry was never far from their minds. Sammi realized the complicated process that was affecting them both.

CHAPTER TWO

As Sammi dressed for her Friday evening dinner, she realized that Jill Harrington was a rather mysterious woman. She felt she knew her rather well, but appreciated the fact that she didn't always open up about herself. Tom and Jill were a happy couple who'd been married fifteen plus years, but they seldom talked about their families. It seemed that their entire lives merged around the police department and their lawful circle of friends. Tom, Jim and Dave were known as the three referees and closer than most family members. Although Tom and Jill didn't have any children of their own they were compensated with her teaching career that many times helped challenged children as a sideline. They had all grown extremely close after Dave had been shot a few years ago and Sammi came to realize how important a part Dave had played in their lives for almost twenty years.

She remembered Dave's account that he had been at the precinct but a short time before Tom came early in both of their careers. They were assigned together almost immediately and had remained so constantly for their entire profession. Jim came along three years later and the entire department knew them as a trio that worked mostly together. Sergeant Brady saw to that.

When he had this caliber of cops working together with such remarkable rapport, he kept them together whenever he could.

Well, this reminiscence had done nothing much except to help her realize that she knew little about Jill. The couples got together regularly, enjoyed each other, but except for the normal support that they gave each other as cops' wives, Jill was the secret one. Oh, Sammi didn't think that she meant to be secretive, yet nothing much was known about her. She knew a lot about Julie, Jim's wife, but then she had known her for a long time. They went to high school together. And it wasn't that Jill didn't talk about herself, because she did at times. She had mentioned that her parents' had died and that she had a brother who lived in another state. Yet except for a few recent happenings, there wasn't much to tell. Possibly it had to do with the fact that she was more reserved and quiet. It was true that she blended in well with everyone, but she was more of a listener and would urge everyone else to be the center of attention. Being in the spotlight herself was a position she usually shunned.

Dave pulled up in the driveway before she was ready to leave and looked at her in surprise as he entered.

"I'm meeting Jill for dinner, remember?"

That's right," he said, recalling their conversation earlier in the week, but also showing some disappointment.

"What's wrong? Something on your mind?"

"Nothing that can't wait," he said and walked into the living room and sat down.

"We've got leftovers in the fridge and I made a new pot of coffee."

Dave smiled and seemed content to relax.

She walked over to where he was sitting on the couch and leaned over to give him a kiss before she left.

He smiled as he said, "You know, I'm so tired today. Think I'll sack out."

"You feeling okay?"

"I'm fine, but I was restless last night for some reason. This'll give me time to recoup. Have fun."

Sammi yelled, "Love you," as she walked out the door. She couldn't help but worry about Dave. He had healed from being shot, but it was a worry that didn't seem to leave her completely anymore.

* * *

Jill was already seated at the restaurant when she arrived. Waiving her over in a casual manner couldn't hide the anxiety on her face. It seemed displaced on her, yet couldn't be ignored.

"Did you beat me by much?"

"No, about five minutes," and then surprisingly admitted, "I wanted to leave before Tom got home. He knows I've had something on my mind, but I can't talk to him yet."

Sammi didn't answer. She gave Jill her complete attention and waited.

"Let's order a drink and then I can relax some. I needed to talk to someone; thanks for coming."

"Of course. We've relied on each other many times lately. Talking can help."

Jill smiled as the waitress took their order.

Sammi realized how pretty she was. Being of medium height with auburn hair and a smile that usually captivated anyone around gave her a pleasant demeanor. But that was missing tonight and replaced with a serious facade as her shoulders carried a weight not usually noticeable. She knew that Jill was agitated and though she would have liked to, she waited until her friend was ready to talk and didn't trespass on her thoughts.

In time, Jill leaned forward with her shoulders still hunched up and prepared to begin talking in her usual quiet and personal tone of voice about a private part of her life that she kept mostly secret.

After an audible sigh, she began. "I think I've mentioned to you that I have a brother, Todd, who lives in Kansas."

Sammi acknowledged that she knew.

"Yes, well, I don't talk about him much. I mean, we're not all that close anymore, but we were when we were growing up. He's two years older than me and he always protected me and made sure no bullies took advantage of me." She smiled in remembrance. It was obvious that she still felt a closeness.

"Tom doesn't like him at all. That's why I hardly ever mention him. And I do keep in touch; we usually call each other every couple of months. But I never tell Tom. He knows we communicate occasionally and lets me do what I need to do, but doesn't intrude or ask any questions about him."

"Why doesn't Tom like him? That surprises me, since Tom is usually so congenial about people and everything."

"Yes, that's true; Tom is known to be agreeable. But Todd didn't want us to get married and tried to break us up. He caused a lot of trouble for Tom with my parents and did everything he could to spoil our relationship."

Sammi leaned back in her chair. "My, my, why on earth did he want to do that?"

"I guess I should back up a little. I was twenty-five when I met Tom. I'd already had one disappointing relationship and another nasty one and that put my brother on alert. He was always trying to make my life easier. Then when Tom came along, he was naturally suspicious of him and believed from the start that he had bad motives. It didn't matter that he was a cop and a good one at that; he didn't trust him."

"Brothers can be protective, I hear."

"Well, you had two brothers, you understand, right?" asked Jill.

"Mine weren't protective of me. My middle brother and I were a little closer, but my older brother and I simply tolerated each other. We were different I guess. My family life was difficult anyway and I always gravitated toward my grandparents for appreciation and understanding."

"Oh," said Jill. "Yes, you've mentioned that. But my brother and I were rather close, although we ran around in different circles. But I met Tom at a party and we clicked immediately. He was always thoughtful with me from the beginning. He was two years older and was ready to settle down. He'd had a few unsatisfying relationships, too. And we merged so well together. I think we were both ready."

"That sounds nice."

"But Todd made everything difficult. I spoke to him several times about it, but it didn't matter. You see, he'd been arrested a few times for drunk driving and for angry, belligerent behavior, so he didn't like cops. He never went to jail, but was on probation twice. Of course, he didn't think he deserved it, so he hated the police."

"Whew, I can see where that must have been a problem."

"It was," said Jill and she paused as if looking back in time. "He wouldn't even come to the wedding. He sent me a nice letter and a gift for me alone, but would never reconcile with Tom. And it's been that way all this time. I sometimes wonder if we had lived closer ... it might have worked itself out in time, but with us several states away, well, there wasn't much chance for that to happen."

Jill shrugged her shoulders in acceptance, realizing now that possibly too much time had passed for anything to ever change. It was obvious by her demeanor that she wished that part of her life had been different.

"He's never visited us and Tom had relented and said that he would behave properly if he came for a short visit, but Todd wouldn't come. Yet, he's always kept in touch, much more so after our parents' died. Before then, my mom would update him on me."

"What does he do for a living? Did he go to college?"

"He started college, but never finished and he never married, at least not yet. He's forty-six, so he still could, but he was somewhat of a loner after he got in trouble in his teens. He sort of withdrew into hurt feelings and shied away from being involved with the world. "

"So what does he do for a living?"

"Well, he's done a lot of things. He's considered quite bright and catches on fast to things. He's worked in computers and never had any classes or anything. But he wandered through many jobs, like day laborer, construction, worked in mines for a while, cement worker, window washer. He even worked as a manager for an insurance company and I understand he did quite well until they found out he lied about a degree on his résumé. So he was let go. I'm not sure what he's done lately. But he lives in my parents' home and has maintained it."

"So, he must be doing okay." Sammi waited after that last comment. There was a reason why Jill was bringing up all this information and she'd get to the point as soon as she was comfortable. However, without any attempt on her part, Jill's thoughts were starting to talk to her. And it was all she could do to wait until she had found her moment of tranquility in order to continue.

"I've brought this up now because I've got a concern about my brother and I don't know what to do."

Sammi couldn't let on that she already knew the problem, but it was one of those moments when the universe let her in on the dilemma, without any effort of her own.

"I think he might be missing," she said as a tear slipped down on the left side of her face; she didn't even bother to wipe it away. "I've called him several times in the last month and I can't get in touch with him. He doesn't return my phone calls. He's always returned them before and usually within a day or two. I've left several messages, and nothing. So I called the only friend I know that he has and I also called his neighbor and no one has seen him lately. In fact, they seemed a little concerned, too."

She saw Jill shift a few times in her chair as she related her concerns. She grabbed her glass of wine a few times and lifted it off the table without even bothering to take a sip. Her nerve center was causing her body to make all sorts of unconnected movements that were not congruent with her mind.

Sammi's interest perked up. This didn't sound like anything Todd would do; he'd at least keep in touch with his sister. She continued.

"He'd never take off anywhere and not tell me. And he would at least return my calls. I did call him at home and left a message, but I also called his cell phone. It's still his voice on the message, but I can't find him."

At this point she let out a few more tears of concern. Her raw nerves were surfacing. She couldn't hold them back anymore, and in truth, she didn't seem to care. Sammi wanted to offer some support.

"And you haven't talked to Tom, yet?"

"No, I know I should, but it's hard because of their past problems."

"But Tom would understand your concern. What would you like to do?"

"Well, I thought I might take some time off and

go down there for a long weekend and nose around to see what I could find out. Someone must know something. And if he's in trouble, he might need my help. I've got to try to find out what's happened to him."

"Of course you do. Who would you talk to if you went? What city does he live in?"

"Our family's home is in Lawrence, Kansas. You may have heard of it; it's a well-known college town."

Sammi shook her head in doubt.

"Well, it's home to the University of Kansas and the Haskell Indian National University. It's about forty miles west of Kansas City, Missouri. That's where I grew up. Back then, the population was less than 60,000. I'm sure it's grown a little today, but it was a nice place to live."

"I grew up in a small town in Ontario, Canada. And I still like that kind of atmosphere."

Jill nodded in understanding. "Anyway I don't know many people anymore, but I do know one of our old neighbors is still there and I know one of his friends. I thought I could also go to his place of employment and make some inquiries. I'm worried about him. He isn't a bad guy and I'm not sure why he and Tom couldn't resolve their differences. Tom was willing and tried, but Todd was so stubborn."

"You know, Jill, maybe he was scared. He could have started down this path that thought that the police were out to get him and couldn't get Tom out of that loop."

Jill was thoughtful for a moment. "That thought crossed my mind a while back, but nothing I said made him want to make an effort. I tried so hard, but nothing worked."

About this time the waitress came and offered dessert which both gals refused. But coffee was in order as their conversation hadn't finished yet. And this would give Sammi time to get Jill in a more relaxed frame of mind.

"When do you think you'll go?" she asked.

"If I still haven't heard from him, I'm thinking about next week. We have a couple of days off at school. The kids are all scheduled to go to special activities for a couple of days. I thought I might schedule it then and with the weekend, I'd have almost four days to see what I could find out."

"That sounds like a good plan. You can't sit here and do nothing. You're getting too worried for that. I know I'd want to get down there and find out what I could. But you'll have to talk to Tom soon."

"Probably tonight. But keep this to yourself until I do, okay? I'm sure he'll tell Dave about it and that's okay. I don't mind you talking to Dave, but I need to get up the nerve to talk to Tom first."

"Wait a minute, Jill. You're talking about Tom, here. He loves you totally. I'm sure he'll be one hundred percent supportive when he hears what's going on. He may even want to go with you."

"Oh God, you think so, Sammi? I didn't want to bring up some old sore wounds again. But I think I'd rather go alone. If everything turns out okay, then I'd like to have some time to talk to him and see if we can finally mend our lives."

"Yes, of course. But I'm sure that Tom will back you all the way."

Jill took a long deep breath. "I'm so glad I talked to you. It does help, doesn't it? I think Tom will be okay with this, but if he isn't, it's still something I have to do."

"Of course it is. Sometimes married people don't always agree. Even the ones that have a strong bond. And that's okay. We can't agree all the time. But you have to do what your heart is calling for, no matter what."

Sammi knew by the way Jill smiled that she needed to hear those exact words from someone. It was the confirmation she needed to reinforce her choice. Her shoulders seemed to relax now and her decision, which had already been made days before, finally felt right to her.

* * *

Arriving home, she realized it was already 10:30 P.M. She found Dave sleeping on the couch, TV still running and an air of halted activity in the room. A smile crossed her face as she looked at him realizing how peaceful and innocent he looked when he was sleeping. Walking over to the couch, she sat next to him and began rubbing his back gently, until he began moving slightly and groaning in contentment. She smiled to herself as he sleepily said, "If I pretend I'm still sleeping, will you massage my back a little longer?"

Sammi laughed. "You're such a tease at times."

Without moving he offered, "I must admit that I heard your car pull into the garage. But I was hoping if I pretended to be asleep that you might come over here and give me a massage. And it worked."

She laughed, knowing his ability to act like a little boy at times.

Then Dave sat up slowly and asked, "How did it go?"

"Okay, Jill has some serious problem on her mind. She plans to tell Tom tonight and asked me to wait until she did."

Dave nodded. "I know they usually share everything. This must be pretty heavy for her."

"It is, Dave. And she's quite agitated right now. Hopefully soon we can talk about it. I'd like your opinion."

"Okay, when you're ready."

"So you said that you had something to tell me. What is it?"

"Oh," said Dave, walking into the kitchen to get a cup of coffee, hoping to become fully a-wakened. "Want a cup?"

"No, thanks."

"Well, it's about the Terry Gonzalez case. I hear that they've retrieved the gun and it's a .38 special. That's not much help ... that gun's so common. It appears that it was wiped clean and then thrown into the water so there's not too much hope for fingerprints. The sarge doesn't think our group would be the best one to work on this case directly; we were too close to him. I hate to agree with him, but I think he's right."

"It can be hard when you've been that close to someone."

"Yep, and about a month ago we brought in a few top notch policemen from Chicago. Did I tell you?"

"No, you didn't."

"Well, we've got LeBron Harper and Tyrone Pittfield. They've already moved their families here. You'll meet them at the next gathering. Anyway they've had loads of experience and of course, working Chicago streets is no picnic. They're both excellent on street talk and street maneuvering. Jim and Tom both admitted they've already learned from them. LeBron was put directly in our group as of last week. I think they're real good additions."

Sammi waited. She knew he had more on his mind.

"But I still want you to listen in on them, okay? I'm planning to do that with anyone new from now on that comes into our group. You never know."

"Okay, when the time is right, I'll see what I can find out for you. Anything new about the mayor's dilemma?"

"No, funny you asked. Jim was asking earlier today and thought it was strange that they've quieted down. No more bad publicity lately. We did find out that fingering us was the tracker's idea. You must have been right about him."

"I think he definitely has to be watched. Something isn't right there, but I don't know what it is."

For almost half an hour they were both quiet. Sammi tried to start a conversation, but Dave didn't hear her; he was so engrossed in his own thoughts. He wiggled in his chair and was trying to bring something to the surface of his mind.

Finally she got his attention.

"What are you so absorbed in?"

Dave was almost startled as he realized he had been somewhere else for quite a while.

"I was thinking of Terry. I wish I had known him better, you know. We all knew him superficially and we knew his working ethic, or at least part of it, but I didn't get to know him under the surface."

Sammi watched him as his concern showed all over his face.

"Well, he was likeable, but I don't think I ever had one deep meaningful conversation with him, know what I mean? We talked a lot about our cases and stuff, but getting down to how he felt about life and other things ... it never happened."

Sammi felt his pain. He was so concerned about what he'd missed.

"I don't think he ever talked about his family."

"That's because he didn't have one."

Dave was jolted. She was sorry that she hadn't been more sensitive in her approach.

"You picked that up? He didn't have a family?"

"I was around him on several occasions, remember? Especially after we realized that he was the mole in the department, I was always tuned in when he was around. He had some personal thoughts occasionally that I picked up."

"Like what?" asked Dave almost emotionally. "What else do you remember?"

"Gees, Dave, I don't remember all of them anymore."

"When you do, write them down. I want to learn everything I can about him."

"Okay, well, I remember once when he was thinking that it would have been nice to have a family. He didn't have a mother or father, at least none that he could remember. And he didn't know of any brothers or sisters. His mind did cross over to one guy he considered a cousin that he was quite close to for a while; I should remember that name in time, but right now I don't. I get the impression that this cousin lived in Mexico and they were very young when they depended on each other for help and support. And he had special thoughts about one girl, occasionally. But that's all I remember right now."

"That's pretty good. If you remember anything else, let me know. Something's bugging me and I can't figure out what it is. But I think there may be something in his background that will be a clue for us."

"Clue to what?"

"Sammi," said Dave in an exasperated tone of voice, "I don't even know. It's a feeling, that's all."

Sammi realized that she would be thinking back over the times that she had been around Terry and testing her memory for more facts. He was a guy who had a lot of jumbled thoughts on his mind on many occasions. Everything was so distressing to her in light of his untimely death. She had liked Terry, too. Everyone did. He was a good-looking young man, dark hair and extremely dark eyes, no doubt from his Mexican heritage, but it did give him handsome expressions. She remembered that he had a type of pain in his demeanor that she hadn't been able to pinpoint, but thought possibly it was because he didn't have a family. She had to admit that there were times she was intrigued with his thought process, and of course now, she wished she had paid more attention to it.

* * *

About midday on Monday Tom came over to Dave's desk and sat down.

He let out a deep sigh and looked directly at him as he said, "I suppose you know what's been going on with Jill."

Dave knew his confusion was obvious.

"Well, seeing that Sammi and Jill had dinner on Friday, I figured she told you."

He leaned back in his chair and hooked his arm on the back of it, "You know, Tom, all Sammi said was that Jill asked her to hold off talking to me until she talked to you."

"Really?" said Tom, but it was obvious he seemed rather pleased.

Tom told Dave the story of Todd, Jill's brother.

"So the two of you never got along?"

"No, I tried at the beginning, but I finally gave up. He tried to cause so much trouble between me and Jill's parents because he didn't like the police. But it was his own fault. Anyway, I couldn't take it anymore and Jill understood. But I felt bad because she was caught in the middle. In later years though, he could have come over and been part of our lives, but he didn't want to. Jill never held that against me, or him for that matter. She said he had problems and she always kept in touch with him."

"But this is a different story now. You say Jill thinks he's missing. For how long?"

"Well, Dave, she doesn't know. They usually kept in touch every couple of months or so. But she hasn't been able to get in touch with him at all. And she's left plenty of messages. He usually returned her calls right away. But there were times that he used to get depressed about life and stuff, you know, and then she wouldn't hear from him for a while. Maybe it's one of those times."

"Still, I can see why she'd be worried."

"I can, too. Anyway Jill gets two days off from teaching at the end this week and she's heading down to Kansas to see what she can find out. I offered to go with her, but she wants to go alone. If he's alright, she'd like to get a chance to talk to him."

Dave could understand that idea.

"He seemed to be an okay kid at times, but he hated the police. We didn't have anywhere to go with a friendship."

"That part isn't your fault, Tom. Too bad he didn't change his mind as he got older."

"Yeah, I used to hope he would, but ..." Tom's voice trailed off as he looked out in space for a moment. Then as he came back to earth he changed the subject. "Well, I guess the sarge doesn't want our group on Terry's case."

"He said not directly, but he wouldn't mind if we nosed around a little for information. Tom, I can't leave this one alone. I feel like there's a veil around this whole thing and I can't get it off my mind."

"I think you were closer to him than anybody

else."

"I felt like he was my younger brother. And I never could hate the guy, could you?"

"No, no, I couldn't, Dave. I didn't trust him anymore and I agreed with him going to jail and getting his badge taken away. But my feelings were so mixed up with him being a friend and then betraying us all. It hurt a lot. Yet, I couldn't hate him."

"I was so surprised at what he did. If anyone, I thought he was one of us to the core. Damn, it's hard not to be able to trust anyone. I'm so glad you and Jim are still with me."

"That's helped me a lot, too."

Dave got a phone call and Tom sat and waited. He had so much on his mind that he was finding it hard to sit still. He was worried about Jill going off by herself, yet he knew it was best. Still, he would worry.

"What do you have in mind about Terry's case?"

I'm not sure, Tom, but I want to find out something about his background. Sammi doesn't think he had any family. She thought he mentioned it once. But I'm not sure. I'd like to find out where he grew up and something about his life. The way things are right now it seems that he's going off being some person whose life didn't matter. And I think it did matter. It mattered a lot."

Tom nodded in agreement. "He was so good at what he did; he was the type that could get information out of anyone. You have to wonder what kind of background he had to get so good at his art."

Dave laughed. "That's exactly what I've been thinking about. I think I'm beginning to bore Sammi on this, but you and I've saw him work people and there was no one better."

* * *

LeBron came over to join them for a moment. Dave had to ask, "Are you going to be first string on the Terry Gonzalez case?"

"No, I'm not. The sarge told me that he don't plan for anyone in this unit to be involved first string in that."

Dave felt exonerated. None of their unit would be on this one.

"What are you guys working on right now?" he asked.

Dave answered. "I've got two fatalities in a car chase and a missing wife in Dunmore that I'm helping on. Tom's with me on these two. What are you doing?"

LeBron chuckled. "It seems that I'm going to be joining you two on that missing wife. She's been gone for almost a week with no trace so sarge wants to put me and Tyrone on it, too."

"Okay, that'll be great. You got your family settled in by now?" Dave asked.

"Sure, the kids are settled in school and that keeps my wife hopping."

"How many kids?" asked Tom.

"Boy's twelve, he's just starting the nasty age and my daughter's seven. She's still kinda nice to be around."

They all chuckled and understood.

"Well, if you need any help, let us know."

After LeBron left, Tom turned to Dave and said, "I think he's a good guy, and likeable. What a great record he had in Chicago."

Dave agreed. "Looks like our group can be tight again. And both Tyrone and LeBron are making great reputations for themselves here. Now if we can get the mayor and his group to realize our potential we could all relax and do our jobs."

"Haven't heard much from his office lately. What's going on?"

Dave said, "I wish I knew. I think the tracker is such a strange guy. And his behavior doesn't seem to ring true to me all the time."

"I thought the same thing last week. But I'll go one step further. I think that guy's weird through and through. Look at how he behaves—he's always shadowing the mayor. I keep waiting for the mayor to turn around fast one day and he'll smack right into him."

Dave had to laugh. The tracker was always one step behind the mayor.

Tom thought of something else. "What does anyone know about this guy? What was his background and where did he come from? No one knows anything about him."

"No," Dave said, "he hasn't been with the mayor all that long. Sammi has her concerns about him. I wonder where his allegiance is?"

Tom interrupted by saying that he had to get back to some files on his desk and he'd talk to him later.

"Come on over for dinner on Saturday. I think Jill would want us to keep an eye on you."

"Thanks. I'd like that. I think that would settle her mind a little. Later, okay?"

CHAPTER THREE

Sammi paced all around the living room in an uneven gait. She felt her home had been violated and wasn't ashamed of the tears that began running down her cheeks. How could this have happened? Dave would have a fit and so would Tom and Jim. She should call Dave immediately. He and Tom had gone down to the precinct early Saturday afternoon to finish up some work. But it was already after five o'clock. They should be home soon for dinner anyway. She would wait and try to calm herself. It would do no good if she showed any signs of stress about this.

She played the answering machine again. She didn't want to hear that voice, but felt she had to get beyond her anger and fear before Dave got home.

"Hi Dave ... I'm sure you're surprised to hear from me. I know I'm not supposed to call you, but I got a chance and couldn't resist. I sure do miss you and I know you miss me. I wonder who misses who the most. (pause and some laughter) I heard you married Sammi, but I guess you needed someone while I was gone. (pause) We can decide what to do with her when I get out. Don't worry, I'm not upset or jealous. She's no competition for me. (a long pause) I hate being in here, sweetie. Can you find a way to help me? I know you can't say any-

thing to anyone, but try and find a way, okay? I still love you as much as ever. We were meant to be together and I'll find a way. Got to go now, they didn't give me much time. Love you and can't wait to be near you again."

Sammi felt an indescribable pain crawling up and down her spine as she listened to the message again. She realized now, more than ever, that their association with Linda Saunders would never end, at least not while she was alive. The entire situation was bizarre. Linda had shot Dave in a sting operation. She was convicted of attempting to murder him, but still felt she had power over him. It was clear to her that Linda would always find a way to contact Dave and she didn't care if more time was added to her sentence. She was convinced that he would try and get her out of prison early. She found herself shaking at the thought of Dave's reaction. But then, suddenly, her thoughts took another turn. What did she know about Linda Saunders? She would have loved to hear some of her thoughts. She'd had so little chance in the past because there was always another reason for her observance.

She poured herself a glass of wine and thought about the feeling she got as she listened to the tape. Before she had listened with shock, dread and definite fear. But now, since her initial reaction was over, she decided to listen again and see if she could gain any insight to Linda's thoughts as she left the message. And surprisingly enough, Linda's thoughts were coming through the recorder. And there were some revealing pauses on the machine. She would listen again, she thought, but suddenly she heard Dave's car pull into the driveway. Although she knew this would be a stressful evening, it was probably true that neither one of them would be too surprised. Tom and Jim always felt that Linda would find a way. And she did live in a different mental world. Sammi would begin to study her thoughts from this recorded message. She now realized that there was much more to this message than she had first believed.

* * *

When Dave opened the door, with Tom right behind him, he knew immediately that something serious had happened. Sammi tried to hide her emotions, but failed totally. Even Tom was looking at her in a strange way. She walked over and gave him a long hug. She hated to let go knowing that Tom understood. Finally she took a deep breath but couldn't help the tear that was escaping from her left eye.

"What the hell's wrong, Sammi? What happened?" Dave got all tensed up looking into her face.

"Let's all sit down first, okay? I'd like you and Tom to get a glass of wine. You're both going to need it."

A few minutes later as they all sat in the living room, Dave could still feel Sammi's agitation. He caught her hesitancy as she said, "I guess there's no way to make this easy, Dave."

"Don't worry about that. Just tell me what

happened?"

"Okay, listen to this message we got on the answering machine today."

Dave was almost uncontrollable when he first heard Linda's voice.

"Son of a bitch, I knew she'd find a way. What the hell? That broad is psycho. How come no one has noticed that? She's crazy."

Dave began to pace the floor as he ran both hands through his dark hair that fell immediately back into place as if by magic. Both Tom and Sammi let him pace and grumble and try to lessen up the stress he was feeling. And the burden was tremendous. First he was beginning to panic for Sammi. *Was there a way that Linda could get to her? Did she have accomplices on the outside waiting for her orders? No one knew entirely what she was capable of, although it was becoming increasingly clear*, he thought. *And what were her connections? Sure, the people from the money laundering and government fraud scheme, but they had only found out about some of them. Were her hands extended into mob activities that would do her bidding for unknown reasons? What the hell was this all about? And this obsession she created about him? It had no firm basis at all in fact. Was she wacko enough to believe her passions or was it a game she played for a bigger prize?* He kept shaking his head as he walked on and grumbled louder.

"Okay, Dave," said Tom with considerable concern, "you've got to settle down now. She's in prison and we all knew she didn't have close touch with reality for quite a while. It might even get worse the longer she's in there."

"I know, I know. But I can't believe she was stupid enough to make this call. That's the most frightening thing. Everything's documented so she knows she'll get another year tacked onto her sentence. But she doesn't seem to care. And you'd better believe there's a reason for that."

"But remember," said Sammi, "she thinks you're going to help her get out earlier. So I don't think she's concerned about that part."

"But who helped her get to a phone and left her alone to make this call? That's number one for us to find out."

"And we'll do that. Do you want to wait until Monday or you want to call the sarge right now?"

"I guess we can wait until Monday for that. I might call Jim later tonight or tomorrow though. I want to get all my thoughts and anger under control before we look into this further. Sammi, I ..." Dave got chocked up and couldn't finish his sentence.

"Maybe, when she finds out that she did have an extra year added to her sentence, she'll see the facts straighter," offered Sammi.

"I don't think that matters to her right now. I said all along that I thought she should be put into a psycho ward, or at least to be watched more, because she doesn't think logically."

Tom added, "The warden says that about a lot of prisoners. If they were logical thinking people, they wouldn't be there in the first place."

"What worries me the most," said Dave, "is not knowing if she's working alone? Is she a wacko broad with an out of whack ego problem or is she the front for something else?" Then he turned to Sammi, "you're going to have to watch it now. She has a vendetta against you."

"But she says she doesn't mind you having someone while she's in prison, remember? She thinks I pose no threat to her anyway."

Dave laughed almost pathetically. "If she only knew ..." and didn't finish his words.

"I was picking some stuff up on the tape, but I'm going to study it at length."

Tom's ears perked up and he looked confused.

Dave looked over and saw Sammi's expression. She said, "I think the time has come. Tom and Jill are definitely the last of our confidantes, but I think the time has come."

Dave said, "That's up to you."

In the meantime, Tom sat there looking back and forth from both of them. He thought he should say something and looked over at Sammi as he said, "I've learned over the last few years that you have talents you don't talk about. You know, Dave, when you were in the hospital, she knew what the doctor was going to say before he said it. I'm not sure exactly what you do, but Jill and I've talked about it."

"I guess being as close as we all are, you'd have suspected something anyway," he said. "Okay, Sammi, you want to tell him?"

He felt her uneasiness as she told her story about being able to hear people's thoughts since she was a young girl. She even added the part about her Grandpa, her mentor, who could also hear what was on the minds of others. Tom didn't even seem surprised. He simply sat back in his position on the couch and asked a few pointed questions.

"So if you're near some people and you concentrate, then you can hear what they're thinking?"

"Yep, that's pretty much how it works."

"And Dave, that's how you always got so much information."

"That's about it. And Sammi doesn't betray her friends. She uses it selectively and responsibly."

"Yes, I do, Tom. I believe there would be a stiff penalty for me if I used this gift recklessly or for my benefit alone."

"Can I share this with Jill?"

"Sure, I've been thinking of the right time to tell her. Adding you and Jill would mean that there are exactly eight people in the entire world who know what I can do and I don't plan to add anymore. Julie I've known forever, as you're aware, and she suspected anyway. Dave found out accidentally and we told Jim because I felt if anything ever happened and Dave was in trouble that I'd need another person to work with to help him out. But all six of us are a team, I feel. And it's good for me to have some people to talk to and relax with. Before I told Dave, no one knew. Well, of course, the few people I've helped knew, but they were sworn to secrecy and they don't live close to me anyway."

"It must seem like a burden at times, doesn't it?"

Dave answered this one and said, "Sammi gets worn out a lot, and I have to back her off. She has trouble saying no to some pleas for help."

Tom understood how that could spell trouble.

"Anyway, back to our recording here. Sometimes Tom, especially in the last few years or so, I can hear people's thoughts over the telephone. So I listened to the recording again and was picking up some interesting stuff. Nothing I want to share right now, but I'd like to study it later and see all that I can pick up, then I'll let you know. It might be helpful."

They were all quiet for a few minutes, wrestling with the latest dilemma concerning their criminal case from last year. This case never seemed to end and its ramifications kept spreading out beyond anyone's control or imagination. When would all this end? No one knew.

* * *

"I'm glad Tom was with us tonight." Dave couldn't seem to be far away from Sammi and insisted she sit right next to him on the couch because he needed her closeness more than anything else. He put his head back and was lost for a while in the enjoyment of the moment.

"How long has Linda's been in prison?"

"It's getting close to a year and then she spent those months before the trial in jail, too."

"I'm not surprised we heard from her. I figured she'd manage one way or another and I don't think it's going to end, no matter what you or the legal profession do to try to stop it. What we need to do is find a way not to get so upset about this. After all, she's going to be in prison for quite a while yet."

"I know, but I do worry about her connections, you know. If I knew she worked alone and she was finding a way to vent her fury, well, that's one thing, but what if she has others on the outside waiting?"

"But these others on the outside must wonder if it would be worth taking a chance and ending up in prison, too. After all, no one in that fraud case last year thought they'd ever get caught. They thought they were too clever for that. I'll bet they'll be thinking twice now and go on to other things rather than help Linda with her vendetta."

Dave thought about that for a few minutes. She had a point. But criminals didn't think logically, although most were the small fishes who were ordered around by others. And he was sure that something else was going on. Considering the Terry Gonzalez murder case, it could be that Linda and her problems were getting to be old news now and they were more interested in something else. Time would tell.

"Anyway, Linda says she doesn't have to worry. She doesn't think I'm any competition for her," she said snuggling next to Dave teasingly.

"Little does she know that you're my whole world," he said and gave her a long affectionate kiss. "And she was never in my life at all, except for what I told you about. It was hardly anything, a brief passing fling. God," he said in total frustration, "who would have known it would come to this?"

"Personally, I think Linda has more smarts than she lets on. She knows exactly that it was a little fling, but has her reasons for trying to make more out of it. Remember, at that party I heard her think, *we need him*, well, something else was going on. And I don't think she's wacko at all. I think she's very clever. Not in a Julie-type way, but for all her illegal and immoral life style, I think she knows what she's doing. And she's in complete control of her emotions."

"I'll bet you're right. I'll be glad to have a meeting with the sarge on Monday. And I want Tom and Jim there. I'd love to know where all this will end."

"I don't know, Dave. But I'm worn out tonight and I'm going to bed. You coming?"

"Oh yeah," he said as he put his arm around her and headed for the bedroom.

* * *

Sammi woke up unexpectedly at three o'clock in the morning. She'd had a dream she couldn't remember, but it had left her feeling confused and somewhat fearful. She waited a few minutes before she realized that sleep wasn't going to come to her easily now. She got up slowly and carefully, not wanting to disturb Dave and walked into the kitchen. She poured a cup of coffee and sat down at the table almost automatically. So much was on her mind. But her thoughts were flashing by so quickly that they didn't make any semblance of logic. She tried to slow them down. It was difficult. So she sat, trying not to think at all, and that seemed to help. Her thoughts began talking to her.

Linda Saunders has more power than anyone realizes. But she isn't connected with the mob, at least not directly. However, she'd like to be and isn't sure why they haven't extended themselves to her. Jerry Macy was closer to mob ties than anyone else. It seems that the mob was quite interested in Dave. That's what they meant when they said that they needed him. And if Linda could get Dave friendly with some of those members, then she was in. That was her main reason for her attempt at affection with him. But in truth, she did care about him. Yet, she knew that she wasn't on the same side of the law as he was, so there was no future. But she still had hope. And, if for some reason, Dave did succumb to mob activities, all her wishes could be fulfilled.

Sammi felt chills racing throughout her body. She was sure that she was picking up thoughts from far away, and from an atmosphere that didn't know any bounds when she concentrated. Even with Linda and Jerry on the outskirts of the mob, she realized there was a lot of reason for concern. And the thought that the mob wanted Dave was so frightening. Should she tell him? Possibly he would be better prepared if he knew. But she hated to do that to him; all of the extra worries he'd have. Still, she felt that she should. Everyone should be prepared.

"What are you doing up at this hour?" asked Dave as he sauntered into the kitchen. She didn't think he looked more than half-awake.

"I woke up and couldn't get back to sleep." She smiled appreciating his concern.

Dave poured himself a cup of coffee and sat

down.

"You know, Sammi, drinking coffee in the middle of the night isn't the best idea."

She laughed. "I know, but it's what I wanted."

"You're worried, aren't you? You always hold back, but it's okay to admit it."

"Sure I'm worried. Linda scares me." She decided at this time to relay some of her thoughts, but not let him know that they had substance to them. He listened, made some expected facial expressions and offered his own thoughts.

"I could believe anything about Linda and Jerry and some of the others. The slate will always be open on them because we don't know what they're all about. You know that line that you told me about her saying 'we need him' has never left me. I didn't think it had to do with the governor's stuff so I knew more would be coming out later. And I don't think it's come out yet. But trying to get some of us either on the take or working with them is an ongoing thing. Criminals all try to do this. That's why Terry was so successful."

Sammi didn't say anything. She was glad that he realized a lot more than she thought. She should have known they'd all be aware. She then realized that she was the one who wasn't aware of even half of what these cops suspected or what their minds took in on a daily basis. And she knew Dave caught something in her expression.

"What? What are you thinking?"

She smiled. "I should have realized how much more you guys are aware of all the time. I'm still rather new at this, but I get worried about anything that affects you. So be patient with me. I know you guys know what you're doing."

"But we always need any added information that you can get us. Sure, we've suspected everything in the world about Linda and Jerry and that F.C. guy. We don't even know where he's at right now."

"Isn't that Ben's job?"

"But that's where we all work together, you know."

"Let's listen to the tape again."

Sammi used her concentration, but was able to pick up but a few scattered thoughts at best. And they were scrambled at that.

"I know there was a guard that helped her get to the phone. She threatened him with people on the outside, but honestly, her thoughts told me that was a hoax to scare him. But the name Sanford did come up. Don't know if that was the guard's name or someone else's name. I couldn't get anymore. She didn't seem to have any emotion in her thoughts at all. There was one thought about the mayor, but I didn't get it."

"The mayor? Well, I'm sure this is all connected. It's a few new ideas. I'm sure the sarge will look into this and I can have them look at the guards on duty at the time. Wouldn't you know she'd find a link to someone?"

"I'm almost too tired to care right now."

Sammi smiled and then yawned a few times right in a row. Dave looked over and said, "Okay, enough, let's go back to bed. I'm not going alone; I need you next to me."

* * *

The next few weeks had the flutter of new and old activities around Dave's office. He'd met on Monday morning with Sergeant Brady, Tom and Jim about Linda's message.

"Shit," said the sarge upon hearing the news, "I'm not surprised, but I did think that some jail time would have put more sense into her."

"I'll bet Sammi wasn't too pleased," added Jim. "Did she get any new ideas?"

Dave gave Jim a straight look which reminded him that the sarge wasn't in on what Sammi could do. It was so easy to forget when they were all together.

"Well," said Dave, more as a deterrent, "Sammi will always worry, but I'm glad that she'll keep more aware from now on. She believed it when Linda said that she doesn't mind we're married, but I think she's being too naive."

The sarge looked concerned as he said, "Should we keep Sammi covered? What do you want, Dave?"

"I don't think we need that, right now. But I'll feel better when we find out who helped Linda with this. How did she manage to get to a phone and be allowed private time? What's going on out there?"

"You can be sure that I'll be finding out about that," said the sarge. "Damn, there's always something."

Tom said, "But I think the prison will be glad to know about this latest breach. And by the way, where did she get your phone number? Unless she made a note of it before she went away."

Dave acknowledged Tom's comment. That was another point. Then he thought, *I wouldn't be surprised if she has an entire file on me. What the hell's her game anyway?*

"Okay, for now, let me know if you want Sammi protected. I wouldn't think she's in any real danger yet, but it's up to the two of you how you want to work it."

"I think we're alright, now; we'll see later."

"And we can help out on that, too," said Tom with Jim nodding his head in agreement. In truth, they all looked out for each other.

The sarge finished by adding, "I'll be talking to the warden today, if possible. I need to find out what kind of prison they're running there in Muncy. I know they have strict rules and a good record. I've met the warden personally, and he's a good guy, but somebody's screwing up and we need to take care of it NOW."

* * *

Tom stopped by Dave's desk. "Jill wasn't able to find out anything about her brother. It's like he disappeared off the face of the earth. No one's seen him and apparently no one knows anything. She's beside herself. He takes off once in a while, but he usually checks in with her."

Tom was clearly distressed. "I mean, he and I've never had any kind of relationship over the years, but I don't hate him. And I'd be willing for Jill's sake to try and be friendly. I sure hope nothing's happened to him."

"What does Jill plan to do?"

"She's talked to the one friend that she knew of and he said that it's not unusual for him to take off like that. He says he's a guy known for his down moods, so he wants to be alone at times. But if he hears from him, he'll let Jill know. And he lives across the street, so if he comes home, he'll know about that, too."

"When was the last time he saw him?"

"You know, Dave, he wasn't sure. He thinks it was about three weeks ago. And then Jill found out he lost his job at this insurance company where he was working. He was laid off though, not fired. Apparently they were cutting back on staff. Plus someone there said that he had been dating someone for a while and that fell apart as well. Seems that nothing is going his way right now."

"How long is she going to wait?"

"I don't know. She'll probably keep leaving messages for the next couple of weeks. If she doesn't hear anything, she'll contact the police and see what they can find out."

Dave shook his head. "Must be hard on her."

"It is. He's her only family. And even with the circumstances and distance that's developed, she's always had a soft spot for him. I sure hope everything's okay."

About this time they got word that everyone was wanted in Sergeant Brady's office.

The entire department was needed and many stood outside his open door so they'd hear his message.

"The mayor seems to be at it again. Not as bad as last time, but he's been talking to the press about having to keep us in line, so I'm going to be sending out our own press releases starting today. We're going to be on different sides of the fence from now on so if anybody hears anything derogatory about our department in the news, I want to know about it immediately. Is that understood?"

Everyone agreed.

"Ron has changed a lot over the last year or so. I don't know what's going on, but I swear we'll not be the scapegoat for his dammed scheme to get reelected. I used to like Ron, but I see as of late, it's everyone for themselves. So we have to stick together. I want to know of anything that you think I should hear. That's all."

As everyone got up to leave, he called back Tom, Dave and Jim.

"I heard from the warden of SCI-Muncy late yesterday. There was a guard who seemed to be playing up to Linda for favors. He's been let go. He admitted to letting her use the phone in private. But he also said that she told him of people on the outside who wouldn't be happy if he didn't help her. We don't know if that was true or if it was an excuse the guard was sending out. Bottom line is she gets one week of solitary confinement for the phone call. And she gets one year added to her sentence as she had been warned not to contact you, Dave, or have anyone else do it for her. And she gets an extra three months for having a big mouth. Apparently, she told the warden he'd be sorry because she had friends on the outside. They already monitor her mail, but that will be doubled in the future."

Dave said, "I wish I knew who she was involved with on the outside. Word has it that she wanted to be part of the mob. Could be she does have connections." And Dave remembered that Sammi had heard on the tape that the guard was threatened with retaliation.

"I know and that's worrisome," said the sarge. "We're monitoring most of her conversations with other inmates as much as we can. Damn, even in jail she's a problem."

"No shit," offered Tom. "But if they keep it so that she can't contact anyone, that should halt her activity for a time."

"But she can't be kept in solitary forever. When she's out of that, she's the type that will find a way. But the warden says he plans to make it as hard as possible for her. And he can be clever, especially now that he's aware of her conniving and deceitful personality."

They all looked frustrated, but hoped for the best.

"She's still someone we have to guard against," said Jim. "In or out of jail, she's got to be watched."

"Agreed, and hopefully together we can keep her under control."

Dave kept silent. Nothing could convince him that Linda would stop in her attempts at whatever she was planning. And he was worried for Sammi. How could they find out what was behind all of this? Sammi could tell them, if she had the opportunity to listen to Linda's thoughts, but that was one method Dave hoped he'd never have to use.

* * *

At home that night, he was in a thoughtful mood. So many things crowding his mind and most wouldn't even come to the surface. He thought after the money laundering ring went down and then with the success in the child abduction cases that he and Sammi could relax for a while. But his mind wouldn't let go of his concern. Sammi was foremost on his mind. Was she in danger because of Linda? This made him angry. It had taken a long time for him to find someone like her after his wife died, and now because of Linda Saunders, they both had to watch over their shoulders and couldn't relax in the happiness they had found.

"You're certainly in deep thought."

Dave was startled to attention. "Sorry, my mind won't relax and let go."

"You've got to find a way, honey. All this stuff is getting heavy for you. How about you and I try yoga?"

He howled at that one. He was sure she must be kidding.

"Right and next you'll want to put me in those little tight pants and have me standing on my head."

"No," she laughed. "But yoga can be quite relaxing and that's what you need right now, or even meditation. They have classes in that, too."

"I know. I think I'd rather try weight lifting again or some of the other exercises we do at the gym. I've been lax as of late, but it does relieve the stress."

"All right. You got on Tom's back for not getting his physical exams; well, you've got to get to the gym, right?"

"Yeah, okay."

He knew Sammi wouldn't give up, but he waited for her to prod him more.

"Again, what's on your mind?"

He smiled. "You're not going to give up, are you?"

Her satisfied smile reminded him that it wasn't in her nature. "No, I guess not."

"Well, okay, several things right now. I guess that's the problem. So many things are on my mind. I'm quite worried about Linda Saunders. I wish we knew what she was all about. Did you ever ask Julie to look up that emblem on the letter she sent us?"

"No, I didn't. I meant to, but ... let's get that to her this week."

"That's one thing. That would give us a better clue as to what she's into. But then again, I can't get Terry off my mind. God, we finally buried him and it should be starting to let go a little inside of me. I'm not the only one who feels bad. It bugs me that he didn't even get a good burial recognizing him for the good police work he did. Because although he was convicted of being a mole, he did do some good work for us, too. I can't seem to let it go." After voicing his thoughts, he got quiet.

Dave still felt a lot of pain about Terry. And he needed to talk about it at times. At least this had been a good beginning.

"I'm taking a shower and then getting to bed. I've got early meetings at the bank tomorrow."

"I'll turn in soon, too."

When she left the room his thoughts began to race around in his head. Mostly they were of Terry. Whenever he thought of him he felt like he had lost a family member. *God, he loved that kid. What could have possibly happened to turn him around?* It was something he wanted to find out. He remembered one time they had been kidding around when Terry first starting working with them.

"So you're going to be my big brother I hear. That's great, Dave. I never had one. How am I supposed to act with you?"

"Keep your nose clean and you won't have any problems with me. That's the first thing."

"Oh sure, that's a gimme. But are you going to monitor whom I'm dating or is that off-limits?"

Dave laughed. "I'm sure I could give you a few pointers there, too."

"No doubt," said Terry. "You sure have a variety of girls that keep flirting with you. But I must say, you're kinda good looking, I guess. I mean, from a girl's point of view, they most likely even think you're handsome," he teased.

Dave laughed and was slightly embarrassed. "Well, I've seen a few look at you, too."

"But that's because they think if they don't get you, I'll be around."

"That's your second worry. The first thing is for me to get you shaped up and first string for police work. We can worry about the girls later."

That was the type of light conversations they had. And Dave did act like a big brother to him. Terry was about twenty-five when he first joined their force from New York. And then there was the discrepancy that had surfaced as far as his record was concerned. There were some irregularities in his behavior in New York that had never been reported to the Scranton Police Department. Dave wanted to find out how and why that had happened.

"You coming to bed or not?" called Sammi.

"I'll be right there."

When he entered the bedroom Sammi was busy packing up her athletic bag with a clean towel and her Nike shoes and other things.

"What's this about?"

"I figured from now on we can eat dinner an hour later. You're going to be going to the gym a few times a week and I think I'll use the exercise center we have at the bank. What do you think?"

"I think you lassoed me into this," he laughed. "But it's a good idea—for both of us."

CHAPTER FOUR

All of the loose ends that Dave had been trying to tie up were still in disarray. There were few leads in the missing wife case, although calls seemed to come in every day creating more questions that irritated his logical mind. He needed facts and details to fall in line and that wasn't happening. He was considering bringing Sammi in when they questioned the husband again. He seemed genuinely worried about his wife, trying to explain things to his two young children, but his thoughts might give additional clues. That's where Sammi was valuable.

In the midst of all his present work, his mind kept wandering off. He was even now thinking about Linda Saunders. *Was she a threat from jail or not?* And the confusion about Terry wouldn't leave his mind either. It was begging him to investigate and follow every lead. But he wasn't on the case. Another unit had been assigned and evidence seemed to be escaping them. It was a painfully slow process, yet ample hours were being allotted to give it fair attention.

Something was still nagging away at him when LeBron approached him.

"Did you hear about the press release the sarge put out yesterday?"

"I heard he put one out, but I didn't see it yet."

"Here I've got a copy of it. The sarge is pretty good in the communications area, isn't he?"

Dave read the notice.

> **The Scranton Police Department has been investigating the shooting death of one of its own. Although we do not always give out the details of how we work for obvious reasons, it is good for you citizens to be made aware of the fact that we are making progress and taking seriously all of the subversive activities in our area. Others talk about our strategies and second-guess our methods, but we are the ones who take the chances to protect you citizens every day and our crime rate has been dramatically reduced over the last few years; others seem to have forgotten. The unfortunate murder of Terry Gonzalez is a high priority and will be dealt with as a high priority, but not at the sacrifice of the safety of any of the citizens of Scranton. We will keep you updated of all pertinent information as it unfolds.**

Dave let a long, deep whistle escape his lips. "I'm sure this wasn't a real favorite with the mayor."

"I hear they've already had words about it," said LeBron, "and it didn't sound good from either side. The mayor said he will be the one to put out press releases and the sarge said that if we're sacrificed in the news for his benefit, then he will put out his own releases. It was quite heated, I hear."

"Would seem so. Sad for them to be at each other like this. We're supposed to be on the same side and they used to work together so well."

"Really? It doesn't seem so right now."

"No," said Dave, "and that's a shame."

When LeBron walked away Dave was thinking of what Sammi had said about part of this new plan for chaos being to get the mayor and the police chief at each other's throats. And that seemed to be what was happening. Something was undermining this entire process. Dave thought that this must be a plan from outside parties not involved in the day to day details of Scranton. Someone had plans in mind to create havoc again in this state. Just then his phone rang and brought him back to the present.

"Hi Dave," said Sammi. "I heard from Jill. Her brother finally contacted her."

"No kidding. So he's okay then."

"Guess so, kind of depressed about losing his job and breaking off with a long-time girlfriend and apparently needed to get away. I'll tell you about it tonight."

"Okay,"

"We've got a few problems at the bank. The president wants me to sit in on a meeting with a few new people and I think it might be late."

"What time do you think you'll be home?"

"Not until at least six o'clock. Should give you time to get to the gym," she teased.

"I think I will," he laughed. "Jim says he's going to start going, too. I think you and Julie are on the same mind set. Did you talk to her about this?"

"No, I didn't. Isn't that a coincidence?"

Dave had to laugh. "Right, right. And you're the one who doesn't believe in coincidences."

"That's true, I don't."

"I might close up here soon anyway. I can't seem to concentrate much right now. My mind is loaded. A good workout would be the best for me today. And I can see you smiling over the phone."

Sammi laughed as she said, "Got to go. See ya later."

* * *

Dave decided he was done for the day. It was after three o'clock anyway and some days it wasn't worth trying to push yourself to concentrate when it didn't seem to be happening naturally. Sometimes it was much better to back off, clear your mind and wait for another day.

As soon as he locked his desk and gathered his stuff, he headed for the front door when he heard one of the officers calling after him.

"Dave, Dave, wait a minute."

He turned and waited for the anxious-looking young officer on reception duty.

"There's a gal at the front desk that needs to see you. She seems kind of anxious and somewhat uneasy."

"I was on my way out the door, Tim. Can't someone else help her?"

"I don't think so. She asked for you personally. She didn't come in and ask for help. She said she needed to see Detective Dave Patterson."

"Any name? What's this about?"

"Wouldn't say. Said it was personal and she could only discuss it with you."

"Well, okay," he said, somewhat irritated at the timing, but also undeniably intrigued. "Bring her back to my desk, but give me about five minutes."

Thinking about the situation, he smiled as he thought that Sammi would say, *there are no coincidences.* And if the truth be told, he wasn't particularly upset about this turn of events, but he did want to get a good workout and get himself physically exhausted to get rid of the tension inside. He regenerated so well that way and the balance between mental and physical always seemed to fall back into place. *Oh well, she probably wouldn't take long,* he thought, but he did wonder sometimes where people got his name. In truth, any officer could no doubt have helped her, yet so many times people picked up a name from somewhere and that was the sole person who'd satisfy them.

Dave was ready and waiting when the officer brought back a shy and delicate looking young woman, possibly late twenties with definite Mexican heritage. She was quite attractive in her simple fashion, yet had strong and unmistakable pride in herself, despite her tender appearance.

After she sat down, she seemed to stare at Dave in a questioning manner, almost like she was studying his face. And she waited until he spoke first.

"You wanted to see me. I'm Detective Dave

Patterson. How can I help you?"

Looking downward in an effort to evade direct contact seemed to help her. She was somewhat shy and her shoulders hunched up slightly as her hands began twisting in her lap. She was having a difficult time stating her problem and made two definite attempts before she began.

"My name is Marlina Katia Valdez," she said and almost expected Dave to recognize her. Her face showed confusion and it was obvious her mission was difficult for her.

Dave sat back and gave her a friendly smile. He offered her a cup of coffee to see if that would help her relax, but she waved him off.

"Okay, Marlina, how can I help you?" Again he repeated his request and gave her his undivided attention. By now he was wondering who this girl was and why she was having such a difficult time. But then she began and he realized immediately what a tremendous task she had been given.

"Sorry, this is a little tough for me," she said. Her English was perfect despite her heritage and Dave realized she must have lived in the States for years.

"Take your time; it seems that you have a tough problem. That's what I'm here for. I'd like to help you."

She smiled at Dave in an almost familiar fashion. It gave him an uneasy feeling. Then she let out a deep sigh and began in earnest.

"You don't know me, Detective Patterson, but I've heard about you for years and you're the one I had to speak to. You see, I was engaged to Terry Gonzalez."

Dave was shocked to silence. He felt his skin react with excitement and concern as the words sunk into his mind. For a moment, he didn't know what to say. He'd wanted to find out about Terry's past, but didn't know where to begin. And then in walks this girl off the street who says she was his fiancée. But he wasn't sure yet; he wished Sammi was here.

"You were engaged to Terry Gonzalez?" That was all he could manage to say for a bit. Then he sat there thinking, *My God, I should be asking all kind of questions, but my mind is blank. I feel numb.*

"Yes, I was engaged to him. I've known him forever. We were good friends most of our lives. We grew up in Mexico and after he became a policeman in New York, he was able to get me into the United States. Legally, I want you to know that. I am now a legal citizen."

He smiled. "We appreciated him at this station. He was a good friend of mine."

"I know what he did, but there's more to it than you know. He loved being a policeman and when he started working here, he knew he'd found his place. He always talked about you; he thought you were his best friend."

"We worked well together." Dave's policeman instinct knew that he had no real proof of what she was saying so he starting playing it cagey and asked a few pointed questions.

"When were you engaged to him?" Dave remembered that Terry said he had been engaged a few years ago, but they broke it off. It was after he got out of prison that he was thinking of renewing his relationship and settling down.

Marlina smiled. It was almost as if she knew he was testing her, but she cooperated. "We were engaged almost three years ago. But Terry was working some difficult stuff and was worried for my safety. We broke it off and he wanted me to go away for a while. But we kept in touch. After he got out of prison, we talked again about getting married."

That certainly checked out with what Terry had said.

"I'm sorry for your loss," said Dave as he saw the devastated look on her face. If this was all true, this gal had lost a lot.

"Do you live in Scranton?" he asked.

"No, I'm from Philadelphia. And like Terry, I've no family. Actually, he was my family and my best friend most of our lives. We looked out for each other. We grew up in the same orphanage in a small town in Mexico."

Dave was spellbound. He listened yet wished he could feel certain of what he was hearing. Then she offered him the proof.

Marlina took a deep breath. Then she picked up her big purse from the floor and pulled out a large and rather bulky manila envelope. She almost caressed it in her hands before handing it to him.

"Terry told me that if anything happened to him, I was to deliver this package to you. I'm sure it has a lot of delicate information in it and he said it would give you some of the answers you'd been wondering about."

He accepted the package and looked at it

without even attempting to open it. He stared at it and relished the feeling it gave him about being close to Terry again.

"This wouldn't be the best place for you to open it. Terry did say that it had some personal as well as legal stuff in it. He didn't talk to me much about his work; he didn't want me involved."

After another moment, he looked up at Marlina and noticed she was already preparing to leave.

"Are you staying around for a while? I'd like to keep in touch with you."

"I have to get back to Philly; I'm working tomorrow. But let me give you my address and phone number. I'd like to keep in touch with you, too."

As she got up and turned to leave, she stopped and took one step back. She put her hand on Dave's arm and said, "Thanks for being his friend. He thought the world of you and your friendship meant everything to him."

"I felt the same way," was all he could offer.

And within a few more minutes she was gone. She'd talked to him about thirty minutes in all, but he felt his entire life had changed. He didn't truly know how to react. Yet he could almost picture Terry there with him saying something like, "Hey, my girl's pretty hot, isn't she?" He had this flippant attitude about a lot of things, but Dave always suspected he had a very serious side that he kept mostly hidden. And now he realized that he was about to find out what that was.

He headed for the gym. This workout was now more important than ever. His mind was bursting with any wild idea that was coming his way. And he needed to settle down. He was glad Sammi would be home tonight.

* * *

Dave smirked as he walked into the gym and saw Jim hard at work on the treadmill. He waved him over.

"Julie's on my back, so here I am. What about you?"

"Same thing. Sammi's thinks I need to get rid of my stress. But she's right. I keep meaning to get here, but never get around to it."

"Yeah," said Jim. "it does help a lot. My ex is having marriage problems again and the girls are upset. She's been married to this one for over two years, maybe three. I don't know, I forget. But I wish she would find what she wants. I don't like to see the girls so uptight, you know. And even Kathy, she's never happy. Can't imagine what she wants."

"Some people have a lot of trouble finding their place in life. Some never find it."

"That's true. Gees, I've been on this treadmill for over thirty minutes now. I don't think Sammi's going to count it good if you simply stand here and talk to me."

Dave laughed. "Guess not. I'd better get to work. But before I go, do you think you might have some time this weekend. You and Julie have plans? I think I may need to talk about something."

"I'm sure we could manage. Don't think we're

booked or anything. Let's try for Saturday night.
Anything okay to talk about in front of the gals?"

"Oh yeah, I'd like them both in on it."

"Okay, later."

Then Dave moved on and began with weight
lifting and on to the treadmill. He ran full speed
for a while until he felt his body fatiguing. He
wanted to feel that physical exhaustion, then his
mind could settle down. It always worked that way
for him. He ended up doing some boxing and hit
that bag as hard as he could. Over and over he hit
that bag full force and suddenly something inside
started to let go. He had accomplished his purpose.

* * *

He still beat Sammi home. It was past six
o'clock, but there was no sign of her yet. He took
out the folder and looked at it. He was anxious to
see what was inside, yet he paused. Some of the
secrets of Terry's life would be held in here. He
knew that, yet still he waited and simply stared at
it. His mind was wandering off thinking of Terry.
Obviously he was involved in something that had
him concerned. He had taken the foresight to let
Marlina keep some information for him. He could
trust her. But the fact that he gave it to her for
safekeeping meant that he was sure there was an
even chance he wouldn't make it. What was so
important to him to take such a chance? Well, he
had wanted to know what Terry was all about and
now he would find out.

Opening the folder, he found several typed

documents, a few pictures of people he didn't recognize, and some legal documents tucked in the bottom of a pocket folder. But on top was a letter addressed to him. He opened it first and noticed that his hands were shaking a little.

> *Dave,*
>
> *If you get this letter it means I'm gone. Marlina was told to give this to you in the event I turned up dead. So, I guess I am. I have so much to tell you and there's so much I've kept from you, but it was out of necessity. You were the one I trusted most. And that's why part of me died a little when you got shot. I still need to tell you how sorry I am for that. But, I must get to the facts that you need to know.*
>
> *Hope you'll be happy to hear this—in fact, I know you will. I wasn't a mole in the police department. I was a double agent. Let me explain. I lived in Mexico until I was almost eighteen. Not sure if you knew that I was an orphan, I never talked about it. A little embarrassed I guess. But in our pathetic little town and with my background, I had nowhere to go. Luckily I made it through high school. But they always told me that I had brains, so I guess that helped. Anyway, many friends*

around me died, most got into drugs or other illegal and dangerous activity. I thought it was stupid, so when I had a chance to get out and get to the States, I grabbed it.

Some guys took a liking to me and got me in; it was illegal. I even went to college, but I was drawn to police work. After two years, I did good and was on my way, but they found out about my illegal status. Yet you know me and my likeable ways—ha ha—well they made me a deal and part of it was becoming a legal citizen. I was real good at getting information out of people, and I could fit easily into any group, so they wanted me to work undercover and they put some crap on my record that wasn't true, but it gave me what I needed. I got sent to Scranton so that I could wheel and deal on the outskirts of the mob, but I reported back to officials in the New York precinct. Some FBI people know about me, too. But no one could help me. They were told hands off so I could do my work. I did tip off people about that Fritz Connelly guy, but mainly I reported to Jerry Macy in that money laundering deal. What I gave him was sometimes the truth, but sometimes it was what the FBI wanted them to believe. I guess you could call me a double snitch, although I must admit I always hated that word.

Dave had to put the letter down for a bit. As he got to page 2, he was beginning to realize what Terry had put up with. He was a good guy and a true cop, but caught up in a tough situation. And no one ever knew. Sammi picked up thoughts about getting information to Jerry Macy, but nothing else. He took a deep breath. Part of him was thrilled that Terry was a good guy, but it had gotten him killed.

Okay, good buddy, that's the background. Now, to what I need you to know. Fritz Connelly isn't done yet. Not sure where he's at but he wants trouble in Scranton and Harrisburg. They screwed up his deal to be governor. The latest is to cause trouble between the mayor and police, and then the governor wouldn't know what to do. They still want that governor out of there and one of their own put in, but it won't be Fritz. I guess they're desperate for this area as their hub of activity.

And, they want to oust our buddy Sergeant Brady. They don't like him at all. He's trouble for them. He's got to watch his back. I'm not sure who's going to do it or how, but I know that's part of their plan. I've been suspicious of that new guy that works for the mayor, the one they call the tracker. He's a real nut. Anyway, I've been trying to get some information on him. So, if you get this letter before November, look into his part in my death. I've been updating these letters regularly. Scranton and Harrisburg, the mayor, police chief and some of the sergeants as well as the governor still have a lot of problems on their hands. Don't let these guys get them at each other's throats. I know that's part of their plan.

Wish I had more for you, but some of this I heard about when I was in prison and was following up when I got out. I need you to do a favor for me. Take care of Marlina. She's got a few friends in Philly, but she's mostly alone in the world. Help her, okay?

I want you to know, Dave, that you were always like a big brother to me. I couldn't have loved you more if we were blood relations and I'll always look after you wherever I am.

Don't forget me,
Terry Gonzalez

I've enclosed some documents that will give some details as to what

I've talked about. I found them use-
ful.

After he read the letter a second time he sat there feeling limp. His body wouldn't function and his mind was failing him. Terry was a good cop. He took a deep breath. It seemed that something inside of him always knew that. Apparently all the cops felt something since everyone was ready to forgive him. It was a shame that even after he came out of prison, he still couldn't set the record straight. And all he got was that crappy little funeral. He deserved a heroes' salute. Sometime in the future, Dave was going to make sure that he got it.

* * *

He heard Sammi's car enter the garage. He was happy she was home. When she entered he went over and held her for a long time. He knew she saw the look on his face and no doubt felt the tension in his body. But she would wait until he was ready to talk.

And he waited until after dinner. He was especially quiet that night and it was considerably later when they sat together on the couch that he was able to open up. His eyes filled with tears as he went over the story, first when Marlina walked into his office and then he slowly handed her the letter. He laid his head back and closed his eyes and let Sammi read the letter quietly. When she turned to him, she had tears rolling down her cheeks.

"Oh my God. What a load he carried. This guy who had no family growing up and learned to wheel and deal throughout his life, was a valuable double agent."

Then she stopped talking and cried some. Dave had a few tears escape from his eyes, too. They sat close to each other sharing the pain. Sammi was the first to speak.

"He died doing what he wanted to do. That's the one positive thing I can say about this. What a loss for all of us. And what you felt for him, Dave, was right. Something inside of you must have known."

Dave nodded. "At least I'm glad we all talked to him after his prison term. I know some departments would have shunned him completely. But we didn't. We all liked him so much. It's like when you have a little kid who does something bad. You still love the kid, but hate what he did. Everyone forgave him. Most couldn't figure him out, but they still liked him."

Still trying to recover they sat together longer.

"I'm so glad I had those few conversations with him before he died. He knew he was taking a big chance and said what he wanted to say to me. God, I loved that kid."

Dave held Sammi and relaxed for a while longer. His body wasn't going to surrender its pain, yet the hurt was a different type now. He wished he had known. That's all. If only he had known.

"I'm not sure yet what to do with this information. I know I have to share some of it with the sarge, but I don't know. I'm not officially on this case. I think I want to talk to him about what you heard because it's confirmed here. This group wants to cause trouble between the mayor, the police department and the governor. It's already starting to happen. I have to let him know that. You picked it up, too."

Sammi seemed to bring up distant memories. "Yeah, I did. I know that part of the plan is getting these groups hating each other. They want to alienate them as much as possible."

"I think it might be hard to get to the mayor already. He seems to have become trusting of those around him. And he's heading for trouble that way."

"What are they going to do about the governor? It doesn't sound like they're going to let him alone either. What do they want?"

"They want control, Sammi, it's got to be that. And they'll do anything they can to get it. And one of the ways is to have their own hand-picked governor in office. "

"You're going to have to find a way to get around that Peter guy."

Dave wrinkled his nose, an old habit he acquired as a kid. "Right, the tracker has too much influence already."

"And it didn't seem to take him all that long to do it."

"He seems to be a big part of this puzzle. And Terry said that if he died before November to look at him for having something to do with his death."

She puckered her lips. "I knew he spelled trouble right away, but I didn't get enough."

"Well, your favorite thing is coming up."

"What?"

"The annual get together at the governor's mansion. Isn't that your favorite thing?"

She gave him her most exasperated look. "When is that?"

"About two weeks, I think. And this Peter guy has to be there, because the mayor will be there. I think you're going to be busy at this party."

"I'm going to be wondering who to concentrate on."

"Just pick up what you can. The rest of us will be clued in, too. By the way, guess where I saw Jim today?"

She shook her head.

"At the gym. Julie's been on his back, too. And I wanted to get together with them on Saturday. I'd like to talk to him before I decide what to do with this new stuff. Probably should get Tom in on this, too."

"That's the best thing. Then the three referees can figure out what to do."

Dave laughed. "You know, it's not as much fun when you use that term against me."

Sammi laughed. "But I enjoy it, too."

"But you're not supposed to enjoy it; you're supposed to be irritated. It's my tease."

"Oops, sorry," she laughed.

CHAPTER FIVE

"Holy Shit, you've got to be kidding." That was Jim's reaction when he found out about Terry. "This guy walked a lonesome road. Hell, I worked the docks for a while and after six or seven months, that was enough. But you guys knew what I was doing. This double stuff is considerably harder to pull off."

"That certainly must be why he joked around so much. It was his way of keeping the tension down."

Everyone had come to Dave's house on Saturday. A big part of him wanted to keep the Terry business private, but he knew he couldn't. And it took away a little part of himself as he began telling the story. But it had to be told. He still wasn't entirely sure what to do with all the information. True, the sarge had to be let in on some of it, but how much? And what? He wanted some opinions and these guys he trusted.

Tom said, "I sure wish we were first string on his murder. That would make everything so much easier. But we're not. So now what?"

"That's the problem," said Dave. "I know I can't keep this to myself, but part of me wants to. I wish the three of us could work this."

No one had any answer. The girls were letting them try to work it out themselves, but it seemed like a dead end. If they gave all of this info to the sarge, well, they weren't sure what he'd do with it. But this could change the picture. They hoped it would.

"I'm hoping Sammi can pick up something at the governor's party. Everyone will be there." He turned to her, "We've got to find a way to keep you around the tracker. He's probably the one who has the most information."

"Is there anything we can do to help?" asked Jill.

"Actually there is," she said. "Dave knows that I have to concentrate, sometimes rather intensely to get the information I want. And when I do I can lose track of things around me. And we don't need anyone to get suspicious of what I'm doing. This is a big operation so we don't know who we can trust right now. But I could use any of you, but especially you girls to keep me on track, give me my space and not allow too many people to interrupt me. Gals hanging around talking together always looks normal. I think this will work out better than it did before, Dave."

"Yep," he said. "We're a complete group now. This is a solid operation and it might be harder for the two of us to work it without being detected. We're going to all need to work together on this one."

So they had a plan in place. It would take all of them at the party to allow space for Sammi to do her job and not allow anyone close enough to get suspicious. But it could work better than ever, with all of them working together.

* * *

The trio talked to the sarge on Monday morning. It was a long closed door session with lots of shock, disbelief and head shaking coming from their boss. At the end he sat down and was quiet for a few minutes. This was entirely out of character for a fast-talking, quick-thinking police sergeant.

"I know what I'd like to do on this. It's against my better judgment, but sometimes I go against the grain anyway. I didn't put you guys on this case because you three were the closest to Terry. I thought a fresh perspective would work better. I felt I needed a more detached outlook. But now, things have changed. I'm going to leave the others on this case, too. It's a high priority, but I'm putting all three of you back on it; we'll call it a backup action. But it'll be a quiet investigation on your part. You don't have to share this with any-one yet. But I do think you've got the best chance of getting a lot of information in several areas."

All three smiled. They were obviously pleased and it was not lost on the sarge.

"I'm sure you'll bring Sammi in on this, too. Never mind answering, you've probably already included her."

Sergeant Brady was quiet, but everyone knew he wasn't done yet. He was mulling things around for a few minutes before he began again.

"Terry's murder is bad enough, but we've got an entire state to be concerned about. Why the hell are they targeting us again?"

Jim answered this one. "It seems that they

want this area to be the hub for the entire eastern part of the States. We're in a unique position for them to hide info, especially if they can get the governor's computer system again. They're good, it's true, but they think they're so much better than us that they can do it this time."

"And of course it's all about control and power," said Tom. "They want to have control of all of the business on this side of the state, then they can easily run their national business from here."

"But I don't get it," said the sarge, "why here, why our state? Why our town?"

"Well," explained Dave, "remember there's a perfect triangle between Scranton, Harrisburg and Philadelphia. The docks give them comfortable access to shipping cargo around the world. Most of their shipments go by sea. The governor and his area would be the main focus. It's a smaller city and easier to control major activities. And Scranton completes the triangle. Within this area will be most of the money laundering, layering, hiding and testing that will continue in an ever-increasing pattern. They did it before and failed, but apparently they believe they can do it now."

"Damn, why not New York? It has similar access."

Dave continued. "True, but within that computer system they would have the stock market and Wall Street to contend with. Any tampering or suspicions even accidentally arising in that area and the feds would be all over it."

"I guess so. Anyway, they already have the mayor and I at odds and I don't think that's ever happened before. Oh sure, we had quick little heat-ups once in a while, but nothing like this. We always had a good working relationship."

"We're going to pounce on the tracker and one of his bodyguards. What does anybody know about them anyway?" asked Jim. "Anyone know anything?"

They all shook their heads. "The tracker definitely has the mayor's confidence; he listens to him, so this could be tricky," said Tom.

"Let's find out who he is first, and anything about his background. Also anybody else new in his unit needs to be looked at. I want a report on them. Something's beginning to smell really bad."

* * *

Sammi was happy that she and Jill found time for a quick lunch. They talked about her brother and Jill got her up to date.

"It seems Todd hit the end of the line for a while. He forgot to contact me and the loss of his job was devastating to him; he was doing well, he thought. And then his girlfriend decided to call it quits. I guess it was done amicably, but it still hurt him a lot. He said that he still can't decide what to do with his life and he's forty-six now. He feels totally lost."

"He seems to be going through some rough times."

"He's so alone in the world. He's always been a loner, but I don't think he wanted to be. So now he's decided to take some time and try to get a new perspective."

Jill seemed concerned about what he was planning to do. In fact, it seemed a little odd to her.

"When we were kids, our parents took a vacation in Prescott, Arizona. We stayed at the Pine Lawn Mobile Park and had a wonderful time. The men and boys went prospecting for gold in the Superstition mountains and Todd always remembered that and said he wanted to go back some day."

Sammi waited as the waitress came and poured more coffee. She felt Jill was only now getting into the reason why she'd wanted to have lunch with her.

"I know he's trying to find himself. And he mentioned that he felt bad that we've been so estranged over time. He admitted to me that he acted badly regarding Tom for no real reason. He was simply an angry and confused kid. Later on, he didn't know how to make it right. I told Tom about it."

"What did he say?"

"Well, Tom was always willing and even now I think he'd do it for me. He could understand how a troubled kid got a thought in his mind and then didn't know how to change it. He's seen it a lot in his work."

Sammi knew how thoughts could affect your life. And getting out of a rut caused by deep ingrained thoughts usually took a lot of effort.

"Anyway, he's decided to go back to Prescott to see if he could find himself. I'm not sure if that's a good idea and I told him so. He'd be alone there. Yet he says he wants to remember those times when he felt good about himself and do some soul searching and add a little prospecting. It might trigger good thoughts about himself. He won't stay more than a month and when he comes back, he wants to begin building a real life for himself. I hope he can do it."

Sammi felt Jill's brother had a good attitude. "It might be important for him to get away; maybe he'll get some new ideas for a future."

"But prospecting can be dangerous. I made him promise he wouldn't go alone. Some people have died there and others have gotten hurt. And with his state of mind, I don't know ..."

Jill seemed quite agitated. She would have liked to help her brother, but this was not the time. This was the moment to be a good sister, show trust in him and wait.

"He has to do it himself, Jill. You can't do this for him."

"You're right; I know. And they do have some prospecting groups that go out together. I think he wants to check out the Old Dutchman's Gold Mine. Have you heard about it?"

She didn't think she had.

"Well, it happened before the turn of the century, but this man found a lot of gold and no one could ever follow him back and discover where it was. After he died, many tried with no luck. And a lot of people died trying to find this gold mine. It's almost a legend and Todd's always been fascinated about it all of his life."

"If he got into a group and went out prospecting it might do him good. He's got to get away for a while. But this time, hopefully, he'll stay in touch with you."

"Oh yeah," Jill laughed. "I made him promise that."

* * *

At home that night, Sammi began working feverishly on the computer. Her thoughts had been tempted to find information about an unknown subject, The Old Dutchman's Gold Mine. She hadn't told Jill, but something about that title tickled her memory. She must have heard about it at one time or another. There were many listings and she got the information she wanted.

> **The Lost Dutchman's Gold Mine is reportedly a very rich gold mine hidden in the Superstition Mountains, near Apache Junction, east of Phoenix, Arizona. The land is presently a designated Wilderness Area, and mining is now prohibited.**

Sammi felt that Jill would be happy to hear that. Her brother couldn't do any prospecting there, but, of course, he could visit the area and bring back some of those memories that he needed.

> **The mine was named after a German immigrant Jacob Waltz who located a rich gold mine in the Superstition Mountains and for years edged out enough ore at a time to maintain a decent living and occasionally splurge on**

items he wanted. He apparently made a deathbed confession to someone and drew a crude map to the gold mine.

After his 1891 death, people have been trying to find his mine, since its vein appeared to be rich. Many died trying and to this day, no one has ever found any trace of it.

Since it was now a Wilderness Park, no one would ever find it, thought Sammi. And it was one less thing for Jill to worry about.

Dave wandered into the computer room to see what she was doing. She discussed her findings with him.

"I've heard about that gold mine," he said. "I know some people get so fascinated and think they're going to find a treasure and live off of it for the rest of their lives. Others are more curious, I guess."

"It's interesting, though, and I had to look it up. I'm sure her brother must know about it being a designated Wilderness area, so possibly he wants to get back there and remember happier times."

"That could help him," he said.

He read a little more about it and then the subject was changed.

"Todd is a good example of the power of your thoughts. Apparently, he didn't get any counseling during his life, but it sounds like he could have used some. I don't know why some people's thoughts get all tangled up like his did. I mean, he was raised in the same family as Jill. Apparently his parents loved him, too, and took good care of him. But for some unknown reason his life took a different turn than Jill's life. Doesn't it make you wonder why?"

"You don't know his thoughts. I know you could if you were around him, but right now, aren't you guessing?"

"I'm going by what Jill told me. He's been a confused guy for a while, never finding what he was looking for. Other than his late teenage years and early twenties, which can be hard on a lot of people, he stayed straight and didn't get into any trouble, but he's not a happy guy. Something's missing in his life."

"That's true of a lot of us. Some people never find what they're looking for."

"I know, but I'd love a chance to listen to his thoughts. Perhaps I could find a negative pattern and help him change it."

"Sammi, Sammi, you can't help everyone in the world. I know your heart goes out to a lot of people, but you can't do it all. Just help those you can."

She nodded. Yes, that was true, but she always wanted to try. And she had to admit, she didn't have all the answers anyway.

"Which reminds me," continued Dave. "The governor's party is this Saturday. Another formal party that you'll love," he teased. "But it's good that we have others working with us now. Getting around the tracker will be difficult since I don't think the mayor will be too congenial with us. But we need you to get anything you can out of that group."

"Remember, I don't have to be right next to the person to hear them. But I do need to be able to concentrate. I think Jill and Julie will be able to help me out there. If you saw three women together, wouldn't you think they were having a tête-à-tête? This will allow me to do what I need to do. I think this will work out quite well."

* * *

"I'm so glad the sarge put us on Terry's case. I was having trouble being on the outer rim of this one. I seem to be living it every day anyway. I can't stop thinking back at some of the times we talked and joked. But he was carrying a heavy load. No one on either side could know what he was doing. That does take a brilliant mind and a fast-thinking person. We saw one side of him and we thought he was extremely valuable."

Dave stopped and shook his head. Terry's story would never leave him. But once they could bring his killer to justice, it would help a lot.

"And even Terry's notes said to check out the tracker," said Sammi. "He's the one I'll concentrate on at the party. Is he married, or dating anyone? That might be another angle to follow."

"I have no idea. We don't know anything about him. And so far any checks we've made about a Peter Armors have come up empty. I don't even think that's his real name. I've got a sinking feeling he's a plant here for somebody else. And Tom said the report on that bodyguard you were concerned about is showing someone with a troubled past."

"What's his name?"

"Josh Logan and it seems he was suggested for the job by the tracker. This is a web that someone is trying to put around the mayor and unfortunately, so far it's working. He's buying it completely."

"I thought everything had been quiet for a few weeks between the mayor and the sergeant."

"It has, and there hasn't been any antagonism between the governor and either one. But you have to believe it's in the works."

"And if they get to the point that they aren't speaking or cooperating with each other, then their enemies can move in and take over a lot easier, right?"

"Exactly. They isolate them and then they're both weaker. And once the ground work is laid, it's a lot tougher to break it up. We've got to stop this one before it goes much further."

"Is Julie seeing anything new coming over the computers?"

"She mentioned the other day that some new and rather bizarre things are starting to happen, so you see, Sammi, here we go again."

Dave moved over to the couch and put his arm around her. He then relaxed and put his feet on the ottoman and rested his head against the back.

"Let's sit here for a few minutes and forget the rest of the world."

"Okay, 'cause we know the universe will continue to unfold as it should."

"Oh no, do I hear some philosophy coming out of this little person next to me?"

Dave laughed as he gave her a hug and let the rest of the world take care of itself.

* * *

Two days' later Sammi got a call from Dave while at work. Could she stop by the police station on her way home? They were bringing in the husband of that missing wife and wanted her in on the questioning.

She arrived a few minutes before John Wentworth. He seemed more nervous and agitated than she expected, but then it had been almost two weeks since his wife had been reported missing and the strain was beginning to show. They had two little children under five and his nerves were beginning to unravel. Sammi picked up the shock that he'd experienced at first, but now it was sinking in that she might not be back. His mind was scared, frustrated, angry and confused. Why did this happen to Vicki? They were an ordinary couple etching out an everyday existence and one day, she leaves her job as a cashier at a local Wal-Mart and doesn't make it to the sitter on time to pick up the children. There was still no sign of her or her car since that day.

Dave and Tyrone conducted the interview and Sammi sat on Dave's left side.

Tyrone began. "Mr. Wentworth, have you heard anything at all from anyone who may have seen your wife?"

"No, of course not," he said. "I would have let you know."

"Okay, but relax. We need to ask you more

questions; some are strictly routine."

That statement didn't seem to help him relax at all. Sammi relayed to Dave that his mind seemed to be strictly on the questions.

"I'm sure this is tough on you, but we keep hoping that you've remembered something."

"No, I sure wish I had. But I'm in the dark. She didn't make it home. Her routine was to leave work and pick up the little ones before five o'clock and she didn't make it. I don't know anything more."

"And your relationship was good, no big fights or problems?" asked Dave.

"No, we were fine."

Sammi signaled he was telling the truth, but got a flash thought from him about a neighbor he had concerns about. She cautioned Dave.

"Is there anyone in your area that you've had concerns about?" he asked.

He shot Dave a startled look. It was obvious that he was hesitant to say anything.

"Look," he said, "we're not going to run out and accuse anyone. But we need to know if there was anyone at all in your area, or anywhere else that you had concerns about?"

"Okay, I need to mention something. I'm sure you realize from her picture, that Vicki is quite pretty. And she was considered quite appealing. We did have this one neighbor who made some suggestive remarks to her a few times when I wasn't around. He made her nervous. And she seldom went outside when he was out and I wasn't home. It was never more than words, but now it makes me wonder."

"I see. Did you ever confront him?"

"There wasn't anything to confront him about. I think he was trying to find out what kind of gal Vicki was. She let him know in no uncertain terms that she wasn't interested and I think he shied away after that. Yet sometimes when we were outside playing with the kids, he would lean on the fence and watch us. It made Vicki nervous."

"How old is he? Is he married?"

"I'd say he's about fifty, and he's married. His wife is quite nice, but you can tell he's the boss and he doesn't always treat her with much respect. And he didn't talk respectfully to Vicki. She didn't like it."

"What's his name?"

"Do I have to tell you? I don't want to create any problems and he's mean when he's angry. He does have a temper, especially when he's been drinking."

"We'll be discreet, but we have to know. We could find out anyway, but you telling us about him would be a big help. We need to follow up on any possibility," said Dave. "Others will be questioned, too. We've already talked to some in the neighborhood."

"Oh, really? I didn't know. That's different. His name is Larry Nielsen and he's a rather big fellow, over six feet and extremely muscular. He isn't shy at all and will tell you what he thinks no matter who you are."

"Okay, is there anything else on your mind?"

As she expected, John's thoughts went immediately to his concern about Vicki. He didn't want to think she was dead, but after more than a week and no one heard anything about her, well he wanted to know the chances.

"You think she's dead, don't you?" he asked.

"We have no evidence that points us in that direction," said Tyrone. "People have been missing a lot longer than two weeks and showed up fine. We simply don't know."

John slowly nodded.

"And in the last two weeks, this Larry fellow has been home. You've seen him?"

"I think he was gone away the first weekend Vicki went missing, but he's been pretty much around other than that."

It seemed that a few other neighbors had expressed concern and sadness about his wife, but none had said much. They'd been in the neighborhood less than two years and a lot of couples had problems and one party left for a period of time. No one knew them well enough to make a judgment.

Other than the questionable neighbor, this session hadn't produced any more clues. When it was over Sammi told Dave that other husbands had been angry at this Larry for his flirtatious performance with their wives.

Tyrone said, "Well thanks, you two. This gives me a few more ideas. I've got to follow up on that neighbor fellow. I'm curious if he has any kind of record with that temper. LeBron has been checking surveillance on that store and now I wonder if he was in that day. We've got to get a picture of him and we need to talk to him."

"Right, and I'd try to be careful on this one. Don't let him know John said anything at all. He seemed kind of nervous about him anyway and he doesn't need anything else right now."

"Agree. I picked that up, too. I know you're mainly on the Gonzalez case now, but I still appreciate any input you can give me."

"Absolutely. And I'm still available for working on this one."

* * *

Later that night Sammi mentioned, "One troublesome neighbor doesn't seem like much of a lead."

"You never know. That's why we have to follow up on anything that comes our way. It doesn't seem that anyone saw that woman after she left the store. With all of our queries out there, still no one remembers seeing her."

She said, "All these dead ends. I'd sure like to be in on any questioning of that Larry Nielsen guy."

"I'd like you to be there, too. What this guy has on his mind could be quite telling."

Sammi then changed the subject. "Did Julie ever find out anything about that emblem that was on Linda's letter?"

"No, Julie's still digging away at that one. Her main sources have come up empty, although they said that some groups or clubs make up their own and they're not always registered so they wouldn't know all of them."

She said, "It's quite imaginative in a way. It has the impression of a few animals, like the head of a lion on a bull. This to me would represent strength and leadership. But then they have a few types of flowers for a gentler impression and finally it ends up with a large sign that almost looks like the infinity symbol on its side."

"You could have something there. They're showing their strength to all, hostile and majestic, the flowers could be poisonous though, and the infinity might mean they plan on being around forever and succeeding."

"Wow, that could be it. This emblem could be an entire message that they have the strength to win."

She remained quiet for a bit trying to understand what they were doing.

"Julie came up with part of this," said Dave. "Her sources say these emblems usually mean a type of total dedication to a mission. And they're not always favorable to the world."

"We'll have to wait and see on that. Anything new on Linda?"

"Not much. She had a rough time with the solitary confinement and when she got out she asked immediately for that guard that helped her. She wasn't too pleased that he was let go."

"This should help her to realize that everything isn't going to go her way anymore."

Dave was more hesitant. "I don't know. She always worries me. I guess she always will at least until we find out who she's involved with. There has to be others here that she has as connections."

"You think so?"

"Sure, look, if that group is coming back and trying for the governor's computers again and trying to get Scranton and Harrisburg as their main hub, you've got to know that Linda is in on this somewhere. Of course, from jail she's not going to play a big part, but she still might be useful to them in some way."

"Do they have any monitor on the visitors she gets?"

"Actually, she's not allowed many, but yes, they have to log in and get checked. She has no privacy even with them or with her mail. And especially now, her mail gets proofed with greater care."

Sammi tried to understand. *Why did some people think this was worth it? People's evil thoughts caused them trouble all of their lives.* She would have liked to know something more about Linda though. *What was her childhood like? Did she have loving parents or was she an orphan or raised in foster homes?* Some of the answers would no doubt give a reason for her choices in life. Her attitude and her direction had obviously gotten diverted to a subversive line of behavior, as well as to a dangerous and detrimental pattern of lifestyles that sooner or later had to end up with her in prison.

She heard Dave next to her starting to breathe deep and noisily. He was falling asleep. She hated to wake him up, but their bed would be much more comfortable. He struggled to wake up and yawned repeatedly before he made it to the bedroom. She hoped he hadn't lost a good dream.

CHAPTER SIX

Sammi knew it would be a festive evening. She'd been to the yearly get-together at the governor's place once before. But neither Julie nor Jill had ever made it inside. They were quite excited and understandably so.

They all planned to arrive at the governor's mansion at 8:00 P.M. and then take time for a quick tour of the place before the festivities started in earnest. Although it was looked forward to as a gala event with food, drink and relaxation on the menu, the guys were always on duty. Policemen never had the luxury to totally relax, yet there was an excitement in the air reserved for these special celebrations.

"I'm sure you'll show the girls your famous '*Gone With The Wind*' staircase," he teased. "I honestly didn't get it when you first mentioned it to me. I think that's a girl thing."

"Come on, Dave, I know you've read the book; it's a classic."

"Of course I read the book, but I didn't make the connection."

Sitting at ease in her beautiful mauve full-length gown and spreading its slightly bell-shaped skirt across her side of the front seat, it was obvious that she was much more comfortable dressed up than Dave. He hated tuxedos and even though he had rented the coolest and most up-to-date rendition, he would have traded back to his blue jeans or even his police uniform in a split second. But this event required formal dress for the one official ball that the governor gave each year to thank all of his work force in the state which included his own work staff, police force, legislators, mayors and numerous other state workers.

"Okay," Dave said, "I think we all have our priorities in order. And I agree that you gals talking together as needed for a cover is a good idea. We'll back you up whenever and wherever you want us to. But the important thing is to get you in a strategic position to hear what you need. Agreed?"

She said, "We're all set. Honestly, the girls know what I need, and I think I've got the perfect cover with Jill and Julie. And, of course, sometimes we'll all be together."

"I don't want to split up too far," he said. "I think it'll look more logical if we're close by most of the time."

"And I hope I'll get to dance with you this time. I think we've only danced together twice in all these years I've known you. They'll have a nice band as usual and ..."

"Gees, I hate to dance at these big parties. I'll dance with you at home anytime you want, okay?"

"Nope, not good enough. You're a good dancer, Dave. I want at least one dance."

Dave smiled at her and she knew he was trying to think of a reason, any plausible reason to get out of it.

* * *

Walking in the front door, they looked at each other as they remembered the last time they'd been there together. It was when they first started realizing they were sharing more than a close friendship and Sammi couldn't help but remark, "We've come a long way, haven't we?"

He looked at her lovingly as he said, "The best part is that we took that long way together."

They had barely walked through the front door when Governor Gary and his wife approached them. Introductions were made as well as wishes for them to relax and have a good time.

He made one extra comment to Dave. "It's nice to see you well and functioning again. God bless you."

When they entered the main ballroom, they met Jill, Julie, Tom and Jim who had arrived shortly before them. Dave's eyes immediately went to the far corner of the room near the huge double windows. He looked at Sammi and said, "I have to go back over there for a minute. It's something I need to do."

"Do you want me to come with you?"

"I would. I'd like that."

They excused themselves from the main group for a few minutes as they walked over to the place where Dave had been shot in a sting operation more than two years ago. They weren't sure at the time whether he was going to make it or not and Tom had stayed by his side all the way to the hospital. He remembered nothing from the moment he went down until he regained consciousness five days later. He couldn't come to this place without walking over to this exact spot. He held Sammi's hand tightly. She had been his anchor throughout his recuperation.

He felt someone behind him. He turned to see Tom and Jill standing there quietly. The moment was surreal.

Dave took a deep breath and said, "Tom, I was lucky you were here with me."

"And you'd have taken care of me as well, like you did in the past."

No more words were spoken. None were necessary.

At this moment Sergeant Brady found his way over and shared in the moment. They all looked at each other, but no one spoke. Then slowly they all turned and went back to the party.

* * *

It was almost an hour later when the mayor and his wife walked in. And of course, the tracker was right behind him, apparently alone. They started to make the rounds of the room. When they approached the sergeant and his group, a stiffness took over as the tracker tried to steer them away from each other. But his wife and Sergeant Brady's wife had always been friendly and they complicated the tracker's plans to completely ignore their group.

"It's good to see the two of you," said Audrey Stillman. "It's been much too long."

"I agree," Norma Brady said, "and we must

rectify this situation. I've missed you."

Then introductions were made and Sammi was busy concentrating on two considerably strong-minded women who could be allies for them, as well as trying to pick up anything on the tracker's mind. And she had a lot of work to do. These women did have a hint of some problems between their two husbands, but didn't know the extent of what was happening. But they didn't plan to step aside and be ruled by the tracker, especially the mayor's wife, Audrey. She seemed considerably aware that he had an agenda. She didn't agree with it and she was not going to let him rule her life.

"Sometimes life can be quite busy, but we can't let our husbands get in our way," Audrey said. "Let's have lunch sometime soon and catch up on our lives."

Norma nodded. "I think it's a great idea."

The mayor kept a stern look on his face, but Audrey's emotions were real and she wouldn't take a back seat to anyone. When the tracker tried to move them on hurriedly, she said, "What's the rush? I'm talking to an old friend."

Sammi caught his thoughts as he realized that she was going to be a problem for him. He made a note to tell the mayor to keep his wife in line. He would suggest that she not have lunch or be friendly with either Sergeant Brady's wife or the governor's wife. Noting the strong personality of Audrey Stillman, Sammi knew that he had a challenge on his hands and that was an angle they could use.

* * *

Moving through the evening, Sammi and the girls found a way to stay in close proximity to the mayor. Where the mayor was, the tracker was close behind. Then the bodyguard came in and what she heard in their conversation was seriously worrisome.

"Josh, I think we have a problem with the mayor's wife."

"How's that?"

"She wants to get friendly with the sergeant's wife again."

"We could put a stop to that real quick," replied Josh.

"Hush up, we don't want to use any muscle here, at least not yet. I want to try other ways first."

Peter's mind was going in several directions. Sammi kept picking up the word Sanford, but couldn't get much else. However, she did hear him thinking about someone named Wayne Ellison and he thought, *he's not going to like this at all. I'll let him decide what we should do here.*

And although he got interrupted twice in his mental world, he went right back to Wayne Ellison as he thought, *I've got to let him know about this right away. He won't like it, but he's got to decide our next move.*

She had been standing next to Jill and Julie as they were pretending to have their own private conversation, but as the guys walked up, it was obvious to Dave that Sammi had heard something alarming. Her face had a startled look and when he took her hand, her palm was definitely beginning to sweat. She held on to him, but wouldn't look at him and kept her concentration open. She was definitely picking up something of value. They stayed there for a few more minutes and even though the mayor and Peter moved several feet away, Sammi wouldn't break her focus. Dave knew enough to let her have her lead and a few minutes later she began to relax. She took a deep breath and looked at the group.

She smiled as she said, "This has been an interesting evening."

The group was happy with her remark and Dave said, "Relax for a few minutes, Sammi. I think you need it."

"I could relax easier if you'd dance with me," she said with a sly look.

Everyone knew of Dave's dislike for dancing at big parties, yet her eager and hopeful expression won him over.

She followed him to the dance floor and attempted to get more of a semblance of normality for the outside world to see.

"I love to dance with you. See Jim and Julie and Tom and Jill, they're all dancing, too. You can't hate it that much."

"No, I don't, but I feel uncomfortable."

"But you're a good dancer."

"Thanks, but it's not what I like to do."

She smiled and said, "Well, I appreciate you dancing with me all the more then, cause I love to dance with you."

She felt him hold her closer and that made it all worthwhile. They danced for two dances and she appreciated the special effort he made for her. And the party moved on.

* * *

Shortly before they were thinking of leaving, a tall, middle-aged man with an interesting face and traces of white beginning to spread throughout his hair walked up to the tracker and called him aside with an obvious take control attitude. It was one of the few times that Dave had seen Peter move quickly and leave the mayor's side.

Sammi leaned over and said, "Let's dance over to that side of the room." After they had manipulated themselves to a strategic area she said, "I've got it."

They were about twenty feet away, but Sammi caught most of the conversation. It was revealing and troublesome. When the men separated, the tracker went right back to the mayor's side and all lost track of the other gentleman. So it seemed that he must have had an important message for the tracker, delivered it and left immediately. However, Dave caught sight of him for a moment when he said goodnight to the governor, who happened to be standing near the front entrance. And, as luck would have it, Sergeant Brady was talking to the governor at that exact moment and shook this man's hand before he left.

"Who was he? Do you know him?" asked Sammi.

"No, I don't think I've ever seen him before."

"Too bad. I didn't catch a name, but I think we need to find out who he is."

Dave looked thoughtful as he said, "We'll talk on the way home. Let's try and keep our expressions festive. We got a stare from the tracker and I don't want him to get suspicious about anything."

At that moment, as if fate had arranged it, Jim and Julie approached them and they switched partners, amidst laughter and merriment. And Dave was happy that the tracker witnessed the fun time they were having.

Sammi asked Jim. "Who was that guy talking to the tracker?"

"Not sure, but I've seen him somewhere. He seems to have some Asian background, doesn't he?"

"But not China or Japan, I don't think."

"Well, this has been a nice party and Julie enjoyed seeing the inside of this place."

"Yes, it's quite beautiful. It's my second time here, but I'm still mesmerized at the beauty."

"I guess so," said Jim, looking around. "I do like to look at the architecture, but I have to admit that all these fancy furnishings don't do a lot for me."

Sammi smiled. "Everyone has their special part to appreciate." After a pause she said, "You're a very good dancer; I don't believe we've ever danced before."

"I think you're right. We almost danced at my wedding, but then the drums rolled for something. I kept thinking I've got to get back and dance with Sammi, but it never happened."

She laughed. "I'm glad we got the chance tonight."

* * *

The ride home had its special charm for both of them. It had been a fun evening, and although, as usual, Sammi had a mission to accomplish, she liked being part of the team that was helping to keep corruption under control. Being married to Dave had made them a valuable duo and they had the help of two other trustworthy couples, whenever they needed it.

"Okay, what was so interesting about this evening?" he asked.

Sammi smiled. "There's a lot going on again. I guess I'm not surprised, but it seems that some of these groups are fighting again for control of this part of Pennsylvania. First, let me talk about the tracker. I got some strange stuff from him. He does not want the wives of the mayor, governor or Sergeant Brady to renew their friendship. It seems that will spell trouble for what he's trying to do."

"Why would that matter to him?"

"I suppose because if the wives are friendly then the husbands might put aside their differences, too. He was quite adamant about it when he talked to Josh Logan, that bodyguard. It was suggested rather clumsily by Josh that something could happen to deter that before it ever began."

"Whoa! Are you kidding?"

"Not at all. The tracker said that he didn't want any muscle used yet. And here is the other interesting part, he kept thinking about a guy named Wayne Ellison. Do you know who that is?"

"Never heard the name."

"He thought about him a few times and

thought that he'd have to let him know about this renewal of friendship between the wives right away and he didn't think this Wayne would like it at all."

"God, here we are again, right in the middle of some crap that's starting to go on. See you were right, Sammi. The tracker wants to cause trouble between the mayor, the sergeant and the governor."

"That's for sure and he thought that he'd have to let this Wayne figure out how they should proceed."

Dave was quiet for a time and Sammi let him mull these new ideas over in his mind.

"I'm going to have to let the sarge know about this right away. But how do we let the mayor in on the fact that he'd better warn his wife so no harm would come to her."

"I don't know, but when you do you'd better let him know that whoever that guy is that talked to the tracker ... Sammi paused for a moment. She knew this would be a shock to Dave.

"What?"

"Well, he gives reports to one of the lead contenders in the fraud case, none other than Fritz Connelly."

"WHAT? Are you kidding?"

"No, he didn't give any hints of where he was at or if he has direct communication with him, but he said that Fritz will want to keep the tension up here until we can cause this governor enough trouble to get rid of him."

"Oh my God. What the hell's going on here?"

"Dave, it sounds like they're trying to finish

that same job. They want to get rid of this governor and they're taking a different route this time. First, they cause trouble between the top officials of the state and follow orders from that Fritz Connelly wherever he's at. We don't know about step two or whatever after that. "

Dave shook his head. "It never ends, does it? Sometimes I think I'd like to find a new type of crime instead of having the same old stuff come at us again and again. They're not going to stop until they succeed."

"So we'll have to keep knocking them down," she said.

Dave reached for her hand. "You're right. They seemed quiet for almost a year, but here they come again."

"And the name Sanford kept crossing the tracker's mind. Don't know if it's a first name or last name or how it's connected. But remember, I think that's the same name that came across on that recording Linda left us. Sound familiar to you?"

"Nope, not at all. At least you got the tip of the iceberg tonight. I think I'll talk to Jim and Tom tomorrow and I'd like both of them to be with me when I talk to the sarge next week. I want him to be aware that their wives might need protection and the sarge has to know of this plan. God, Sammi, it never stops."

"Well, they think they're good. But you guys are good, too."

Dave appreciated that comment but was silent for a time. They had a good police force, he thought, but they had been blindsided. But so had the mayor and the governor, and with Sammi picking up bits and pieces, they'd have a plan in mind to be ready for this new set of problems.

* * *

Dave looked over at Sammi. She hadn't said a word for the last twenty miles. The road back from Harrisburg to Scranton was almost hypnotic at times and he realized that it had lulled her to sleep. He liked the way she curled up her body in comfort and was totally relaxed. He was glad. Her concentration episodes exhausted her stamina and sometimes sleep was not always easy for her after a long session. But tonight, possibly the movement of the car and the hum of the engine had created a monotonous atmosphere that had hypnotized her into restful slumber. He smiled as he thought about their life together. Sometimes he wondered how it would have turned out if he had married her right after college instead of her friend Kelly. Would they have been as happy? He'd never know, but often wondered.

"Are we home yet?" she asked, definitely not awake.

"No, we've got a ways to go. Get some sleep and I'll wake you later."

"You don't mind if I sleep?" She asked this question amidst three yawns anyway.

"I think you're still half asleep. Get back to some good dreams."

She smiled. "Only if you're in them."

He still had about thirty miles to go. The trip had gone quickly, but several miles back he'd lost track of Jim and Julie who were on the road ahead of them. Sammi had to make a stop and they had a quick cup of coffee. But now the road ahead of them was clear, with no traffic and no trouble. His mind wandered.

The information Sammi had gathered tonight was troublesome. Most of it had brought up the possibility that the same group, but with extra people and a lot more effort, were trying to take over the southeastern part of Pennsylvania again. And although Julie had noticed some strange occurrences on the computer system, this time they were not touching the governor's computer or playing games with the ledgers and state budgets. Yet their end target seemed to be the same, merely a different approach. The surprising part to him was that most of this was discovered because he wanted Sammi to get information that hopefully would help to solve Terry Gonzalez's murder. Then his mind took in an obvious idea. It probably was all connected. Maybe Terry had found out some information concerning their latest plot and the tracker found out about it. Who was this guy? Peter Armors seemed to be a mystery man and a strange one at that. But he'd had no problem eliminating Terry figuring that no one cared about him any longer. After all, he'd been convicted of being a mole in the police department and they were soured on him anyway. But that would be the biggest mistake he had made up to now.

* * *

"Holy Shit, you mean that Fritz Connelly isn't

out of this picture yet? What the hell's going on?"

The sarge was clearly vocal when he heard the latest. "I thought he was off in some other state causing trouble somewhere else. I don't understand what's so great about us. We're still the target?"

He wasn't sitting at his desk anymore. He was stomping up and down his small office and waving his hands in the air trying to figure out what all this meant.

"Where's that Ben Collier? Isn't he supposed to have him under surveillance?"

"Don't know," answered Dave. "I think he lost him for a while, but hopefully he found him by now."

"Well, I'll give him a call later. We've got to find out what's happening? So this tracker guy is in it as far as he can be. You say he reports to someone named Wayne Ellison. Anybody know him?"

They all shook their heads.

"I'll bet he's not even from this state," said Jim. "They're bringing in people from all over the place again."

Dave asked. "Who was that guy that the tracker talked to; you shook his hand before he left. I think he stayed for a short time and then left."

The sarge wrinkled his nose and scratched his head as he tried to remember. There were so many people at those parties. He was back sitting behind his desk again and when Dave described his Asian look he answered, "Oh that's Kris Kaphle. Don't any of you guys know him? He's the state senator from District 16. I think he's in his second term."

The sarge was so agitated he didn't catch Dave's troubled expression, but Tom and Jim did. Their boss seemed more interested in letting them know that he served on some banking committees and recently had added some communication technology to his expertise. Dave whistled quietly, almost under his breath but Jim heard him.

"I want to talk to Ben Collier. He can clue us into what's going on here. This is a hell of a mess we're in. And the mayor doesn't have a clue. He wouldn't believe anything I'd tell him anymore. Don't know how to handle that, but first things first. I'll meet with you again, after I've talked to Ben.

* * *

"Okay, Dave, what gives? I saw your reaction to that Kris Kaphle guy," said Jim.

"Seriously, neither one of you know him, right? Don't know anything about him?"

Both Jim and Tom shook their heads.

"It's more problems. Sammi said that this Kris guy sends reports to Fritz Connelly." He waited to let that information sink in. The ramifications were obvious.

"Damn, that would mean they have someone in the senate," said Tom.

"At least one," said Jim. "Who's to say there aren't more?"

This was the beginning of an increasingly complicated situation. These groups hadn't given up at all. They were coming at them from all sides.

And although Sammi had been able to find out some secret information, would it be enough?

Jim took a deep sigh as he said, "I don't even know where to begin on all this stuff. It's possible that's what Terry found out—he could have discovered something about a new attempt to oust the governor and everything else and it got him killed. What did that final report from the sarge say on what Terry was doing?"

"It was vague. He had told the sarge he had some hints of wrongdoing, but he wasn't that specific. He said it had to do with something called Windmill."

"Windmill? Obviously a code word, but what the hell does it mean?"

"No idea," said Tom. "So, guys, where do we go from here?"

Dave was the first one to speak. "Look, we all wanted to investigate Terry's death, but investigating all this new information is doing the same thing. This has got to be all connected. So we have a Wayne Ellison, whom we don't know; we have a Peter Armors who's definitely a problem and we don't know anything about him either. And now we have this Kris Kaphle whom we also don't know much about and he has his hands in a lot of things. I think we need to find out about our own state senator who may not be what he seems. What do you think?"

"You're right. We could use more help on this, but I think we need to be a little secretive here," said Jim.

"Right," added Dave. "Except for bringing in

Sammi for some interviews about that missing wife, I'm going to have to let LeBron and Tyrone handle that case. We can assist when needed, but this new stuff is a serious priority. I'll run all this by the sarge, but how does it settle in with you guys?"

"Okay with us."

About this time, someone came to tell Tom he had an urgent phone call. He excused himself as Jim and Dave looked at each other. They spent a few minutes looking over the notes and realized they had a lot of work to do.

Tom came back hurriedly, excited and obviously worried.

"That was Jill. Her brother's been in a bad accident. They're not even sure if he's going to make it. He went to Prescott to get away for a while and get himself together, remember I told you both about that. Well, he was doing some mountain climbing with a group, something he's done many times. But there was an accident. One of the guys was killed, and there was another one hurt slightly besides him. But Todd's injuries are serious. Look guys, I hate to leave you now, but Jill needs me. I can't let her go down there alone. God, I'm sorry."

"Tom, we're sorry for you and Jill. Take off, will you? None of this stuff's going to get settled this week. You take all the time you need."

"The sarge isn't even here right now."

Dave said, "We'll explain it to him. Keep in touch, okay? Let us know what's happening."

"Sure, it's going to be tough anyway. Todd and I weren't exactly close, but Jill loved her brother and, gees, I hope he makes it. He's about forty-six."

"Anything we can do to help, let us know. We'll hope for the best."

And suddenly Tom was gone. Jim and Dave looked at each other and both had some serious drooping of the shoulders beginning to occur.

"Well," said Jim, "this does change things. How do you want to do it now?"

"I was serious with Tom," answered Dave. "This whole thing is going to take a while. Let's see if we can get an overview this week. Let's start trying to get some background information on these guys. And I'd like to find out who Wayne Ellison is."

"Are you telling the sarge the latest?"

"I don't know. He's got a lot on his mind about the mayor and their wives. I think I'd like to hold off for a while. What do you think?"

"It wouldn't hurt. We can let him know later as definite clues develop. I think he's got all he can handle right now."

"Okay, then ..."

They were interrupted by LeBron. "You wanted to know when we were going to interview the neighbor of that missing woman. We're bringing him in Wednesday around 1:00 P.M. You want to be there, I understand."

"Sure do," said Dave. "I think there's a connection with him, but I can't figure it out. Did you get a chance to look over the surveillance tape from that Wal-Mart store?"

"In the process, but we're not finished yet. I'll let you know the results as soon as I get them."

"Good enough."

"Later," said LeBron as he walked away.

* * *

Jim left to go back to his desk. Dave put in a call to Sammi.

"Hi there," he said.

"I hope this is good news; my day's been tough," she said.

Dave laughed. "It's in the middle. Is that okay?"

"Yep, that's fine."

"That interview I told you about regarding the missing wife is going to happen on Wednesday about 1:00 P.M. I need you here. Can you get some time off?"

"Oh yeah, not a problem. No clues yet?"

"None. She's been gone almost two weeks now. We need to find something fast."

"Okay, I'll pick up what I can. Hopefully he can give us some clues. Hey, I've got to run. We're having another meeting. You'll be home tonight?"

"I will," he said.

"Are you working out first or not?"

Dave laughed. "Well, since you reminded me, I guess I will."

"Great, see ya later."

Dave had to laugh as he put down the phone. She always managed to remind him about his workouts, but she did it in a subtle manner. She had a positive effect on him, and despite his serious and often nerve-wracking profession, she managed to keep him in a good frame of mind.

He hadn't forgotten about Jill's brother. He needed to tell her, but it wasn't something that he wanted to do on the telephone. Tonight would be better and by tomorrow he hoped that Tom would have called with more positive news.

CHAPTER SEVEN

Getting off the plane at Prescott Municipal Airport was surreal for Jill Harrington. She held onto Tom's hand tightly and used it as her anchor to stability. The last twenty-four hours had been traumatic and her mind had not yet adjusted to the shock. It was but a few weeks since she had finally located her missing brother, at least he was unaccounted for from her side of the picture. He had at long last returned her phone calls and his slow response had to do with the turmoil in his life. When she found out that he had been laid off from his job and that had corresponded with the breakup with his girlfriend, she understood his need to get away and to try to put his life in order. But to return to Prescott, Arizona where they had vacationed a few times as children, seemed a little odd to her. But as long as he kept in touch, it would be okay.

She had been expecting a phone call from him, since he was about ready to return home from his excursion, per the agenda he gave her. Instead, she got a call from a nurse at the Yavapai Regional Medical Center in Prescott telling her of a serious mountain climbing accident. She was sure that she didn't get all the details straight in her mind as shock engulfed and numbed her entire system. All she could do was call her husband

and he took over immediately. He got the reservations and although she offered to go alone, he wouldn't hear of it. His nonexistent relationship with her brother was of no concern; he wouldn't let her face this situation without him. And so, as they got off the plane, she took his hand and never let go.

"I'm so glad you came with me; I hated to ask."

"You didn't ask; I'd have never let you come alone."

She looked at him and realized that he was the world to her.

They checked into the Pine Line Court motel and headed immediately for the hospital. Even though Tom had placed another call to the center, they still weren't sure what they were about to face. Information given over the telephone was veiled and cloaked in secrecy. Tom felt that until the hospital was certain they were talking to the next of kin, information would be sketchy.

As they entered the hospital, he realized that the last time he'd been to one was when Dave got shot. He remembered how they all hated the smell of the place and the trauma that usually accompanied visits. They walked immediately to the Information Desk and asked for the location of Todd Mayfair. The receptionist looked at them almost detached as she gave them her answer, which was in the form of a question.

"Are you next of kin?"

Jill felt her knees buckle a little noting the look on the greeter's face as it conveyed desperation.

"Yes, I'm his sister and only relative."

"I'll call Dr. Owens. He's asked to talk to any relative that came. Please have a seat, it'll be a moment."

It was hard to describe the feelings that were crawling throughout her body. Fear, remorse, anxiety, anger; everything was crossing her brain and every imaginable thought found its way into her psyche. She tried to keep her mind blank and she heard Tom's voice in her ear.

"Hold on, Jill. Let's wait until we talk to the doctor."

"But we already know it's a serious accident. God, I hope he didn't die." Her face went blank at the thought. "I wanted a chance to get things right between us and between you and him, too."

She saw Tom look down at the floor and realized that she had put him in an awkward position.

"Oh Tom, I'm sorry. I know you tried. I'm not blaming you. But I was hoping we could all have another chance."

"I'm always willing. I must admit, mainly for your sake. But if he's willing, I'd give it a try."

Jill gave him a quick kiss on the cheek. "I love you, Tom."

He simply smiled and they waited.

It was almost fifteen minutes later when a middle-aged guy wearing a white coat and with a stethoscope around his neck approached. It seemed much longer. He immediately put out his right hand as he introduced himself.

"Hello, I'm Dr. Rick Owens. I've been put in charge of your brother's case."

He was about to continue, but Jill couldn't

wait any longer and asked quickly, in desperation.

"Is he still alive, Doctor?"

"Oh yes," he replied hastily noting her high level of anxiety. "What have you been told?"

"Nothing," answered Tom. "We were simply told it was quite serious and we should get here right away."

He nodded his head in understanding.

"Okay, let's sit for a moment and I'll catch you up."

They all sat down on a nearby available couch and Dr. Owens leaned forward as he began his story. "Several guys had gone mountain climbing in the Superstition Mountains. It seems a large bolder shifted ever so slightly for some unknown reason, but it was enough for one guy to fall to his death, and another to obtain significant injuries. But Todd was the more serious of the two. We believe he will make it in time, barring any serious complications."

Tears were already rolling down Jill's face and she brushed them away automatically. She never blinked, not wanting to miss one word from the doctor.

"He has quite a list of injuries. He broke his right leg both above and below the knee, but the breaks are clean and that's considered good. He fractured his left leg slightly above the ankle. His spine has been bruised in a few places and although we think it will mend appropriately, that will be a main concern for us. It could mean the difference between him walking again and not. And last, but certainly not least, his jaw is fractured in two places and will be sewed shut for some time. Oh and his hands were injured, but we're still figuring out what's going on there. He won't be able to talk to you, and until his hands heal, communication will be rather difficult if at all."

"So it was a freak accident?" asked Tom.

"It would seem so. Some areas of the Superstitions can be quite dangerous, but all of these guys were experienced climbers. I'm sure they were following protocol in such a dangerous area. It was considered a rare occurrence and nothing these climbers had done wrong. Sometimes nature throws a curve ball."

"Can we see him? Is he awake?"

The doctor paused for a moment. Then as if he made his decision he said. "He's still in intensive care for at least another twenty-four hours, probably longer. He's been awake a few times, but he's still highly sedated. I'll let you see him as soon as he wakes up again. I'm sure it will do him good to see you. But don't upset him in any way. We must keep him quite calm right now. Understood?"

Jill looked over at Tom. Their eyes showed agreement in what they would do. Tom told the doctor. "I think at first it would be better if Jill saw him alone. They're quite close, but I'd like to be able to look through the window if I could."

The doctor seemed to understand and appreciated their being honest without pushing the issue further. He went with them as they first approached Todd's room. Jill had trouble letting go of Tom's hand, but the doctor let her grab his arm for steadiness.

* * *

Todd was awake, if you could call it that. His entire body was bandaged from head to toe. His middle torso was wrapped up totally and securely in an effort to keep his spine intact. His jaw was wired shut and the bandages around his head led Jill to take Dr. Owen's word for the fact that this was her brother. Both legs were wrapped as were his arms and hands. Yet with consciousness looming in the distance, he remained peaceful and quiet. The sole thing he could safely move were his eyes and when they rested on Jill as she entered the door, a calmness overtook his body and he wouldn't even blink.

"Todd," she said softly. "You're going to make it. Your body took quite a beating when you fell, but you're going to make it. And I'm going to be here for you."

Todd closed his eyes and a tear wet his eyelashes. He opened them again in an effort to make sure she was still there. When he was satisfied, he went back to sleep.

"That's enough for now," said the doctor. After they walked out he told them both, "He's got a good, strong heart and his lungs weren't damaged. His main organs made it through. He's got a long recuperation period ahead of him, but he's young and luckily in decent health. I think he was one lucky guy."

After they thanked the doctor, he left and Jill grabbed onto Tom. The nurse asked them to let her know where they'd be in the hospital at all times and she'd let them know when he woke up again. They all agreed that for him to see his sister when he woke up was its own type of therapy.

* * *

Dave and Sammi met for lunch on Wednesday. They would be heading back to the station together in order to interview Larry Nielsen, the questionable neighbor. Dave told her that he'd gotten a call that morning from Tom and that Jill's brother was holding his own. He was still on the critical list, and his serious condition would require a long recuperation period, but indications were positive.

They arrived at the station in time to see the neighbor enter with his lawyer. Larry seemed rather cocky and smug realizing that everyone would be surprised that he had hired an attorney so early in the investigation. However, he stated immediately that his neighborhood was against him and he wanted to be prepared.

Entering the room, Sammi again sat down on Dave's left side and took her few moments to get used to the atmosphere of the room. Dave was calm and LeBron was relaxed, but the vitality around Larry was electrifying and he was ready for combat.

"I haven't done anything wrong, but I need to protect myself," he offered arrogantly before any questions were launched at him. His lawyer immediately cautioned him not to say anything. Then he shut up.

"Okay, Mr. Nielson," said Dave. "We're interviewing everyone in the neighborhood, just so you're aware. We're trying to find out if anyone has information on the disappearance of Vicki Wentworth. Understand?"

He had caught the hint from before and checked with his lawyer before he answered, "Understood."

"Okay, then, when was the last time you saw Vicki Wentworth?"

He paused before he said, "She went outside in the morning to put out the trash that day. I remember because she was dressed in some real tight pants; I'm sure you get my drift." He had a sneer on his face that he was ready to share with the guys in the room, but avoided glancing over at Sammi.

His lawyer hushed him up and cautioned him to simply answer the questions and not elaborate. He took a deep breath and waited.

Sammi let Dave know that was a lie. He had been to the Wal-Mart the day Vicki disappeared. He had been there in the afternoon with some buddy named Spike and he had pointed her out as she worked the cash register. His buddy Spike thought she was quite a looker.

Dave excused himself for a moment and talked to LeBron. Had they finished checking the surveillance tape?

"Yeah, and we have a couple of guys, one that kind of looks like this Larry, but no positive I.D yet."

Dave said, "I'm going to push it anyway."

Returning to the table he said, "We seemed to have seen someone like you on the surveillance tape of the Wal-Mart store late in the afternoon of the day Vicki disappeared. She was still there when you guys left, but didn't make it home. You think that might be a coincidence?"

Larry had a panicky look as he consulted with his attorney immediately. He took a moment and then offered. "Okay, okay. Maybe me and a buddy did go to Wal-Mart's that day, but that's all."

"Why did you hide it?" asked LeBron.

"I didn't hide it; I forgot."

"And who was this buddy of yours?"

Sammi let Dave know there were two buddies with him.

"Okay, it was this guy Spike. I don't know him all that well, but sometimes we have a beer together."

It was obvious to Sammi by Larry's thought world that all three had low opinions of women and that was what coupled them up.

"And who was the other guy?"

Larry looked shocked. He hadn't planned on talking about the other guy, but felt now that he had to.

"I had met that other guy once before. He seems kind of rough, even to me. His name is Brian and I think he's been out of prison about two months. But he's no buddy of mine. He and Spike are friends. I think they met in jail."

"We want last names, phone numbers, addresses, where they hang out and anything else you can tell us?

"I could get killed over this. I mean, I have beers with them occasionally; we have a lot of laughs together. But I wouldn't want to get caught crossing them."

* * *

Dave and LeBron conferred with each other privately. LeBron said, "We've got to check their records. This smells real bad to me."

"I'll follow up on this," said Dave.

When they came back in, Dave had some advice and choices for Larry to make.

"Larry, you can either tell us what we need to know or become an accessory after the fact when this goes down. If they were involved, you could still help this Vicki. But it's your decision."

Apparently he got some good advice from his lawyer. "I'll tell you what I know, but I wasn't involved."

And he proceeded to tell them that he thought Vicki acted high and mighty and needed to be taught a lesson. "That's what I told the guys, but it was trash talk with me; I didn't mean anything by it. I think she does fling it out there and it bugs the hell out of me. But I didn't mean for them to do anything and I don't know that they did."

Somehow Larry didn't seem so smug and over-confident anymore. When he left the station he turned and looked back twice at Dave adding again, "I didn't mean anything by it."

* * *

When the coast was clear, LeBron said, "If these two guys are involved, I can't help but believe that Larry here should be considered as an accessory before the fact. My God, it's obvious he has no respect for women and it sounds to me that he goaded these guys by telling them that she was high and mighty and whatever else he said. Some guys don't get it."

He heard Sammi take a deep sigh. "I often wonder what prompts guys to think like that, don't you? Could be an abusive mother, a tragic childhood. Something happened to set them on this way."

"No doubt," said LeBron. "But lots of kids have less than perfect times in their early lives and still manage to keep a decent attitude. To me, there are no excuses."

"Perhaps," said Sammi. "But maybe a little luck would have helped."

LeBron had to laugh. "No doubt that would have helped."

Dave said, "He's definitely on the edge with this one. We'll have to get an APB out on this Spike Evers. We need him in here fast for questioning. You said there was nothing on the parking lot surveillance tape."

"No, we asked where she usually parked and unfortunately nothing shows her leaving. Dead end there."

"Okay, but we do have these three guys on the store tape, right?"

"Yep, we recognized Larry Nielson and there were two other guys with him."

"Okay, then that's where we start. Find this Spike Evers. That's top priority."

"Got it, and when I do, I'll make sure you're informed. I'm assuming you two want to be in on the questioning."

"Absolutely," said Dave.

LeBron was glad he had more information to follow up. This had been an interesting and revealing interview.

* * *

Dave got a call from Tom on Thursday night. Jill's brother had passed the critical stage and would be moved out of intensive care within a few days. He had a lot of healing to do and would probably be in a rehab center for quite a while. In the meantime, it had been almost impossible to communicate with him. He did have the little finger on his left hand that was mobile, and used it to tap once for yes and two for no, but that was all. It was frustrating at best. Then Jill asked to speak to Sammi.

"I know this is a lot to ask of you, but Tom will be leaving tomorrow to go home. I was wondering if you could come up for a few days and talk to Todd. You're the only one I know who could communicate with him. You don't have to let him know what you can do, but we need to know what's on his mind."

"Of course I will. You sound so worried? I thought the doctors said he was out of danger."

"They did and he is, but his frame of mind is questionable right now. And the doctors say they have to wait until they can talk to him. Remember, he came to Arizona because he was depressed and this type of injury would be devastating to anyone. I have to wonder what his state of mind is now."

"It must be tough. And they can't help him much without being able to communicate."

"They come in and tell him nice, encouraging things, but I want to know what's on his mind. Honestly, Sammi, they mean well, I guess, but they're so rigid and careful in everything they say because they don't know what he's thinking. But you'd know."

"I think I could help at least determine that. I'll get an early flight out and meet you at the hospital sometime tomorrow. I'll be in touch."

"He was shocked when I told him Tom was with me and concerned about him. When Tom walked into the room the first time, well, I would have loved to know what he was thinking. And I'd still like to know. You'll come then, even for a few days."

"Sure, I'll come tomorrow and stay the weekend, at least."

Dave understood. This was a chance for Sammi to help someone without being under the tremendous pressure she usually experienced. This would be a healthier encounter for her.

* * *

Sergeant Brady called in Dave and Jim. Ben Collier had informed him that they had Fritz Connelly under surveillance and he was on the Board of Directors for none other than the Primer International Construction Company. They called Julie into this meeting as well.

Jim looked the most surprised. "That company is still operating?"

"Oh yes," Julie said, "that company has never gone down completely. We did get it out of our area for a while and managed to do a lot of damage. But they're international and won't ever go away completely. Ben was telling me last week that Colorado had big problems with them earlier this year. In fact, he thought they might move their national headquarters out there. But Pennsylvania has a lot more to offer them so they changed their minds and came after us again."

"No kidding. Amazing how they change their minds and turn up in different places all the time."

"Their mob ties are quite extensive," said the sarge. "So, crappy as it is, we'll never get them all. This is a forever game. But we do have to get them out of our area again. That's what everyone has to do."

Silence overtook them all for a few minutes. Dire thoughts loomed and they were all calculating their own participation in this operation.

"The reason I called you in was because we found Wayne Ellison. And this one is really worrisome. The tracker apparently reports to him and he's the right hand guy for Fritz Connelly."

Grumbles were heard around the room. Dave wasn't ready yet to tell them that the senator from District 16 also reported to Fritz Connelly. It seemed that this mob group had infiltrated the state in several areas.

"So what have we found out about the tracker? Dave tells me that the bodyguard Josh Logan has a questionable record, but we can't find out anything about this Peter Armors who is always with the mayor and has tremendous influence over him. That's our first priority. Find out who this guy is and let me know."

* * *

Jim didn't mince words as he followed Dave back to his desk.

"Okay, Dave, you've got something more. What is it?"

"Right. Sammi says that Kris Kaphle, that senator, sends reports to Fritz Connelly. They know everything we're doing. They're coming at us from everywhere. What else don't we know?"

"That means that the senator is on the take. Who can we trust right now?"

"No one unless I run them by Sammi. And she'll be gone until sometime next week. She's going up to help Jill communicate with her brother."

"Oh yeah, she'd be real helpful there."

Dave nodded. "I can't help but believe that Terry found out about some of this and that's what got him killed."

"I'm thinking the same thing. So where do we go from here? I feel we're buried. And we have to be careful."

"Our group is okay. I had Sammi listen in at the last few gatherings and LeBron and Tyrone are solid. So other than the sarge, we stick with our group for now. It's the one safe way."

"Does Ben Collier know what's happening here? I think the FBI should be in on this one, if some of the crap we're getting is coming from international areas, too."

"I think you and I need to have a private meeting with the sarge. We'll let Tom know when he gets back. But if the FBI know everything we're doing.....isn't that why they put out phony information? Julie knows more about that than we do. We'll bring her in on this, too. I hate not to trust our own people, but ..." Dave put his hands through his hair. He was utterly frustrated. *What was going on?* He knew they wanted to oust the governor, but felt there was much more involved this time. They wanted to oust the mayor, the governor and the sarge. The only one who knew was Sergeant Brady. This was one complicated mess.

"Dave, I hate to say this, but we're dug into a deep hole right now. The mayor doesn't trust us at all."

"And wasn't that part of their plan all along? See what's happening. The money laundering stuff will probably show up again in the future somewhere, but this time they're undermining us from the inside out. I think it's time we get with the sarge about all this. I think he's guessed some of it, but he still has a shock coming."

* * *

Dave and Jim went back and talked to Sergeant Brady. Julie was allowed in. And Dave told him about the senator and his connections to Fritz Connelly.

"Holy Shit. What's going on here? They've got

one of our senators."

Dave said, "They may always have had him and possibly they've got more. I want to check his background. But the important thing to me is that we have to let Ben Collier know the extent of what's going on around here already. I get the feeling he doesn't know how they're going about it this time."

"Probably not. He was very direct with me when I talked to him, and didn't mention anything about me watching my back or not. And I know he would have. It's time for all of us to lay our cards on the table, but how can we do this without getting someone around here suspicious. Hell, we don't even know who's on our side anymore."

Dave looked over at Jim. They were in agreement on that. Dave began. "That's what Jim and I were talking about. The only people we can trust right now is our own group, plus Sammi and Julie. That's it. So that's the ones we talk to, except, of course, Ben Collier. I have a feeling he might be sending someone down here to work with us."

"That wouldn't surprise me. Dave, you and Sammi know him quite well, why don't you give him a call tonight? I want him to know everything. If we all work together we can figure out the best plan of attack."

Leaving his office didn't alleviate any frustration they were feeling. It was good to be working on a plan, but Dave was getting nervous about something else.

"Could Linda be involved in this ... even from prison? If this involves the Primer International

Construction Company, which is obviously a front for all of these companies hoping to control everything, I'm sure she's still in the picture. I think I want to listen to that tape again. What was behind her words?"

"Really, Dave. Don't read too much into that right now. She was a broad that needed her claws into some guy, sometimes many guys. Right now it's you. But I wouldn't be surprised if she was involved, yet I couldn't imagine how. For God's sake she's in prison. She'd have to have a heavy out here working with her. I don't think that's happening for her."

"I'd never underestimate her again, ever. But she's a small player at best. God, how can this type of stuff happen?"

"The greed of these companies wanting to form their own empires and control prices and production and everything. It's probably never going to stop."

"I'm going home. Sammi's leaving tomorrow for Prescott and I still have to make that call tonight."

* * *

By the time Dave got home, Sammi was packed and had dinner on the table. She wanted to have a relaxed evening with him before she left tomorrow. But when she saw him walk in the door, she realized that was not going to happen.

"What gives?"

Dave discussed the latest.

"None of this surprises me. You can't be

surprised either."

"No, I'm not. But how do we get around them? I wish we could get to the mayor and have him play along but that's not going to happen."

Sammi looked somewhat complacent for a moment. It took Dave by surprise.

"Okay, what? I know that look."

"Nothing, right now. But as soon as I get back, I may have an idea, depending, of course, on what's going on."

"I shouldn't be surprised at you anymore."

"Oh, but you should. I always want to be able to surprise you."

Dave had to laugh. Lately, whenever he was thinking down in the dumps, she found a way to turn the situation around.

After dinner they placed a conference call to Ben Collier. He was aware of the efforts to oust the governor again, but didn't know about the mayor or the sergeant. And he was surprised about Senator Kaphle.

"Oh, they're serious this time, aren't they? Coming at us from all sides. Julie says that nothing interesting has been crossing the computers and that was surprising me. Now I understand. They're trying to get other things in place first. I'm glad to know this. I'll let you know soon what we plan to do. We've got to move before they get too much further into the inroads. Damn, Scranton and Harrisburg are so juicy for them; they can't let it go. And we caused them serious problems last time. We better make sure this time that they won't think another attempt is worth it."

Dave took a deep breath. It carried over the

phone.

"I think this is more global than you're used to. But we deal with this quite often. We'll have procedures in place real soon and I'll keep you aware. But keep this to yourself."

"We have a small group of confidantes, Ben. At this end we find it hard to trust anyone."

"That's the best. I'll get back with you both soon."

* * *

The phone line went dead. They both stared at each other. It did help to talk to Ben who seemed to have a different perspective.

"It's like in that last case with the abductions, once we gave them the information, even Ben had to step back and let the agents do their work. They're certainly more used to this stuff."

Dave said, "I know. I look at the governor, the mayor and our sergeant and I don't want them hurt. I don't want bad things going on in their units. We need to run a clean city and to work together. We've got to get control of our city again; that's my main concern. I guess I don't look at the broader picture."

"You're doing your job, but now, for a while, we do have to look at the bigger picture and I don't like what I see. There are so many details to watch, but we'll have a group working with us."

Dave relaxed on the couch, stretched out his legs and sighed as he said, "I hate to see you go tomorrow."

"I can take a cab to the airport and then you

..."

"No you won't. I'll take you to the airport. No arguments."

"Okay, okay," she paused and then added, "I like that idea, too."

They sat for a few minutes quietly. Sometimes you could have so much on your mind that nothing made any sense. So they sat there quietly thinking of what was ahead of them.

"One day at a time. This'll all work out," she said.

"And we'll keep trying until it does work out in our favor."

Sammi agreed.

"Enough about that," he said. "How do you feel about talking to Todd?"

"I want to get some private time with him. I realize that Jill is his sister and she loves him, but people still have a right to their private thoughts. I can't afford to breach that and in this case it might be tricky."

"Jill will want to know what he's thinking and how he's feeling?"

"And part of that will be okay, but some of his personal thoughts ... well ... I have to do all this without letting him know that I can read his thoughts."

Dave puckered his lips. Yes, he realized this could be a delicate situation.

"But Professor Harley and Father John Meyer knew what I could do and they both kept my secret for years. I may have to do this with Todd. I can never figure this out ahead of time. It's usually at the moment that I know how to handle things."

Dave tightened his arm around her. "Yes, this could be rather complicated."

"I just can't betray his trust and relay his thoughts without his permission. That wouldn't be right. I've never done that. I'll figure it out when I get there."

Then the conversation ended. They sat there for a long time together waiting for the evening to end and looking forward to when they'd be together again.

CHAPTER EIGHT

In one way, arriving in Prescott, AZ was like a breath of fresh air. Sammi was almost happy to get away from the daily complications that were occurring in Scranton and the continuous under-handed activities that were commonplace for them lately. It gave her a chance to clear her mind and renew her balance. She had never thought about all these illegal activities before; they hadn't been part of her life on a day to day basis, but now, with her marriage to Dave this was a big part of her life and would be, so she had to learn to take it in stride.

Her ride to the hospital brought a pleasant change in the beauty of the earth that she was experiencing. It actually exhibited a slightly red-dish tone with glittering shimmers of possibly fool's gold that she had heard about. She couldn't help but notice the hills that climbed higher and higher and seemed to go on continuously. Each surpassed the other in size, ruggedness and ma-jesty. Although the Pocono's were a welcomed attraction back home, it was good to get away and find something else to fascinate her mind. Every-thing felt small in comparison to these moun-tains, even the mischief that was presently sur-rounding her life.

Jill was waiting for her at the hospital entrance. They hugged and exchanged pleasantries before they got down to business. She wanted to have a cup of coffee and talk for a few minutes before they went to see Todd. Presently he was sleeping anyway.

"You just missed Tom by about two hours," she said.

"I'm glad to be here with you. How are you holding up?"

"I'm doing okay. Of course, it was a shock at first, seeing him all bandaged up like that, and he still is, so be prepared for it. But now that I know he'll make it, it helps a lot. But we're not sure about his spine yet. The doctor is still concerned and said if he could get a few answers from Todd it would help. But that's been hard."

Sammi acknowledged.

"I was hoping you could find a way to be able to tell the doctors what they need to know. He does have the little finger of his left hand usable, so he taps out yes and no, but it hasn't been as much help as they would like. So we wait."

"Does he seem comfortable enough?"

"Yeah, and he says he's not in much pain at all. Of course, he's on pain medication, but considering everything, he seems to be doing okay."

"Sure sounds like it."

"Well, if you're ready, I guess we can go up and see him. After he gets used to you later in the day, I thought I could leave the two of you alone. What do you think?"

Sammi smiled inwardly. That was something she had hoped for and Jill was sharp enough to realize it would be a good idea.

She answered, "Yes, when the time is right, I think I could work best that way."

Jill nodded. "I kind of thought so."

* * *

Nearing Room 303 at the Yavapai Medical Center brought on a nervousness for Sammi she hadn't anticipated. She had been told what to expect, that was true, but seeing it first-hand was still difficult. To observe any human being in a totally vulnerable condition felt like a personal attack; it was something that could happen to any of us.

Most of this guy's body was wrapped up in one type of bandage or another. His right leg was in a cast from the bottom of his toes clear up to his hip. His left leg was wrapped in a semi-cast type apparatus that took in his entire foot, except for his toes and ended well past his knees. Neither of his arms were broken, but were suffering from bruised muscles and then both of his hands were in casts except for the little finger of his left hand. It almost looked peculiar all by itself, sort of abandoned in a way. And his head was entirely wrapped. Apparently there was no concussion, which was great in itself, but with the complicated breaks in his jaw bone, he was wired shut and everything in his head area was covered. He could see through large slits in the bandages that did leave room for slight expressions, but that was all. The scene was a shock to Sammi, even though Jill had tried to prepare her.

She took her arm. "It's hard to see, isn't it? I was prepared, too, but it's still hard."

Sammi was glad that she saw Todd through the window before she entered the room. Now she could handle the situation better.

"Hi, Todd," said Jill. "I told you my friend Sammi Patterson was coming, remember?"

He seemed calm and wasn't surprised. Sammi knew he remembered what Jill had told him. And that was a good sign for the condition of his brain.

"Hi, Todd, I see you remembered that Jill said I was coming." She decided from the beginning that she would give him signs that although he couldn't speak out loud or express his thoughts in writing, that communication was taking place. It would become obvious to him in time, but at a pace he'd be comfortable with. Since he was on strong medication she felt it wouldn't shock him and by the time he realized what was happening, hopefully it would seem like the norm.

Although he was fully bandaged from top to bottom his head was producing some slight movement, which in moderation was considered okay. Sammi knew that he felt that this was the first time someone knew what was on his mind since his accident. He felt he was finally communicating with someone. And he seemed comforted and peaceful.

The first thoughts she heard on his mind after that was how glad he was that Jill had someone with her. He was comforted she was not alone.

Sammi said immediately. "I'll bet you're glad your sister has someone with her, aren't you?"

And he tried nodding his head slightly. They

both saw it and Jill was thrilled. Then his mind wandered somewhat, almost into a semi-sleep condition. His eyes closed and as they both waited, Sammi could hear him contented in the fact that he was near his sister again. He had missed her a lot.

He went into a deep sleep again, so they moved over to the couch in the room and waited. Sammi clued Jill on to some of the latest happenings in Scranton that Tom would be facing when he got home. She shook her head.

"These groups never stop, do they? Tom was telling me that he was worried about all of the inferences that were coming out before he left."

"Well, we're learning some things now. And apparently only our small group will be in on all the details. We don't know who to trust right now. So it will be the six of us, the sarge, LeBron and Tyrone. That's about it. These guys are so worried for the sarge and the mayor and the governor. I have to keep reminding Dave to take it one day at a time."

Jill understood. "That's what I keep trying to tell Tom."

"I've got Dave working out in the gym now. You've got to talk to Tom about joining him and Jim. It relieves so much stress for them, and God knows they need it right now."

* * *

Sammi took a deep breath before she approached the next subject with Jill. She didn't want to be secretive, but it had to be said.

"I heard Todd think about the fact that he was glad to be near you again. He has missed you all these years."

She smiled. "If anything good comes out of this, I hope we can all get a good relationship going. Tom's always been willing, but I'll have to wait and see."

"I need to tell you something, Jill. It has to do with my personal feelings of what I'm allowed to do with this gift I have."

Sammi could tell she realized the seriousness in her person at approaching a difficult subject for her.

"I'm willing to help out in any way I can with Todd. If I can be of help to the doctors without them catching on to what I do, then I'm happy to do it. But I do have a limit as to what I feel justified to do."

"What? What's bothering you?"

"Well, I'll know what's on Todd's mind; that's not a problem. And most things should be helpful to both of you and the doctors. But I have a line that I don't cross; I need you to know that."

Jill simply listened.

"Each of us have private thoughts that we don't tell others until we're ready. For some people that time never comes. I imagine I'll be able to have some telling conversations with Todd, but if I don't feel that I have his permission to discuss certain things with you, then you'll have to wait until he's ready to tell you himself. I can't trespass on other people's privacy. Do you understand?"

She felt Jill understood. She looked down at the floor for a moment and gathered her own thoughts.

"I've been told by everyone how responsible you are with your gift. Todd, like all of us, probably has a lot of secrets in his life that he should be allowed to tell when the time is right, if ever. I wouldn't ever expect you to betray him by telling me his personal secrets."

"I was sure you'd understand, but I needed to mention it."

She gave Sammi a pat on the back and they both relaxed as the time crawled by.

* * *

Tom called Dave immediately when he got back to Scranton. They had dinner together and he was surprised at how many new events had happened since he'd been away less than a week.

"Dave, this movie we're in, it's moving too fast. Okay, let me think for a minute. Senator Kaphle reports to Fritz Connelly? My God. And the tracker, whoever he is, reports to someone named Wayne Ellison and he in turn answers back to Fritz Connelly. Help me out here, Dave, I think I'm drowning."

Dave almost laughed but it was too serious. "That's about it. But that's why we have to find a way to make the mayor aware of what's happening. We still have a good relationship with the governor and I'm thinking to mention to the sarge that we better let him in on what's happening fast, before he gets soured on us and on the mayor. He could possibly help us out with the mayor."

"This Fritz Connelly is still pulling a lot of

strings?"

"Jim thinks he might be the top guy in the States ... internationally no one knows. Even Ben Collier wasn't aware of some of these details. So, what exactly do we have? We have a police sergeant and a mayor who used to be good friends and respectful of each other. They used to work together easily, and now, they're at each other's throats and don't trust each other at all. And that was the plan. That's what Terry said in his folder."

"Sure and if they get the mayor's position and the governor and they manage to get the sarge out of there, they'll have control of most of the major activities around this entire area. It would be clear sailing for them."

The waitress came around for more coffee and dessert. They both declined.

"That's why I'm so upset about the mayor's behavior. I've been so stressed lately ... this has all been getting to me and I've had trouble settling down. Sammi's been upset. She thinks I should get in better shape so I'm working out lately at the gym to relieve the anxiety. So is Jim. It does helps. Honestly, I look forward to it once a day now. You should think of it, buddy. These are heavy days we've got going and they won't end for a while."

"I know. But I can't figure out how the hell we're going to get the mayor to listen to us. He avoids us at every possible turn. Remember at the governor's ball, he would have walked away immediately if it wasn't for his wife. I can't imagine how to do this."

"Sammi said she had an idea. She plans to come back by Tuesday, I think."

"What does she have in mind?"

Dave laughed, "I have no idea. But Sammi has her own procedure. She doesn't talk at all until she's ready."

Dave's phone rang. It was LeBron.

"I wanted to let you know that Spike Evers has been spotted and he's still around Scranton, or at least nearby. He was spotted in Dickson City. He was in what looked like a dark-colored truck that was so filthy with dirt and grime all over the tires and underbody, we couldn't even tell the color for sure. The license plate was full of mud and wasn't clear either."

"Interesting. That could have been on purpose."

"But we don't have him yet. We were shocked when he surfaced and honestly, we weren't ready. We lost him. However, we've put more guys in the area. It shouldn't be long now. I'll be in touch.."

"Thanks, LeBron. Keep me informed."

"Will do."

Dave related the story to Tom. "If we get him by early next week ... damn, I need Sammi in on his questioning. She's the one that told us the neighbor Larry wasn't alone at the Wal-Mart store. She'll be able to clue us in about the missing wife."

Tom agreed. "We can keep him under surveillance until she gets back. We don't want to miss an opportunity of having her in on the questioning."

"That case is a worry. It's more than two weeks now since she was last seen. I'm hoping she's still alive, but we've got to find her soon. It's possible she's dead already, but sometimes these lowlifes keep them around for a while for their evil purposes. At least if she's still alive ..."

Dave stopped and put his head down. Tom could feel for him. This case was hard on all of them.

* * *

Dave was tired when he got home. He did work out and that helped; it was one routine he would continue. And he took his shower and relaxed for a while. He felt much better.

God, so much was going on. He had two main questions on his mind at this time. To him, the most critical part was the missing wife. He felt with the interview he'd find out what they needed, that is, if these two guys were involved. His gut feeling said that they were, and he had learned to listen to his suspicions.

The second was finding out about Peter Armors. There was no history on him at all that they could find, so he wondered what possibly could have been disclosed for the mayor to hire him. *Had the mayor seen a different file?* There had to be some history on him. But it seemed like he was someone who simply materialized about three years ago and then finagled a job as the mayor's right-hand person about a year or so after that. It didn't make any sense to him.

The phone rang. It was Sammi.

"Hi honey, how's it going?"

"It's slow right now. Todd's not awake that much. But I'm finding it fairly easy to read his thoughts. So, in time, I should be able to help the doctors and Jill."

"That's good. How's he doing?"

"I think it's amazing he's still alive. He's bandaged from head to toe and can move one little finger, that's it. Honestly, Dave, it's hard to see a human being in this defenseless position. He's so totally dependent on those around him."

"It must comfort him to have Jill around."

"It does and he's missed her so I think his thoughts will tell us a lot shortly."

Dave was quiet for a moment. It prompted Sammi to ask. "Did you work out today?"

He laughed. "Yes, I did and it does help. How long do you think you'll stay?"

"I honestly think that I can accomplish a lot in the next two or three days. Although his body is immobile, his thoughts are all over the place. Rather slow, right now, but he's still heavily sedated. They're going to start slowly pulling him off the strong stuff tomorrow."

"That's a good sign, right?"

"Absolutely, but I'd like to do most of my work in the next few days. My idea is that I can talk back to his thoughts and he's already responded to that realizing he is communicating with someone. But when he gets off most of the pain medication, he'll undoubtedly think a lot of these happenings were hallucinations, or something on that order. Know what I mean?"

Dave was impressed. "Yes, that's a great idea. You always think of something."

"And Jill was wise enough to realize I need some time with him alone. That should start tomorrow, so I'm going to try and find out medical stuff and stability inclinations. But I think his thoughts are responding rationally and rather calmly right now."

"That's great, Sammi. I'm proud of you."

"Thanks."

But she knew his train of thought was very erratic right now. She wasn't listening in, she didn't have to, but she knew his mind was heavy.

"So, what's on your mind anyway?"

Dave sighed. "You always know, don't you?"

She waited.

"Well, they've found Spike Evers and they've got him under surveillance. I don't want to bring him in until you get back. We can get so much more if you're here. I know there's no proof we've got the right guys, but my gut says we do."

"Okay, and your intuition has proved quite valuable. I hear things, but you almost know things. Same thing, different technique."

"We'll see."

"Right now I plan to come home Monday night or Tuesday. I think that's all the time I'll need. I can always come back again if I can help out any further."

"Good, the sooner we question these guys, the sooner we'll know. I'm hoping that Vicki is still alive. And if she is, the sooner we get to her the better."

Sammi took a deep breath and it carried over the phone.

"What?"

"I feel bad for the husband and the little kids."

"Me, too. But together we're all doing the best we can. We'll get them."

Dave set his jaw in a hard line. *Yes, he* thought, *one way or another, we'll get these guys.*

* * *

The next day Todd woke up with a little more awareness. Jill took a few moments to say something significant to him and then added, "I'll be back in a little while. Sammi will sit with you, okay?"

His little finger signified yes.

When Jill left the room, Sammi smiled at him and waited. His thoughts were a little scrambled at first, but soon started to slow down and become connected. He thought, *That's right, I talked to her before and she answered me somehow. I wonder what she knows about Jill and me.*

That was her cue and she started. "Todd, I've known your sister quite a while. Tom and my husband Dave are both policemen. That's how we met."

Todd tried to smiled as he thought, *I wonder if she knows the rough time I gave Tom when he wanted to marry my sister. I know he hates me; he has to. He came here because of my sister, so that must mean he loves her a lot.*

Since Todd was still heavily sedated, Sammi took advantage to converse with him. "I think Tom was happy to see you're doing as well as you are. He was quite concerned."

Todd looked at her strangely. His eyes closed a little as in deep, careful thought. He couldn't believe Tom would care about him one way or another. He was so angry at him when he was younger and now he didn't even remember why. Well, he sort of remembered, but it seemed silly now.

"Jill has missed you a lot. She hopes that you can all be friends from now on. I know Tom is willing; I hope you are, too."

A small tear appeared on his left eye as he thought, *There's no way that Tom would want to be friends with me. I treated him so badly. I hated cops; they had made my life miserable. I was so angry that life didn't turn out the way I wanted. I always felt left out of everything, with my friends, with my family, especially with my dad, and then Jill was going to leave me, too. She was my anchor and she wanted to get married and move far away. I felt so lost. I didn't want it to happen.*

Sammi couldn't pass up this opportunity. "Sometimes growing up can be hard. I don't know why it's harder for some than for others. And Jill told me that you didn't want her to marry Tom. I can't help but wonder why. He's a nice guy and he so adores Jill. But I know you love your sister. You obviously didn't want her to move far away, right?"

Todd actually moved his head slightly up and down. *No matter what*, he thought, *he could communicate with this person. How could this happen?*

"I'll bet you felt a little lost as a teenager. It happens to so many of us. I felt that way at times, too. And it hurts. I'll bet you showed anger; I know that's how I expressed my frustration."

He looked at her in amazement. Again his head moved up and down. *She knows*, he thought, *she really knows.*

"But then, for a while, I got myself into such a mess that I didn't know how to get out of it. Know what I mean? I didn't know how to stop the angry behavior and be nice again."

Todd was relaxed now and simply listened to her. "I'll bet you could start over now, if you wanted to. This could be a good time.".

His little finger signified yes. But he thought, *How do I do that? I'm going to be a cripple for a long time, maybe forever, and I don't want Jill feeling sorry for me. That's not what I need. This is my chance to grow up and finally accept my fate in life. But how do I do it?*

"Take your time and wait and progress physically first. In the meantime you can let your mind wander and meditate, and keep your thoughts on the positive things that you want to accomplish. You can get some great ideas that way."

Suddenly Todd thought, *How can she talk to me when I can't talk back to her. Something funny's going on here.*

The good part was that Sammi realized his mind was functioning perfectly. His reasoning power was sharp even with the heavy sedatives. His thoughts came slow at times, but they were on target. So she had to change directions, but she realized that he was one smart guy.

"Are you in any pain anywhere, Todd?"

He signified that he wasn't.

"Can you feel your toes in your left foot? Can you move one of them?"

He tapped out yes, that he did have feeling

and he moved his toes slightly.

Sammi smiled at him and said, "I don't think you have to worry about being a cripple at all. It will take time, but you have feeling in your legs, right?"

He tapped out yes.

Sammi smiled at him again. "I think you're progressing very nicely."

Then the thoughts began to crowd in on Todd's mind. *It's like she knows what's on my mind. She talks to me about what I'm thinking. This is weird, but I'm glad she's here, at least she knows.*

When Jill walked back into the room the atmosphere changed. Todd began concentrating on his sister and had to let go of his suspicions about this captivating stranger. Was he imagining that she could understand him? She seemed to be able to answer the thoughts on his mind. *Probably the medication,* he thought. *I've been feeling rather weird lately.* When he looked over at Sammi, she smiled and it was like she knew again what he was thinking. He'd need more time to think about this.

* * *

Back in Scranton, Dave and Jim both ended up at the station on Sunday afternoon. Dave needed to go over some files, mainly the lack of file on Peter Armors. That was making him crazy. *Who was this guy? Where did he come from?* And possibly, most important, *Who was he involved with?* Yet inquiry after inquiry couldn't pull up any information on him. His file had shown that he had attended some little-known college in New York, but never graduated. And when they checked, the school had never heard of him. Everything was a dead end. Other information for a Peter Armors had pictures of a different person. This was ridiculous and Dave was beginning to feel his frustration when Jim showed up.

"Hey, are you scratching your head about the tracker again?"

"This one drives me nuts."

"That can't be his right name; that's got to be the answer. But who is this guy?"

Dave mulled over the idea for a few moments. Then he said, "I've been feeling for a while that he's a plant anyway—that's a no-brainer. The way he manipulates the mayor quite shrewdly and doesn't leave his side for a second, he's got to be connected with Fritz Connelly and the others. And he was buddy-buddy with that senator so now we know what we're dealing with, don't you think?"

Jim was quiet for a few minutes. He was wrinkling his brow as was his habit when his mind was being crowded with conflicting thoughts. He wouldn't be rushed to share his ideas as he needed to assess his own opinion. Now it seemed he was ready.

"I've thought for a while that Peter was in the shadows and never up front with anyone. It wasn't one thing, but too many to name and some were simply hunches. But from the beginning something wasn't right about that guy. How come the mayor doesn't see it? He's a bright guy. When he used to deal with the sarge regularly I was sometimes amazed at the ideas he came up with. And he ran a crafty campaign when he got elected. So what happened? His first assistant left because of family problems or something and moved away. And where did this Peter come from at that time? None of us had ever heard of him."

All of a sudden Jim stopped talking. He had worn himself out. He'd let all of his inner thoughts reach the surface and simply plopped them out there. He was confused, angry and hated not knowing what was going on.

"I think the secret of what is going on around here lies with this Peter guy," said Dave. "His trail can't be that secret. Someone's got to know something about him. I tell you, Jim, we've got to find out his true identity before we can move forward."

Jim nodded, but said that didn't make him feel any better. They had all been trying to find out who he was and no one was successful yet. These people had covered their tracks quite effectively.

"If we could get to the mayor. He could tell us how and why he hired him. But you see they cut us off from him rather quickly, didn't they? We've got to find a way to get to the mayor again."

"Well, it's not going to happen today. I wanted to double check on a few things and I think I'm ready to leave. I've got to talk to Sammi tonight. I hope she comes home tomorrow."

* * *

Dave's phone rang. It was Marlina Valdez,

Terry Gonzalez's girlfriend.

"Yes, hello, how're you doing?"

"Thank you, I'm fine. I trust you're the same."

"Yes, I'm well."

There was a strange pause on the line. Dave waited somewhat impatiently to hear the purpose of her call. Her voice sounded different, more alive than when she had seen him in his office.

"Is there any progress on finding Terry's killer?"

"No, there isn't. But we're working on it and we won't give up. Have you thought of anything to tell us?"

"No, but I did wonder if the folder had helped you at all."

"It did give us some good information. We're still looking into it."

"Oh, okay," she wondered.

She seemed hesitant to Dave, different in some way, but he couldn't pinpoint what it was. Her voice wasn't quite as edgy, but the words were still of concern for Terry.

He did have questions of his own to ask. "Marlina, I wanted to ask you about someone in Terry's past. He sometimes talked about a cousin that he had grown up with. Would you know who that is?"

She paused for a moment before answering. "That was probably Amilio Hernandez. He grew up at the same orphanage we did. They weren't exactly cousins, but liked to pretend that they were. They were so close and looked out for each other and they both looked out for me. Amilio was about two years older than Terry and he thought of him as a big brother."

"What happened to him? I'd like to talk with him."

This time there was a long pause on the telephone. When she continued her voice was a little shaky. "That's not possible. He died when he was sixteen. You see, he got into drugs and stealing stuff. Terry never did. He hated all that stuff and was always worried about Amilio. And when his cousin died, it made a big dent in his heart that he never recovered from. I know for a fact that's why he decided to become a cop. He wanted to stop all this crime that caused his cousin to die so young."

Dave didn't speak. There was nothing to say. He looked at the phone and thought again of his younger brother whom he missed desperately. He was angry, but knew this was part of their jobs. They always took chances and some had horrible endings.

For some reason Marlina did seem a tad upbeat. Something was different about her today and then she ended the phone call with the following.

"I'd like to keep in touch occasionally if you don't mind. I know Terry loved you a lot and it helps me to talk to you about him."

Dave said, "You call me anytime, Marlina, anytime at all. I'll keep in touch, too."

* * *

Sammi looked around the hospital area as she waited for Jill to return from a meeting with the admissions nurse who had more forms for her to fill out. She had been impressed with the facility which seemed to have its share of professionals with a good attitude and knowledge to follow up. As she saw Jill approach, she prepared to ask Jill her own questions.

"How did Todd get along with your father?"

Jill took a deep breath and had slight disappointment cross her face before she answered. "Mostly, they didn't. He treated me differently I guess because I was a girl, but he was quite rough on Todd. When he was little, Todd cried a lot, but my dad would never give in. Mom says that he wanted him to grow up and be strong, but it didn't work. I think Todd hated him."

Sammi looked down for a moment. She didn't want to trespass any secrets but felt that she was still within allowable territory. "I've gotten some hints from Todd. He felt alienated from everyone, especially his father and that's why he didn't want you to get married and move far away. He depended on you."

Jill had a tear forming in her left eye. Her head nodded before she continued. "I could understand that. Dad ruled our home. That's how our household was. Dad was always hard on him, and Todd had such a tender heart. He didn't recover from some of the whippings he got." Jill let out some tears. "It was awful, Sammi. Dad was from the old school and anything Todd did that didn't measure up got him a whipping or embarrassed him to tears. I sometimes wonder how he turned out as good as he did. I know I was younger, but I used to put my arm around him and tell him everything would be okay. "

Sammi simply listened. Some people awhile back believed that the best discipline was using a heavy hand instead of trying to nurture a breaking heart. How sad.

"I know he likes you being around. That means so much to him. And he can't quite believe that Tom could forgive him and want to be friends. So that's one barrier that you'll have to work on."

"I've been thinking of something. I've got to run it by Tom yet, but I'd like Todd to recuperate in Scranton. I know within a short time he'll be going to a rehab center. But it doesn't have to be in Kansas; it could be around Scranton. And then I'd be close by and who knows, him and Tom could make some inroads. I hope Tom will agree. What do you think?"

She smiled. "That's a great idea. You can't be forever taking planes back and forth to Kansas and that's what would happen. It's a good idea. And I'd like to keep visiting him, too. I can't imagine Tom disagreeing with that."

"I think I'd like to call Tom right now and see what he thinks about it. It would be so great to have him around. He's my brother and he needs me right now."

Sammi went back in to talk with Todd while Jill made her call. At first she thought he was asleep and looked around the room, but when she glanced back, he was staring at her.

Hi, he thought and smiled. *I was hoping you'd be here today.*

"I enjoy talking with you, Todd, and you're looking better every day.

I think I'm doing better, at least I hope so. Then

he stared at her and didn't even think anything for a bit. Finally he offered, I think *it's strange but I know I can communicate with you.*

She smiled and said, "That's because you're one sharp guy."

She knew that made him feel good about himself, something that had been lacking with him for a long time.

I'd like to do something good with my life, he thought, *But I'm not sure what.*

Sammi said, "I hear you've got a real good brain in your head. And Jill told me that you've had some college. You could go back to school. In fact, while you're recuperating you could probably take some classes on line. That might help you decide what you want to do. And here's something I'd like you to remember. Always keep your mind on the things you want in life, and off the things you don't want. People don't realize how important thoughts are in determining their success. But I think you're beginning to understand, aren't you?"

Todd nodded. And he smiled at her. She knew he was excited about school, but he wondered how he could do it. Who would help him? He'd need somebody and sooner or later Jill would go back home.

Just like clockwork Jill walked back into the room. She smiled at Sammi and gave her a thumbs up. "Tom was truly excited and thought it was a great idea."

Then she turned to Todd and said, "We want you to come to Scranton, okay? I've discussed this with Tom and he agrees wholeheartedly. You'll be recuperating for quite a while and you'll need someone to watch out for you. Whatever rehab center you're at, I don't care, but I want it to be close to us. What do you say?"

Todd started crying and both eyes showed tears as his emotions overtook his demeanor. His thoughts were so tangled that even Sammi had trouble deciphering them. But he was happy and he felt wanted. When his thoughts became coherent again he was thinking. *They want me around—I can hardly imagine this—They want me around them.*

"Todd, your sister will be happy to have you around. She's missed her big brother; she's told me so."

And Jill stood there nodding, as she knew that Sammi had answered his thoughts.

And that was the biggest smile that they'd seen cross his face yet. Sammi's job was done and she told Todd that she would be leaving for Scranton on Tuesday morning, but she was looking forward to visiting with him again there.

And when Sammi left the room for the last time, she was happy to share with Jill her brother's final thoughts. *How could I get to be this lucky? I'm going to get a second chance with my sister and Tom, too. I'm so lucky.*

CHAPTER NINE

Sammi felt satisfied to be home. She'd missed Dave, even though she had been gone less than a week. When she walked in the front door she took a deep breath, looked around and smiled. How could one average-sized unpretentious home mean so much to her? But it did. Then Kali came running up to her and left no doubt as to how happy she was to have her home. It was almost four o'clock in the afternoon on Tuesday. She had time to take a shower, unpack and sneak in a quick nap before Dave got home. There was something about your own home, she thought; it had a personal scent different than any other place.

She placed a call to Dave letting him know she had made it home safely. He wasn't at his desk. She left him a message. *"I'm home, honey, but I'm tired. Wake me when you get in."*

And that was all it took to get her moving and finishing up her chores. As she relaxed, stretching out on her more than generous bed, thoughts moved sporadically across her tranquil mind. At first they centered on Todd and how his recuperation would unfold. Then her curiosity wandered to Spike Evers. Were they ready to bring him in? That was one case she wanted solved and quickly. And that was the last thing she remembered until

Dave was waking her up about two hours later.

"I wanted to say hi. You sleep longer if you need to. I'll get dinner ready."

"Oh no you don't. You come right back here for a few minutes." She laughed and gave him a hug. "I've missed that lately. God, I hate it when you're not around."

He smiled and welcomed the attention. He happily held her and they enjoyed each other for a few minutes and then Sammi got up. She wanted to know the latest.

"I'm calling LeBron right now. I want him to pick up our Mr. Evers and bring him in tomorrow. We've got to get that interview done now. We've got to know if he's the one or not."

And Dave excused himself and went immediately to call LeBron who said he'd call back as soon as he had more information.

When he returned, Sammi was full of questions. "Tell me what I've missed. What's going on?"

Dave smiled at her inquisitiveness. "Okay, we've been concerned that they might get to the governor. Right now, he's still friendly with us, but we all know what happened to the mayor. So I told my concerns to the sarge and he went up and had a meeting with Governor Gary on Sunday to clue him in about the problems that are starting to occur again and what to watch out for. We're not sure if we can use him to connect with the mayor or not. That could be too risky. But the governor was shocked. He couldn't believe that we were being targeted again."

"So he's still cooperative with us."

"Oh yeah and apparently he noticed something at the ball and mentioned it. He said it was his observant wife who clued him in about the coldness of the mayor."

Sammi gave him a clever look. "Yes, some-times women notice subtleties better than men. Anyway, I'm glad we're still solid with him. Did you talk about Senator Kaphle?"

"No, we decided to hold off on that one."

"He had enough to digest as it was."

"You said you had an idea on how to get to the mayor."

"And I do, Dave. I do. But I think I'd like to get this interview over with tomorrow. I still have a little thinking to do about my contact plan and then we can move ahead on the other part. Okay with you?"

"Sure, in the meantime, the sarge tried to call the mayor and guess what? The tracker sent back a message saying that all communication with the mayor would be filtered through him in the future. He wanted to know what the call was about and the sarge hung up. He was shocked that he can't even get a call through to him."

Sammi wrinkled her nose in surprise. "I guess I am, too. That seems pretty extreme, but I'll bet that's what that Wayne Ellison wants. Remember? The tracker said he would let him decide the next move. It seems they are tightening up the circle."

"Seems that way."

"Has anyone found out anything more about that Wayne Ellison?"

"Jim is running some background on him. I haven't heard yet."

"That could be telling. All these new characters and we don't know anything about them. Too bad I couldn't get to him. Bad enough about the mayor."

"Unbelievable, isn't it? Our own sergeant can't even get through to the mayor. What's that mayor thinking?"

"Maybe he doesn't know that his calls are being intercepted."

That comment stopped Dave. "You could be right. Well, let's eat."

* * *

The phone rang around ten o'clock. LeBron informed him that they'd have Spike down at the precinct by 1:00 P.M tomorrow. And he couldn't help but mention that upon being informed about his forthcoming questioning, Spike was one unhappy and angry dude who was screaming lawyer.

"If he comes in with a lawyer already, that's going to hamper us a lot."

Dave answered. "Let's wait and see how cooperative he'll be."

As he hung up the phone, Dave turned to Sammi and said, "I can't believe how much I depend on you these days. If this Spike guy brings in his lawyers, you can still catch his thoughts. I've got to be sure to ask the right questions to trigger his mind activity."

"This is one interview that I'll be writing notes to you, as we go along. If I can grab enough thoughts from him, I'm hoping we'll have a direction to take real fast. You can put him on the spot immediately. We don't have time to waste. If Vicki's still alive, we've got to get to her as soon as possible."

Dave's face was tense. "And we have to be ready to move fast."

"Was he alone or was that other guy with him?"

"LeBron said he was alone."

* * *

Spike Evers sauntered into the station with two well-known lawyers. Apparently he had used them before and had a deal with them that they would be available at all times in the future. Dave had trouble figuring that one out. Spike's connections were limited at best. He had done time for stalking women, molestation and other such activity. He couldn't imagine who or why anyone out there would be helping him. And since these lawyers were expensive, he doubted Spike was paying for them.

Dave was to lead this investigation, although LeBron could jump in anytime with his own questions. Sammi, as usual sat on Dave's left side with her writing pad. Most newcomers thought of her as more of an assistant or secretary who would take notes and offer nothing more significant. That was their first mistake.

"Now, Mr. Evers," started Dave as he looked over his file, "we're investigating the disappearance of one Vicki Wentworth. Do you ..."

He didn't have time to finish his question. Spike was all over the place in his denial. "I don't know her, never heard of her, don't know anything about her."

Spike's lawyers hushed him up fast and he settled down. But it was already too late. Sammi got a clear thought of him accosting her in the parking lot. *Snooty bitch,* he thought. *Me and Brian are teaching her a lesson. Wouldn't even look up at us when we passed her.*

Dave caught Sammi's notes. "Weren't you at Wal-Marts on September 21st with Larry Sinclair and your friend Brian?"

His head did bounce back a little at that question. He turned to his lawyers who told him to answer truthfully yes or no.

"Yes, I was."

His arrogant attitude suddenly disappeared. He waited anxiously for the next question.

"And didn't Larry Sinclair point out his neighbor whom he said needed to be taught a lesson?"

"Yes, Larry says she's a snooty bitch and high and mighty acting ..." His lawyers hushed him up again. They asked for a quick conference with their client.

His face was somber when he returned and simply answered, "Yes, Larry pointed out his neighbor."

"I'm sure you've heard she disappeared. Do you know what happened to her?"

He conferred with his lawyers. And while this was happening Sammi let Dave know that they had the right guy. He had approached her in the parking lot and Brian and Spike got her into their van. But they needed to know where they had taken her and where she was now. This could be tricky.

"What happened next?" asked LeBron.

"Nothing. What do you mean? Larry pointed out his smart-ass neighbor and that was it." His lawyers were on him again. They could be heard telling him that his negative attitude toward this woman would hurt him.

He answered. "But she was a bitch. I hate those females who think they're better than anyone else. God damn."

Apparently Spike didn't know what it meant to whisper. And both Dave and LeBron heard him. His lawyers looked angry, but also somewhat embarrassed.

Dave veered away for a moment. "What's your friend Brian's last name?"

"Don't know," he answered.

"Where can we find him?"

"Don't know."

"Where can we find Vicki Wentworth?"

He took a deep breath, and then smugly answered, "I don't know that either."

Then Dave paused for a moment. And LeBron was almost going to ask a question, but Dave cautioned him to wait a moment. Sammi was obviously writing feverishly and she was getting crucial information.

They decided to break for about ten minutes and confer with each other.

* * *

Dave was able to confer with Sammi privately

as LeBron excused himself for a few minutes.

"I got a last name on that Brian, it's Hatterly."

"Great, hold on a minute." Dave went over and got one of the guys to run a quick check on him. "He's been in prison. We should get something fast."

When he came back, Sammi was ready with her latest information. "Okay. I get the impression Vicki is alive. His thoughts said that they were teaching her a lesson like it was present tense. When we return I was hoping you could keep asking him questions related to Brian and where Vicki is now. I got an impression that they don't leave her alone. So if Spike is here, Brian is probably with her."

About this time the sarge came in along with Tyrone. They wanted to know how things were developing. And then the report came through. Brian Hatterly got out of prison two months earlier. His record consisted mostly of violence toward women. And a note in the record stated that he could easily be provoked by any female who didn't show humility and submission to him. His psychological profile was chilling. He had been severely abused by his mother as a child and even with extensive therapy his anger toward women never lessened. He was considered to be dangerous, and although he had served time for his latest molestation charge, he was let go with reservation.

Dave had an unsettling feeling inside and devised a plan for Sammi when the interview was finally over. The meeting resumed with the sarge, Tyrone and LeBron becoming observers.

"Where is Vicki Wentworth?" he asked.

"I told you I don't know."

But Dave waited a moment or two and gave him time to worry in his thoughts. Then he continued.

"Where is your friend Brian?"

"I'm not his keeper. I don't know."

Again Dave waited. Even the sarge thought this was peculiar. But he did notice that Sammi was writing feverishly.

"When was the last time you saw Vicki Wentworth?"

"In the store."

Another purposeful pause by Dave.

"You mean in the Wal-Mart store?"

"Yes, that's what I said."

The pauses were beginning to get to Spike, and that was part of the plan.

"You didn't see her in the parking lot when you and your friend Brian abducted her?"

"That's a fairy tale for you to prove."

At this point, his lawyers were all over him again. They wanted him to answer the questions and nothing more, but he had trouble with his ad-lib-type personality and his sneer had returned.

"Where is your friend Brian now?"

"I told you I don't know, and I don't know."

"So you don't want to help us find Vicki. We'd go easier on you if you'd cooperate."

"Can't help you and I wouldn't if I could. That bitch deserves anything she got."

Now his lawyers were livid. They said this interview was over and they were not happy with their client. They were already arguing with him as they got up to leave, but they were stopped.

Dave told his lawyers, "We're holding him overnight."

"On what charge?"

"Withholding information in a kidnapping."

"You can't make that stick. We'll have him out by morning."

Dave smiled as he thought, *That's all the time I'll need.*

Then he turned to Sammi and said, "Okay, Ms. Evans. I'll need you to type up your notes immediately."

"Right away, Detective Patterson. I'll get right on it."

And she rushed out of the room over to a computer and started typing.

It prompted Spike to say, "That's how a woman should act."

And that's exactly what Dave wanted to hear.

* * *

Dave had a conference with the sarge and the other officers. Jim wandered in, after he had finished with his daily routine, and joined them.

"I've gotten some clues, but I want to wait until Sammi types up her note. She hinted that she might have a direction for the location where they're holding her. Don't know if we have enough, though."

"Sarge," called one of the officers, "we need you over here."

He excused himself and Tyrone and LeBron

needed to check out other things they were working on exclusively. That left Dave and Jim.

"Does Sammi have something?"

"I think so, but I'm not sure it's enough."

At this moment Sammi joined the group with some basic notes.

"Did I exit okay?" she smiled.

"Look," answered Dave. "I wanted Spike to see you as an obedient female so he wouldn't give you another thought. And you did good."

"I know," she teased. "Anyway, from what Spike was thinking, Vicki is definitely still alive. She's being held at some cabin near the base of the Poconos, but I need more. I was upset his lawyers shut down that meeting when they did. I need more. Can we get to him again, like now?"

Dave wasn't sure. "Let me check with the sarge."

* * *

As Jim and Dave wandered off, Julie came over and joined Sammi for a cup of coffee. She'd been working feverishly on some new information coming over the computer system. It seems she was able to intercept two memos from Fritz Connelly.

"Honestly, Sammi, they're getting careless, which leads me to believe they may want me to catch these memos. They may be bogus. Anyway I'm working with Ben right now so he can decide."

"Wait a minute, Julie. That's how we all think. The tracker said that he would have to let Wayne Ellison decide what to do and you said the same thing about Ben. I always check with Dave and Dave checks with the sarge. So this Wayne Ellison has to be a major player higher up in this scheme."

Sammi paused for a moment feeling slightly self-conscious. "Sorry, Julie. I guess this is all obvious, but it helps me to talk about it out loud."

"I understand. I do the same thing."

Then Jim and Dave returned, along with the sarge.

"I understand you want more time with this Spike guy. I'll be going along. All we can do is ask him up front if we can talk to him or if he wants his lawyer again. Then we'll see."

"Okay," she said rather awkwardly.

Sammi was having a problem with this.

"What?" asked the sarge.

"Well, I was hoping that there wouldn't be a group around. Dave and I might do better alone with him for a few minutes. That's all we'll need, a few moments."

Knowing her reputation for results, the sarge had a plan.

* * *

Walking down to the holding cell area, the sarge immediately confronted Spike.

"We need you to answer a few more questions. Do you want your lawyers or not? It's your right, but we'll have to hold up your dinner if you do."

"I don't know. God, I'm hungry and they tell me they're bringing me something soon."

"Well, I need your answer," said the sarge.

"Just a few questions right? Same old stuff again. Okay, I don't need my lawyers."

He looked over at Sammi who kept a low profile. She had her notepad in hand and looked quite subdued, looking down mostly at the floor acting in a submissive manner. Spike glanced at her and thought she was okay.

The sarge left immediately and then it was Dave and Sammi. They had discussed the specific questions he was to ask in order to trigger his thoughts.

"Okay, now once again. Do you know where Vicki Wentworth is being held?"

Spike laughed. "This is one of the questions you want to ask? Same question. Same answer. No, I don't know and I wouldn't tell you if I knew."

"Your truck was all muddy so I thought you'd been out in the mountain trails around here somewhere."

That shut him up completely. But his thoughts went directly to a mountain trail near Milford. He pictured a cabin hidden from the road that belonged to an uncle of this Brian Hatterly. He was allowed to use it occasionally, since no one else went there anymore.

"I have nothing to say, except that you have a cute assistant here. And she's not mouthy like that other broad."

Dave didn't answer, but Sammi could tell that comment made him nervous. He moved on fast.

"When did you hear that other broad was mouthy?"

"Well, she has a bad mouth on her and ..." He stopped immediately and looked worried. "This questioning is finished. Oh yeah and just in time. Here comes my food. Anything else will be done in the presence of my lawyers. Now, I've warned you and we're finished."

"Okay," said Dave.

They immediately left as they didn't want to get caught in dangerous territory. But Sammi smiled as they walked out the door.

She repeated what she'd heard. Dave went to work fast as he talked to an assistant. "Find out about a person, last name Hatterly who owns a cabin somewhere near Milford. We need this information yesterday."

They both walked into the sarge's office and he got LeBron and Tyrone in.

"Look," said Dave. "We've got some good information, but mostly it's been your case lately. What do you want to do?"

LeBron said, "I thought we worked as a team here. Let's all take these guys down."

"Okay," said Dave, "let's do it together."

It wasn't twenty minutes before the location of the cabin was obtained and the units were sent out within a half hour. Dave and Jim chose to go, but Sammi was going home, a decision that made Dave happy. She'd be available for the interrogation in the future, if and when needed.

* * *

When Sammi arrived home she had the usual chores to complete. Kali needed to be fed and clothes needed to be washed and she was returning to work at the bank tomorrow. She was

half-way through completion when the phone
rang.

"Hi, Jill. How's it going?"

"It's good. Some of Todd's bandages are being
removed so we can see a little of his skin now. And
they've kept up some of his pain medication for a
few more days. But the doctors say he's doing
quite well. They think they can release him to a
rehab center in the next few weeks."

"That's wonderful. Have you been able to talk
to him at all?"

"Well, I keep talking, like you did, but I don't
know what he's thinking. If I ask him yes or no
questions he taps out his answer. He kept looking
around earlier today so I asked him if he was
looking for you and he was. He forgot you left and
went home."

That felt good to Sammi. That would mean
that he would have forgotten how they communi-
cated. But she was quite sure that he wouldn't
have forgotten the gist of their talks.

"I'm sure a lot of things will go in and out of
his mind while he's on that medication. That's
pretty normal, I'm sure."

"I think so, too. So I'm going to start looking
for a rehab center around Scranton. This has
worked out so well."

"Yes, it has. And who knows? He might like
Scranton."

Jill laughed. "Wouldn't that be something?"

Sammi thought that life had a strange way of
making things right at times.

"I talked to Tom a few minutes ago. He told me
that they might have found that woman who

disappeared?"

"The units are out right now. I'm waiting to hear anytime. We located the cabin and if they're there ... I hope she'll make it. Indications were that she was still alive."

"Wow, that sure is something. You must feel so proud."

"I'm proud of my part in it. But the guys are the ones doing all the hard work. This is a team effort."

"I know, I know. But still, what you do seems so satisfying to me."

"It does have its good moments, but there are other times that things don't turn out so well."

"Let me know what happens. I've got to go now."

* * *

Sammi finished her chores, stopped for a cup of coffee and read the mail. More bills, but that was usual. And no, they didn't need any new windows. She was about to toss one letter in the trash, but the addressee caught her eye. It was addressed to Ms. Sammi Evans. She never got mail like that anymore. Everyone knew she had married Dave Patterson. Intrigued she opened the letter.

> **Ms. Evans,**
> **I thought I'd call you by your real name. That's who you are for sure. That's all you'll ever be. Dave could never truly love you. You're not his**

**type. He likes glamorous, beautiful
and effective women. And you'll
never be that.**
   **Enjoy him while you can. It won't
last forever.**

Sammi was shocked. She read it again. She couldn't believe it. There was no signature and it looked like it had been typed on an old manual typewriter. Of course she thought of Linda Saunders. She'd be the one who would send something like this. But there was no return address and no other way to trace this letter. She decided to put it in a plastic envelope and hold on to it for a while. Now was not the time to show it to Dave. He had too much going on.

It did unnerve her a little, but not as much as before. She knew this would keep happening since Linda obviously had others on the outside helping her. But why? What would be the point? Obviously they wanted to keep her on their side for some reason. But what that reason could be she had no idea. She'd be in jail for years to come. How could she be of any use to them? She had made up her mind that this would never end and she'd have to find a way to deal with it.

She decided to put this letter out of her mind. They wanted to use fear and worry against her. She'd have to fight that. She decided to take a shower and possibly a nap before Dave got home. She didn't want to keep this from him; that went against what they were all about. But she could wait at least a few days.

* * *

Once they knew the exact locality of the cabin, they had no problem arriving from all sides quietly, yet effectively. They had found out the precise location from a township map and although hidden from ordinary view to naive travelers, to the suspecting eye it was quite accessible. Two vehicles were spotted outside, a grey van and Vicki's red Jeep. The grey van is what Sammi had heard about so they knew Brian had to be there. But they needed to know the circumstances. They couldn't give him time to harm her, if she was still alive. So they sent up three policemen to scout around and see if they could spot any activities inside.

"Nothing in the back," called in one officer on his phone. It was his duty to inspect around the back of the cabin which ran along the edge of a rugged ravine. The trickiest part was the underbrush and trees, which made walking difficult. But it also gave a lot of cover which helped.

"Nothing on the west side," called in another officer. He also mentioned that his side had the kitchen area in view and no movement was seen in there.

The officer on the east front of the cabin reported, "They're both in here. She seems to be tied up to a post of some kind so she's sitting there on the floor, and he seems to be eating dinner on a couch at least ten feet away from her. It's the living room area and he's watching TV."

"Can you spot any guns?"

"No, can't see anything like that."

After a quick discussion it seemed that the best idea was to rush the place. With Brian's background, if they tried to talk him out, he would probably kill Vicki or seriously harm her. Given any chance at all, his instinct was to harm a female.

"Is she mobile? I mean, can she walk or run?"

"No, I don't think so. He seems to have her tied up with handcuffs. She can't get away from that post."

"Okay, I guess we're going in and fast."

Since all knew exactly where both were located inside the cabin, four officers blasted through the front door and one window simultaneously. Brian was so shocked he hardly moved. He didn't even put down his plate and try to run. When he did get his wits about him, he had four guns pointed directly at him and he simply laid down his food dish, put his hands up and said nothing. But his mouth was still open in shock.

He was yanked up as they searched him for the key to the handcuffs, but nothing was found.

"Where's the key?" they demanded. But he simply laughed.

"Great, one more charge we can levy against you."

But he simply laughed more.

Vicki had a black eye and tons of bruises all over her body. She had open cuts on her back and face and obvious dried blood covered many areas of her clothing. She seemed quite dehydrated. The medics immediately began to tend to her wounds.

They asked her, "Have you any idea where he keeps the key to these handcuffs?"

She simply shook her head. She had one tooth missing in the upper front left side of her mouth, which still showed signs of swelling and caused her trouble talking. It was obvious that she had been aggressively abused.

It was at this point that Dave walked through the front door and saw the commotion.

"What's going on?" he asked as he noticed a helpless and abused woman who was still handcuffed to the poll.

LeBron said, "We can't find the key. I guess we could cut them off ..."

"Wait a minute. Hey, Jim, get in here! We need you." He turned to LeBron and said, "This guy can pick any lock you've got."

Jim came in and Dave simply said, "There's no key. Get those handcuffs off of her, will you?"

It didn't take Jim more than a few seconds on each hand and Vicki was free. She began crying uncontrollably and the medics took care of her from there. She was in their rescue truck within a few minutes and on the way to the hospital.

It gave Dave a lot of pleasure to call her husband and report that his wife was found alive. But he added that she had been severely abused and was on the way to Mercy Hospital on Jefferson Street. He added that she was coherent, but letting loose of all the emotions that she had obviously kept inside. And Dave's answer to the profuse appreciation was, "We were doing our jobs."

Then turning to Jim he heard him say, "Looks like the referees did it again."

LeBron was in charge of the unit that was

gathering the evidence, so they left.

On the way home, he placed a quick call to Sammi to tell her of the happy ending. She said she'd have dinner ready and a glass of wine.

Dave was well satisfied with his day. When things worked out so well, it made all of the failures in their jobs seem distant. That's what his father would have said. He was a cop, too, and reminded Dave not to concentrate on the failures, but to remember the successes and victories. That's how he kept from getting bitter in a devastating profession. He would forever remember his feelings when he first saw Vicki, tied up to a post, forced to sit on the floor. Bruised, yes. Traumatized, definitely. But she would survive. She had a loving husband and two children who needed her and that alone would give her a reason to fight to regain herself.

* * *

When Dave walked into his home Sammi was waiting for him. He gave her a long hug and had trouble letting go. He held on and on. Finally, after a deep breath he said, "Boy, I needed that."

"Me, too."

He smiled as he brushed her hair back from her face and looked at her. "We work so well together. Sometimes I think of us as one person, and not two. Crazy, huh?"

"No, it's not. We each have our part to do, that's all. You must be starving. Go relax," and turning she handed him a glass of wine. "I'll call you when it's ready."

Ten minutes later, when Sammi called she got no response. She walked into the living room and Dave was sleeping on the couch. She looked at him resting peacefully and thought, *He can eat later. He needs this more right now.*

She sat in the big lounge chair opposite him. What a great ending to this story. She couldn't wait until they got a report on Vicki. But he said she seemed coherent and thinking rationally. But her emotions gave way as usually happens when people are rescued. Dave stirred on the couch. He was completely stretched out and his lengthy body took up the entire sofa. She laughed as she thought that her body took a little over half of the space, even when she extended herself as much as she could.

Thinking of Brian Hatterly she realized that he'd had a thinking process of hate toward women most of his life. It was true that his young life gave him reason for distrust and fear, but if only someone could have gotten to him and helped him realize that not all women were like his mother. If only he had learned to change his thoughts to good feelings about other women and that could have helped him feel worthwhile. If only he'd had some helpful therapy. *If only ... if only.*

Then the letter crossed her mind again. She knew she would have to tell Dave, but it wouldn't be tonight and she couldn't see having time for the discussion tomorrow either. They needed a few days to settle down. And they had other problems looming in the near future.

CHAPTER TEN

"I need to get together with the mayor's wife."

Dave slowly put down the sport section and turned to look over at Sammi's determined face, wondering what brought about this sudden remark. And he silently questioned her impulsive desire to get with Audrey Stillman. He knew she wouldn't answer until he asked, as she was waiting for his interest to kick in.

"What brought this up?" he said knowing she had been thinking about it for a while.

"I remember her thoughts at the governor's ball. Of all three women, she had two things going for her. One, she was knowingly suspicious of the tracker and his motives and two; she wouldn't be pushed around by him or her husband. Remember, when the tracker tried to rush them away, she said, "What's the hurry? I'm talking to an old friend.""

Dave nodded; he remembered and looked intrigued.

"I think the best way to get to the mayor is going to be through his wife. Luckily, they seem quite devoted and although she definitely has a mind of her own, I got the feeling that he trusts her. The question might get to be who he trusts more, the tracker or his wife. That'll be interesting. And since we can't get any calls through to him, who knows what else is going on? I've got to tell you, Dave, if anyone knows what's happening around there, it's going to be Audrey."

"I think you've got a point there. You certainly could determine what's on her mind as you talk to her, but how can we do that? We can't get through to the mayor."

"I'm going to have to find out where she gets her hair done, or where she shops or what else she does. Anything at all, but preferably shopping. I think I could do better that way."

Dave had to smile at that idea.

"I have a plan in mind and it gets a little tricky, but first things first. I'm going to talk to Julie and see what she can find out on the computer."

"Okay, but if not, we might be able to put her under light surveillance for a short time to find out where she goes regularly. That's a good idea, Sammi."

"I think I could relate to her. I liked the way she was thinking at the party. She won't be bullied and if I can make some inroads I was thinking ... well, I'd better wait and see. But one way or another, she's the one who can help us. I knew it back then and with the tightening of the circle around the mayor, it might be the best way. But I wonder if the tracker has her followed, too. "

"I'm sure he does, but it's still worth a try. We've been wracking our heads trying to figure out how to stop this estrangement before it goes any further. The sarge and the mayor used to be real good friends and they trusted and helped each other. We did some great work that way.

Luckily, we got to the governor so he's aware of the situation and it definitely has him worried. We still can't find out anything about this Peter Armors. It's so frustrating. Where did this guy come from?"

Sammi scratched her head and shifted in her chair. "He bothers me. Who is he? What's his background and most important, who's he connected with?"

"I think we know who he's connected with up the line, but why did they pick him for this position? This is a tricky and pivotal spot, so why him?"

"Anyway, even if Audrey is followed, two women having a cup of coffee and talking and laughing, and I'll make sure of that, should seem harmless enough. I know the tracker won't like it, but I don't think he can stop it. And if her thoughts get into a certain direction, well, with a little prodding, I might be able to clue her in."

"You'll have to be careful, Sammi. You can't tell her too much."

"I know, but she's already suspicious of the tracker. I thought the best thing would be to add to the doubts in her mind. She already has concerns and if they begin to cross her mind, then I'll jump on that, in a tactful way of course."

Dave was thoughtful. "I'm going to keep this quiet for now; I can tell the sarge later. Let's see if we can get anywhere first. If you can get to her; then we'll discuss how she's thinking and how open she is to your suggestions. Hopefully we'll have an avenue to follow."

"It's one step at a time, like you told me. Then

we'll see where the next one will lead."

"Well the sarge doesn't know how to proceed right now anyway and he's worried that it'll get worse if we do nothing."

"Okay, then, let's see if we can find out what she does. She must have certain activities she does regularly and that's where I'm going to be."

* * *

The next few days were mostly routine activity and much to Dave's appreciation, he had time to relax and get caught up on his paperwork. He always hated that part of his job, but detested getting so far behind that he would have to spend a week locked in his chair writing reports. Intermittently there were questions and details that got him up and busy, but by Thursday afternoon his work was done and he sighed with relief.

"Damn, Dave, I can't believe you've caught up on your reports. Good job," teased the sarge.

He smiled realizing he did have a reputation for delaying his files and procrastination was part of his personality, at least as far as filling out forms was concerned.

"We're going to question Brian Hatterly again in about an hour. You want to be there?"

"And I've got time," then added smugly, "since my paperwork is up-to-date. "What's he been saying so far?"

"Since he was caught red-handed, he's been thinking up excuses as to why she deserved what she got."

"Oh, he has reasons for that, does he? Can't

imagine."

The sarge gave a rather disparaging look that took in all of the sickening feelings he was experiencing. "How's Vicki doing?"

"Jim and I stopped by last night, at the request of her husband. She wanted to thank us. God, she went through hell. Nothing was broken, but I heard that hardly any part of her body was free from a bruise or some kind of cut. She was smashed in the mouth and lost a front tooth, and as you can expect she was repeatedly raped by both Spike and Brian. It was disgusting. It's a miracle she survived. She'll heal physically, but mentally her resilience amazed me."

"You wonder how she kept it together."

Dave added. "By picturing her children and husband, she said. And she didn't take her mind off of them and it got her through."

"She's one tough gal."

"Yes, she is. And to have to put up with ... I guess it was mainly Brian. I was reading his file earlier and it's amazing they let him out on the street."

"Dave, he's definitely wacko. You're right; he shouldn't have been let out at all. He seems to sincerely believe that if women don't act submissively that they need to be taught a lesson. And unfortunately his record shows that he's tried to teach a few others some lessons, too. This will be his third offense against women. Of course, this one is the most serious with the kidnapping and all, so he'll go away for a long time. Still, his attitude is bizarre. Where do they get these ideas?"

"Sammi thought that Spike Evers' childhood

explained his reason for erratic behavior. His mother was quite abusive and he never got any therapy to get his thinking back on track. Maybe this Brian has the same type of problem."

"That's a point. Some people should never be parents anyway. They start these kids on behavior patterns that have them terrorizing society and they end up in jail for the rest of their lives."

"So whose fault is it then?"

The sarge thought for a moment but didn't answer.

Dave continued. "Then we get to why their parents were so ineffective and abusive and the answer usually lies in the fact that they were abused and abandoned themselves. A vicious circle, isn't it?"

"And it's sad. But our job is to stop that circle. We can't get into feeling sorry for these people. We have to stop the circle of crime; that's our part of the job. Let the system get them the help they need."

Dave didn't answer. They both knew the system hardly ever gave adults any therapy. Even children were too often left out in the cold. A lot had to do with funding. And so the circle continued.

* * *

That evening Sammi knew that it was way past time and she had to show Dave the letter she'd received. She hated to do it and was still wondering if she could hide it for a while longer. But, she knew that wasn't a good idea. She looked over at him. He had been fairly content lately, more relaxed and working out regularly. Everything was moving along nicely and she hated to break the tranquility that surrounded them. She was about to speak, when he beat her to it.

"I forgot to tell you something. I was in on an interview with that Brian fellow today, and guess what?"

She looked over intrigued.

"He said that Larry Nielsen was in the parking lot when they took Vicki and saw the whole thing. He wasn't in on it, but he saw everything. So he knew from the beginning that she'd been kidnapped and had a decent idea where she'd been taken. And then we questioned Spike again, and he confirmed everything."

"So what does that mean?"

"Well, at first we thought we could push the idea that he was an accessory before the fact because he mentioned to these two lowlifes that she needed to be taught a lesson. That was a thin line, but this guy is trouble waiting to happen. His attitude toward women is warped, although so far a lot less violent than the other two. A little legal trouble could help him straighten out a bit, or at least scare him into acting better."

"And now what?"

"Well, Sammi, he lied to the police. And he saw an abduction occur and did nothing about it, and lied when asked about it. He's definitely an accessory to a crime and he'll do time for this."

"Wow, I'll bet Vicki will be happy he doesn't live next to her when she gets back home."

"I understand they'll be issuing an arrest

warrant for him within the next few days. I imagine he'll be one surprised guy."

"It could turn his life around. Maybe something like this is what he needs."

"There's no reports that he's been abusive with his wife, at least there are no reports on file. So far it's simply his big mouth and lack of respect."

"I know these people aren't happy inside, Dave. They don't know how to work their lives. They want to bring everyone down so they'll be as miserable as they are."

"Really, you think so? Hmm, I guess it's a thought."

They were both silent after that. Sammi's conscience was bothering her. This was another chance to tell him about the letter. They prided themselves on being open with one another. Although she thought she had good reason, she had been secretive and held something back. And she wouldn't like it if Dave had done it to her. It had to be done.

"Dave ... I need to tell you ..."

The telephone rang. *Damn,* she thought, *I want to get this over with.*

After a few polite words, Dave handed her the phone; it was Jill.

"Sammi, we're moving Todd to the Allied Rehab Center on Morgan Highway by Friday. We're coming home."

"That's great. That's actually quite close. How's he doing? Any improvements?"

"They're still small, but they've lessened his pain medication a lot now and he seems to be okay. He's seems more coherent. We still can't communicate that much, but he listens to me and I know he understands what I'm saying. So that's something."

"Yes, it is. Well, it'll be good to have you home, both of you. Will you be allowed to ride back with him?"

"I think so. He's requested that I ride with him and the doctor nodded his head, so I think that means yes."

"I think that'll make it easier on both of you."

"Right, look I've only got about another minute. He knew I was calling you and wanted me to say hi."

"Oh, really? Well, you give him my regards and tell him that I'll be visiting with him soon."

"Thanks for everything, Sammi. It helped so much."

"Okay, and if you need me, you call."

Sammi turned to Dave as she put down the phone. He had heard the conversation and he nodded in approval and went back to the sport section of the newspaper.

* * *

Sammi took a deep breath. She knew she should tell him, but changed her mind. It wasn't her favorite subject anyway and she felt she could wait one more day.

Then Dave said, "Weren't you about to say something when the phone rang?"

Now she felt she was caught. And he noticed the look on her face and didn't know what to make of it.

He added, "Sammi, what gives with you?"

She took a deep breath. "Okay, Dave, I do have to tell you something. You're not going to like it and ..."

Dave never seemed to have much patience for this type of comment. "Sammi, tell me."

"Okay, but I have to go and get something first."

She left the room and came back with the letter in the little plastic bag. She was hesitant. She knew he'd be upset with her and they so seldom argued. But what choice did she have?

"I got this in the mail late last week. But before I show it to you I want you to know that I always planned to discuss it with you, but you had just got back from rescuing Vicki that night and you were exhausted. You fell asleep on the couch, remember? Then I was going to give it to you the next day but you were so busy that I waited."

By this time, Dave looked concerned. "I get the feeling you've been keeping something from me, right?"

"In a way. But I always planned to tell you. See, I'm telling you now."

His voice was dry as he said, "Let me see it, Sammi."

She handed him the letter and sat down on the couch and waited. He must have read it a few times and then put his head down. She knew by the movement of his shoulders and position of his arms that he was upset. She thought it best not to say anything and gave him time to adjust his temper.

"I'm not happy about this, Sammi. You should have shown me this right away no matter what. Since when do you keep me out of the loop? What possessed you to keep this a secret from me?"

He was angrier than she thought he would be. His voice was much stronger and deeper than usual and his tone was adamant. In fact, she felt that this was the first time she'd seen him this angry with her. She reacted with fright inside, but it wasn't for anything physical. It was worrisome that he'd lost a little confidence in her. What could she say to make him understand? What could she possibly say?

For a few moments they were both at a loss for words. Dave got up and walked out of the room. Sammi knew he'd be upset, but hadn't imagined he'd be this infuriated. She heard him pound on the kitchen table. She sat and waited. It was almost ten minutes before he returned. He was still holding back his emotions and she couldn't understand the extent of his irritation.

"I don't understand what possessed you? We're supposed to share everything, the good and the bad. You don't pick a time when it's okay to tell me things I need to know. You simply tell me."

"The first night you fell asleep right away, as soon as you got home. You were exhausted. I wasn't going to wake you up and tell you."

"Why didn't you tell me first thing the next day?"

"You took off before I was even awake, remember? You left me a note and said you were meeting Jim for breakfast and would be interrogating Brian and Spike all day. And I had to go to that late meeting at the bank. I wasn't home when you got home and you were asleep by the time I got back."

Dave waived his hand. She knew he remembered that they'd had a few unbelievably hectic days. But he felt excluded and that hit him hard.

"But you weren't left out. It's not like I discussed it with anyone else. And it's only five days later."

"But I need to know everything immediately, Sammi. Promise me in the future you'll tell me right away, even if you think it'll upset me. I need to know. You held this alone and that's not right."

"I'm sorry, Dave. I know you're very mad at me, but I was waiting until things settled down a little, that's all. God," she said as her eyes began to water, "we've had so much going on, I thought, what's a few more days?"

Dave was still quiet and he hadn't made a move toward her yet. Something inside of him was having a problem letting go of his concern.

"A few more days is a lot to me."

"Then you'd better tell me what's bothering you. I didn't think a few days would be a big deal, but now I see that it is. So I won't keep anything back in the future, I promise. But you're keeping something back right now, aren't you?"

She sat still as Dave pulled up a chair in front of her and took both of her hands in his. His voice was steady, serious and totally sincere and he kept full eye contact as he spoke.

"Sammi, in this entire world, you're the one person I totally trust. Oh, I trust Tom and Jim, but in a different way. You not only have my whole heart and soul, but also my emotions and feelings. There's nothing about me I would ever keep back from you and I want you to be the same way with me. It's that closeness you and I've always talked about, but to me it's so much more. I see too many who go through the motions of what a marriage should be. I did it myself with my first wife. I don't want that to ever happen to us."

She nodded. She remembered when Dave had discussed his first marriage and the emptiness he felt because there was no closeness, little sharing and not enough trust.

"Remember when I was in the hospital and you wanted me to recuperate at your house and I thought I'd do better at home?"

Sammi puckered her lips. She had never forgotten that.

"I know I did a miserable job of explaining it and you left the hospital that day hurt and feeling excluded. I tried to call you a couple of times that night but you were so upset with me and feeling shut out that you couldn't even talk to me until the next day. That's how I felt just now."

She now understood how he felt.

"At first, this incident scared me quite a bit, but after you reminded me about those extremely hectic days, I can begin to understand why you waited." Dave paused for a moment and almost smiled. "But it did scare me, Sammi. I can't deny it and it took me a few minutes to put my emotions aside and get logical again."

Sammi repeated. "I'm so sorry, honey. I had no idea how this would affect you. I thought it was something unpleasant that I had to tell you, and I'd simply wait until a better time." She paused, with tears coming down her face. He wiped them away.

"I know the contents of this crappy note had to upset you. I was thinking that's why you waited."

"No, that's not why. I was waiting for a better time. Honestly, Dave, we know who's behind this, but ..."

"And that's partly why I need to know right away. Anyway, we can put this behind us. I think I better understand now why you waited, but don't do it again, okay? I won't do it to you. We've got to stay open with each other. There's no one in the outside world I pull into my trust like you. We're solid and I need to keep it that way."

"Understood," she said. And then he joined her on the couch and gave her a tender yet affectionate kiss and a satisfying hug.

Sammi had no idea that he would take it this hard. In her mind, she was still surprised. There had to be another reason, too, but she wouldn't listen to his thoughts. She would never do that.

"I think part of my anger was the content of the letter, too," said Dave. "I guess I was hoping that this would go away, at least for a while."

Sammi figured that was possibly the real reason he got so angry. "I don't think that's going to happen. She'll always find a way. But who could she have found to do this?"

Dave shook his head. "I can't imagine. But I think in the future, and there will be more coming, I'm sure; they'll all be anonymous. It was smart to

put it in a plastic bag; I'll have it checked for fingerprints. I do want this to get on record."

"Good idea."

"How did you react when you first got it?"

"I almost didn't open it. It looked like junk
mail and I was close to tossing it in the trash when
I noticed it was addressed to Ms. Sammi Evans. I
don't get mail like that anymore."

"Were you upset?"

"I wasn't even surprised. I told you she'd find
a way. And if we can find out how she did it, it
might give us a clue as to how she fits in this
puzzle."

Dave nodded. Then he put his head back on
the couch, his feet on the ottoman and relaxed. It
was the first time he'd relaxed in the last twenty
minutes. She joined him and they sat quietly
realizing that they'd made it through an important
acknowledgement tonight.

Slowly Dave looked over and said, "I love you,
Sammi."

"And I love you, Dave Patterson."

He smiled with satisfaction and continued to
enjoy the moment.

* * *

The telephone rang. Dave answered.

He listened quietly without any return conversation. Finally he said, "Thanks," and that was
the end of it.

Sammi wasn't surprised. Dave got a lot of
calls where he was given information and barely
responded. She waited. If she was involved, he'd

tell her.

"Every Tuesday Audrey Stillman gets her hair done at the Transition Salon on Lackawanna Blvd. Afterwards, she takes the opportunity to go shopping and do personal stuff. It seems to be her afternoon out."

"Okay, well, that's a beginning. Do they know where she goes shopping?"

"She has several places so that could be tricky for you."

"I'm going to call and find out what time she gets her hair done. And I'll be around that place when she leaves. I think it's in the mall and if I work it right, we could easily find a place for a cup of coffee and chat time."

Dave was thoughtful and said, "I'm not saying anything to the sarge right now. But if you make an inroad with her, it might be our best chance.

* * *

Sammi still felt exhausted when she got out of her hot shower on Sunday night. It had been a hectic week and another one was facing her. She hadn't been getting enough sleep and she knew it, but so much was going on. *Well, tonight would be different*, she thought. Lights would be out by ten o'clock and that should make a new person out of her.

She peeked around the corner of the living room and sure enough, Dave had fallen asleep stretched out on the couch. She was surprised he hadn't succumbed much earlier. The hours he was keeping lately were too much. She'd begged him to take a day off, but he wouldn't hear of it. He did work two half days after a couple of all night shifts and that seemed to help him get more rest. Sammi always worried about him. Last week she noticed him favoring his left shoulder again. And she worried. But he caught the look in her eye and said that he'd had been to the doctor and checked it out. Everything was fine, but his tendency of a slight weakness where he'd been shot, would always be there.

She tiptoed into the living room. She wanted to read for about a half hour and had no intention of waking him until it was time to go to bed. After a moment or two she decided on a cup of coffee.

When she entered the kitchen she found a present, beautifully wrapped in lilac paper with a large white bow on her side of the table. She was shocked and simply stood there for a moment. She turned to see if she should wake Dave and there he was right behind her, smiling broadly.

"I thought you'd never get done with your shower. I kept waiting for you to get out here." He seemed so excited and it showed on the impish look he gave her.

"What's this about? It's not our anniversary." She almost panicked for a moment wondering if she had forgotten some celebration.

"No, it's not that. It's something else. Open it up, will you?"

Sammi smiled. She couldn't imagine what surprise awaited her as excitement entered her body.

Well, it seemed that the first box had a smaller box inside it and then there was still another smaller box. There were a total of four boxes by the time she got down to a ring sized box.

Her face looked at him questioningly. "What on earth?" she said.

"Will you open the last box?"

She opened it slowly and carefully in time to see a gorgeous diamond ring.

Her mouth did drop open a bit and she stared and didn't say anything for a moment.

"Dave, it's so beautiful," she said with tears in her eyes. "But I don't understand."

"We got married quickly for our own reasons and bought attractive matching bands, but I always wanted you to have a diamond ring. I look at Julie and Jill and they both have nice rings. I wanted you to have one, too. Do you like it?"

"I love it. I mean, what's not to like? Dave, it's stunning. I had no idea ..."

"I wanted to surprise you. If I'd asked you, you would have said no, that you didn't need one. But you do need one. It puts the finishing touch on our marriage."

"I don't think I ever knew you were so sentimental."

Dave looked slightly embarrassed. "Well, a little is okay."

"I love it. Dave." And she came around the table and gave him a satisfying kiss.

Trying to fall asleep that night wasn't easy. It should have been; she was relaxed and felt pampered and loved. Dave and she were solid again. Actually they always were, but occasionally they still had learning curves about each other to work out. And slowly they were getting the little glitches straightened out and their marriage was secure. Oh, she knew that nothing would be perfect, but the road they were following was satisfying for both of them. They were heading where they both wanted to go.

* * *

While trying to fall asleep, Todd crossed her mind. She'd stopped at the rehab center to see him for a few minutes. It wasn't planned, but she was passing by on her way back from grocery shopping. Jill and Tom had already left so they had a private chat. It wasn't exactly a conversation, Todd still had trouble communicating. But he was much more aware of things since his pain medication had been lessened. When she walked in the door his eyes lit up. He was glad to see her.

She knew she had to be a little more cautious when she talked to him. But she didn't yet realize what a clever young man he was.

"Hi Todd, I was passing by so I thought I'd stop in to see you."

He smiled. The bandages around his face were almost gone and his expressions could be seen. His jaw was still wired shut and would be for a while yet, but he did have the semblance of smile when he chose.

"I understand you're improving quite well. The doctors are proud of you. Are you feeling better?"

He tapped out yes. But his thoughts were suspicious. It was almost as if he knew something, yet he didn't. His thoughts were full of expectancy. He was happy to be in Scranton and

Tom and Jill both had come to see him. He was glad that Tom was giving him a second chance.

"I'll bet you're glad to be back near your sister, right?"

He nodded.

"And Tom's been congenial, too, right?"

Again he nodded. And he was thinking that his thoughts about him had changed considerably. He now realized that his sister had married an upstanding guy. Too bad he'd been so stubborn all those years. To be honest, it wasn't that he was stubborn exactly, but he had created a complicated quagmire and didn't know how to change it so he left it alone. Still, he now realized that they had lost a lot of time that couldn't be retrieved. But if Tom was willing, he could make it up to him.

"I think you're going to find out that Tom is a good-natured guy. And he's been happy that the two of you have a possibility of a friendship in the future. Now, I won't be dishonest with you, part of it is because it would make Jill happy. But he told me the other day that he felt you were a sharp guy and looked forward to getting to know you better."

Todd looked happy. He was thinking, *Wouldn't it be nice if we became friends.*

Sammi said, "It would be great if you guys found something in common and became friends."

Todd looked at her in a strange way and thought, *She's done this before, it's as if she knows what I'm thinking.*

Sammi picked that up fast and didn't answer his thoughts but totally changed the subject. Then he began doubting again if she knew what was on his mind.

"Do they treat you good here? It does seem like a nice facility, but you're the one who lives here."

He tapped out yes but thought, I wish that they would bring me some newspapers to read. Sammi knew that she had to keep him off guard and didn't answer his thoughts again.

Instead she said, "Have you thought about what you want to do when you get better?"

He tapped yes and thought about going back to school. Again Sammi ignored his thoughts. This was her best diversion right now.

"I'm sure when you're hands are better and you can write out some notes, it will help a lot in communicating, right?"

Todd was looking confused and thinking, *Maybe she was more sensitive before, but it sure seemed like she knew more.* Then he relaxed and enjoyed listening to her as she talked to him for a few more minutes.

"I think you've got a great attitude, Todd. After all, you've had a horrendous accident and many would let this get them way down, but it seems to me that you're ready to give it your best shot. You're impressive. When someone can keep positive with all that you're going through, well, you've got my vote."

Todd tried again. He thought, *And you've got my vote. There's something about you and someday I'll figure it out.*

Sammi didn't react. This was intriguing to her. He was the first one she knew who suspected something and was trying, in a kind and friendly way, to trap her. She enjoyed the game.

She knew he had a lot of intuitive powers and noticed a lot. Jill was right when she'd told her that he was quite bright. It would be interesting to find out in the future what profession he would end up in. She was sure he could master several.

On her way out, Sammi talked to one of his nurses.

"His sister told me that he would enjoy reading the daily paper. Can we sign him up?"

"No need. I'll take care of it. Should be good for him."

"Be sure and tell him his sister ordered it for him. That'll make him happy."

"He seems to be happy getting some visitors. It's true he has a long way to go, but he's a fighter."

"Yes, he seems to be. And that should work in his favor."

As Sammi left she saw the nurse jotting down some notes on her pad. She was sure that newspapers would be a good idea for him since it would keep him abreast of what was happening around Scranton. And his mind had let her know that he wanted to find out about Scranton for more than one reason.

CHAPTER ELEVEN

"Audrey Stillman, isn't it? I'm not sure if you remember me. I'm Sammi Patterson, Detective Dave Patterson is my husband; he works for Sergeant Brady."

"Of course, I remember you. We met at the governor's ball. It's good to see you again."

They were standing outside the Transition Salon in the Viewmont Mall in Scranton. Sammi had been waiting at a discreet distance and when she noticed Audrey paying her bill, she purposely walked past the front of the salon corresponding to her exit. And they had almost bumped into each other which made it impossible for her not to take notice. She laughed, happily and seemed genuinely pleased to see her.

"I get my hair done here every Tuesday. It gets me out and I need my freedom every so often," she quipped.

Sammi made sure to place herself in the lane of traffic so that two people almost bumped into her within the next few minutes.

"I like this mall. It's close to me and it's easy to find your way around," Sammi said. She had noticed a stern looking man looking at them from a distance. No doubt that was one of the tracker's men.

"I like it for the same reasons," she said.

Sammi continued. "I sure enjoyed the ball. Such a beautiful home they have. I hope to have time to see more of it in the future." And with that Sammi's hopes were answered. Bringing her mind back to the ball triggered an unpleasant memory for Audrey. She was thinking that she didn't like the coldness that had developed between the two men, her husband and the sarge. She had questioned her husband about it, but he wouldn't say much. That's what Sammi needed to hear.

"I understand you and the sarge's family have been friends over the years," she said. Immediately she wondered if she'd overdone it. She didn't want to appear nosy, but she had felt a friendly atmosphere around her and went with it.

"Yes we have and I like Norma. She's a delight. But lately, I don't know what's wrong with these men."

At this moment Sammi got bumped again which prompted Audrey to say, "Would you like to get a cup of coffee? We could talk easier that way, if you have time."

"I'd enjoy that," she answered. But as they started heading to a little nearby coffee shop the tracker's guard approached her and said that she would be late getting back home.

She answered, "Then call them and tell them I'll be late." And she walked away without one backward glance.

"Sorry, Sammi," she said. "Some of these guys are so bossy lately. It didn't used to be like this. I feel that I have to ask permission to do anything. I don't mind conferring with my husband, of course, but these guys are so pushy. I don't understand it."

Sammi needed to jump on this immediately. "Who's he anyway?"

"Well, I've always had a protector, so to speak around me, but they were always in the background making sure I was okay. But these guys try to create my agenda and that's got to stop."

"Oh, I see." But she quickly added, "Do they work for your husband?"

"No, and that's the strange thing. They were hired by that Peter Armors. Are you familiar with him?"

Sammi shook her head.

"Well, he's one strange guy ..."

Then all of a sudden she seemed to want to change the subject. Sammi heard her thinking, *I probably shouldn't get into this with an almost stranger.*

So she changed the subject hoping to bring it up later. "You must have a busy schedule?"

"I do keep busy most of the time, but I almost always have to ask permission for what I'm doing these days. It didn't used to be like that. Politics are not what they used to be."

Audrey had a lot on her mind. "I shouldn't ramble on with this, I know, but there's no one to talk to. They keep me on a short leash now and I don't like it."

Sammi felt that Audrey's strong personality and intense desires would be a good asset to her. She definitely had a mind of her own, as she should, and it would make for a good bargaining point.

The waitress came and coffee was ordered.

Conversation seemed to flow easily between the two of them. And with conversation came a lot of thoughts that Sammi was privy to as her concentration accelerated in such a relaxed atmosphere.

Audrey's thoughts conveyed a lot of irritation about the tracker. She didn't like him; she didn't trust him and she didn't think he was doing the best for her husband.

In an effort to relax her, Sammi managed to get on a more positive subject for her.

"I understand you have a boy and a girl?"

"Yes, they're both away at college and I'm glad. My son especially would never have put up with being pushed around. Sorry."

"What's he studying?"

"He likes engineering and my daughter, right now, is studying nursing. She's changed her mind a few times already, but we'll see."

"Yes, well, sometimes it's hard when you're only eighteen or nineteen to decide what you want to do for the rest of your life."

Audrey looked over and smiled. "That's exactly what my Lindsey said. And it's a valid point. Anyway, they usually come home only between semesters right now, so I miss them."

"I can imagine," was all she replied.

"I've enjoyed talking to you. I hope we could do it again sometime."

"I'd love that," answered Sammi. She knew that Audrey appreciated having someone on the outside to talk to, so she was thinking that this had worked out better than she hoped. But she needed to throw out a hook to her. And she had the chance with her next remark.

"Let me give you my number and you call me," said Audrey. "I'd love to set something up with you."

Sammi answered. "I hope I can get through to you." When she saw Audrey's surprised look she added, "Well, I understand Sergeant Brady tried to get in touch with your husband a few times and Peter said all calls had to go through him. I was wondering if you had the same setup?"

"What?" she said. Her thoughts and words were in unison and she was definitely shocked and surprised. Sammi was sure now that although she had suspicions, she was beginning to believe that things were out of hand and she thought, *I wonder if Ron knows about this. I doubt it. He always took care of his own business. I'll bet he doesn't know what's going on.*

Sammi knew that Audrey was seriously concerned now and that's what she wanted. But she didn't want to overdo anything so she tempered her words with, "I didn't mean to upset you. I wanted you to know that if I didn't get through to you, you'd understand. I guess I shouldn't have said anything. Gee, I'm sorry."

"No, no. Sammi. You don't know how happy I am that you did. Something strange is going on ..." and then she stopped. But Sammi caught her thoughts, *I'm going to have to talk to Ron. He'll be hard to convince, he's so stuck on this Peter guy, but this almost seems like a conspiracy to me.*

Sammi still felt she had to protect her plan. "I probably shouldn't have said anything," she offered and acted as if she was worried that she had divulged a secret. She was pleased with Audrey's thoughts even before she spoke the words.

"Don't you worry, Sammi. I've got some work to do, but no one will ever know how I got suspicious. Listen, why don't you give me your phone number? I'll get through to you and it might be better if you don't call me. I'm not afraid to tell you I'm concerned, in fact I'm a little nervous about this entire matter. I've had misgivings for a while, but kept everything to myself. Too many things are not right. We could help each other. It's not good that Ron and Sam don't even talk anymore."

Noticing Sammi's surprised expression, she asked, "What?"

She smiled and said, "I never knew the sarge's first name. He was always Sergeant Brady to me."

"Oh," she smiled in understanding. "I need to think things through. I think we're on the same side here. I know I can trust you; I feel it."

"Well, I'd heard that these two men had become estranged and I wondered how odd. They should be working together. They used to be confidantes, I heard from Dave." Sammi felt she had to let her know where she was at. Her thoughts had been wondering.

"I'm going to call you. I'll need to talk some more, but I want to look into a few things. I trust our conversation will go no further."

"I was going to ask you the same thing," said Sammi. Immediately Audrey felt that both of them were in the middle.

"I'm worried now more than ever. I'm thinking about a lot of things that haven't fit together lately. I think we're going to need each other in the future and these guys need our help, whether they know it or not."

Sammi nodded.

"Okay, here comes my bodyguard. I guess I don't want to make him too suspicious cause I know he reports to Peter."

Sammi said, "I think we should start laughing a lot as we leave. It might be better if he thinks we're two females being silly and gabbing about nonsensical things, like they think a lot of females do."

Audrey jumped on that in her thought world. And by the time they waved goodbye the bodyguard was shaking his head and his expression showed that he thought this meeting was nothing but silliness. And that's exactly what she wanted.

* * *

Sammi had missed a call from Ben Collier. When she tried to return his call, he was away from his desk. He seldom called her. She had worked with him on some cases and found out about the intriguing world of the FBI. She wondered what was happening now. He always had a reason for calling. Well, it was his turn so she'd wait until he got in touch with her.

She was anxious for Dave to come home. She wanted to tell him about her conversation with Audrey Stillman. Her plan had worked better than she had expected. They had their coffee, conversation and the beginning of a friendship, and because Audrey was a strong personality, her thoughts were quite telling.

She had picked up Audrey's thoughts of suspicion regarding the secretive people around her husband. A while back his right-hand man was Tony Baran. He was a good, loyal friend and in those days their lives moved along in a straight forward direction. Everything seemed more open and above board. She never felt pressured about her schedule and never told what her agenda had to be. But Audrey was concerned after Tony had to leave and he hired Peter Armors, who brought in a few of his own people. Sammi caught some thoughts that even from the beginning new rules were added and her role was much smaller in her husband's administration. He didn't consult with her as much and she felt that Peter was inching into her most favored status. Oh, she knew her husband still trusted her, but she felt she had lost her preferred status and with it some of the dependability that made her feel needed.

Losing herself totally in deciphering Audrey's thoughts, Sammi was startled to hear the door open. She hadn't heard Dave's car pull into the garage.

"What's up?" he said, noting the look on her face.

"Gees, I was so caught up in thinking about things that I haven't even started dinner. What would you like?"

"It's not always your job to cook. I felt like Chinese food today so I stopped and got some on the way home. I even got some fortune cookies. Let me plop down this paperwork and then we can eat."

She smiled, "You're such a thoughtful guy at

times."

He laughed, "Glad you think so. What's up? You seem to have lots on your mind."

"I do, but let's eat first and relax. Then I think we need time to discuss some things."

"We do. I got a call from Ben Collier today."

Sammi reacted. "He called me, too. But I wasn't there. So he went to you, huh? Must be important."

"Not desperate, but some matters need to be taken care of. Let's eat first, okay? I'm starving."

So they sat down to Egg Drop Soup, her favorite. And then they had sweet and sour chicken with fried rice. And, of course, fortune cookies.

"You first," said Dave. "I'm going to predict a good fortune."

Laughing she opened the fortune cookie. "Your life becomes more and more of an adventure."

"I can't deny that, but that's good. Adventures can be enjoyable, right?" she said.

Then Dave opened his cookie and read, "You have a secret admirer." His face soured.

Sammi immediately quipped, "Yes, you do and it's me. But it's not really a secret."

They both laughed as they cleaned up the kitchen.

* * *

"What did Ben want?" she asked. She had been anxious to talk to him, but they never connected.

"He needs us to come back to Philly for a few

days. They've had a lot of loose ends with the Donnie Fedorick and Sergei Ivanov cases."

"When are their trials?"

"They've been delayed so many times. I mean it's been well over a year since they were arrested and charged with all those abductions and, of course, they were also charged with the robberies."

"Is that all happening at the same time?"

"I don't think so. They're going after them for the abductions first; that's the more serious crimes. But it seems their lawyers have requested more time on several occasions and now that their trial is getting close, Ben wants to double check with us, mainly you I think, on several key points."

"I see. When does he want us up there?"

"Within the next couple of weeks. And I thought I'd like to have dinner with Marlina, if we can manage it. Did I tell you she called me last week?"

"No, you didn't mention it."

"It was a routine call. More that she wanted to keep in touch and find out what was happening as far as finding out about Terry's killer."

"How's she doing?"

"She seemed lighter than before. I got the feeling that she was more on an upbeat note. It didn't seem strange to me exactly, but she didn't seem as down in the dumps as before."

"Well, time has passed. Sometimes that helps."

Dave nodded. But his mind was wandering. It was obvious that something was bothering him, but he had trouble speaking about it.

"Sammi, she seemed different. I can't even put my finger on more than that, but she didn't seem the same as before. I don't know how to explain it; just a feeling I got."

Dave got quiet now. She knew he was thinking of Terry. He always quieted down whenever their conversation turned to him in any way.

She went back to reading the newspaper for a while. There needed to be a lull in the conversation before she brought up her subject. And she needed to get her thoughts together, something that was getting increasingly difficult considering the happenings around Scranton.

* * *

"Dave, I got my meeting with Audrey Stillman today?"

"You were able to get to her?"

"Yep, I did. I waited until she was ready to leave the beauty shop and I almost bumped into her, on purpose of course. She was quite congenial and wanted to talk. Her thoughts told me a lot from the first moment. So we had a cup of coffee and I've got to tell you, I think we have an ally in her."

He looked impressed. And he was happy. "Only today, the sarge was mentioning that he wanted to work on a way that he could get to talk to the mayor."

"Well, I think we may have one."

She proceeded to tell Dave about their conversation, especially about the fact that Audrey had always been suspicious of this Peter Armors fellow, almost from the beginning. She also proceeded to tell him how she had been able to sneak in the fact that she might have trouble calling her, as Audrey suggested.

"You do impress me sometimes. That was a great way to do that. And her reaction shows that she wasn't aware of this net that's closing in around the mayor."

"And she doesn't think her husband knows either. Now she didn't tell me that in words, but that's what her thoughts said."

"So she wants to see you again."

"Yes, and she said that she'd call me to make sure that there would be no problem. And the important thing is that she wants to look into a few things and she thought we could be helpful to each other. Her thoughts told me that she wants to make sure that her husband knows that Peter is controlling his phone calls. I think our next meeting will be extremely interesting."

"Wow, this is great. I don't know if I should mention this to the sarge yet?"

"I think I'd wait. She seemed to have meant what she said, but let's wait to see if she follows through. I think she will. She doesn't think this Peter guy has been doing the best for her husband for a while. But now she's angry. There were times that her thoughts were moving so fast over a few things, I couldn't catch them. That doesn't happen often, but usually when people are entirely livid about a situation."

"Okay, then, we'll certainly hope for the best on this one. If she does call you and wants to work out a plan, then I'll pull in the sarge."

"That would be better. But she sure sounded like she wanted to get to the bottom of this confusion that was going on around her husband."

Dave came over and sat by her. "You're so impressive to me. Some days I forget that what you do is so great and unusual. It's not that it ever feels like the norm to me, but I'm sort of used to it by now. And I don't tell you that often enough."

She smiled. "What you and Jim and Tom and the others do every day is the hard stuff. True, I've got this gift, but I turn the information over to you and you actually do something with it. So I'm impressed by all of you guys, too."

"That's what teamwork is all about."

* * *

The next day at the office Dave let the sarge know that Ben Collier would need them in Philly for a few days. They planned to leave next weekend and be back by the middle of the week. But they wanted the weekend as free time to enjoy the city.

"That's right," said the sarge. "In a way going to Philly must feel like going home again."

Dave smiled. "And I wanted to set up dinner with Marlina, Terry's girl. She called me last week to see how things were going."

"Too bad you didn't have much to tell her."

"We've got a lot of background checks going on right now, and you never know when things are going to start to turn up. But I wanted to talk about something else. Before this Peter Armors was hired by the mayor, he had that other guy ..."

"Tony Baran. He'd been with him in different capacities for years. He was a great guy. God, he was with him when Ron was city commissioner, even before then. It was sad when he lost him."

"Why did he leave?"

"Not entirely sure. I heard it was something to do with his family. Why?"

"I'd like to find him and have a talk. I want to know if he left on his own or not."

The sarge raised an eyebrow. Then his brows produced a pucker. "I never thought of that. That might be something to know. A few people thought it was strange when he left, but not much came of it. But that's a good point. Let's see if we can find him now; he could have something interesting to tell us."

Dave was happy that the sarge was beginning to see the big picture. If Peter was a plant, Tony could have been forced out of his job. And that could lead to valuable information. And he hadn't yet let the sarge know about Senator Kris Kaphle. The time didn't seem right, but soon things would start to fall into place. At least, he hoped so.

"Were there any fingerprints on that latest note that Sammi got?"

"No, it was a clean note and a clean envelope. I figured it would be. But you've got to wonder who Linda has doing this and why? Is it a vengeance against Sammi? I doubt it. I think there's a deeper reason for this reminder and I don't think it's going to stop."

"Doesn't make sense to me. She may still be after you, but I can't believe she'd want to bother from jail, although she was a strange and proud woman. Could be that she couldn't stand the fact that you got married?"

"Who knows? But I seriously think there's more to it. We'll have to wait and see."

* * *

As Dave left the sergeant's office, Julie called him over. She'd been getting some suspicious movement across the computer this morning.

"What's up?"

"Look at these last two memos. One is slated for F.C. and we know who that is. That alone isn't a surprise. I've seen several of them coming across in the last few weeks."

"What about before then?"

"Nothing. They haven't been targeting the computers at all. But last week they started with a few F. C. memos. And the strange thing is they're talking about Pittsburgh. Now we know that Pittsburgh isn't in this triangle so that caught my eye. And today it was more than F. C. memos. There were a few going to W.S. At first I didn't think anything of it; I don't know who W. S. is, do you?

Dave felt confused.

"But look here. This last one says W.S. and it's going to W.E."

"Could that be a typo. Who's W.E.?"

"I don't think so. They haven't made any typing errors that I know of. If they did I think it was on purpose."

Dave had to agree with that. If anything, these

people weren't sloppy.

"I know it's not much, Dave, but I think the communication part is starting up again."

Dave thought for a moment and said, "That would mean that they think their internal plan is getting pretty solid and they can start to move ahead again. Let me know if you get any financial data."

"I will, but this is a slow process. They may stop completely for a few weeks and then come in stronger. It's a pattern they used last time."

"We need to stay on top of this. Sammi and I have to get back to Philly for a few days next week."

Julie looked interested.

"Those abduction cases are getting close to trial now and they need to check a few things. We'll be gone four days and of course, Jim and Tom need to know about this. I almost hate to leave now. Sammi's working on something, too, and we need to be ready for them when they come at us."

"I think we'll be ready. I'm catching a lot of stuff here and I'm working with Ben, too. He's already clued me in on some stuff that he knows is bogus. So I've put some bogus stuff out from our end. It's getting tricky."

"So you don't think this will go for another week?"

"It's getting closer, Dave, but I think it'll be two more weeks or even a month before they put their plan into action."

"But we don't know for sure what that is yet, right?"

"You're going to Philly. Talk to Ben about it. I know there's some stuff that I'm not privy to yet, but he was telling me the other day that they've figured out part of their plan. And he said it's not pretty."

"Okay, later," he said as he left.

* * *

At his desk, he had a message from Tom. He was at the hospital with Jill and wanted him to call right away.

"What's up, Tom?"

"Look, Dave. Would it be possible for you and Sammi to stop by the hospital tonight? Todd got quite upset about something and he can't seem to get the message out to any of us."

"Is he alright?"

"Yes, it isn't anything medical, but when asked if it was important, he tapped out yes. He seems so concerned about something and it doesn't seem to have anything to do with him, not his health nor his predicament. I'm totally confused. Do you think you guys can stop by for a few minutes? We need Sammi."

"I'm sure we can manage. You're going to stay there, right?"

"Oh yeah. I want to know what's got him all charged up. He was fine when we first got here but then, I don't know. We had the TV on and suddenly his eyes got real big and he's been agitated ever since. We can't figure it out."

"Okay, I don't know what time Sammi will be home, but we'll head over as soon as we can."

"Thanks. See ya."

Dave put in a call and told her what Tom wanted.

"I wonder what it could be."

"They've no idea. But it has them concerned."

"I'm sure. Okay, I've got to go. See you when I get home."

CHAPTER TWELVE

Audrey Stillman knew her husband Ron was a stubborn man. He was particular about his lifestyle, wanted things his way and had a definite plan for his life. But he was also of fair disposition and when he entered into public service his ambition had been coupled with a true desire to improve life in Scranton. And he had improved the police force, parks and recreation centers, community services and was a good liaison with the governor for general areas of improvement.

He was ambitious, that was true, but having passed his fiftieth birthday last year made him realize that he still wanted to make a few more steps up the ladder. Audrey remembered what he was like in college, strong, dedicated and true to his beliefs. She was counting on that part of him that was more than a little out of sight lately, but definitely the solid base he ruled from. That's what she was hoping to awaken again. And she was stubborn, too.

"Ron, what's on your agenda for tonight?"

"Not sure, why?"

"We need to talk. I've got things on my mind that won't wait."

She saw his concerned look. This wasn't like her. She usually was more placid in her approach to life. But she had been tossed in the background long enough and the time had come to assert herself in a way consistent with her position.

"Let's have dinner here together and get whatever it is off your mind," he said.

She knew he was assessing her attitude. He always did that. It was natural for him. But she knew he loved her and counted on her and she planned to use that to her benefit.

"I'd rather go out somewhere, the two of us. Is that even possible nowadays?"

"What do you mean? I meant for it to be the two of us."

"No, you always have Peter around."

"Well, yes, he'd be around."

"No, I'm saying I want it to be you and me; that's it."

She knew he saw her agitation. He probably was wondering what was wrong with her. He always needed Peter around; she knew that. But she saw him look at her searchingly.

"I want an evening out like it used to be. Remember when Tony was still with us, we used to go out the two of us occasionally, and although someone could be in the background, we'd have some privacy. That's what I want tonight. It's what I need. What do you say?"

She knew how to get to him. His eyes even sparkled slightly in reminiscence. And it always worked. Lately though she had to admit that it had been harder and harder. She could almost read his mind. He was thinking that Peter wouldn't like it. And he wondered why he couldn't be around. He depended on him.

"I like to have Peter around. I never know

when I might need him."

"But for tonight let's have it like old times, okay?" Her smile could still melt him a little. And finally he gave in.

Yeah, he thought, *that would be fun. Tonight could be like old times—the two of us.*

"But we can't go out without the bodyguard."

"Well, pick a different one tonight. Before Peter and Josh were around, your favorite protector was Jimmie. Let's take him with us tonight and we'll have our usual driver, okay?"

She looked eager and knew it. She hoped he'd have trouble saying no. She had him off guard because she was acting differently. And she was different and had some heavy thinking on her mind.

"Okay, we'll go back to old times."

"I know that Peter will have a problem with this," she said letting him know she was aware.

"But I still run this show, don't I?"

He couldn't have known how much she wanted to hear those words from him.

* * *

As expected, Peter was not happy. And when he found out that Josh wouldn't be going either, Audrey heard loud and strong conversation coming from the inside of the living room area. But it ended in a positive note, for her anyway.

"Listen, Peter, I still make the decisions here. I don't think I realized that you thought you made them for me. But you don't. So for tonight you can have an evening off. Audrey and I'll be fine."

She came out in time to see Peter exit. As he passed by her, he said nothing and his look toward her was not friendly. Even Ron noticed it.

"God, he wasn't even civil with you. What's wrong with him? I'm thinking now that this was a better idea than I thought at the beginning. I almost got the impression that he thinks he makes the decisions for me."

And as he scratched his head, she caught a look in his eye that was calculating. He had picked up something and was mulling it over in his mind. He hadn't noticed how Peter had casually directed his life lately, because he never questioned it.

And out they went to a favorite restaurant that they hadn't frequented in about two years. During dinner, Audrey started discussing her suspicions.

"Look, Ron, I've had suspicions on my mind for way over a year now. I've held back a lot, but I can't anymore."

He looked at her somewhat surprised. "Audrey, if you've got something on your mind, why haven't you talked to me about it?" He stopped suddenly. "I know, I know. You're right. Lately, we haven't had much time." He caught her look and added, "Okay, not for a long time, it seems. That's not good."

She took a deep breath and he noticed. "That's why I needed tonight. We never talk anymore. There's always someone around, namely Peter, and, truthfully, Ron, I don't trust that guy."

"You don't trust Peter. Why not?" He definitely looked taken aback.

"Think of how our lives have changed slowly but deliberately since he's been around. At first, I didn't even notice it. It was so subtle, but when I look back to when Tony left and compare those days to now, well, think about it, we don't control our own lives; Peter does."

"That's a little extreme, don't you think? I agree he has a different approach or at least a different way of running my office, but I think he's been above board."

Audrey knew it was time to lay her cards on the table. "You've got to be kidding, Ron. I've always prided myself on the fact that you could always see what was going on around you. But this guy is shrewd. And he and Josh together are a disturbing combination to me."

Ron put his fork down and looked into Audrey's eyes. She knew that he realized the depth of her concerns and he shifted his position. She had at long last caught his attention.

"Okay, look back to the governor's ball. He tried to determine who we were going to spend time talking to and who he thought we should avoid. You must have noticed that."

"Well, he wants me around people who could benefit me."

Audrey simply looked at him in disbelief and made him look inside himself.

"And since when does he determine who will benefit you? It seems to me that you've done a great job on your own most of your public life. And it's not that there has been any magic happenings since he came around. Actually I thought we did much better when Tony was around."

"Really, you don't think he clears the way for me that well?"

"For one thing you're losing some of your most valued partnerships."

This time Ron looked at her in a puzzled way. She could tell he still didn't have a clue.

"If I have to spell it out—Sam Brady. How many times in the past twenty years have the two of you been at odds with each other? Hardly ever, until Peter took control. And I don't even understand what gives with you two. And did you know that Sam tried to call you several times in the last month and was told that all calls to you had to go through Peter? Were you aware of that?"

The look on Ron's face said it all. He had no idea. His expression went from doubtful to unbelieving. He would have laughed it off, but his wife was a bright woman and she was quite intuitive. She had studied law, had minors in social services and governmental affairs and he considered her a treasure of information, at least he did in the past. His mind looked back quickly, and he realized things had changed. He was beginning to see a pattern of faint manipulation that he never gave much thought to before.

Audrey backed off for a few minutes as Ron had gotten very quiet. She knew how his mind worked and it was working overtime. She'd have to wait until he was ready for more.

* * *

It was later that same evening, after they'd

gotten home and were at last relaxing alone in their room that Ron brought up the subject himself. She was happy to see that he had taken her seriously and given careful thought to the ideas she had presented to him.

Suddenly he said, "What's going on here, Audrey? What's happening?"

"I don't know for sure, Ron, but I have my suspicions. And I'm not too naïve to tell you that I'm worried. Remember over a year ago when the police broke up that ring that was trying to oust the governor, you remember that?"

"Of course, who could forget that?"

"I have a feeling that they're trying again, but this time they're working from the inside out."

"What do you mean?"

"They want everyone against each other like you and Sam and others as well. It's not a good idea for you and Sam to be at odds and not to be working as a team. If they can get that to happen, they won't have any problem taking over."

"Where did you get these ideas?"

"I've noticed a lot of things in the last year, especially the last six months."

"Why didn't you talk to me?" He saw the look in her eyes. "Okay, I guess I know why, but you found a way tonight, why not before?"

"Because I didn't and still don't have anything concrete, but I'm worried for you and for Sam. Something is going on, Ron."

He was quiet for several minutes. He took a sip of coffee, but his mind never stopped turning around episodes in his mind. Audrey knew it; that's how he worked. She gave him all the time he needed because now, he was thinking for himself.

"Audrey, a couple of things come to mind. I hate to say I've been blinded, but some things didn't seem that big of a deal at the time and Peter took a lot of the little matters off of my hands. But some of them weren't handled in the way I wanted. And as far as you're concerned, I owe you an apology. I used to confide in you first and foremost. You're still the one I trust the most; you're aware of that, aren't you?"

"I'm happy to hear you say it. Things have changed so much, it's made me wonder. But listen to this. Last week, I bumped into Sammi Patterson when I got my hair done."

He wrinkled his nose.

"She's Detective Patterson's wife." He nodded. "And we had coffee, at least we tried to have coffee and talk for a few minutes. But as soon as we headed for the coffee house, Josh came up to me and said I should get back right away that I'd be late for something or other. It's like they don't want us associating with anyone outside of their realm. That and a few other things got me thinking. I believe we have reason to worry."

"I should call Sam and talk to him."

"Honey, I know you trust me and I think that wouldn't be the right thing to do right now. Tonight was a shock for Peter. Enough already. I think we should maintain the usual schedule, except that I'm going to work to find out things through Sammi Patterson. We hit it off well. We decided to get together again and I told her to give me a call. Guess what she answered?"

He shook his head.

"She was worried if she'd even get through. She had heard that Sam had tried to call you and Peter wouldn't put his call through. That got me to thinking."

"Son of a bitch. You think we might have another conspiracy going on here?"

"I don't know, honey, but something's happening."

"This definitely is odd. I'm going to keep things the same right now, but I'm going to become aware of what's going on around me instead of letting Peter handle everything. And some way in the near future, I've got to find a way to get to Sam."

* * *

There was a call on Ron's cell phone. It was Peter. He decided to upset him; it gave him pleasure. He called Jimmie, his bodyguard for the night, and told him to relay a message to Peter that he'd talk to him tomorrow.

But he looked at his wife with newfound respect, and wondered how he could be so blind. Something was definitely in the works and he had been acting like a sacrificial lamb.

"What's with the two of you anyway?"

"Who? Oh, Sam and I? Well," he said with an amused sneer crossing his face, "Peter thought we should use him to get us good publicity."

"But you were making him look bad, right?"

"And I'm getting stupid in my old age, because I wasn't even thinking that far. Yet Sam is level headed and he was probably seeing through this charade. No doubt that's why he tried to call me. I think I've got a lot of work to do in the future and not all of it's political."

Ron felt foolish for a moment. *Why hadn't he noticed any of this?* True, his mind had been so much on his reelection that he didn't see anything else. He let Peter take care of all other matters. *Well,* he thought, *that's was going to change.* And he hoped it wasn't too late.

* * *

When Sammi and Dave entered the rehab center, they had no idea what was in store for them. All they knew was that Todd was agitated, wouldn't settle down and no one could figure out why. And they all knew that Sammi could hear his thoughts and hopefully clear up this situation.

But she was cautious. Not wanting Todd to know what she could do could be tricky, so she tried other ways to accomplish what they wanted without being obvious, a difficult feat in this situation.

"I'm so glad you're here," said Jill. "He's settled down some, but it's obvious that he's got something he needs to say and none of us can communicate with him."

Sammi walked over to the bed and said, "Hi, Todd, how're you doing?"

He definitely smiled as he thought, *Now I'll find out for sure if she knows what's on my mind. The others didn't.*

She smiled slightly. He certainly kept throwing out the gauntlet to her, but she had other ways to work with him.

Jill said, "Should we leave the room?"

"Oh, I don't think it's necessary, do you, Todd?"

He was playing her game, but he did have something important to say. This hadn't been a ploy of any kind.

"Now I understand that something on TV got you upset, right?"

He nodded and thought, *I'll bet if I think about it, you'll know. And then I'll know, too.* And so his thoughts purposely concentrated on the message he wanted to convey.

Although Sammi was shocked in one way, in another way she was ready for his surprise. And instead of reacting to his thoughts, she got the newspaper and felt she could accomplish her mission that way.

She simply pretended she hadn't heard his thoughts. And shortly Todd was confused again. *Could I have been wrong?* He thought. *Suppose she's simply particularly intuitive.*

That gave her the edge. She knew what he had found out and she was anxious to relay it to the others, but not willing to give up her talent to Todd.

"Okay, then, since the TV story is gone, whatever it was, is there something on this page of the paper that says the same thing? Most of the media talk about the similar stories." She began leafing through the newspaper pages with him and waiting for a reaction.

Todd looked confused, but finally relaxed and seemed to accept her answer. And then she showed him a picture that got his eyes to open wide, his body to react with definite agitation, and his voice grumbling as well as it could beneath a wired up jaw. It was a picture of Mayor Stillman and Peter Armors.

"Now what is it that bothers you about these guys?"

Of course Sammi knew and the group in the room knew that. But she wanted to keep her talent a secret so they let her work in her own way.

She pointed to the picture of Mayor Stillman. "Does this person upset you?"

He shook his head.

Then she pointed to Peter Armors and his face got red and his anxiety and excitement increased considerably. He nodded with considerable exaggeration.

"Okay," said Sammi, "he bothers you. His name is Peter Armors and he works with the mayor."

Todd did all that he could to refute that statement. He shook his head and even tried to move his shoulders negatively. It was obvious what he was telling them. And his thoughts told Sammi the rest of the story. This guy's name was not Peter Armors; it was Willie Sanford. He had known him briefly in Lawrence, Kansas when they took a few classes together. He was trouble then and not allowed to return to school. He didn't know him well, but knew he had been in jail. He and another guy, Wayne something or other stuck pretty much together and didn't socialize with anyone else. He often wondered why they were in school.

After Sammi found a way to decipher the name and most of the story without adding to Todd's suspicions she said, "I'll bet you never thought that you'd be helping out the police someday."

He smiled and seemed pleased. And Tom thanked him before he left which meant a lot.

Back in the hallway, Sammi related everything that she'd found out. Everyone looked at each other.

"That's why all avenues turned up empty. I figured that wasn't his real name, but ..." Dave said. "Now we've got to check up on a Willie Sanford."

"But don't forget," said Tom. "He was friends with a guy named Wayne. Dave, that's got to be this Wayne Ellison that we think is his contact. Now those two along with Josh Logan are pretty much running this show right now, at least in Scranton."

"And Julie says that computer activity is starting to accelerate so they're beginning to move. Good God, Tom, we'd better get with the sarge tomorrow."

They all looked worried. But Dave ended with "But now we've got something definite to work with."

Sammi excused herself as she wanted to go back in and talk to Todd alone. He seemed surprised to see her back again.

"Well, I hope you understand that you've given the police some important information. I'm not sure I know exactly what they'll do with it, but I know they appreciated getting this help from you."

Todd smiled. He looked satisfied and he thought, *Who would ever have guessed that I could have helped the police? That's amazing.*

"The police could always use somebody like you. Think about it for some future stuff. In the meantime, if you remember anything else, let them know."

Todd almost couldn't believe what he was hearing. *The police wanted his help and they appreciated it. Wow, he did have a new direction to go. This one felt so right. Why hadn't he seen it before?*

As she turned to leave Sammi stopped and said, "I'll be seeing you soon. You take care of yourself."

Todd smiled. He liked her a lot. But she confused him. He thought for sure today he'd be able to figure out how she knew things. But he was still in the dark.

When she caught his thoughts and waved goodbye at the door, she realized that she enjoyed the game they played. Although she knew, for Todd, it wasn't a game.

* * *

"So what more did you have to talk to him about?" Dave asked on their way home.

"I wanted to give him encouragement and let him know that the police appreciated the help he'd given them."

Dave smiled. "That was nice."

"Well, I also wanted to mention if he remembered anything else to let us know."

"Good idea. So Peter Armors' true identity is Willie Sanford. I wonder what we'll pull up on him."

"I was thinking there wouldn't be much. But remember that was the name that I pulled off that message from Linda. So they must know each other. And that's the name that I heard him thinking about at the governor's party. "

Dave looked surprised. "That's right. I forgot about that. But why don't you think we'll pull up much?"

"If the mayor hired him, someone must have cleaned up his history."

"Well, they may have cleaned it up for the mayor, but we should be able to find his record, if he had one."

"Todd remembered that he or Wayne Ellison had been in jail."

"That's right. God, Sammi, this case is taking a lot of funny turns. But I wish we knew more about what they were thinking of doing. We've guessed the final result, but we have to stop them before they get there."

"And I think we will. I'm hoping that Audrey will call me by the time we get back next week. She's a sharp woman and I think she's noticed a lot of things over the last year. She probably has lots of clues for us that she's not aware of. And if she gets Ron to realize he has problems, well, I think we'll all be working on the inside against them, like they're doing."

"This is getting so complicated, isn't it?"

"In one way, but when you stand back and

look at the complete picture, they're trying to pull us down from the inside and the best way we can stop them is by doing the same thing to them."

"That's a great theory."

* * *

Sammi and Dave were leaving for Philadelphia on Friday. That gave them two days to clear up loose ends and get ready for a slight getaway. There was another meeting with the sarge for the three referees.

"Holy Shit. You guys are digging up some useful stuff here. So Peter Armors is Willie Sanford. My oh, my. Why does a person use an alias? Because there's a lot in their past that they don't want people to know. So someone picked this guy as a plant."

"Seems that way," said Dave. "But what's his entire purpose?"

"To undermine the mayor and he's done a great job of it so far. We have to get to Ron and make him aware. I know they want to take him down, but I don't think they want to harm him, do they?"

Dave puckered his lips and said, "Sarge, nothing is beyond them."

"That's true. But how do we get to Ron? That's the main thing right now."

Dave clued him in to what Sammi was trying to accomplish. He asked for a few days after they got back to see if it was working.

"Sure, that seems like a good idea. I'm not even going to ask how and why Sammi got in on this. I'm beyond that these days. Just keep me aware of what she's doing. I don't want Ron and his wife to be in danger."

He thought this was the time to tell him about the senator. And that didn't go over well at all. He was totally infuriated.

"You mean they've got one of our senators working with them."

Jim said, "Could be more than one, who knows? But at least one, which means that's more proof that they're working us from the inside."

The sarge shook his head. "These games nowadays are tricky. What's their plan? Damn it. We've got to find out."

"Julie's been catching some stuff on the computer and we're hoping that Sammi gets another meeting with Audrey soon. She thinks she's a sharp woman."

Sergeant Brady looked up. "Audrey Stillman is quite a shrewd woman. And she's no dummy. I'll bet she's noticed things for a while now. She's hard to fool, that one."

"That's what Sammi thought, so we can start putting things in place for our benefit."

"In the meantime, I still have a city to protect. What's new with that kidnapped woman?"

"She left the hospital last week but she's got a long way to go. Her prognosis is good for a full recovery. That's great, isn't it?"

"You guys and Sammi did great work. And for those out there trying to get us crappy publicity, we lucked out and got some good reviews on that one."

* * *

Julie came up to Dave as soon as he got back to his desk.

"Listen Dave, I've gotten some interesting memos intercepted. I'll have a copy of all of them for you by the time you get back. But this particular one caught my attention. Look at this."

It read:

Windmill operation is stalled. One more month needed. More background imperative to success. Then it'll be a go.

And it was sent from WS to WE.

Dave let out a low whistle. He remembered that Terry had talked about Windmill in that file he left for him. He wished he knew more about it.

"When are you leaving for Philly?" asked Julie.

"Tomorrow afternoon, and we'll be back by Tuesday night."

"They're slowly starting to move but with this memo it does seem we've got a little time."

"But how much?"

Julie simply shrugged her shoulders and shook her head.

"Any financial happenings going on the computers?"

"Not in the last two weeks. It looks like they had a test case going on regarding the state budgets back then, but it fizzled away. Ben seems to think that was bogus and simply used to see if any of us were paying attention."

"So what happened?"

"We ignored it and nothing has come of it since. Ben said if we had reacted at all that they would have sent more stuff out to confuse us. And, of course, when we're concentrating on the state budgets, we're not thinking about other things."

Dave's phone rang. Julie was finished anyway so she returned to her office.

"What's up?" he said.

"Can we leave a little later tomorrow? I got a call from Audrey Stillman and she wants to meet tomorrow. She says it's important."

"No problem, that's great. I'll call Ben. I'm sure he can get us a later charter."

"Honestly Dave, it sounded almost like she was whispering somewhat. This is the meeting that I think will tell us if and how we can work with her."

"Great. I'll let Ben know we need a later flight. What time do you want?"

"We're meeting at three o'clock. Could be a longer meeting, but I don't know how to judge it. It'll depend on her."

"I'll work it out with Ben. I'll tell him eight o'clock, but to have them wait for us until we get there. Okay?"

"Sure, that'll work. See you tonight."

* * *

When Sammi arrived at the restaurant, Audrey was already there and it was obvious that she was anxious to talk to her. After pleasantries she immediately began with her concerns.

"Okay, Sammi, I'm going to lay my cards on the table today. You and I've got to trust each other. I talked to Ron and he didn't know anything suspicious was going on. He didn't know his phone calls were being filtered and he was furious."

Sammi listened at this point. Audrey had so much on her mind that she started talking in a swift pattern and didn't slow down for a while. Suddenly, she took a deep breath and stopped.

"Gosh, I'm sorry. I've got so much on my mind. But we've got time to talk. It's simply once I start ... well, we really need to get some things straightened out and attempt to put a plan into work. He regrets the problems with Sam; can you tell him that? He wants to work things out with him in secret. He thinks it would be wise to let Peter and the others think that they are still at odds."

Sammy smiled. They were thinking like she'd hoped. And she knew that Audrey's thoughts were honest and in line with her words. She was worried about her husband and felt that some dire happenings might be in the forecast.

"Ron told me of several things over the past year that Peter took over and didn't respect his wishes. They were small deals and he let them go, but as we looked over a lot of things we could both see a pattern. Now, Ron believes this adds up to one thing: conspiracy. It almost blew him away because it's been so subtle. What do you think they have in mind and who are they anyway?"

In the last twenty minutes as well as in the previous meeting, not one conflicting thought had crossed her mind. Sammi was comfortable with her. And in her discussion with Dave the night before, they both felt that if she had congruency between her thoughts and words, then it was time to let them in on what was going on.

"Okay, Audrey, I think the time has come for you and me to start this interior war in another direction. And believe me, this is a war that they're creating to win the position of mayor, sergeant and governor and they are fighting it from the inside out."

Audrey seemed a little confused.

"Let me back up. Last time, remember when they tried to oust the governor?"

She nodded and said, "Oh yes, Ron and I discussed that. It seemed to us that they're trying to do it again."

"You're right. They are. And to answer your question we don't know who all is involved, but we do know some of the key players. One, of course, is Peter Armors and his bodyguard Josh Logan. They have gained a lot of influence in the last year and a half."

Audrey nodded and couldn't take her eyes off of Sammi. She was mesmerized.

"But Peter Armors is not loyal to your husband and never has been. He reports and gets his orders from a guy named Wayne Ellison. Do you know him? Have you ever heard of him?"

"No, I don't think so. Who is he?"

"We don't know much about him but he's higher up than Peter and he seems to call the shots for Peter."

"But what is the purpose of all this?"

"Okay, as we see it now, they want the mayor, Sergeant Brady and the governor gone. It's a mob activity and they want this entire part of the state to run their global affairs."

Audrey look worried. "How do they plan to do this?"

Sammi clued her in to how it had already started in getting her husband and the sarge at odds with each other and then they would both look bad. They wanted her husband to lose the next election as well as the governor.

Audrey, who had been leaning forward on the table intent on everything Sammi was telling her, suddenly pushed up and sat way back in her chair. She brushed a long dark strand of hair away from her face and simply stared at her. She was having trouble believing everything she was hearing.

"This sounds like something out of a bad movie. I'd suspected a few things, especially over the last six months, but nothing like this. What are we going to do? What can we possibly do here?"

"Actually, Audrey, we need you. You're the one who will keep your husband aware of things because we want Peter to think nothing has changed. Like you said, your dinner with your husband a while back threw him for a loop and we don't want anything else to concern him. Let him think your husband is following his orders and you, too, but with our side aware we will be infiltrating and undermining their purpose. Everything is not in place yet, but you and I are going to be the liaisons. It's the only way. We'll have to meet whenever we can and again; I don't want to call you."

"How can we keep doing this?"

"They're going to think that we've connected in a friendship and get together on a regular basis. I think we can get away with that for a while. I'm sure Peter and Josh won't like it, but if he thinks it's two women simply gabbing and being silly, well, we can get our information up to date."

Audrey took a deep breath. She was a strong woman, but this was getting scary for her. She felt her husband was so vulnerable. Sammi didn't want to tell her yet that she was quite vulnerable, too.

"But what if you need to get to me? There may be a time you need to tell me something."

"Don't worry about that. I'll find a way. But I do have one request."

Audrey looked at her and waited to hear.

"I need you to invite me to your home for dinner or tea or something. I need to be around Peter and Josh for a time. Can you manage that?"

"We could have you and Dave over for dinner?"

"No, I think that would send the wrong message. I would like them to think of it more as you and I getting together as friends. I don't think I even want your husband to join us, but I need to be around Peter and Josh. How can we do that?"

"Oh, Ron has this one big room where he works and of course, Peter is always there and Josh is usually close by. I could work it out with Ron to let us have one side of the room for our get together."

"That would be perfect, but do you think it would look suspicious?"

"Oh, no it's quite a huge room and I've had a few friends over in the past and Ron worked at his desk and I was entertaining on the other side of the room. It was fine."

"Great," she said excited. "I've got to get to Philly this weekend with my husband, but we'll be back by Tuesday night. Anytime after that let's have this meeting. It could give us valuable information."

Audrey looked over at her and smiled and then held the look for a moment or two causing her to feel uncomfortable.

Finally she said, "I know this will put you on the spot for a moment, and I don't mean to, but I know that you've helped out the police many times. And there always seems to be a confusion as to how you do it."

She didn't answer and kept as low a profile as she could.

"I want to say that for anyone else a meeting like this with my husband and Peter and Josh around would seem a strange request. But I know you have your reasons and I won't question them. But from what I've heard, it'll be a pleasure working with you."

Not to be outdone, she said, "And I've heard you're quite clever yourself, Audrey, and I'm sure I'll enjoy working with you."

As they were about to leave she grabbed Sammi's arm and said, "Be careful and thanks for all you're doing."

"And you take care of yourself and your

husband. When this is all over, I hope we can have that dinner."

CHAPTER THIRTEEN

Getting on the charter plane brought back memories of when Dave and Sammi lived in Philly for a time while working on some abduction cases. In fact that's why they were going back this weekend; they needed to review their testimony. They'd had good results, even though there were still some missing children that hadn't been found yet. But they had cracked a big kidnapping ring and although they knew these crimes never ceased, they had put a big kink in one of them for a long time to come.

But Philadelphia had another added charm for them. It was at that point in their relationship that they decided to get married and they'd worked as a valuable team ever since.

"I've gotten to appreciate these charter jets," said Sammi. "The first time I was somewhat nervous, but I didn't want to admit it to anyone. It seemed so small, but now I prefer them."

Dave agreed. "They're small, but quite powerful and perfectly safe. And you don't have all the busyness of a big airport and the noise of a lot of chattering passengers to contend with on the plane. It's more relaxing."

This particular charter had only four passengers, although it seated ten. She was used to it by now. Remembering a few times when she was the sole passenger made her feel special in a way.

"We'll check into the motel, get some sleep tonight and go directly to Ben's office in the FBI building first thing in the morning. He said he'd be there waiting for us."

"Okay, I'm not entirely sure what they want, are you? We haven't been asked to go to court to testify, at least not yet."

Dave said, "Ben led me to believe they want to go over our testimony one more time. It's been a long time since these guys were arrested, over a year now, and I think they want to refresh everything."

"Is Ben going to invite anyone else? Oh, wait, probably Jeff Slade, too. It'll be good to see him again."

Even though it was a short flight, she succumbed to the motion of the plane and Dave woke her up before they landed. She was surprised.

"It didn't take much to get me to sleep."

"You've had a busy day. I think we should grab a sandwich and take it back with us. I'm tired, too. We'll get to bed early."

"It'll be almost ten o'clock by the time we get there, and I'm beat."

And when the plane landed there was a car available, per Ben's arrangement. It took about twenty-five minutes to drive to the motel. They picked up food on the way and it was lights out by 11:30 P.M. But now Sammi was awake.

"Dave, Dave," she said quietly, but he answered.

"What?"

"I wondered if you were asleep yet."

He laughed, "Not now."

"I'm sorry."

"That's okay. I think you're too wired to relax, right?"

"It was quite a session I had with Audrey. But she's sharp, Dave. She'll be good to work with."

"We're lucky that worked out so well. And now she's got Ron watching his back, too. At least he's aware and he'll notice a lot of things."

She told him about having Audrey set up a dinner or some type of meeting at the mayor's house for her. Dave was a little concerned.

"Do you think that's a good idea?"

"Well, yeah, I do. Then I can listen in on Peter and Josh. As long as they're in the same room, I'll catch what they're thinking. And my presence alone should trigger some wandering thoughts with them. That's what we need to know."

Dave took a deep breath. She knew he worried about her.

"But remember, Audrey and I plan to play silly women again. That got us by Josh last time and I'm sure it'll do the same with Peter. These guys don't give us women that much credit. And right now, that's good."

"But Audrey doesn't know what you can do. How are you going to manage that?"

"Dave, that woman is shrewd. She told me that she's heard I've obtained amazing results at times, but most people don't know how I do it. She looked me in the eye and smiled and didn't push me in any way for information. In fact, her thoughts told me that she assumed I wanted to keep my methods secret. So all she said was that it would be a pleasure working with me."

"You're certainly getting a reputation."

"But I plan to bring in one of my lined pads and write down notes in my special shorthand. They'll think we're planning something and that way I won't miss anything. I'm hoping I have a lot to tell you when I'm done."

"When are you going to meet with her?"

"Don't know. She knows we get back on Tuesday night so whenever she calls after that."

"I'll be anxious to hear what you can learn from them."

"Me, too."

There was silence for several minutes. Dave was sure that Sammi had finally relaxed and fallen asleep. *Now,* he thought, *I can fall asleep, too.* But then he heard.

"What did you arrange with Marlina?"

He yawned loudly and slowly and was barely audible as he answered, "we're going to have dinner with her on Sunday night. Ben wanted to get the preliminary work done on Saturday at his office." Another set of yawns ensued before he continued. "Then on Monday we can meet with his lawyers and go over stuff and hopefully be done by Monday night."

"Right. He'd told me it shouldn't take more than a day to go over everything with them and make sure that all the details are right."

Sammi yawned herself. Dave leaned over and gave her a kiss on the cheek. "Can you relax now and get some sleep?"

"Yep, I can. Thanks, sweetie. Good night."

* * *

Ben Collier thought it was good to see everyone again. He had set up a conference room approach with coffee pots and sweet rolls available; this would keep interruptions to a minimum. Jeff Slade came in about a half hour later.

"This is like old times," said Ben. "All three of you are my favorite people to work with."

And Jeff was happy to see the two of them. "I've missed working with the two of you. Results seem to start happening whenever Sammi's around."

"Everything's in the timing," she said. "But we did get some good results, didn't we?"

Jeff said, "And we're not finished searching for the missing children yet. We've got almost a seventy percent success rate right now, but it'll get higher before we're done. That's amazing in itself."

Ben added, "But it had a lot to do with those missing files that you found, Sammi. That's what made the difference."

"We all worked together. To me, that's what made the difference."

Everyone had to agree on that.

"And Dave, I hear there's a lot of happenings going on in Scranton right now. Sounds like a tough situation developing there."

"We certainly have our work cut out for us. And we have several units working on this. Quite confusing right now."

Jeff said, "I almost got assigned there myself, but then someone else came along that the uppers found more suitable. Sure sounds like a perplexing web."

Ben said, "It's that and a lot more. We've got a lot of holes to plug up and we need to do it soon."

He poured coffee for everyone and they relaxed for a few minutes.

"What are you working on?" Sammi asked.

"I'm still on the abduction cases and I'm almost exclusively working with these lawyers right now to make sure they understand what we did, minute by minute. It can get quite tedious going over the same stuff again and again."

Dave nodded, "I can imagine."

"And you, Sammi. I'm sure they've got you working on the Scranton dilemma. But you still work at the bank?"

"Yes, that's my main job; always has been. But I try to keep aware of what's going on. Honestly, Jeff, this is a confusing case in a lot of areas."

"Well," Jeff said, "They're lucky to have you and I know you'll make a difference."

"I hope so, in time. It takes time."

Ben smiled. More than anything else he appreciated Sammi's unpretentious attitude. She did have a special talent, which he had never figured out, but was happy enough with the results she could obtain. And she had her two feet planted firmly on the ground. There was no reason for anything but plain, simple, straight talk with her. She understood as much as any of the agents or policemen and usually picked up more information than they did anyway.

"Okay, let's dig in and get these preliminaries out of the way."

And so they covered the tremendous amount of details that referenced the abduction cases and also some robberies that were connected to Scranton. They broke for lunch at two o'clock, had it sent in for convenience, got back to work by three and finished around seven. It was a long day, but a fruitful one. Ben was pleased with everything and felt on Monday, the meeting with the lawyers wouldn't suffer any surprises.

It had been a complicated case; it usually was when children were involved. They'd been grabbed off the street and sold. At the time Sammi was brought into the situation, everything had been irritatingly stalled with no new leads surfacing for a considerable length of time. But when they all worked together results began to emerge.

"Are you going to want us to appear in court?" she asked.

"I'm not sure right now. After Monday, we'll have your official depositions recorded and the lawyers seem to think that's all we'll need. Honestly, we've got so much evidence against these two that they've been screaming for a deal for months now, but the details can't seem to be worked out."

"What do they want?" asked Dave.

"Well, Sergei wants a lot less jail time for his information, but he's willing to give them stuff on his international ties, which is quite important. I personally still hope that we can make a deal."

"How much chance for a deal is there now that the trial is starting?"

"A lot. That's usually when reality sets in and they accept whatever they can get."

"How much jail time is Sergei looking at?"

"It always depend on a lot of things. But we have him involved in a lot of kidnappings, not just one, so he'll serve some time for each abduction. That could add up to a lot of years."

Then Sammi had to ask about Donnie. He was a young man of about twenty-one, caught up in a mess. He'd never had a good life, grew up in foster homes and Sammi had taken his case seriously. She felt for him and the fact that he'd never had a real chance in life.

"Well, they're being tried separately. But he'll definitely go to jail. It should be a lot less time though; he certainly wasn't the main character. I'm not sure what will happen because these courts can be strange."

"I was sort of curious," she said.

Dave threw in, "Yes, Sammi always thought his was a sad story and with some help he could have made it."

She had one more question. "And, of course, I need to ask about Lena. What's the news on her?"

Another child with a background that didn't leave any room for self-esteem or good thoughts about life. But she had played a minor role and since she was only sixteen she had a chance after juvenile detention, to make a clean start.

Ben began, "Well, the last time you saw her was over six months' ago, right?"

She nodded.

"Yes, well, she's gotten some psychiatric help from that Dr. Regan that you recommended. Apparently, he's real good with kids like her. And she's made some important improvements, I'm told. But she'll definitely remain in custody until she's twenty-one. After that it'll depend on the psychiatrist's assessment and the court and I guess other things. But she should get a new lease on life in time. How she uses it, well, ... but her adoptive parents are still in the picture, so that should help."

Sammi nodded. She was happy.

"I always felt they both deserved a second chance," said Sammi.

Even Ben agreed with that. "Yeah, they both had sad stories. But let's wait and see. It'll be interesting to see how this all plays out."

* * *

Ben joined Sammi and Dave for dinner that night.

"I'm glad we've got a chance to talk about what's going on in Scranton," said Dave. "This is getting more complicated by the day."

"Yes, well, they want that area real bad. It would make all of their lives simpler and if they could get control of the mayor, the sarge and the governor; their game would be complete."

"But the sarge would never succumb," said Dave. "They'd have to prove him incompetent to get him out of there."

"They've started that already. I heard that you found out Peter Armors' real name. Well, whoever he is, we've found out that he was involved with some unsavory characters, namely Spike Evers and Brian Hatterly."

Dave sat back in his chair. "How did that get

into your hands?"

"Because I've got an agent in the area poking around. We haven't told anyone, not the sarge nor anyone else. He's undercover; that's the way he works best. Anyway, there's a connection between those two guys and Peter."

"Why?" asked Sammi. "How are they connected at all?"

"Honestly, I'm not entirely sure how, but why is because they want to make Sergeant Brady look as bad as possible. But luckily you foiled that plan. I understand that this latest kidnapping was supposed to be an unsolved case."

"No kidding," said Dave. "That type of publicity looks bad if it gets in the papers."

"Right, but if it had, that plus the killing of that ex-cop, which is still unsolved, could be the start of a campaign to make him look like he's not up to the job. Now since that didn't work, I'm a little concerned that something else will happen to make the sarge look like he can't keep things in his city under control. And it will keep escalating until the end."

"Wow," said Dave. "In all my imaginations of what that kidnapping was all about, I never thought of that."

Sammi added, "But it does follow a pattern of ruining positions from the inside out. They're still following the same theme. I wonder what they've got in mind for the mayor."

"That's a hot one, but I don't know yet. They're keeping that one quiet and it has us worried. Somebody at your end should hear something soon, possibly even my agent."

"We're all keeping our eyes and ears open."

"It's a tough one, Sammi. That's all any of us can do right now."

"In the meantime," Dave had a question. "Have you located Fritz Connelly?"

"We've got him under surveillance. He's in some small town in Colorado and he's keeping a low profile right now. But I've been working with Julie and all of a sudden his computer system is one hot item; it had been quiet for months. Now it's starting to produce some serious movement. Julie was joking a few weeks back that she was starting to get bored. And we don't want that."

Sammi laughed. She, more than anyone else knew how Julie hated to get bored. She was extremely bright and needed to be pushed constantly to expand her capacity.

"What's Fritz's doing?"

"He talks in riddles, Dave, he always has. That's what makes him so difficult to understand. But Julie has his pattern down pretty good and that wasn't an easy thing to do."

Sammi sat back contentedly in her chair. She knew that she had a satisfied look on her face. Having someone appreciate Julie made her proud.

"We're lucky we've got someone like her. Boy, that gal is smart. I have to say that both Julie and Sammi here absolutely amaze me at times. You gals make these hard jobs a lot easier."

She absorbed the compliments and Dave looked over with pride.

"We'd be hard pressed without them."

"Okay, thanks you guys, but we're a team, remember?"

"I'm only saying," continued Ben, "that before the two of you came along, operations didn't run so smoothly. Now, I know, I know," he said waving his hands, "every ending isn't perfect, but our success rate has improved quite a bit since you both came on board."

That was about all the compliments she could handle at one time. She turned the subject back to Fritz Connelly. "But what's Fritz doing right now?"

"From what we can figure out, he's the one coordinating everything. He deals personally at one time or another with everyone on our short list, Peter Armors, Josh Logan, Wayne Ellison, that senator and even with those two kidnappers, but I must admit that he did that through other people. He's also reporting to some in the international spectrum. We've got names, but they seem to come in mainly if and when Fritz gets his game accomplished."

"Wow," said Dave. "So this is international again."

"If Fritz is involved, we can guarantee that it's got international hands in the mix. Most of the cargo that gets shipped out of Philadelphia goes to other countries. They have a big stake in them winning."

Dave simply shook his head. Sometimes the extent and complexities of criminal life amazed him. He figured he'd never get blasé about some of the surprises that life kept throwing at him. And he thought about Senator Kaphle; he was from Nepal, originally as a kid. He might be part of the international flavor of the movement.

* * *

On Sunday evening, Dave and Sammi arrived at the restaurant first. They'd picked a table in an obscure corner so they could talk to Marlina quietly and without interruption. Even though it had been a few months since Terry's death, it was still dramatic for all of them.

He always got serious when talk turned to his young friend. "I still feel numb when I think of him. I so wish I'd known him better."

"I guess that's why we learn as we grow older to appreciate everyone as much as we can, cause you never know."

"You're right. Cause sometimes by the time we understand the value of a person, they're gone."

Sammi nodded. "I felt that way about my grandpa. And I did appreciate him while he was living, but he was the only other person in my life that I ever knew of that could also hear other people's thoughts. But I was only fourteen when he died. I can't help but wonder how much more I would have appreciated him if I had been considerably more mature before he passed. I had so much more to learn from him."

"Yeah," said Dave, "especially since the two of you shared this special gift. But I felt the same way about my father. I was an adult when he died and we were able to share police experiences, but looking back, I wish he had been here to see the work I do now and I know he would have loved you. He would have been amazed at our performance as a team."

She knew how much he loved and missed his dad. We all had someone special in our lives that we missed, she thought, but thinking about them kept them alive and active in our life. That's how thoughts worked.

* * *

About this time the waitress brought their wine and they waited for Marlina to appear. And she was right on time. Sammi noticed a very attractive young girl of obvious Mexican ancestry approach their table. With Dave's description, there could be no doubt.

He got up and she gave him a warm yet shy hug. And he introduced her to Sammi.

"Yes, I've heard about you. I think I caught Dave off guard when I told him that I knew a lot about him, but that's because Terry always talked about him, almost everyday. Terry felt very close to you, Dave. He had mentioned you also, Sammi, and thought you two were perfect for each other."

Dave's expression showed strong emotion rising and he quickly said, "Well, we thought the world of him, too."

Marlina answered, "I know you did and Terry knew it, too."

Then the waitress came around again and she ordered a glass of wine. Dave thought that Marlina looked steady, much more so than the day she first entered the police station to talk to him. Tonight she seemed poised, relaxed and in control. It had only been a few months since Terry's death, yet she seemed to be accepting her fate with maturity. Looking from Sammi to Marlina, he felt comfortable and welcomed what she could tell him about Terry.

"What type of work do you do?" asked Sammi.

"I work for an insurance company; I'm an underwriter. It's been a secure job for me; I've been there for three years now. Actually Terry had known someone in the company who helped me get the job. It's worked out rather well."

"How do you like Philadelphia?" Dave asked.

"It's a great city. Lots of history and lots of important things to see. I still like to visit some of the museums and buildings on weekends when I get a chance."

Dave got the feeling that she was moving on nicely with her life. She was treading slowly into a new life without Terry, but she seemed secure. That relaxed him somewhat. Terry had asked him to watch out for her.

"Where are you living?"

"I've a rather nice apartment on the south side. I moved into it about six months ago and it's a much nicer area than where I used to live. I'm pleased with it."

Dave noticed that Sammi had gotten quiet. And she seemed rather thoughtful. He knew she'd worked hard this past week and felt she must be somewhat tired.

Marlina asked, "Do you still work with Tom and Jim? Terry used to talk about the three of you and said you always stuck together. He said that was important in police work."

"Yes, we're still together and Terry could have fit nicely in our group, too. But his agenda was a little different. Yet he was so valuable to us."

Dave thought Marlina seemed slightly withdrawn at times. Possibly she was a little more timid than he thought. In the beginning of their conversation at the police station, she seemed nervous yet reserved, but at that time she had a difficult task to perform. Later, she seemed to relax. However, tonight she did seem tense to him, but he felt they were bringing back a lot of memories. He would always do that to her.

"Have you made any good friends here, I mean people you can trust. Terry wanted me to look out for you," he said.

Marlina smiled. "That's just like Terry, isn't it? But I do have some friends I can trust and a few of the guys at work watch out for me. But, if I ever need you, I'll let you know."

"Anytime, you know that."

Marlina nodded.

Dave was overcome with sadness at times. It prompted Marlina to bring up another touchy subject.

"Terry always liked to take chances. He did it all his life. He had a few close calls when he worked in New York and he always volunteered for the tough assignments. That's just who he was."

"Yeah, I know. But it still hurts. And it really hurts to have never had a chance to personally acknowledge him face to face for who he really was."

"I understand, but he knew that when he took those double agent assignments. He used to say that it was just a part of everything."

And with that they all got silent and rehashed

their own personal memories of Terry.

* * *

Then the waitress came around again. They ordered their dinners and relaxed in the enjoyable atmosphere of a quaint, yet contemporary café. And they talked more and more about the old days with Terry. Dave got more insight into his childhood, which Marlina shared from their orphanage days.

"He knew how to get people to trust him. And everyone liked him, the caregivers, the adults who ran the home and even visitors. He knew how to talk to them and get the positive results he wanted. He was always one of the favorites."

Dave nodded. "He could weave in and out of any group around. He was worth a lot to us."

Marlina seemed pleased with that comment. "He could impress anyone that came to the orphanage. He got his cousin Amilio out of trouble on more than one occasion. He had a way about him that people couldn't resist. Everyone that was an enemy to most of the orphans became a friend to Terry. That was the real gift he had."

And on and on the evening progressed with Terry as the main topic of conversation. Dave noticed that Sammi had been listening most of the time and realized that he and Marlina had truly controlled most of the talk. But they had a pleasant evening. And they ended talking about keeping in touch and Dave promised he would make her aware of any new developments in Terry's case.

And Sammi liked her a lot. She was a sweet person who was also caught up in the intrigue of a serious situation. As everyone got ready to leave, she realized a closeness had evolved around Terry; that wasn't a surprise. It's what Terry had been able to do most of his life.

* * *

Sammi was quiet as they rode home. Dave looked over at her a few times and apparently decided to leave her alone in her thoughts. *He most likely thinks I'm being emotional,* she thought, *and I am. But I have my own reasons.*

After about ten minutes, Dave couldn't take it anymore and asked, "Are you alright? You're so quiet."

"I'm fine, just a little tired. But it was a nice evening, wasn't it? I enjoyed meeting Marlina."

That comment helped Dave to relax some. "She seems to be handling the situation quite well. I mean, it's been more than a few months now, and she's so alone in the world. That's what Terry was so concerned about. And he asked me to watch out for her. I have to do that."

"Of course you do. It's a little more difficult because she lives in Philadelphia, but she said if she ever needed anything that she'd call you. And I think she will. But right now, she seems to be doing quite well."

"And that's good to see. But you were so quiet tonight. Is everything okay or did you hear something I should know about?"

Now Sammi knew that he had her. She should

have known that she couldn't fool him; he knew her too well. But she didn't want to tell him right now. Later would be better, if there was any good time to tell him.

"Well, I did pick up something quite interesting, but I'd rather wait until we get home to tell you."

"Home in Scranton?" He seemed surprised.

"No, no. When we get back to the motel. As soon as we close the door, I'll tell you."

Dave looked intrigued and she was glad he had accepted her answer so easily. But then she wasn't delaying or hiding anything from him. She was waiting until they got home and relaxed and could get his undivided attention.

"What time do we have to meet with Ben and the lawyers tomorrow?"

"Didn't he say he'd call us first thing in the morning? But I got the impression it wouldn't be until ten o'clock, which is good. I need more than six hours sleep tonight."

Sammi began yawning at the thought. She was tired as well and looking forward to crashing when they got home.

"It seems funny to be driving around Philadelphia again. We spent so much time here that it seemed like home for quite a while. And of course, this is where we got married," he said as he reached for her hand.

"Yes, they were good times despite the burdensome work we were doing. It helped working as a team and knowing we could do that in the future.

Dave nodded and said, "Well, here we are.

Home Sweet Home, at least for now."

* * *

When they entered their room and Dave closed the door, he said immediately, "Alright, we're home and the door's closed. What did you hear?"

She had to smile as she led him over to the two chairs provided in the small sitting area. Sammi began. "Now Dave, you're aware that I never believe any thoughts that I don't hear more than one time and in more than one way. And I check colors and other things before I believe them."

Dave nodded, but his face showed an expectation that was getting increasingly suspicious.

"Okay, I can tell you what I heard ... but I can't always confirm that it's one hundred percent true in reality, but it is true in the mind of the person thinking the thoughts."

"Yeah, Sammi," he said, "I understand all that. You've explained it to me before. What's bothering you so much?"

Dave was getting anxious and she couldn't figure out how to tell him her discovery in any delicate way. She couldn't imagine what his reaction would be. He looked at life from a different perspective than she did at times.

"I can't find an easy way to tell you this."

"Sammi, tell me, okay? Enough already, just tell me."

"Okay, this is what I heard many times tonight and in many ways." She paused a moment and then threw out her shocking discovery. "Terry Gonzalez is not dead. Terry is very much alive."

CHAPTER FOURTEEN

Dave amazingly jumped to a standing position. It was like his body did an involuntary leap from his chair. And he unwillingly stood there looking down at Sammi unable to say anything. His arms went limp and they hung down at his side as if they had no previous experience of movement. He couldn't focus and his face showed unmistakable strain while trying to connect his thinking with his hearing. His eyes, although staring at his wife, were many miles away and not even fixated. The onslaught of the shock to his mind had put him in a temporary trance and didn't let go until Sammi's voice got louder and louder.

"Dave, DAve, DAVE," she said. Finally she got up and put her arms around him. He slowly and almost mechanically put his right arm around her small waist and then his left arm followed suit. It took a few moments before the warmth of her body got through to him and he gradually came back to consciousness and held her for real. He took a couple of deep breaths and shook his head as if trying to throw away any disbelief that had entered his body. His shock had been quite intense.

"Are you okay? Dave, talk to me," she said feeling increasing concern.

"I guess ... I'm okay," he answered gently. It

was almost another minute before he could ask coherently, "Did I hear you correctly? You think that Terry is still alive?"

"That's what Marlina's thoughts were saying to me."

She started to pull away, but Dave coaxed her back. "No, I need to hold you," he said and enclosed her in his arms with a newfound emotion; "I'm so numb right now. I can't believe this. And you, you were able to keep your expression straight in the restaurant." Then Dave let go deliberately and they both sat down again.

"How did you do it? I knew you'd heard something. That much I knew, but I can hardly believe my own reaction right now." Dave took another deep breath. It was still shaky coming out. "It hit me so hard that I felt something had assaulted my mental logic. It really threw me. But you handled everything calmly and kept on talking sensibly. How?"

"Remember, I never take thoughts for reality on the first pass by. I have to hear them a few times and I check colors and other stuff. So I was not only busy being logical, but also assessing the situation. That gave me time to realize what she was thinking, and by then I could accept it."

"Wow, you think it's true? Or, maybe Marlina wants it to be true."

"That's always possible. And I see now that you do understand that thoughts can be tricky. But I think this is for real. Let me tell you why."

She certainly had his complete attention. He wasn't even blinking.

"First of all, do you remember when you told

me how nervous she was when she brought you that folder from Terry? From her thoughts tonight, at that time she believed he was dead. It was a little over two weeks ago that she got the shock of her life and found out he was alive. And a few times tonight, once when she put her head down for a minute and a few other times she was thinking, *I've got to act more despondent and unhappy. I don't want them to catch on.* She had trouble keeping her emotions sad and gloomy. She's quite worried about Terry 'cause he's in an extremely dangerous position, but she's thrilled that the love of her life is still around."

"What the hell's going on? I'm obviously tickled he's still alive, but what the hell's going on here?"

"Okay, I caught a few other things. I don't think Marlina knows all that much about what Terry's doing. But I do know that Ben Collier is working with him. Now, don't quote me on this next one, because it's a feeling, but I think Terry is the undercover agent that Ben's got working Scranton right now."

"Holy Shit," he said, but he had a strange look on his face. "Why are we being kept in the dark here? Why didn't they tell us?"

"I'm sure they had their reasons."

He was quiet. She knew he understood. But he looked like someone had kicked him in the gut and the pain was hanging on. He made a decision.

"I want to have a meeting with Ben before we leave. I can't stand being in the dark like this. I don't think it's right. I mean we know anyway. He should talk to us."

"Now Dave, be logical. Ben wouldn't run around telling anyone, not even you, unless there was a reason. Isn't that right?"

He hated to agree. "But we had such a close connection."

"I know, I know. And after it's all over I'm sure the referees and the sarge would be the first ones to be told. But you must respect Ben right now. He's a good guy."

"He is. But we're going to confront him tomorrow. Let's do it after our meeting with the lawyers, but before we leave. Damn, damn," he said as he ran his hands through his hair. "This is almost too much to handle. He's out there taking chances again."

Dave had a few tears escape from the protection of his eyelids. He loved Terry and it was a lot to accept that he wasn't gone, he wondered why had they kept it a secret, especially from him? And Sammi knew that the referees were planning a heroes' funeral for him once they realized he wasn't a rogue cop. Dave must be thrilled and so confused.

"I guess you won't get those eight hours sleep that you wanted," she said.

He laughed. "I don't think I'll sleep at all. I'm so God damned thrilled he made it through whatever, but I need to know what's going on. And who the hell was that guy they pulled out of the water? I don't think I'll relax until we talk to Ben tomorrow. And it'll be hard enough getting through the day as it is."

"How about we order a couple of glasses of wine? Would that help?"

"It might. But talking to Ben tomorrow, and understanding what this charade is all about is the one thing that will ease my mind."

Sammi came over and stood behind his chair and began to give him a neck and shoulder message. He had to admit that did help a lot. They forgot about ordering the wine.

* * *

"Sammi, Sammi, are you asleep? he asked.

She smiled and said, "Not now."

He had to laugh. This was a repeat of what they did to each other at different times.

"You can't sleep, right?"

"Well, I almost get asleep and then I think of some funny thing that Terry did or said. God, I'm so thrilled he's still alive."

"Remember, you might not be able to get to him ... if he's undercover. How does that work?"

Immediately Sammi was almost sorry she had asked. She felt Dave would go through a long explanation of how undercover cops worked. But he didn't.

"Too much to explain tonight and they're all different anyway," he said and then gave out a big yawn.

He started to say something and didn't finish. Sammi waited a bit and looked over only to realize he had fallen asleep. She was so glad for him. A good night's sleep would help him accept everything. She turned over, but wasn't comfortable and then turned over again. Finding a comfortable position was impossible; she was completely awake now. She could have been irritated, but realized the humor in the situation. She looked over at Dave. She was happy to see him content in dreamland somewhere. So she thought about her grandpa and how the different worlds affected each other. It was an amazing universe, but her biggest concern was always the thought world right here on earth. Working with that was a full time job for her.

* * *

Luckily, they beat the lawyers' arrival at the FBI center by fifteen minutes. It was enough time to let Ben know that they needed to have another private meeting with him before they left. He seemed somewhat surprised, but had to let it go as Jeff Slade entered with one lawyer and three others followed within a few minutes. Ben did have a strange look on his face, but he had to bury his concern and let the present situation gain his complete attention. And with one final questioning glance, he addressed the lawyers and put his uneasy thoughts on the back burner.

Most of their testimony was straightforward and details were addressed over and over again with particular precision. They didn't want any loopholes and most important, they didn't want any surprises. All the warrants had been issued and presented to the workers at the warehouse prior to confiscating all of the files that were taken.

"But how did you realize there were hidden files?" asked one lawyer.

"Sammi had told us ahead of time," answered Ben.

"Okay, but how did you know about them?" he asked, turning to her.

She shifted in her chair. Noticing that Ben was about to answer she took over. She could give him a satisfactory answer. "There were three small boxes of files that were obvious and we felt there had to be more. Those three small boxes couldn't contain all of the information. And when we questioned the suspects outside asking if there were any more files, well, their faces told us they had more. When I asked a point blank question, "Where were the other files?" one of them said, "We'd never tell you, lady."

The lawyer smirked and relaxed.

"So we went back in and began searching and discovered a secret panel. That's where we found several rows of boxes and files."

That seemed to satisfy them and it was surprising to both Sammi and Dave that getting their mind back on the abduction cases did lift their concentration away from Terry.

"Okay, and we had the warrants and they were shown to the suspects, right?"

"Oh yeah," Ben said. "They were visible at all times. In fact the main worker took it from my hand and read it. He seemed to be fairly thorough and somewhat familiar with legal stuff."

"Which one was that?"

Ben pointed out his picture. The lawyer nodded, made a few notes and moved on. And so went most of the day. A break was taken when lunch was brought in, but otherwise it was questions and answers all day long. And mainly they were dealing with details. Sometimes it was the smallest seemingly insignificant point, but the lawyers treated those with utmost care.

One explained. "It can be the least and tiniest aspect that the defense can jump on and get everything going in another direction. That's why we can be tedious and I know," he laughed, "boring as hell about all these little details."

They all relaxed, understanding that they would continue until they felt satisfied that they knew everything was under control.

"Will you be asking us to testify in person?" Sammi asked.

"At this point, we don't think so. We have a lot on these guys and they want a deal so it looks like this one is sort of locked up. But you never know, so we have to be prepared. I've been told you'll be available if needed?" He stared questioningly at both of them as he asked.

They both nodded. "Yes, of course we will."

The positive comment was acknowledged and they continued through the piles of pages that were ultimately dwindling.

It was around 5:30 P.M. when the lead lawyer called it a day. He thanked them all for their patience and cooperation and ended the session.

* * *

After the lawyers left and Jeff Slade said his final goodbyes, Ben invited Sammi and Dave back into his office. They all settled down with coffee and Dave didn't wait, or mince words but got directly to the point.

"We have reason to believe that Terry Gonzalez is still alive and that you're aware of it."

Ben sat way back in his chair and stared at both of them. "I should have known if Sammi was involved in some way, you'd figure it out."

"Then you're admitting he's alive."

Dave was quite anxious; that was obvious. But he was treating the situation like an FBI secret venture, which it was. So he waited to see what Ben would offer out to them.

"Okay, at this point, there's no reason to lie about it. Terry is alive and well. But I need to know, how you found out."

Dave said, "That almost goes under the heading of how Sammi finds out things, so we can't tell you directly. But we did have dinner with Marlina last night."

Ben seemed slightly surprised, so Dave reminded him of a few facts.

"You knew she came to see me after Terry was declared dead and brought me a folder from him."

Ben nodded in remembrance. "That's right. I almost forgot about that. He wanted someone to know what he'd found out and needed to pass it on to you if something happened. But Marlina didn't tell you, did she?"

"My God, no," said Dave. "She put on a good act, and still wanted to be kept informed regarding his death."

"Okay," Ben said, rubbing his chin and pausing for a moment. "And I'm not going to ask Sammi how she knew, so you can relax. Let me tell you what happened as far as I know. I'm beginning to think that there are even more details than I know. These secret activities can be so tricky."

They sat with forced patience and waited for Ben to continue. He took a moment to give everyone a refill of coffee and then with a thoughtful countenance slowly began to unravel an intriguing mystery.

"I've talked to Sam Brady a few times ... he doesn't know Terry's alive, but he did tell me about the folder Terry left for you. You must have been surprised to hear that he was a double agent. I've only met him about five times myself, but he's unbelievably good. It's my superiors who know all the agents thoroughly and they made the decisions about him. He was onto something big, concerning Scranton. He found out about that Peter Armors, didn't know his name was a phony, but had picked up what he was about. Apparently Peter was the one who put out a contract on him. He felt he was dangerous to their cause and wanted him gone, permanently."

Sammi was in shock. Dave was more familiar with contracts and such, but was still in disbelief.

"So Terry had found out about the plans to get rid of the mayor, governor and the sarge, right?"

"I'm not sure if he knew about all three, but he knew about the overall plan to control that part of the state. And he had heard that they were going to get rid of the mayor in such a way as to make the Sergeant Brady look bad enough to lose his job. But it was when he found out about Peter's involvement that they wanted him gone."

"What do you know about Peter?" asked Dave.

"Not much, he's part of the mob ... well, they all are. And they want their control to be in place before much longer. So they were taking drastic measures."

"But how did you work it out about Terry?"

"Okay, I wasn't in on all of it, but Terry had to disappear or he would have been killed. We've had him in total protective gear anytime he moved out anywhere. We knew there would be an attempt and we knew pretty much when and how. It was sloppy when you think about it. It was a drive by shooting, but of course, they have their expert marksmen. Anyway, when it happened, he went down fast. But we had our own people around him quickly; they simply realized that the police arrived on the scene immediately, so they had to get out of there fast and had no time to check and make sure he was really dead."

Dave puckered his lips. "So it was sort of planned from both sides."

"Oh yeah, and they had already tried to get to him a few days before, but the attempt was foiled because of too many pedestrians in the area. Anyway, we got the police around the body fast so they had to leave. They covered him up and one of their men, the only left behind, confirmed that they pulled the sheet over his head and took him away."

"So everyone thought he was dead, right?" Sammi asked.

"That's right and since we were ready for them, we had another body ready to take his place."

She looked surprised.

"Philadelphia's a big city. There are homicides every night like Los Angles and Detroit."

"But they weren't positive that Terry was dead, were they?" Sammi seemed confused.

"He'd been shot through the head, supposedly. They wouldn't be able to recognize him except for his clothes. So we put his clothes on another body. You see, we knew there would be an attempt to steal his body from the morgue to confirm positive I.D. These mob guys don't play guessing games and they needed to be sure. We made it easy for them to steal the body, but we had his identification and similar marks on the body as well as his trademark vest that he always liked to wear and they bought it. And we've had Terry stashed away for a while now."

"So when they stole the body and confirmed it was Terry, they had to get rid of the body again."

"Yep," said Ben. "I've no idea why they put his body in the water near the Philly docks, but we couldn't have asked for a better scenario. He was found promptly, identified as an ex-policeman and it was all over the papers. Now the mob had no doubts at all. But we've had a feeling that's what they wanted, too. It was like a double authentication for them. "

Dave had to get up and stretch for a minute. It also relieved a little of the pressure he was feeling. Ben stood up, too and smiled. These were tense moments for all of them.

"But why is he ..." Dave had started to ask a question but was interrupted.

"Good God, I forgot to ask you people something on Saturday; I can't forget to ask you now.

It's about those problems in Scranton, and we've got some characters we're trying to identify that's part of this whole group. We need to find them fast." Ben turned to his file cabinet and brought out six pictures of some guys they were desperately trying to locate. "Have either one of you seen any of these guys?"

Dave and Sammi stared at the pictures. Then Sammi looked up at Ben as Dave was still studying the photos. She gave him an understanding look.

Dave said, "Sorry, Ben, but give me a copy of these photos and we'll keep an eye out for them when we get home, but I don't know any of them. Who are they? What do you think they're doing?"

Ben, who by now was aware of Sammi's shrewd abilities looked at her and said, "Do you want to tell him?"

She smiled. "Dave, one of these guys is Terry, right, Ben?"

"Actually two of the pictures are of Terry."

Dave was shocked and looked at the pictures again. He still couldn't be sure and Ben had to point them out.

"No shit," said Dave. "That's Terry and that's Terry, too? He's so amazing. Even knowing, it's difficult to recognize him."

"I know," said Ben. "So when my superiors wanted to send him back to Scranton, at first it worried me. But they brought this guy, whom I'd met several times before, into a meeting with us and I never knew. After the meeting concluded, and it was at least a thirty minute meeting, they came back in and told me. I was totally shocked."

Dave laughed. It was the first time he'd been relaxed about Terry in a long time. His sense of humor was coming back.

"He now talks in a thick Spanish accent, goes by the name of Amilio and I don't think anyone would doubt that he wasn't recently snuck into this country from Mexico."

They both knew why he had picked the name Amilio. Even Sammi was amused as well as pleased. Dave had to chime in with, "I knew he was good ..."

"He's terrific," Ben said. "He's definitely one of a kind. He even fooled his girlfriend for almost ten minutes before he told her."

That had to bring a smirk from both of them.

"So he's in Scranton now. What's he doing?"

"I don't even know, not for sure. I'm not his contact, but I get information about him. He's presently quite worried about the mayor and his wife. I'm able to get information to him and I'll let him know that the both of you are aware. That might be important at some future time. But you have to keep all this a secret, right now. I'm not even telling your sarge. Not yet. That's got to be Terry's call."

"Understood," said Dave, still shaking his head.

"I would have never told you at this time, but I felt I had no choice. This is ongoing until further notice and we don't want anyone thinking he's still alive."

Leaving Ben's office, they realized the many ways that their lives intertwined. He shared her secret talent and she was aware of his police

business. She never could have foreseen how her life would be, and she wondered what her grandpa would be thinking about her talent right now.

* * *

On the plane, Sammi fell asleep almost immediately. It did give Dave some time to think about his life and career and how mixed up everything could get. They still didn't know the entire plan for the takeover of Scranton and Harrisburg and that was worrisome. They needed to find out and fast. Then they could have everyone in place waiting for them to make their first move. But what was their first move?

Julie had been intercepting memos regularly, but nothing was ever specific. They could be talking in codes that no one was aware of. Well, with Terry doing his thing, you could be sure that he'd be finding out something. He always could. But he had to be careful. He was walking such a thin line and had to be thinking out of both sides of the situation at all times. Tough job, but if anyone was up to it, he was.

Dave remembered back to a time when they were working a job together. They sat waiting in their scout car; they were on stakeout. And it was at times like these that they mused about their lives.

"Dave, are you ever going to get married again?"

He was caught off guard, but still had to laugh. "That's the most important thing on your mind right now? We're in a fairly dangerous sit-

uation here; we could get shot or killed if this doesn't go down right, and you want to know if I'll ever get married again?"

"I was wondering what your attitude was about marriage? It's always sad when one doesn't work out, and then Kelly's accident made it even tougher. So I was wondering how you're holding up inside?"

"Haven't given it much thought. I still liked Kelly, but the marriage didn't work out."

"And you've been quite busy with a string of rather nice looking ladies, I might add."

Dave had to stir in his seat. "I'm playing the field right now, Terry. I don't know what I want, but I hate to be bored."

"Me, too."

"What about you?" asked Dave. "Do we have a marriage in the future for you?"

"Not right now, at least not for a while. But I think I'd like to get married and raise some little ones. Can you imagine a little Terry out there some day?"

They both laughed at that. And some of their conversations were honest as well as revealing.

Terry finished with, "I think some lady's going to be pretty lucky to get someone like you."

Dave looked over and smirked. "Are you trying to win points here? I already put in your evaluation last week, so you're too late."

"I'm serious. I think you're a great guy. But then you have to be, you're my big brother right?"

And then their suspects moved and the talk was over for a while. It was funny how all of these old conversations kept popping up in his mind.

And someday, he thought, they'd get to talk some more.

* * *

When they arrived home, Sammi had received another letter addressed to Ms. Sammi Evans. It was derogatory about her and was another reminder that she didn't have much more time to enjoy Dave. She was told her marriage days were numbered.

Although it was distressing, they decided to get it on record more as a proven point that Linda in some way was still involved. That night Dave seemed to accept the fact that this irritation would always be with them.

"I guess I don't understand the purpose of these letters. That's what gets me the most."

Sammi agreed. "It doesn't make much sense. I have a feeling that they're not even coming from her."

He wrinkled his brow at that thought. "You mean that someone else is sending them, even without her knowing, for another purpose."

"I do. And I think it's to keep the police department frazzled on this and therefore not concentrating on other things."

Dave said, "This would be more like a diversion? Well, that's the first thing that makes sense to me. I think you've got it."

She nodded.

Dave had to smile. "You don't seem to let these letters get to you anymore. I'm glad."

"You'd better not either. That's what they

want. We have a much bigger puzzle to figure out."

"We do and we need a good night's sleep 'cause we've got a lot of work ahead of us tomorrow.

"Think you'll sleep better tonight?" she asked.

He laughed, "I'm sleepwalking already. God, I'm tired. Crazy, huh? I can't believe it. We haven't done that much physical work in the last couple of days."

"Dave, emotional stress and the energy we've used to try and figure out everything that's come across our minds in the last couple of days uses up more energy than any physical exertion I know of. It's a different kind of exhaustion."

"I imagine the world of thought taught you a lot about that."

She smiled, but had to agree. Yes, she had learned a lot from listening to other people. That and a little communication with her grandpa from the other side.

* * *

Dave had an early meeting with Sergeant Brady on Wednesday morning. He had to inform him about yet another letter that Sammi had received. Another glitch that had to be reported. But Dave wanted to know what was happening in Scranton.

"Honestly, Dave, things have been pretty quiet. We're not getting any new information at all. I wish we'd hear something; I don't like it when it's this quiet."

"What about Julie? Anything coming across?"

The sarge simply shook his head in a worrisome manner. "Jim and Tom aren't picking up anything either. They said the other day that things seem too laid back ... like before something big was going to happen."

Dave asked, "What's happening with those kidnappers? Are they talking about anything?"

The sarge looked slightly surprised. "No, but we caught them red-handed. What would you think they'd be talking about?"

Dave felt he was caught up in something that he shouldn't have mentioned, but he continued carefully. "I was thinking it was strange that Brian, recently out of prison, would have pulled such a stupid thing and Spike was in about the same position. They didn't mention any other names?"

"Oh, I see what you're getting at. Somebody else could have been involved ... someone who initiated this crime? No, they haven't mentioned anyone else."

Just then Julie knocked on the door. She was immediately waved in.

"Interesting memo came across. Although they use different ways to hide their identity, I'm quite sure this one was sent from Senator Kaphle and it went to F.C."

The sarge let out a low whistle and waited for Julie to proceed.

"It's starts out rather casually by acknowledging that another memo was sent out. Now, most of it was in code, but did Sammi get another letter?"

Dave nodded.

"Okay, then later on he said that more distractions were needed. This was tough because part was in code and part wasn't, which is strange to me, but it seems to mean that the memos are definitely a decoy to keep the police engaged in other areas. And the name that came across is particularly important. At the end he said 'Windmill' would be another two weeks, at least."

Dave jumped on that immediately. "That's the code name Terry had talked about in his report, right?"

"Yep, that's it. And if they're saying another two weeks, that means that we can expect some smaller irritations to distract us. Okay, at least we've got a timeline."

"But a timeline for what? We still don't know what they plan to do."

Julie added, "Well, another memo might spell it out more."

"That senator seems like such a laid-back player. I get the impression that he lays low most of the time and simply passes on information to Fritz. What kind of a player is he anyway?"

The sarge thought for a moment and said, "They probably don't want him involved much at all so no one will suspect him. He's in an important position to see things and pass on information.

Dave nodded. Julie left and went back to her office.

It gave them more to think about and more to worry about. After talking about a few more minor details, Dave tried to reassure the sarge that something would turn up soon. Then he went back to his desk.

* * *

Tom and Jim were there quickly. They needed to know if the sarge gave out any more clues or if this mission was still at a standstill.

"Gees, Dave, I know the sarge is concerned, but we can't find out anything. It's too damn quiet out there. Something's about to happen; I can feel it," said Jim.

Tom said, "We need more spies out there. We're not getting anything at all."

Dave had to keep everything to himself, but he felt they had one of the best spies of all time out there, Terry, but he was certainly laying low right now. He would have loved to know where he was and what he was doing. You could always be sure that he would be in the middle of something.

Shortly after lunchtime, Sammi called. She had heard from Audrey and she was going to have dinner with her at the mayor's house on Friday. The mayor would be home and that meant that the tracker and Josh would be around, too.

"I'm a little concerned, Sammi. You feel alright about this?"

"I'll be okay. Audrey said that she'll make sure I'm escorted to my car when I leave. It's the mayor's house, Dave, you can't seriously believe that they're going to try anything there."

Dave was quiet for a moment. He didn't put anything beyond them and that prompted Sammi to say.

"I think you should let the sarge in on what

I'm doing and Jim and Tom also. If I come back with some pertinent information, I'd like them to have had a hint ahead of time what was going on."

"I'll do that today. It's time they all know. And the sarge was telling me that everything is too quiet around here as far as he was concerned ... they all think so, and it's got him worried."

"I was talking to Julie and she says everything is too quiet on the computers right now, too. It seems like everyone's got the same idea. "

Dave remarked, "That's exactly right. It's weird. Our friend should relay something soon. But it's hard to tell. It seems to me that he'll wait until that crucial moment and then surface."

"That's probably how he'll work it. But I hope that Friday turns up something. I'm getting edgy about things, too."

Dave called a meeting with the sarge and the trio to let them know what Sammi was doing in regard to her connection with Audrey.

"That might produce some sort of info. Whenever Sammi's involved interesting facts seem to turn up. God, I hope she can find out something. We need a lead, some kind of direction."

The sarge seemed to sum up what was on everyone's mind. They remained quiet for a few moments and then slowly went back to their individual duties. But the mayor was never far from their minds. He seemed to be the first and central target.

CHAPTER FIFTEEN

Sammi had never seen the inside of the mayor's residence. Audrey met her at the door and showed her around in a rather proud though cautious manner. She'd had a lot to do with the furnishings in the last few years and it showed a blend of good taste mingled with knowledgeable refinement. She knew how to make this a home for her family, yet a welcoming arena for all of the business events and happenings that her husband was involved in.

"This is lovely," Sammi said. "I could tell immediately that you must have had your hand in a lot of it."

She smiled, pleased that her efforts had been noticed and appreciated.

"I do like to keep my hands in the decoration of our home. It's hard for some people to realize that this is our home. It's the mayor's business retreat, but it's also our home and when the children were here I wanted to make sure that they knew that."

"Of course," she answered.

They walked along the entire inside and Audrey pointed out a few artifacts that she held in especial esteem. They even took a few moments to walk outside in the back of the mansion. The landscape was breathtaking and she noticed the protective overhead area where cars could pull in and out without much detection from the outside world. It was possible for someone to completely escape the public's exposure in this area. This home and that of the governor was a different way of living from her own, and she was keenly aware how different their daily lives could be.

When they entered what Audrey referred to as the great room, she was amazed at how huge it was. She had been told that the size was of significant value in allowing them to have dinner and their privacy at one end, while allowing her husband his privacy with business meetings at the other end. Her husband insisted that they be together in the main room so that any of them might be privy to important information. He, as well as his wife, had heard of Sammi's prowess, and though neither one would ever confront her directly, they wanted to give her every advantage that she might need to do her work.

"Hello, Mrs. Patterson," said the mayor. "It's good to see you again." As he spoke he extended his hand and she did receive a firm yet gentle handshake. His eyes were keen and alert, yet careful and she knew that he, too, would be on guard during tonight's proceedings.

"Please call me Sammi," she said and as she was introduced to Peter and Josh, she was taken aback as to how the atmosphere could change by looking from one person to another. Peter and Josh were forcibly polite, but that was all. Their irritation couldn't be hidden. They were thinking that she shouldn't be there and couldn't understand why the mayor allowed these things to happen. The good part was that this wasn't the first time that his wife shared the room with him for different entertainment scenarios.

* * *

As they began to retreat to their individual area for the evening, Sammi caught Peter in some worrisome thoughts. *I can't understand why those two became friends all of a sudden. She's married to that detective and I don't like this. But I guess we can still conduct business, after all, she's way on the other side of the room.* With that his thoughts changed immediately to some local business that the mayor was asking about.

Audrey knew ahead of time that Sammi would be taking notes. They covered it with occasional loud talk and laughter that kept Peter and Josh off their mark. But happily Sammi realized that the mayor was one sharp character. His awareness brought on shrewd conversation and she couldn't have asked for a better partner, except Dave, of course.

So with occasional giggles to keep the men distracted, Sammi was writing notes, as if they had some gala event being planned. But she felt rather than saw Peter occasionally looking at their end of the room. At one point, Josh pretended to walk around the room looking at pictures and admiring furnishings as if he'd never been there before. It was such an amateurish attempt, it was almost funny, and so Peter called him back realizing that ploy wouldn't work at all.

Peter's thoughts were scary. He was assessing

the situation and wanted to make sure that Ron wouldn't allow this type of happening again.

We've got to be able to complete our business now. There's only another week or so. Wayne is on my back daily. This has to come off without a hitch. If it fails, we'll all go down, probably even Fritz.

And it went that way most of the evening. Sammi was able to catch little tidbits of what was going to happen in the future, but the main plan hadn't crossed his mind. Sammi needed to know that so she was particularly pleased when Ron called them over for their opinion on some up-coming events.

"What do you think Audrey? What would work out the best, a barbecue or a lawn party?"

"I like the lawn party idea, myself. It's worked out so well in the past."

The guys didn't care about the details, but they were more interested in the outcome. This was a party scheduled for one month in the future. Then Sammi heard it. She was shocked, but had to hold a straight and congenial countenance. And she managed to look right at Peter's face when he was asked what he would prefer and he answered out loud in words, "I don't think it matters that much." But then his thoughts gave him away, *If all goes according to plan, neither one of you will be around to enjoy it anyway. The time is near now, so this party crap won't even matter. Wayne says Fritz is getting restless.*

Sammi had to keep calm and poised. She couldn't give them even the slightest hint that she knew anything. And she hadn't yet heard what she wanted to know. No thought had yet crossed

Peter or Josh's mind as to how this would be accomplished. So she started to push the conversation and pin down more about the party and plans. This kept Peter thinking they wouldn't be there and she hoped his thoughts would slip and give her what she wanted.

"I think a lawn party is the most festive, and gets people mingling more. After all, isn't that what you want? Everyone mixing and circulating and keeping the enthusiasm alive for your re-election?"

Peter's thoughts almost laughed out loud to her. *What reelection? That's almost funny.* And then he finally gave himself away because of his angry, sick mind that loved death and murder and seemed to linger on the method of killing. *I hope you both go off in a bunch of little pieces when that bomb explodes under your car.*

Sammi felt quite nauseous for the moment. But she covered it up by sneezing a few times in a row. The maid came in and she accepted some water as they retreated back to their side of the room.

Audrey was very astute. She knew Sammi had figured out something. She couldn't get any straight expression out of her, but agreed when she felt it was time to end the evening. Dinner had been over for a while and they ended with the silliness that was so effective before. Yes, yes, they were two silly women and Peter wondered how Ron could stand his wife at times.

But as they left Sammi had to push the envelope one more time. "Ron, this party isn't for another month. Why don't we all meet again, say in two weeks, and finalize everything?"

But Peter was adamant in his thought world. He thought in two weeks they would be dead. So she refined her question, "Next Friday might even be better. What do you think?"

At this Peter recoiled adamantly. *Fritz wouldn't want any complications. Windmill might start next Friday or at least next weekend. I'd better steer them away.*

"Isn't next week-end the first fund raiser?"

Ron turned to look at him, "What are you talking about? I've never heard anything about that?"

Peter was almost embarrassed. "I don't think we've got it on the books yet, but I think they're planning one at the Lackawanna Hotel. Both you and your wife should be attending." And with these statements Peter was thinking, *I've got to keep them open for next weekend. No little meeting with other people around. They've got to be alone.*

And that's exactly what Sammi needed to know. Peter was sure that they'd be gone in two weeks and wanted them to adhere to his schedule next weekend. As far as she could figure out, the next weekend or the first part of the week after had to be a go.

* * *

When Sammi walked out to her car, she wasn't saying much to Audrey. She had to push herself to remain calm and coherent.

"Aren't those guys a trip? They're quite bossy, but they try to do it in a subtle way so we won't catch on. But Ron is more aware now."

Sammi knew by listening to her thoughts that she didn't have a clue as to the dire circumstances that she and her husband were involved in. Sammi wanted so much to tell her, but then she'd have the problem of her wondering how she'd found out. Also, she didn't know if that was the best course of action. She felt that she had to talk to Dave first. Yet, she stood there looking at her in concern, but not knowing what to do. They needed to be warned and fast, but what should she do? She had to get home; Dave would know how to handle this.

"At least they still think that we're two silly females and that's what we need. We don't need them to suspect even in the slightest that anyone here is on to their tricks."

"Yeah, I know. I do wonder how they plan to oust my husband. He does have a good approval rating. I suppose they need to make him look bad, right?"

This was a hard question for Sammi to answer. She stood there looking into Audrey's worried face and knew that her best option was to leave everything alone until she talked to Dave. Yet she couldn't help confirm Audrey's suspicions.

"They're in with some bad people, Audrey. You and Ron have to watch your back at all times. When are your children coming home?"

"Not for at least three more weeks. That'll be mid-semester break."

"Okay, I'm going home to talk to Dave about a few things. Can you have Ron call Sam on Monday afternoon? I know Sam won't get through to him. And if for any reason Ron's call doesn't get through to him, let me know immediately. We're going to need to talk. I'm sure plans will be forthcoming and we need to be able to get in touch with one of you."

Suddenly Audrey's face took on a different look. "You think we're in danger, don't you?"

Alarming her unnecessarily wouldn't accomplish anything. Being as truthful as she could, she said, "Not immediately, but they've got something in mind and we have to be ready."

On the way home, her mind was spinning and she still felt that she could puke. This was so frightening for her that she couldn't wait to get home. Involuntarily she started crying. She couldn't believe that she had lost control of her emotions. But she had to be understanding with herself. This had been building up for quite a while. She had finally let go; that's all. And she knew Dave would be waiting for her. He would know what to do. Audrey and Ron had to be protected as soon as possible.

* * *

When she saw Dave's was car parked in the garage, Sammi took a deep breath and let it out slowly. It hadn't dawned on her until this moment that he could have gone out. Usually he would let her know if something came up, so she'd assumed he'd be home. And she needed him now. She tried to wipe away her tears; they were still some coming down her face. But he would know what to do. He always knew.

And he opened the door as soon as she got near it. He had been nervously awaiting her return. Taking one look at her, he wrapped her in his arms. That's when Sammi was able to let go. She cried she guessed for at least five minutes and couldn't stop. He got her sitting down in the living room and disappeared for a moment.

"Don't you say one word," he said upset at her condition. "You drink this glass of wine, settle down a bit and then we'll talk."

She tried to smile, took a few deep breaths and surprised herself by beginning to relax. She tried to clear her mind, which wasn't easy with all of the dismal thoughts that were crossing it at a rapid pace. But she couldn't keep silent any longer.

"Oh Dave," she said. "We've got some big problems here. And Ron and Audrey are in extreme danger."

She relayed to him all that she had heard. She went over every detail and consulted her notes to make sure she hadn't forgotten anything.

"So he even thought about the word: Windmill. We're getting somewhere. It's getting real close now. Julie said today that two more memos were sent, but they were so camouflaged that she wasn't sure about them. But the last one did use the word: Windmill."

"How can we possibly protect them, Dave? Is somebody going to let Ron know? And what good will that do?"

"Sammi, you got us the information we needed. I'll be talking to the sarge tomorrow morning and I think that Ben will be in on this one. We need help from the feds. You're not to worry about the ways and means. You've done your job and you did great."

Feeling somewhat satisfied, she sat still for a while longer.

"Nothing was mentioned about the sarge, right?"

She shook her head. "Nothing, what does that mean?"

"Well, it could mean a couple of things. He didn't cross Peter's mind because they're not that worried about him yet. If they're able to assassinate the mayor and his wife, that'll make him look so bad, he wouldn't get reelected anyway. He might even get recalled. You see, then they've got both of them out of the way."

Then he sat and held her for a while. What a complicated mess they were involved in this time. The good thing was they were pretty sure that they had a week or at least until next Friday to get their plan in place. After that, Windmill could happen anytime. But Dave had to get Sammi to settle down. She had gotten so emotional since it did concern people she knew.

"It makes it harder when it's people you're close to, doesn't it?" Dave said.

"I want them to be safe and protected and there isn't anything I can do."

"But you've done your job. With a heads up like this, we can get in there and protect them."

"But there's no guarantee, is there?"

He looked at her worried face and said, "Sammi, nothing is guaranteed in this life. Audrey

could go out driving tomorrow and get in a car crash and get killed. Nothing in life is certain. But with the information you've given us, the odds are on our side."

She took a deep breath and put her head back. She fell asleep within a few minutes. Dave hated to wake her to get her to bed, but realized that was the best idea.

She teased him. "Aren't you going to carry me to the bedroom?"

"Sure," he said as he got up and came toward her.

"No, no, I was kidding. Your shoulder's been a lot better in the last six months. We don't want to hurt it again."

"You don't weigh that much."

"I weigh enough, but thank you for being a gentleman."

They ended the evening on a lighter note with both of them needing to get their minds off of the serious business at hand. First thing in the morning would be hot meetings with desperate plans put into place immediately.

* * *

Sammi took a couple of deep breaths. Luckily Dave had fallen asleep immediately. And though he'd never admit it, he needed the rest even more than she did. She looked over at him. He had such a serene look on his face that you'd never know that his dreams were probably playing chaos with his mind at this exact moment.

She thought back on her life. She couldn't do

that without bringing into her conscious mind the people she'd known. She thought of Lena, the little girl adopted from Russia, who'd had a troubled childhood. Because of it she didn't trust anyone and didn't have the capacity to love anyone. And her repetitive angry thoughts were taking her life in the wrong direction.

Then she wondered about people like Peter Armors, Josh Logan and of course, the never-ending concern of Linda Saunders. In truth she didn't know anything about their childhoods. That could have got them going the wrong way and without any professional help, they had little chance in changing their direction.

Still, she had known others. She thought of Lydia Jensen, a gal she'd helped last year. She'd had a lonely childhood, raised in foster homes since she was fourteen and after marrying a good match for her, ended up having to support him when he went to jail. The fact that he wasn't guilty gave her even more reason to turn to anger and hate and rebel against the system. But she hadn't. She was still able to believe that life was ultimately good and justice would prevail.

And so, what was the difference between all these adults? What was it within them that made some choose the good life and others to choose chaos and destruction? Her grandpa used to say that people decide who they want to be not out of desperation, but out of desire. Everyone had the power to choose their thoughts and therefore choose where their life would go. But she still wondered why, and that was the last thought on her mind as her dreams took over.

* * *

Dave had called the sarge to make sure that he'd be there to meet with the trio on Saturday morning. And all were stunned at the latest information that came their way, but realized that this was a shocking operation from the beginning.

"The file came through on Willie Sanford," said Jim. "He's been on the outskirts of the mob for years. He may be knee-deep in it by now, but that's all we could prove. He went to jail twice, once for attempted murder, but with the plea deals only manslaughter was proven. And another time it was assault of some kind. Now those are the main felonies on his record, but there were numerous misdemeanors. And Wayne Ellison has a longer record for racketeering, fraud, and an attempted murder charge, which was also lowered to manslaughter and the list goes on and on."

"How did Peter get to work for the mayor?"

"Rumor has it that Tony Baran was forced out under threat and then Senator Kaphle recommended Peter. But I can't figure out how this senator fits into the entire scheme of things. He seems to have a clean record, yet he's involved with these guys and relays information to Fritz Connelly regularly. I really don't get that one."

"Have you talked to Ben lately? I'm wondering if we can get Fritz on something this time. That guy has to go away."

The sarge was a little baffled here. "Ben says that he's under surveillance and that with all of the proven emails and stuff that he's connected

with, we should have enough to get him charged with something. But what and how much is still kind of iffy."

"Can we prove he's the one ordering the hit on the mayor?"

"So far there are innuendos, and Ben's hopeful before it all goes down that there will be solid proof."

"Okay," said Dave. "So what do we do about mayor and his wife? Sammi's beside herself on this one."

"I'm putting a call in to Ben right away. I've got to know what he wants done on this. We're not working alone here. We'll meet again as soon as I talk to him."

* * *

Dave and the guys were working out details of other jobs that hadn't gone away either. Spike Evers and Brian Hatterly were talking up a storm to anyone who would listen. They had apparently been approached by a liaison that worked with none other than Peter Armors.

"This is getting to be such a sweet little web," said Tom. "It seems that they're the ones behind most of the crime in Scranton right now. But why the hell kidnap a woman and all that? That doesn't make any sense to me."

"I understood it was to keep our attention on other things and also to make the sarge look incompetent. She wasn't supposed to be found and therefore would have been another unsolved murder."

Tom nodded his head. "Oh, I see, and then if they were able to assassinate the mayor and his wife, the sarge would start looking real bad. Okay, I think I get it now."

About this time the sarge called Dave back into his office. He was on the phone with Ben and he wanted to talk to him.

"Okay, Ben I'm on."

"Dave, can you talk right now? I need to clue you in on something. Sorry Sam, Dave's already aware of something and I can't divulge any more right now. I'm under orders here. But you'll know as soon as I get the okay."

"Understood," said the sarge and left room.

Dave waited patiently then said, "Okay, Ben, what's going on?"

"We're bringing in Amilio or ...Terry. Shit, I don't know what the hell to call that guy. Anyway we both better get used to Amilio because that's who he's going to be from now on. I understand that he's going to be assigned to the mayor's landscape group. I believe he already has. No one will know, so this is what I need you to do. Can you find a way to let the mayor and his wife know that he's the one person they can trust?"

"Sure, Sammi can do that."

"Okay and this is crucial. When it goes down, it will happen fast and they may have only seconds to make a decision as to whom they should believe and follow. They have to know to go with Amilio, that he's the one to trust. Are you sure you can get to them?"

"Yes, I am. Does Amilio know that we know about him?"

"He knows that you and Sammi have been told. He joked and said that Sammi probably figured it out. When this is all over I have plans for him, but even at that time it will be only your group and the sarge who'll know. We have to keep his slate clean. It'll be more obvious later. But for now, make sure the mayor knows who to trust. I can't stress that enough."

"Okay. When will he be there?"

"Dave, he's there now. He saw Sammi and he says that she looked right at him when she left on Friday night."

Dave wasn't even surprised. "No kidding."

Ben continued. "Although he's been hired as a helper to the main gardener—that was all that was available, we're making sure that he's being used as a type of bodyguard so he has access to the mayor and his wife. And get this, Peter likes him and trusts him. And he doesn't even know."

Although Dave shook his head, he wasn't surprised. None of them had any idea what this guy had done for years. He was amazing. And the fact that they could still use him was even more unbelievable. He was walking around associating and staring people right in the face and they never recognized him. After all, it was Peter who had put out the contract on him.

"He told me to give you and Sammi his regards. He hopes to be able to be friends in the future again, but it will be as Amilio Hernandez."

Dave was quiet for a moment which prompted Ben to ask, "Dave, are you still there?"

"Sorry. I still get emotional and so amazed at

the talent of that guy. And to think none of us had any real suspicion of what he was doing."

"I know you're his favorite; he still refers to you as his big brother."

Dave laughed. "Right. He can run circles around me."

"Okay, then, let me know as soon as everything's in place. We don't have much time."

"I know Sammi thought it could be anytime starting with this coming Friday. In fact, there's supposedly a fundraiser at the Lackawanna hotel for the mayor that night."

"And," said Ben, "Amilio says that it was put together rather quickly by Peter, so we're all suspicious of that one."

"Right. Okay. I know Sammi made plans so that Ron would call the sarge on Monday afternoon. The mayor's calls are being filtered through Peter and Sam can't get through to him. But I'll see if we can get to him sooner."

"Okay, clue him in on everything. He's got to be aware and stay vigilant about everything around him. This whole thing is one of the worst schemes we've encountered lately."

"Got to go," said Ben. "Keep me posted as soon as you find out anything."

"Right."

* * *

When Dave put down the phone, the sarge immediately walked back into his office. He had a look on his face that said, *I know you can't tell me things right now and it's okay.*

"I hate this secrecy, but ..."

"Dave, there were times I've had to hold things back. It needs to be done. So I'm assuming that one way or another he's got a plan to help the mayor."

"Yeah, he does."

"When all this is over I hope that Ron and Audrey can get together with my wife and I like we used to. Those were good times and it helped a lot when we were all good friends."

"Why haven't we heard anything about the governor? I hope he's safe and not targeted right now."

The sarge was thoughtful and concerned. He didn't like any loose ends.

Dave added, "I didn't think to say anything to Ben about it. But I imagine he would have brought it up if he had any suspicions."

"You'd think so. But I'll be talking to Ben later today on another matter. See, I have secrets, too," he laughed. "I'll ask him then."

"Okay, what do we know about the detail that protects the governor? I lost track after Charlie Freeman was arrested last year."

"I'll look into that today. Good point, Dave. And you're right. We need to keep all of our bases covered."

* * *

Dave was having a tough time with this assignment. Tom and Jim were his best friends and most trusted confidantes and yet he couldn't tell them about Amilio. He didn't know it would be this hard.

When they approached him, he threw up his hands and said, "Guys, I'm bound here."

"Hey, we know that. We've all been there."

"But to me, it makes the job a lot harder."

They both understood, and they agreed. When they could be open with each other and share the burden, everything seemed easier.

Tom got called away for a phone call and Jim tried to get Dave to settle down.

"Listen, we're all buddies, but there are times ..."

Dave had so much on his mind. His thoughts were scrambled most of the time these days. God, he wanted this caper to go down fast and be finished.

"Jim, you stopping at the gym tonight? I am, for sure."

"Me too. Later, okay?"

When Tom came back he asked Dave if he'd have time to stop at the rehab center with him tonight. Todd was asking for both of them.

"Sure, how's he doing these days?"

"Pretty good. They took the stitches out of his jaw now and he can actually talk a little. He's still bound up by something, but you can make out his words. And the rest of his body is healing nicely. We've talked a few times and I think we've got the beginning of a relationship. I think he wants it, too."

"Isn't that something?"

"For sure. Who would have known? Jill's pretty happy about everything."

"I'll give Sammi a call and tell her I'll be a little

late. By the way, do you have any idea when he might get out of the rehab center?"

"No decision on that right now. But at least he's coming along nicely."

* * *

"How's your day going?" he asked. He was hoping that she had settled down some from last night.

"Okay, I'm doing laundry and housecleaning, the fun stuff. So what about you?"

"I've got stuff to tell you, but I'll wait until I get home. I'm going to work out; I'm sure you're glad to hear that. Then Tom says that Todd wanted to see him and me. I'm going to swing by before I come home, so I'll be a little late."

"Okay, any idea what Todd wants?"

"No, but I understand that he can talk a little now, so that's good. You feeling better today?"

"Yes, but I can't wait until this thing is over."

"I was thinking the same thing. Hey, I've got to go. See ya later."

When she put down the phone Sammi got a little philosophical. She needed to draw emotions from the past which always helped her see things in a clearer view. The universe was progressing the way it should. And though these problems seemed gigantic to all of them at this time, when you thought of the entire world and the universe, they were but a handful of people involved here, trying to get a job done. And either way, life would go on.

* * *

Tom was already in Todd's room when Dave arrived. He was amazed to see him talking and laughing but then realized that he hadn't seen him in a while and the difference was remarkable. If all went well, he might start walking therapy within the next few days. And he could communicate now, which made him happy, but there was no guarantee of smooth sailing, although all of the encouraging possibilities were there.

"Okay," said Tom. "You wanted to see the both of us. What's up?"

Although he talked slowly, his voice was steady and clear. "When I realized a while back that Peter was in this area, I wondered how long he'd been here. Like I said, that guy's bad news. So I asked for copies of papers for the last two years."

Dave looked amused.

"Well, Dave, I've nothing but time here so I thought I'd amuse myself and see if I could come up with anything else that might be helpful."

"But newspapers for the last two years," Tom seemed amused as well.

"It gets pretty boring here and I'm not one to get into soap operas."

Now that amused them all.

"Anyway, I found out some stuff and hopefully I didn't get you guys down here for nothing. I've had this on my mind for a few days and it keeps bugging at me. I'd thought I'd tell you both and if it's nothing or something, at least I wouldn't worry about it anymore."

"Okay," said Dave. "What have you noticed?"

"Okay, way back when, there was a picture of this girl in the paper ..." and Todd pulled out the pertinent paper. It was a picture of Linda Saunders with her arm around Peter. That didn't surprise Dave by now. She apparently knew all of the guys connected with this group. But it was one more connection with her.

"Okay, well," said Tom, "we should tell you that this Linda Saunders is in jail right now for attempted murder and fraud and a list of other things. She tried to kill Dave here in a sting operation."

"Wow, I hadn't heard that."

Dave said, "Well it was a while back. She's been in jail well over a year now."

Todd got very thoughtful and quiet. He seemed to be struggling with himself.

"Why, what's wrong?"

"Okay, see this picture a few months later? This time she's friendly with this other guy. Does he look familiar at all?"

Both Dave and Tom shook their heads.

"Who is he?"

"That's Wayne Ellison and unless I'm completely wrong here he and Linda got married quite a while back. Now it was a marriage of convenience I understand. I think that he liked her, but she wasn't that crazy about him. But he had something on her and he needed her to do some type of undercover stuff. What I'm telling you is the rumors that I'd heard. But it was common knowledge around Lawrence, Kansas that they were both bad news."

"Gees," said Tom. "This kettle of fish keeps getting thicker.

"And one other thing that bothers me is that Wayne Ellison was a tricky character in those days. Truthfully, I'm sure his name is not Wayne Ellison, but for the life of me, I can't remember what it is."

"No kidding," said Dave, realizing that everyone seemed to be using an alias. "Who might know his real identity?"

"I don't know. Not the college, that's for sure. He went by the Ellison name back then. And I think he went to prison under that name. But that's not his real identity. Sorry, I wish I could be of more help."

"You've done great. Thanks a lot. I'm glad that you used this method to keep from getting bored. It's been helpful," said Tom.

Tom turned and looked at Dave who was trying to make sense of all this latest information.

"I think this is a web that has no bottom to it."

Turning to Todd, Dave said, "You're quite good at doing research. Might be something you could look into if it interests you."

Todd looked pleased. It was obvious that he felt satisfied when he realized that he might have been of some help to the police.

Before he left Dave said, "Keep reading these papers, if you will. It might trigger something else in your memory. If you think of anything else, do let us know. And thanks."

Tom leaned over and said, "Good job, Todd. I'm glad you're on our side now."

Obviously, Todd was tickled. He felt like he

belonged and was seriously considering some kind of research work, especially if it could be related to law enforcement work. Who would have ever guessed he would ever be considering this?

* * *

"What the hell does this latest stuff mean?" asked Tom looking totally confused.

"God, I don't know. These people are all part of the job, as we know it. There's probably a lot of them using aliases for a lot of reasons. But it still amazes me. I mean he thinks Linda is married to that Wayne Ellison or whoever he is."

"That's what he said was the rumor back then."

Dave shook his head. "But this Wayne guy had something on her. I wonder what that was?"

"I remember when they were still investigating Jerry Macy and Linda when they went to trial, the lawyers said that she was mixed up in some other murders, but they were never proven. Possibly Wayne was holding some type of proof over her head so she'd cooperate with them."

"Hey, that's a thought. She was certainly involved in a lot of things back then."

As they left the rehab center they realized that their work was far from over. Dave was the first to comment.

"I'll let the sarge know about the latest. Who is this Wayne Ellison? And why does he need an alias?"

Tom nodded as they parted. Dave thought everyday brought more questions than answers.

And the Windmill date was getting closer. What else was in store for them? What possible underlying connections did Wayne Ellison have except the obvious ones? He was tired now; this case had lasted a long time. It was well over two years, and he wished with all of his being that it would be over soon.

CHAPTER SIXTEEN

"You mean I saw Amilio at the mayor's house? I can't believe it. I saw his picture in Ben's office and saw no one that looked like him. I think I'm usually fairly observant."

"If he didn't want you to recognize him, you wouldn't. We're all beginning to realize that this guy is a master at what he does."

Sammi felt deflated. She simply couldn't believe it. It was like Amilio or Terry was always one step ahead of them.

"When I look back on when he first started at the police station, well, he seemed like a rookie kid and I took him under my wing. He acted kind of green, like a true rookie, and it never would have crossed my mind that he was anything other than what he seemed. Yet, even at that time, he was setting the stage for what was to come later."

"So he'll be the one waiting to get Ron and Audrey out of harm's way when the time comes."

"So I hear, and in the meantime he has to come face to face with Peter and Josh, who knew him quite well before, and apparently they don't have a clue."

"Yet if I was Terry," she said, "I think I'd be concerned. What if some little thing got them thinking? His type of work would make me so nervous."

"Remember Ben said that part of Terry's philosophy is that he totally believes who he is at the moment. And with that attitude, others believe him, too."

"If he has the confidence, I guess he's the best one for the job. He already knows all these people, how they think, how they work and now he's aware of the final plan. I hope he can pull it off; and I have to admit he's the best one to get it done."

Then Dave told her about Linda's marriage to Wayne Ellison or whoever he was.

"Sometimes I wish I could get to her. I'd love to have a chance to listen to her and hear her thoughts. They would no doubt answer most of our questions."

Dave was thoughtful. "I wonder where this will all end up. After this weekend or early next week, when the attempt is made, all hell should break loose. And then, maybe the secrets will come out."

Sammi looked over with confusion setting in. "What do you mean the secrets will come out? We know what they want, they want control of this part of Pennsylvania; you think there's more?"

"I don't know, it doesn't feel right. They could get control here in a lot of different ways, through elections by using nasty and even illegal tactics to make the good guys look bad and put their own people in. They could tamper with the votes, which happens more than we like to admit. They could have eliminated other people long ago before it got this far. No, no, Sammi, something else is going on here. I know they want to get control of this part of the state; that's been going on for a while, but I have such a feeling ..." and Dave's voice trailed off.

"You know Dave, Josh Logan had some thoughts about the Pattern Papers. I don't think I got the right name, but it was something like that. Could have been Pastern Papers. Have you ever heard of anything like that?"

"No, why didn't you mention it?"

"Because I was concentrating on Peter and trying to figure out how they were going to eliminate the mayor. And truly I thought it was nonsense."

"Do you remember anything else?"

"Not really, his mind was quite placid without too much activity crossing over. He was concentrating quite intensely on Peter's ideas. He's sort of the follower and Peter's the leader. And the leader is the one that gets most of the thought activity."

And she knew that Peter's thoughts were the ones to concentrate on.

* * *

Dave stroked his chin. He was trying to get a big picture outlook on this entire situation. What the hell was going on here? He knew there was more than they had figured out. But then, these groups always had a bunch of goals they were aiming for at the same time. Mainly they wanted to take over everything in the world. They probably had a lot more operations going on right now and this was only a small part of the big picture.

He didn't feel that their plot was international anymore; it was global.

He was pulled out of his thoughts by Sammi's voice. "Dave, Dave what are you thinking?"

"I think this is so big that we'll never know. But our main job right now is to take care of the mayor, the sarge and the governor."

About this time the phone rang. It was Sergeant Brady. Dave spent almost ten minutes on the phone with him and Sammi caught but a part of the conversation. He looked concerned when he put down the phone.

"Sarge is adding two units under cover at the governor's place until further notice. Some strange things have come across the computers that Julie made them aware of, and more unwarranted activity is happening right in the governor's home. His family will be taken away by tomorrow for precaution. They'll make it sound like a holiday, but the governor will stay behind. Word has it he's a target now, too."

Sammi was beside herself. "Is this entire world going crazy? God, what's happening?"

Dave settled down almost immediately. He got up and went to sit down beside Sammi. He took her hand in his and said, "Look, these possibilities have always been around. We don't talk about it on a daily basis, but you realize it, too. It's the good guys against the bad guys; the white hats against the black hats. It seems like it's hitting here big time right now. But I don't personally think the governor is in danger. But that's simply my opinion. And I believe that if we can foil the plan on the mayor, and reel in Peter and Josh and

Wayne, possibly Fritz and that senator, they'll recoil from here again for a long time. Their plans will never end and they'll try again here or somewhere else sooner or later. It'll never end. And that's the way it is."

His words helped Sammi get a better perspective, too. It would never end. There had been trouble with crime and conspiracies since the beginning of time and it would continue until the end of the world. The days that were seemingly pleasant and comfortable didn't mean that underlying problems weren't forming and ready to spring up at any moment.

"I know it's not a positive way to look at life, but it's realistic," she said. "And you're in a profession that has to be aware of this. Evil has always been around, but it doesn't mean we have to concentrate on it. Right now, perhaps, but in a few weeks when all this is over, you and I are going on vacation somewhere that's fun and romantic and exciting."

Dave laughed, "Sometimes, Sammi, being here with you is fun and exciting."

That changed their mood into a much needed amusing turn. But Dave remembered one more thing.

"You said that Ron would call Sam on Monday. If for some reason he doesn't get through, we have to get to them. They have to know about Amilio and they have to be told that when something happens, he's the only one they can trust."

Sammi understood. "We'll make sure that happens."

"And now for the romantic part of our even-

through the door.

She yelled over at her in surprise and they did everything possible physically to look like they had surprised each other. After their loud hellos, they moved to the side and quieted down for a few minutes.

"I don't want to take much time. Dave's across the hall in the men's store and he wants to come in before we're finished. Sam thought the phone was tapped, so he hoped Ron understood. He heard noises at his end, but wasn't sure if Ron could hear them or not."

"Yeah, he heard them, too. And he was on his cell phone. They must have everything tapped."

"Okay, here it is. Have you met Amilio, yet?"

"Oh, yes, the new guy. He got hired to work with the gardener a few weeks ago."

"Audrey, listen, and this is of extreme importance. He's a cop working undercover. If anything happens around your home, he's the only one you can trust. Do what he tells you immediately. Understand?"

She definitely paled.

"Is it that serious? We're being targeted, aren't we?"

"We think so. You need to be protected and you're to listen to Amilio. Got it?"

Audrey seemed serious when she nodded her head.

About that moment, Dave walked in, looking somewhat uncomfortable in a beauty shop. He played his part well and as he called out to Sammi he said, "Oh, hi there, Audrey, it's nice to see you."

When he got closer he said, "Any questions?"

She shook her head. Then Sammi took her cell phone from her purse and asked Audrey to do the same. They pretended they were comparing them and when they were put away, they had made the exchange. That's the one phone they could use to call them and they still had to watch what they said.

Dave said, "I know this is scary, Audrey, but they aren't going to play their hand right now. We think we've got a week and our plans are in place. Listen to Amilio."

Then Dave said in a louder voice, "Good to see you. We'd better get going. Bye Audrey."

* * *

Audrey was nervous when she confronted her husband that night. They began whispering anything important to each other. Yet they had to keep up some conversation, too. Ron relied on her strength since she was his backbone many times, but he did hold her for a while when he saw her losing courage. She was a strong woman and her strength came back without delay.

"I know what it is, Audrey, they're trying to take over Scranton again. I'll bet they've got the governor protected, too. But why me?"

"I think they want to put their people in all of the key positions. I'm scared, Ron. I'm not ashamed to admit it."

"I'm not a warrior either."

"And Sammi gave me her cell phone. It's the only one we can use to call them. God, what do you think they're going to do?"

"I don't know, but you should go away for now. It'd probably be safer for you, I think."

"I'm not leaving you; forget it. And who knows if I'll be safer anywhere else."

"That's true and I trust Sam. Damn, I wish I'd have trusted him more. I can't believe how this Peter got into my confidence. He was so slick. Now we're in a mess."

"It could have happened anyway. I can't believe these are the total number of people involved; there's gotta be more. This must be a huge operation."

"I'm afraid it is. I guess politics isn't what we thought it was going to be. I knew there was always some underhanded stuff to watch and a lot of nastiness if you're beating someone, but I never thought about anything like this. I should have stayed in some of those lower political jobs; no one targets you there."

"Don't be talking like that, Ron. You're a good man and you've done a lot of good things for this city. We're going to beat this thing. We've got a lot of people on our side, too. But remember, Amilio is the one we trust. He's our ace in the hole."

Ron had to smile. He knew Audrey was trying to put on a brave face, but she was scared to her core. And although neither one would say it out loud, these people didn't want them out of their job; they wanted them dead.

"I've talked to this guy maybe one time. He's been here less than a month. I think he's helping out the main gardener."

"But he was the one in the background watching over me when Sammi left last Friday."

"I see. One of those multi-talented guys. Who hired him, do we know?"

"No idea. But I did see him friendly with Peter yesterday morning. Peter seems to like him."

"Probably has no clue who he is."

"Well, let's try and get some sleep. We've got to be alert and aware from now on."

* * *

Jim checked out Audrey's cell phone the next day. It was definitely wired, but they left it alone. They didn't want anyone to know that they had discovered anything. Even if Peter was suspicious, they didn't want him to know beyond a reasonable doubt.

"Dave, so what the hell's going on at the mayor's house?"

Jim was the first one to start asking the questions in the latest meeting when they had been briefed on the newest happenings.

"From what I can tell, they've got all the phones tapped," said Dave. "They've closed the circle on the mayor so he has hardly any outside contact and they still believe that he doesn't realize it. That's mainly our ace card right now. They think Ron isn't aware of anything."

"So, has he noticed anything? What can he tell us?"

"Nothing, he has no way to communicate with us. But ..."

The sarge had been on a phone call and when it ended he had some surprising news. "We've got word that there will be an attempt on the mayor's life, probably on Friday night on his way to the Lackawanna Hotel for that fund raiser. They plan to kill his wife, too."

Jim and Tom looked at each other in disgust. They knew this was serious business, but they didn't think an assassination attempt was on the agenda. Why and how the hell had everything escalated to this level?

Dave waited until the sarge continued. "Now Ben Collier has an agent in the area helping out. But we need to all work together. This agent is under cover and will only surface when he has to. He's already sent his plans ahead. He says it will be a bomb under their car. That means whoever is driving the vehicle will be killed also."

"This is serious stuff we're getting into here," said Jim. "All because they want to take over this part of the state. Isn't this quite extreme?"

The sarge shook his head, but Dave took over. "In talking to Ben lately I'm beginning to realize it's much more than that. We foiled their plans last time. Taking over Scranton, Philly and Harrisburg, is the tip of the iceberg. That begins their control on some of the shipping business and the computer systems in our state. After that is locked in they want to branch out to other states. But for some reason they believe that they must get our state secure and firmly fixed in their agenda first."

"You mean they want to spread out ..."

"Yep, everywhere. They want control of the United States. It's a global plan. From here they believe they can control the world."

Tom wrinkled his nose. "You're not kidding, are you? First Pennsylvania gets under their control and then they slowly start across other states, right?"

"Yes," said Dave. "And they know it could take years and they might have trouble with other states, like ours, but we're the beginning as far as we know. Colorado's had trouble with them, but they control nothing significant there."

"And Linda Saunders, Jerry Macy, and that entire group as well as Peter Armors, or whoever the hell he is and Josh Logan and of course our favorite Fritz Connelly is part of everything?"

"Yep," said the sarge. "Think of the first group as the first wave that tried to take over. Now, they did cause us some damage, but we got back in stride real fast. But this time, they're working from the inside out and murder is just another word to them. They want us and they want us now, at all costs. We're apparently halting their progress."

"What's on our side?" asked Tom. "How do we find out what the mayor knows?"

"Right now," Dave said, "Sammi's our liaison with Audrey and so far that's it."

Sergeant Brady had an added comment. "On Thursday night there will be a planned demonstration in front of the mayor's house. It'll be a surprise to them, we hope, and will throw Peter a large curve ball. We need to get an inroad there."

They all looked at each other with blank expressions. This was the first time that they'd heard about this and wondered what part it would play it the total picture.

"We plan to get our group there to halt the protest, but give us enough time for some contact."

Even Dave took deep breath. Anything that took precision timing had room for error and reason for concern.

"Ben wants you three to be there as part of the police stabilization group. I can't help but think that his agent will try to contact one of you."

"But how'll we know," asked Tom.

"He'll know," said the sarge. "And he'll give us some information if he thinks it's necessary."

* * *

Sammi was amazed when she heard the latest. She hadn't picked up any global thoughts on world takeover. She felt she hadn't done her job all that well.

"Most of these guys don't even know what the final goal is, so they can't think about it. Oh, they may have some fantasy, but Peter, for example, is thinking exclusively about this job, right now. I doubt if he's thinking that far ahead."

Sammi listened. She felt she had much to learn.

"And it wouldn't matter anyway. The rest of their plan is in the future. Right now is what we have to be concerned about. And their immediate concern is the takeover of this area."

"Wow," was all she could say. Then she added, "I sure do think in smaller terms. They think about the takeover of the world."

"Don't forget, these are the small fishes here, doing the dirty work. Even Fritz Connelly isn't that high on the totem pole, I don't think. The top people are quite high up in the world."

"Really? Well, in a way that makes sense, they'd be the ones who'd have a good reason to want to take over everything."

"They're dead serious about getting their goal accomplished this time. I'd imagine they think they've been hindered long enough and want to move forward."

"Now it makes me wonder all the more who Wayne Ellison is?"

"Yeah, that'll be interesting to find out."

"So no one has picked up any information yet?"

"Not that I've heard."

"I wish that Todd could remember something more."

Dave nodded. "It would be nice, but it wouldn't matter that much."

Sammi looked surprised.

"Look, honey, whoever that guy is, we know he's with the mob and he'll be doing his dirty work. So whether he's Wayne Ellison or has some other name he goes by, the results are the same."

The phone rang. It was Audrey.

Dave listened for less than one minute before the line went dead. Sammi was anxious to know.

"I don't think they know what's being planned for them. But Ron found out that they'll be getting another limousine for their use for the party on Friday. It seems that the present one has suddenly developed some mechanical problems. Seems like the plan is in action."

"So they have no idea, do they?"

"Don't think so. Give me a second; I have to let

the sarge know."

Dave clued in the sergeant and waited for the circle to complete.

It took no more than a half hour before the phone rang again. This time it was Ben Collier.

"Dave, put Sammi on the line, too."

"Okay, I'm here."

"Right, the message of the switch in limousines came from Amilio. He's on top of this. I told him about the demonstration tomorrow night. Dave, he wants you to be around the left side of the group, along the west side of the long porch. Try to be in about the third row back. He doesn't want anyone to see him talking to you. He'll find a way to get out in front along with the others. He thinks this surprise will have them all off their game. He'll take the opportunity to get out a message as to what exactly he needs us to do."

"Okay, I'll manage that. When we go in to disperse the demonstration, I'll be in the third row on the west side of the house."

"And he said not to look for him or to make any waves; he'll find you. Although he'll have to find a way to get sent out there, they'll be watching him carefully. He's still the new guy on the block."

"Got it."

"Dave, you know when you're into this kind of demonstration thing, anything can happen. If he misses you or can't get to you, he'll find another way. But he said, do not, under any circumstances make it seem that you're looking for someone. Try to keep the demonstrators under control and he'll do the rest."

"I understand."

"We're getting to the crucial time here and we've got to get this right. There aren't too many second chances available."

"I know. I'll do my best. I think I'll do like he does and just live out the part. I'm there to squelch a crowd from becoming out of control, concentrate on that, then I'll be playing my part right. The rest is up to him."

"Exactly. Oh, and one other thing. He said to tell you that even though he's the little brother here, he's giving the orders this time. He said you'd understand that line."

Dave laughed, "Yes, I do."

* * *

Dave could feel the anxiety coming from Sammi. She was always worried when he would be put in a precarious situation. And the demonstration was not a delight for her.

"Sammi, you can't always get so uptight. It's my job."

"I know, I know."

"And Tom and Jim will be there. We always look out for each other. And honestly, I don't think they'll even be any shots fired. This'll be a peaceful demonstration."

She wondered, "What's it supposed to be about anyway?"

"I think it'll be about citizens trying to push the mayor to do more about crime in a certain part of the city. Now, that should go over real well with Peter, but I can't imagine how he'll want Ron to respond."

"That seems to play up to him quite well."

"That's what the sarge thought."

Sammi was quiet for a few minutes. It was unusual and Dave had to comment.

"Okay, what's on your mind?"

Sammi had to admit her feelings. "I feel so out of it. I could be in the crowd and then I might pick up something valuable. What do you think?"

Dave looked at her in disbelief. "You've got to be kidding? In case you're not, the answer is No. If anyone recognized you it would send the wrong signal. And besides that, it's too dangerous for you. You've done your job and you did it well. Now it's our turn."

"I guess I want this to be over."

"Me, too. I especially want Friday night to be over."

There was nothing further to say. That ended the discussion for the evening.

* * *

Thursday, life at the precinct was hectic and stressful. Not everyone knew what was planned, yet the sarge had to keep enough police around so he'd have ample officers to dispatch to the mayor's house when the time came, making everything seem like a legitimate response. In the meantime, they had their usual duties and their usual routines of unruly characters, police chases with suspects being brought in and filling up their holding cells. People always wandered in off the streets needing different kinds of help and although the referees moved throughout the day in their usual official capacity, their minds were never far from the Thursday evening. They waited anxiously.

LeBron and Tyrone were not part of this event. They would go home after their shift around 5:00 P.M. and the officers on the afternoon shift would be the ones sent out. The disturbance was scheduled for seven o'clock. That meant that they would be dispatched by 7:30 P.M. or even sooner, depending on the reaction of the mayor and his people. The waiting was tough. Jim was on edge and Tom was somewhat anxious. Dave had to admit that he felt both of those feelings plus a little more.

Julie was working late and picking up a lot of activity on the computer. Memos were going by quickly referencing the fundraiser on Friday night. She came in right around six o'clock with coffee and a light snack. It was the right touch.

Sergeant Brady called them in around 6:15 P.M.

"Okay, now we're all in sync, right? Everybody knows where to go and where to be. Dave's going to be on the left side of the building or the west side, and he's to be there alone. You, two must work the crowd from the middle and the other side. I've got two units ready and waiting. That should be enough. I understand they'll have signs, about "Stop City Crime" or something like that. They plan to be quite loud and will create a lot of attention."

"Is this demonstration for real or not?" asked Jim.

"Yes, it's for real, but it was supposed to happen next week and we managed to get them to move it up to tonight. This'll work good for us."

"Okay."

"Any questions?"

They all shook their heads. This was a straight-forward assignment. It had a special purpose true, but they had all worked demonstration crowds many times in their careers. Every time was different, but the basics were the same. Usually they stuck closer together but other police would be around them and no one foresaw any problems. It was obvious that the sarge had a special reason for his placement of personnel, but no one questioned his reasoning.

No one but Dave and the sarge knew for sure that he would be getting a message. This undercover guy was kept almost hidden from the group as well. It was simply safer that way.

"Okay, we'll meet back here later and compare notes. That's all for now, except Dave, stay a minute longer."

"Look, we can tell Jim and Tom when we return, but I couldn't take a chance to tell them before. That was Ben's call. A look, or the semblance of a search, could tip them off. So far this agent's been perfect and Ben says that we play the game his way."

"Sure, okay by me. I'd have to agree anyway. But I won't look or search. I'll be working the crowd and that's all."

Dave thought the sarge looked quite nervous as he left the room. This was a big gamble they were taking, but there was no other choice. Oh sure, they could have taken the mayor and his wife out and hid them, but sooner or later they'd be caught and the results could be disastrous. No, this had to be done this way. And if they could take down enough of the main group on Friday night, they would have succeeded in returning Scranton to its proper ownership, at least for the foreseeable future.

* * *

Jim approached Dave. "Look buddy, I know you've been approached for something and I wanted to say good luck. I know the sarge has his reasons."

Dave looked worried. "This has to turn out okay. We've got to win this game."

Jim put his hand on Dave's back and said, "Hey, remember we're the referees."

Dave nodded as they both went to sit down and wait for the call. Their busy work was nothing now and their mind and attention was watching the clock pass that seven o'clock hour.

CHAPTER SEVENTEEN

Ron Stillman was in his huge great room when he noticed people begin to file across the front lawn. He called over Audrey immediately.

"What the hell's this about? You got any idea?"

"No, for God's sake."

About this time Peter came running into the room. He was never far from her husband and had seen some of the commotion from the window in the adjoining area.

"What the hell's going on?"

He turned to look at Ron. "You know anything about this?"

"No, I was hoping you did."

It didn't take more than another minute for Ron to hear the footsteps that he knew must belong to Josh Logan.

Josh seemed satisfied when he realized that both Ron and Peter were looking out the window. They were aware and that's what he wanted at the moment.

It took no more than fifteen minutes for the crowd of people to increase to a substantial number that deserved serious attention.

"What do they want?" asked Ron.

"I can't read the signs from here. Can anybody?"

They all shook their head. Audrey seemed quite flushed and agitated. She didn't know what to expect. Peter was taking count of the amount of people that kept increasing.

"There must be more than two hundred people out there."

Then the yelling started. It didn't even start off slowly, but began as a loud angry mob and didn't subside at all.

Peter said, "I'm calling the police. We've got to get some backup here in case we need them. Those people are angry."

* * *

The three referees were all together when the call came through. Sergeant Brady came out of his office and said simply, "It's a go. I'll send out the other units immediately and I want you guys to wait about five more minutes. Let them get there first."

They nodded in agreement. As they heard the sirens blaring out of the lot, they slowly walked to their vehicles.

Dave had to admit that his adrenalin was starting to move. He felt excited, nervous and stirred, but he was focused. This is how he usually reacted and he was glad that his normal behavior pattern was in tow. He worked best this way. His mind stayed fixated and his body followed the normal reactions that it had to go through in order for him to function properly. Yet at this moment, his mind was racing; he knew this contact meant a lot. But he had to remember to concentrate on controlling the mob. That was his only job. And he had learned a lot from Terry on this. *Just do your job, Dave*, he thought, *because Terry is more than capable of doing his.*

When he arrived at the mayor's house there were vehicles all over the place. Most of the mob had parked a ways away, some had been dropped off, but other police cars were situated part way into the circle driveway. As he stepped out, he saw that the crowd was definitely getting restless and although the earlier units were in place and handling the disturbance with precision as was expected in their usual pattern, they could have used extra help. About twenty policemen were expected to handle a crowd of more than two hundred people who were yelling and screaming and creating enough commotion to incite others who had remained calm up until this time. Crime in general was their topic with their friends and neighbors being killed and no obvious solutions, but they also were concerned about certain neighborhoods that were getting increasingly violent and this was their main focus. The signs read, "Save Our Children, Save Our Neighbor-hoods" and more of the same.

Dave crossed the lawn in time to situate himself in about the third row of people on the west side of the building. It seemed that more and more people were coming and he thought that this chaos must have Peter and Josh shocked and unprepared for what they should do. They'd had no advance warning and it must have thrown their plan off balance. He was thinking that this is why Terry would be so valuable to them at this time.

* * *

"What the hell are we supposed to do?" asked Josh. "There's too many of them for us to handle."

"Hold on, Hold on," said Peter. "The cops are out there, too. They'll keep everything under control; it's their job."

"But it's hard to tell from up here," said Ron. "We have to know what's going on? Where did this come from? The police have been investigating those areas and solutions were starting to happen."

"Obviously not quickly enough for some of them."

After a few more moments of watching the uproar from their window on the second floor, Peter said, "Josh, where the hell's Amilio? Get him up here right away. I need him."

Neither Ron nor Audrey looked at each other, but both knew they felt more secure if he was involved.

As he entered the room, he started talking immediately.

"A lot of commotion out there, amigo? What are those people upset about?"

Although Amilio spoke with an especially thick Spanish accent, no one had trouble understanding him.

"That's what we want you to find out. Get down there and see if you can help the police get some calm on this group. We need them to disperse and go home. But find out what it's all about? Can you do it?"

"Sure, you want me sneaking around in that mob and talking to them like I was one of them, right? Then I find out what they want and come back and tell you, right?"

"Yes, that's right, can you do it?"

"Of course, Peter. I do it for you."

"Go out that front door and let them know we mean business," he ordered.

"Boss, I give you what you want, but I work the way I want, comprendes?"

Peter looked surprised that someone working in his group wouldn't obey his orders immediately. But Amilio had caught him off guard; there was no doubt. Looking confused he asked, "You don't want to go out the front door?"

"No, no. That not be good. They see me coming out as part of your group ... that not good. I go out the back and sneak around into the crowd. I find out better things that way. Comprendes?"

Peter looked at him and was still thinking it over when Amilio added, "Okay, boss? You like my idea?"

Peter, in spite of himself almost had a slight smile cross his face. And this was unusual, even in better times.

"Okay, Amilio, you work your way; but find out what this damn commotion's about."

"Okay, Boss, Adios," he said and he slightly bowed to Peter as he left the room.

Audrey thought that Amilio knew how to work him. Sometimes she was beginning to wonder who was ordering who around. Amilio had his way of doing business and it included making people want to help him do it his way.

* * *

Amilio almost melted into the cement wall that covered the west side of the building. He caressed it with his body as if it held special powers for him, and in a way it did. It obscured him perfectly as he made his way around that side of the house toward the front. There were huge towering pampered bushes that had been over-grown for years which created a perfect hiding place for him as he made his way around one area in a concealed manner and then around to the next. He had to keep hidden so he could swiftly melt into the ever growing crowd that was already making its way around both sides of the building. They were spreading rapidly and he didn't want to get caught alone by himself. He needed to move fast and he did at the precise moment when one person dropped their sign. He was there to pick it up and gave it back receiving an appreciated smile. He became one of the group instantly.

Now he had to find Dave. He wasn't worried about finding out what this demonstration was all about. He could hear the people talking all around him and he'd have plenty to tell Peter to satisfy his confusion. No, he needed to find Dave. He looked for the uniforms and then he spotted him doing his riot prevention work as he should. He came up to him on his left side and said, "Don't turn around, big brother. I need you to face away from me right now."

Amilio was proud when Dave didn't react but

continued working the crowd. He nodded slightly and continued to subdue one person after another in a sensitive yet persuasive way. As he talked softly to some people to keep them under control, he was able to reason with others. He was doing as he was told. Amilio heard him talking to this one and that one and staying active in the surrounding group. Then he again managed to get close enough to Dave and relay a message in his left ear saying, "Friday, when we leave the driveway, there will be two cars following us, Peter and Josh. You've got to get rid of them right away. When we turn the first corner I'm doing my thing and they can't see me do it. The bomb will go off within five minutes of us leaving so I have to move them out fast. Got it."

He saw Dave nod again, then a nearby protester grabbed Dave's arm and spun him around. He found himself facing Amilio, but was able to fend off his enthusiastic supporter and didn't give one bit of attention to his contact, who moved away quickly. Dave was concerned because he didn't know if he had gotten the entire message. So he kept up his job as was part of his reason for being there. Shortly the crowd became quieter and the mayor, Peter and his bodyguard came out on the porch to address them.

"Folks, please be calm and stay in control. We are addressing these exact issues that you're demonstrating about."

One man in the crowd yelled, "We haven't seen any results. My kid got beat up real bad last night and he's in the hospital. He's only twelve. You've got to do something about these roving gangs."

"I'm sorry, sir. I promise you right now that we'll double up our efforts in your area and the surrounding areas by early next week. But we've got patrols out there more than ever before. We need some organized help from your neighborhood. Can we get some of you to help out, too?"

The crowd did quiet down after that. It seemed that in the last three weeks that several teenagers had been targeted and nothing seemed to be working. But with a discussion of help with the people themselves involved, they began to reassess the situation. It was the promise of meetings in the next week to set up patrolling with police and citizens that helped them believe they could finally work together.

Dave took a deep breath and looked around. He couldn't see anything else he had to do. He was worried about the message. Did he have it all? Did he understand what Amilio wanted? Then as he started to walk away from the crowd that was definitely thinning, he heard, *check your pocket when you get home.* He kept walking as if he'd heard nothing and thought that he must be getting better at this.

It was all he could do to leave the premises without checking his pockets. But he knew if anyone saw that, it could spell trouble. So he followed Amilio's instructions to the letter.

* * *

They all met back at the station where Sergeant Brady was waiting for them. Everyone was pumped up and the sarge told the trio that Dave had been designated to get a message from their undercover agent. He relayed the information.

But then he said, "Wait, I've got something else." He pulled out a piece of paper from his pants pocket and read it with surprise. It was actually a drawing of the front of the house, and it showed where all the cars would be as they left. It also had a picture of the first corner they would turn and then Amilio would stop the vehicle, get the mayor and his wife out and let the car blow up. Then everyone would think they were all killed.

"But I didn't think our agent would be the driver of the limo. How's he going to manage that?"

Dave said, "I've no idea, but I'm sure he will. He said he's got about five minutes after they leave the house before the bomb goes off. And he doesn't want Peter or Josh to see anything. They can't be allowed to see that he and the Stillmans made it out."

"Right," said the sarge. "That's what Ben said. He wants them to appear to be dead until we reel in a few of these characters. When we've got as many as we can, they'll resurface and hopefully we'll have foiled their plans for many years again."

"How long will they be missing?" asked Jim.

"Not more than a few days. Then we can say that the mayor and his wife were at the hospital being checked out and not too many will be suspicious. We want this to look like a random attack. We don't want to start a riot in our town and have people know what's been going on."

"Sure," said Tom, "if we get this under control again, there's no use scaring the public. This is such a cat and mouse game with these people."

"Okay, then," said the sarge. "I want all of you to get home and get a good night's rest; tomorrow is going to be one hell of a day."

* * *

Driving home Dave realized that the sarge must have been joking when he said to go home and get some rest. Who could sleep tonight? Sure, he needed it, but didn't think it would be possible for him. Terry was in extreme danger as was the mayor and his wife. And there was nothing they could do about it. Not yet, at least. But he knew that each had their job to do and that's the way the system worked. He smiled as he pulled into his driveway. Sammi would be waiting anxiously to find out what happened tonight.

And she was there waiting for him at the door. "I was getting worried."

"I know. I worry about you, too. But every-thing went smooth. The demonstrators got their point across to the mayor about a week earlier than anticipated, but that's okay, and I got my message from Terry...er...Amilio." Dave looked frustrated. "I'm going to have problems with that."

"So the plan is in action, right? Everything's set?"

"We're all set."

Dave told Sammi what the latest information was and how they planned to work it. She took a deep breath.

"Wow, that's so scary. I shouldn't say this, but what if the bomb malfunctions and detonates early?"

"We've all thought of that. I'm sure Terry has, too. But we have to work with what we've got. And that's it, right now."

Sammi nodded. "I feel so helpless."

"God, Sammi, without you this wouldn't have gone smoothly at all. You can't do it all, remember? We've all got our part to do. That's why we're a team and you're part of it, like Julie and Jill."

Sammi agreed but couldn't stop a few tears from forming in her eyes. "I guess I'm real nervous tonight, that's all."

"Me, too. We all are. But we've got a war to fight out there. Now the sarge said to get some rest, but I'm not sure about that. So let's relax tonight. That'll have to be good enough."

"Okay," and Sammi got out two glasses of their favorite wine. "I made us a snack and it'll be ready soon. Now you go take a rest on the couch, will you?"

Later she tiptoed into the living room hoping that Dave had fallen asleep. He laughed as he saw her. "No, I'm awake. I don't think that's going to happen tonight."

"Well, after some food and your glass of wine, you'll get more relaxed and that should help."

"Either way, I'll be ready to go tomorrow."

* * *

The next day everyone was sleepwalking through their usual routine of duties. No one was concentrating on their daily stuff. Their minds were on seven o'clock that night. And they all hoped that everything went off without a hitch.

Julie came over to Dave, "I've got some memos that are quite telling. This should tie some of them in with this latest adventure. Fritz is getting bold at the last minute, or he's nervous and not thinking. Even Ben doesn't think it's bogus. He's already talking about who the new mayor of Scranton will be. Personally, I think that's pretty dumb."

"But his lawyers could say that he was thinking that Ron would lose the election."

"No, he says he wants the new mayor in within one month."

"Holy shit, that seems so stupid."

"And part of it was in code. Maybe that's why he's relaxed. We've given no inkling that we know his code."

"I sure hope he has some surprises coming and soon. We need this character out of the way."

He looked up at Julie and said, "What?"

"There will always be others."

"I know, but I really think that they're going to leave us alone for quite a while after this. It will take them time to get some new leaders in place."

Julie nodded in agreement as she left. Yes, they probably would go and do their evil deeds somewhere else. And she hoped the others would be up to the task.

* * *

It was busy around the mayor's house that

Friday. Other than the usual duties they both had to do, they had to get ready for a fund raiser that was semi-formal at the Lackawanna Hotel. The banquet room was fairly spacious and they hoped to get a crowd of at least five hundred people and with any luck, closer to seven hundred and fifty. All the arrangements had been made and although Peter wouldn't admit it, this had been a last minute decision to hold this fund raiser tonight. Ron still wondered about that.

"This party wasn't on any of the agendas I'd seen. It was a last minute choice, but Peter won't admit it."

"He's a strange person and he always made me nervous, more so nowadays. I wonder what he's got in mind for tonight."

"Who knows? But I'll be glad to get this one over with. I'm tired today and could use a few days rest. I'm going to check my schedule and see if you and I can get a couple of days of R&R somewhere. We both need it."

Audrey smiled at Ron, came over and gave him a big hug. "Wouldn't that be great if we could work it out? We need to get away from all this activity once in a while. Oh, I'd love that."

Ron laughed out loud. "Me, too. And from now on I'm going to make sure that we have our time again like we used to. I've missed that. Sometimes I forget how much I miss it." Then he seemed to get embarrassed for a minute and added, "God sometimes I act like a stupid college kid."

"Well, it's that not-so-stupid college kid that I fell in love with years ago. So don't change too much, okay?"

There was a knock on his door. It was Peter. "It's already 6:30 P.M. and the limo driver hasn't shown up. We can't seem to get in touch with him. We may have Amilio drive you instead. I wanted you to know."

"Okay, Peter" said Ron. "We'll be down at the entrance at 7:00 P.M."

When he left Ron turned to Audrey. "Something funny's going on here. I'm always glad when Amilio's around, but that limo driver has never missed a day in all the time we've had him. And did you catch the look on Peter's face? It was like it was life and death if he didn't get us to that fundraiser."

"Well, if something's not running perfectly, that's how Peter reacts. Anyway, I'll feel better having Amilio with us."

"Yeah, I will, too. But it was that look on Peter's face. I don't know ... something."

"You mean more than usual. That guy's always a little strange. I hate the way he always trails right behind you. It looks weird."

"He sure is different."

"Okay, I'm ready. Let's make our way down to the driveway."

And when they left, arm in arm, Audrey, too, had a strange feeling that she chose not to share with her husband. And try as she may, she couldn't help her arm shaking a bit. She was sure he noticed it, too, but he didn't say anything either. They were both trying to keep a strong demeanor for each other. Yet each one knew that something serious was coming, if not tonight, real soon.

* * *

Amilio held the limousine door open for them. As he was about to close the door he slyly put his head halfway into the vehicle and said, "Be ready to move when I tell you, and move fast."

They both looked taken aback and slightly frightened, but nodded.

He smiled as he closed the door because Peter had suddenly appeared within five feet of him. He turned to him and said, "Amigo, what a beautiful evening. Great night for your party."

Amilio knew from Peter's mannerism and expression that the plan was in full gear. Too bad Peter had never learned to read people that well. For Terry/Amilio, that's what he had to do starting with his very young life. It's how he had survived in that poor Mexican orphanage, and now he had become a master at it. So when he looked at the facial expression that Peter gave him, he knew, without a doubt, that there was no change in plans, but that tonight was a go.

As he got into the driver's seat, he saw Peter head directly for his vehicle behind them and Josh was in another vehicle beyond that. He couldn't say that he wasn't nervous, but this present nerve-racking position was not unfamiliar to him. He had found himself in similar situations many times in the past. But this time he had two people he was responsible for, besides himself. So even though his palms were sweaty and his heart was racing, he forced his muscles to calmly perform their functions and turned on the ignition, waited for a moment and then slowly started driving down the long driveway to the street.

He looked into his rearview mirror. Peter was right behind him and Josh was behind Peter. When he reached the edge of the driveway, he looked both ways, but saw nothing as he turned the limousine to the right and started inching his way down the long block to the first and most important corner. He was gripping the steering wheel with clammy palms and counting the seconds in his mind. There was no room for error. He drove as slowly as he could and suddenly, as he'd hoped, there were cop cars pulling up behind him and stopping Peter's car and therefore halting Josh as well, giving him the protection and isolation he needed. He kept going as planned, increasing his speed slightly and turned the crucial corner. With one quick sweep of the area his eyes took in everything, and confirmed the grassy knoll to his right that held the large bushes that would give them temporary shelter.

He quickly pulled over to the curb and yelled to Ron and Audrey, "Get out NOW on the right side and head for those bushes."

He got out on the driver's side and purposely left his car door slightly open. Then he also ran for the bushes.

The Stillmans made it to the bushes in time, but Amilio was only part way there when the bomb went off. The debris came in all directions and a few pieces narrowly missed him. He quickened his steps and joined them out of sight, in safety behind a large tree type shrub that hid all three of them. Ron was visibly shaken and

Audrey was crying uncontrollably. They looked at him, and although he wasn't exactly calm, he was under control. He had to calm them down and move them on their way.

"Look, I knew what was coming, you didn't. Now we've got to get you both the hell out of here fast. We need people to believe you were killed."

"But when they see an empty car, they'll know," said Ron.

"We've got that covered."

Ron and Amilio held a stare for a moment. Ron then realized that this man had everything under control.

"Dave said you're the one to trust, and we do."

"Good. See that car over there, the white one," he said as he pointed. "Okay, here they come now. Go with them and they'll take you where we want you for the next few days. Someone will be in touch later tonight."

As they got up he said, "Oh, and we've got your children protected, too. And they'll know immediately you're alive."

"You've thought of everything."

Amilio looked concerned and said, "We hope so. We certainly hope so."

* * *

With sirens blasting and an ambulance showing up less than five minutes later, Amilio walked crookedly over from the knoll area as he looked bruised and acted confused and disoriented. Leaving his driver side door slightly open had caused it to blow off completely in the blast and gave the impression that Amilio had been blown several feet away from the vehicle himself. His unsteady gait and his confused mannerism confirmed this. His speech was slightly slurred and his answers didn't match the questions. The paramedics put him on a gurney and took him immediately to the hospital.

It was a short time later that Peter and Josh showed up excitedly beside him and began to ask questions, "What the hell happened?"

Paramedics and nurses shoved them in the background, but they still managed to find their way beside him.

"Don't know, amigo. I think it may have been a bomb."

"Where's the mayor and his wife?" asked Peter.

"Don't know. They went ahead of me. Not sure they made it."

The look on Peter's face said it all. That's what he was waiting to hear. He couldn't have been more pleased.

"What happened to you, amigos? You were supposed to be right behind me?"

"There were all kind of police cars that showed up and stopped us saying some stupid stuff about driving too close behind an official limousine. It was pure crap. We didn't see anything when it happened."

"You're lucky. I'm sure it wasn't fun to see."

Then Peter and Josh were pushed aside by the police and couldn't make it close enough to hear the important questioning. And the police weren't at all concerned about the ranting and ravings that they caused.

Amilio went through a long session of questioning about every detail for their reports and he was tired from raw nerves and exhaustion when it was over. He'd heard that Peter and Josh wanted to see the mayor and his wife's bodies, but were refused. Peter was quite angry and tried to insist, explaining his position as the mayor's chief of staff. He was escorted out of the premises while he was still yelling that it was his right and that he wanted to confirm their deaths as part of his official obligation.

Peter and Josh remaining free was Ben's call. They needed a few more pieces of the puzzle to fit in order to tighten the noose around their necks and they didn't want Fritz or Wayne Ellison to suspect anything at this point. No arrests would be made for now. All in due time; everything would be handled by the book.

* * *

After a few hours, Dave finally had a moment of privacy with Terry/Amilio.

"Hey, big brother. Good to see you again." He had the same lilt in his voice and the same quirky attitude that Dave had so loved about him in the past.

Dave could only shake his head, but couldn't stop tears.

"Hey, no tears. I wasn't in the limousine. I got out in time."

"But I already mourned you once when you were shot and drowned," he said trying to make light of the situation, "How many times do I get to do that?"

Amilio got serious. "Sorry about that. It was out of my hands." Then seeing the caring and affection crossing Dave's person he said, "I love you, big brother. I'm glad we're together again."

Dave was choked up. "I love you, too, little brother and I hope in the future you'll listen to me."

Amilio smiled and shrugged his shoulders. "It's what I do."

"I had no idea how terrific you were at your job. You certainly put me to shame, actually all of us. It's hard for me to call you little brother now."

"Oh no, I want to be your little brother," he said seriously. "Remember I don't have any relatives and you mean so much to me. You took me under your wing when I first came here. You accepted me and looked out for me, and honestly, Dave, I do love you like a brother. I want you to be my big brother."

"My pleasure," he said, but he couldn't hide his emotions.

"So what did you think of Marlina? Pretty sharp, right?"

"Yes she is. She's a lovely gal. A little crazy, though; she's in love with you."

That made him laugh. "And I'm going to marry her. And besides that ... No, I don't think I'll tell you yet; I'll keep that as a surprise."

"I don't think I can take any more surprises from you."

Then the door to the room opened and Amilio started talking in his best Spanish accent. "I tell you I don't know any more. God, all of you officers keep asking me the same thing. I don't know any more than that."

Dave turned in time to see Peter and Josh enter the room. They simply nodded to him.

"We wanted to see how you're doing."

"I'm okay, amigos, but tired of all these questions. I've got one hell of a headache, but no broken bones. But they want to keep me here for a few days. I guess they like me."

That made them all smirk, even Peter.

"Okay, well you call me when you're ready and I'll come and get you. We have a lot of work to do."

"Oh yeah, what you got for me now? I mean, we've got no mayor."

"We've got an acting mayor right now, but we have to help out to establish who will be the new mayor."

"Oh yeah, we get to do that?"

Peter seemed nervous as he realized that he had probably misspoken and suddenly restrained himself.

"Well, we don't personally decide, but we have to keep things running smoothly here."

He and Josh left quickly after that.

Turning to Dave he said, "I think he slipped up on that one, don't you?"

"He thought so, too," said Dave. "I didn't know they wanted to keep you for a few days."

"They don't know it either," he said with a wink.

Dave had to laugh.

"I think protecting myself is second nature to me. Anyway, I don't think they're onto me, but I can't take that chance. To what Ben said, they'll round them all up within a few days. Then I'll be able to leave."

"That's a good idea. I spoke with Ben earlier today and he's waiting on a few more loose ends."

"Speaking of that, I think we're going to need Sammi in on the questioning and stuff. Then we know we've got all of them."

Seeing the surprised look on Dave's face he said, "Look, I know she's the one who took me down. She's one smart lady. But I'm a lot like Ben. We've talked about Sammi at length and neither one of us can figure out how she does it, but she's good. She's got to be to keep me fooled. We need all the help we can get in order to discover their secret data. This group needs to go away for a long time and Ben says that information seems to start floating in whenever Sammi's around."

Dave shook his head and said, "She's got a lot of people fooled."

Amilio said, "And I hate puzzles I can't solve."

"You won't get it out of me. By the way, who knows about you around here?"

"Just you, I think; and Sammi, right?"

Dave nodded.

"But I'll have to see what Ben has in mind in the future."

When he finished, Terry/Amilio had a strange look on his face. He definitely had a secret he was holding back and this time Dave couldn't imagine.

* * *

It took less than three days for the FBI in

connection with the Scranton police and the Pennsylvania State Police to realize that they had enough to round up these guys before they got too suspicious and started scattering. No one was more surprised than Peter Armors, especially when they arrested him under the name of Willie Sanford. And now he had no one to track; no one to follow. His entire world had fallen apart and he was going to jail again, and this time it would be on three counts of attempted murder, plus a string of other charges. Also his memos to Wayne Ellison were forwarded on to Fritz Connelly, so the trail of memos was further proof of the entire connection of the higher ups.

Josh Logan was an accomplice who allowed and helped in the commission of the crimes. So he was going away, too. But Senator Kris Kaphle was off the hook. It was found out that he was an unwilling participator in everything. They'd had two members of his family back in Nepal abducted and threatened to kill them if he didn't cooperate. They had them rounded up before making their move in Scranton. That was also part of the three-day delay. And now with his family safe and secure, he had a lot of information and testimony that would be helpful to the police. He was happy to be on the right side of the law; this was the place he cherished. And he would do all he could to help in the arrest and conviction of these criminals.

Wayne Ellison turned out to be Fritz Connelly's adopted son and together they had been trying to be as close to the kingpins in this part of the country as they could be. Other than these latest crimes, they were responsible for several more and now that they had been found, they would be held responsible and charged for other crimes as well. The net had definitely closed in tightly.

"We sure brought down a lot of this operation, didn't we?" said Jim. "It feels good."

"And even though we know it'll never end, several pieces of this particular group are out of commission for a long time, and maybe they'll never make it out in time to commit more," added Tom.

Dave sat there with LeBron and Tyrone enjoying the success of the moment. If his dad had been there he would be saying, *Enjoy the successes. That's what makes this job bearable.*

"Next week they're bringing down Fritz Connelly and Wayne Ellison from Colorado. I understand Ben wants Sammi in on questioning that group."

"Yep," said Dave. "She'll be working with us again."

Tyrone said, "Who's that guy who worked for the mayor? They said he was quite good."

"Yeah, he was," said Jim. "I think he's new around here."

"Good thing he was on top of things. Otherwise, the mayor and his wife wouldn't be enjoying the rest of his tenure. God damn, that was a close call. Somebody out there knew what they were doing."

Dave sat way back in his chair. He felt a lot of pride for what Terry/Amilio had accomplished. Whoever his parents were, they should be proud of him. He was definitely one of a kind.

Then the call came and the referees were being called back into the sarge's office. What could possibly be happening now?

* * *

The sarge looked strangely at Dave as they all walked in and sat down. He got up and closed his door.

"This is not a meeting that anyone else should overhear. It's entirely confidential," he said.

Everyone caught his look of astonishment because he kept eyeing Dave; they knew he was involved. Dave on the other hand was hoping that these three would finally be brought into the loop. It had been a hard burden to carry alone.

"Well, I've been given some rather shocking news a few moments ago. Dave has known for a while, but was under orders to keep quiet." Turning to Dave he said, "This must have been tough. Even Ben felt bad forcing you to hold this alone."

Jim and Tom shifted in their chairs. They looked at Dave and back to the sarge waiting anxiously for the word to get out.

"Terry Gonzalez is alive."

Sergeant Brady threw it out there. He felt it was the best way. There was no easy way to alleviate the shock so he plopped it out there and gave them a minute to have the information settle into their brain. At first they seemed in a daze. Then the questions began and he told them the story and they all discussed the cleverness of this one cop/agent.

"Holy shit," was Jim's first reaction. "You mean Amilio is Terry. I talked to him directly for several minutes at the hospital after the bomb thing and I never guessed anything."

Dave said, "He's great. He fooled his fiancé for almost ten minutes before he told her. She thought he was dead at first, too. He's a master at what he does."

Tom said, "And we used to think of him as a rookie."

"That's because he wanted us to think that. He's so damned good at what he does."

"Lucky for us," said the sarge. "Lucky for him, too."

Jim said, "Must be a hell of a worry for his family."

"He doesn't have any family, Jim," said Dave. "He was raised in a Mexican orphanage and had to learn early on how to wheel and deal. That's how this started out, as a survival technique, and look how high he's come."

The sarge had to present a reminder. "Only the four of us know about this and that's the way it must remain. No one else. Terry will now be known as Amilio, a totally different person."

"Of course Sammi knows. She's the one who became suspicious," said Dave.

The sarge looked over at Dave and said, "Sammi always knows."

The shock was still lingering for the sarge, Jim and Tom. It was like he had been resurrected to them.

"What's he going to do now?"

"Haven't heard," said the sarge. "But anybody

would be lucky to get him."

Dave was silent again and then he had something unpleasant to say, "Sammi got another note yesterday. Same type of crap. I don't think it'll ever end."

"Still, bring it in and get it on record."

Dave nodded. "I think Linda set this up before she went away after the trial as kind of a vendetta, so it'll keep happening. She has a crusade against us and we'll have to live with it."

"But I'd think they're empty threats now, don't you think?" said Jim.

"I hope so, but Julie told me the other day that the emblem on top of that letter that we tried to identify for so long, well, she's pretty sure that it's connected with this group that wants global takeover of the world."

"No kidding."

"Of course, their fight will never be finished. When Fritz and Wayne are gone, others will take their place. And it will go on and on, long after we've left this planet."

"That's true, but we can hammer away at our little part of the world."

With that comment, their discussion returned to Terry/Amilio as he had mesmerized them all and they were all trying to pull up memories which confirmed how talented he was. And because of his talent, the mayor and his wife had been returned to their home, albeit a special unit would be in place until further notice. But trusted and known aides were in place. Tony Baran, who had been forced out almost two years ago, was returning to help out and bringing with him his trusted associates. The mayor's office, in Scranton was once more on steady ground.

CHAPTER EIGHTEEN

"What the hell are we supposed to do? We can't cancel the plans now. Some of those people out there would be suspicious and want to know why. It's already been announced in all of the newspapers and it's played out in every TV news show I know of. No, no. That would send the wrong message." Dave was exasperated and it showed.

They had all gathered at his house to discuss another hot topic. No one could decide what to do. They seemed locked into another happening. So they all sat there shifting in their chairs, looking at each other and wondering what type of craziness were they involved in now. They had to continue and pretend.

Sammi spoke next. "I have to agree with Dave on this one. We can't cancel this funeral now. Most of the plans have been made. What else can we do?"

"Does seem silly, but that's because we know the reason. Look, Terry ... or whoever's in that putrid little nothing grave will get moved and given a heroes' funeral. That's the one thing that makes sense. It will look like the police department found out that Terry wasn't a mole, but a double agent, and wanted to give him a good policeman's burial. We have to do it." Jim was quite adamant.

"I don't think there's any question. Does anybody disagree?" asked Dave.

No one spoke.

"Okay, then, on Friday, we're having a first-rate funeral procession to the burial place for this top-ranked cop. We have to do it. And he's getting a special burial plot reserved for heroes. It's been set up for a while now."

Tom shook his head. "Only Terry could get us in this position. But honestly, that will convince anyone out there who's paying attention that he really is dead. This funeral will acknowledge that and help our cause at the same time."

Jim laughed. "You've got to see the humor in this because it's kind of funny in a way. I'm glad he's alive and someone who was a pauper most of his life will be getting one hell of a burial."

"Has anyone decided what the inscription on his grave will be?" asked Sammi.

Dave blurted out, "Maybe we should ask Terry."

Jim wanted to know, "Where's he at these days?"

"I heard he went back to Philly to spend some time with his girlfriend."

Dave said, "Oh yeah, and she'll be coming to the funeral. I know, I know," he said as he looked around and saw the glazed expressions, "but she has to be here and play her part. Basically, this is crazy, but we've got a war going on out there and Terry has to be protected and indisputably believed dead for his safety and so he can be of some value in the future."

Jim laughed. "I know, but something about this sounds like an episode of the Twilight Zone."

* * *

A few days later work at the precinct started out routinely, which was a pleasure to most of the officers. But then, as usual as of late, Sergeant Brady called his main staff into his office.

"Looks like we're going to be getting another addition to our group. The chief thinks that with all of the business we've had to conduct lately, well, they've found funds to hire a few more cops and we get one. He'll be in later today. That's all for now."

They all congregated at Dave's desk for a few minutes.

LeBron says. "That's good. We need all the help we can get. Lately it's been a nightmare. As for me, I'm glad.

"Sure, we are, too," said Jim. "I hope he has some experience. A rookie is always hard at first, but everyone has to start somewhere."

Just then word came through that the trials of Brian Hatterly and Spike Evers would be starting next week. Everyone would have to be available for that, even Sammi. So it didn't seem that there would be much chance to relax. They all knew that the interrogations on the attempted murder case of the mayor and his wife would be starting in a few weeks as well and wouldn't stop anytime soon. There was so much work to be done and the defense lawyers were already screaming for more time and more information to be released. That mob group had so many lawyers and each with their own expertise. They knew this would be a battle to the end.

Dave felt bad when he told Sammi that they'd have to postpone their vacation again for a while. But she planned a four day weekend to a secret location and they both felt satisfied with that. They could take a longer vacation later on.

"Here we go again," said Jim. "We never work on one case at a time. It's always several things."

"Could be worse," said Tom. "You could have a boring job."

Dave laughed, "Not much chance of that around here."

Then Dave got a call from Ben Collier. "I never got much of a chance to thank you and Sammi for all you both do, but consider it done. Sometimes I wish the both of you would consider working for the FBI."

"I thought we did," said Dave, "at least it seems that way sometimes."

"I'm sure it does," Ben answered as he took the teasing lightly. "But we work so well together. At least you guys come to our help when we need it. I don't ever want to lose that."

"And you won't."

There was a pause, which made Dave wonder if there was another reason for the call.

"So you called to thank us, or is there something else?"

"You're getting to act a lot like Sammi these days, did you know that?"

Dave laughed; Sammi would enjoy that one.

"Honestly, I needed to talk for a moment. You

and Sammi have got to be the most intuitive people that I work with. I've been mulling around in my mind about Fritz and Wayne. We've got them and the evidence is solid, but you never know. And I wonder who's right behind them waiting to take over."

"You sound like me and Sammi. Can't tell you how many nights we've moved that around in our conversation. But the way this game seems to be played is that we have to wait until a problem arises, then we have to try and solve it."

"I know. I wish we could ..." and Ben didn't finish.

"I think you need a few days off, Ben. When was the last time you had a vacation?"

He laughed. "Not for a long time. My wife says the same thing."

"Sammi and I'll be taking one before long. You have to do it, too. And when another problem arises, we'll all work together again and give it our best shot. That's all any of us can do."

Ben was quiet for a moment then said, "I think that's why I called you. I needed to hear something like that."

"We all do. Hang in there."

* * *

Late Tuesday afternoon, the sarge called his entire department into the conference room. When Dave walked in, he nearly fell over. There sitting on the far side of the room next to Sergeant Brady was Amilio Hernandez, alias Terry Gonzalez.

"Okay, everyone. I wanted to introduce you to the newest member of our department. This is Amilio Hernandez. I'm putting him in Dave Patterson's group and I'm sure he'll be an asset to our section. Some of you may recognize him; he worked for the mayor for a while and was the limousine driver that made it through that bombed out vehicle. So he has a pretty thick head. He also has tons of valuable experience that I'm sure he'll share with us. We want to welcome you, Amilio, and hope you'll like working with our group."

And in his thick Spanish accent, Amilio said, "Thank you, Sergeant Brady." Then he began, "Amigos, it'll be my pleasure to work with all of you. I've looked forward to it for a long time. I know that I'll have a lot to learn and I'll do my best for you. Gracias."

With that most of the officers went up and shook his hand and introduced themselves. When it was over, Dave told Amilio to follow him and he'd show him his new desk.

"Can't I have my old desk back?" he asked.

"No, Tyrone has it. But we brought up another one and it's right on the other side of me. It's fairly new and it's close by so I can keep my eye on you."

"Seems like old times, right?"

Dave looked over and said, "Much better."

"What are we working on?"

"Only car chases and speeders, right now. We've got to sort out all of the interrogations from the mayor's stuff and oh yeah, you missed that kidnapped woman case."

"I heard about that. Sarge says that it was part of the diversion, too."

"Here you are all Mexican, talking Spanish, looking the part. How can you do it all?"

"Well, Dave, I am Mexican so that's natural to me. But I've always been a good pretender. It got me through some tough times growing up. And now, I guess I'm still a little kid at heart."

"I'm not going to push this with you, but I think you're amazing."

"That's because you're my big brother. Big brothers are supposed to believe in their little brothers. You see, I told you that you were a natural."

The week moved on and Amilio got into the swing of business quickly. But then, it was like coming home to him. Dave even thought they might have to rename their group the four referees. Jim and Tom liked the idea, too. And they prepared for the coming weeks that would be quite difficult. Amilio had special and unique testimony that would be impossible for them to refute, but Sammi had gathered her own set of details that were proving to be extremely valuable. And as it turned out, Amilio was still quite impressed by her.

* * *

Friday morning about 9:30 A.M. the routine changed. Amilio asked the question at a time when Tyrone and LeBron were within earshot. So he got an answer that was meant for Amilio, the new kid on the block.

Dave said, "We're all getting ready to go to a funeral. In truth, the funeral has already taken place, but we had a cop a while back who was thought to be a mole in the department. So he got a shameful uneventful burial, not acknowledged at all by the police department. We've found out since that he wasn't a mole, but in fact, was a double agent. So today we're moving his casket to a special unique place reserved for heroes. We want to give him a heroes' burial."

Dave couldn't believe it, but that was the first time that Amilio kept his mouth shut. He couldn't think of anything to say. And Dave felt justified in throwing a smirk in his direction. The sarge and the referees had purposely kept this funeral a secret from him.

When the group scattered some, Amilio was right beside him.

"I don't have to go, do I?" he asked.

"Of course you're invited, we want the entire department to attend, no exceptions." He said his comments rather loudly so anyone in ear shot could hear.

Amilio shifted his position a few times.

"Marlina will be there as well. She felt she had to attend and show her respects to her dead fiancé."

Again, Amilio said nothing, but his expression remained serious as well as stunned.

"Dave, you're pushing this thing too far."

"The funeral change and reason for it had already been announced in all the newspapers and reported all over TV. We decided we couldn't change our minds now without arousing suspicion. You're stuck."

"That means I have to attend my own funeral.

I feel like Tom Sawyer."

"Today, you are Tom Sawyer."

Amilio took a deep breath and remarked, "I think I've been had. This is the price I have to pay."

"And you can ride with me, little brother. I know it must be tough to attend your own funeral, but it will prove to everyone who might have any doubt left that you really are dead. This isn't a game we're playing and you should know it more than most."

"I'm done. I can't even think of a reason to refuse."

Dave looked at him searchingly. "I can hardly believe that."

And they laughed as they got into the squad car.

* * *

The funeral service at the grave site was impressive. All of the officers were there in their best uniforms and the coffin was draped in the proper policeman's burial cloth. It was a beautiful sunny day and Sammi, Jill, Julie and Marlina all sat close together in the front row. Dave and Amilio pulled back a little.

"Kind of hard to see yourself going into the ground. Well, I know it's not me, but ... Did you ever find out who that guy was?"

"Personally, I didn't, but I think Ben knows. He was a vagrant and no one really knew his story, but it seems fitting to me that he'd end up with this nice burial plot, don't you think?"

"Yeah," said Amilio. "I like that idea. Kind of like sending him off in style."

Marlina was given the casket memorial drape and she did shed tears that were not manufactured. She had mourned his death once and knew that the second close call could have ended in a real funeral for him. Her tears were of fear for the danger he faced every day.

But Amilio had a different take on it. "I know why she's crying. She told me that ever since she was a little girl that she wanted to be Mrs. Terry Gonzalez. And although, she's glad I'm still alive it does change things. I can never be who I really am."

"That must be hard."

"But it's okay. All for a good cause, and this way I can keep Amilio alive. He was so important to me in my early life. I don't think I would have made it without him, or at least not as easily. He was a great kid, helped me out and he overcame a lot. But he got caught up in that drug stuff. So now, every time I can do something good using his name, I tell him silently, it's for him."

"That's nice."

"But I told Marlina that when we get married I'm adding Terrence as my middle name. Amilio didn't have one so I'm giving him mine. That way I can still be who I am, sort of. Does that make sense?"

"It does. I understand."

As they were walking out of the cemetery, they all met up and decided to go somewhere to eat.

The guys stood and talked for a few moments. "This isn't over by any means. There are still so many loose ends to be tied up," said Tom.

Jim said, "And I'd like to know about those Pastern Papers. I'm not sure I have the name right, but Sammi was concerned."

Dave said, "Sammi was never sure she got the name right either, but it does seem to be a log for this organization. Would be great to find out about that."

"And Linda marrying that Wayne Ellison. What was that about?"

Jim offered, "Not sure yet, but it seems she was around when they killed someone and they threatened to testify that she was involved if she didn't cooperate with them."

"Nasty business," said Dave.

"But she chose her life ... I mean, she targeted that cop." It was obvious that Tom held no sympathy for her.

* * *

As they walked toward the cars, Amilio singled out Sammi. He wanted a few words with her, but she started the conversation.

"Amilio, you're really something. Dave is so proud of you."

"And I'm proud of him. He was a good teacher for me. He taught me a lot."

She smiled proudly.

"But I want to talk about you. I know you're the one who figured out I was the mole. You took me down alone. That's amazing to me. I'm not sure how you did it."

Sammi didn't answer.

"Oh, I'm not asking for your secrets. But I wanted to tell you that I think you're very good, too, because I can't figure you out at all. Ben and I've talked about you. We thought that either you're psychic," but then he saw her wrinkle her nose. "I know, Ben says you hate that word, so I thought you could be one of those intuitive people or you simply know things. Anyway, I think you're a good match for me. You've become my biggest challenge and someday maybe I'll figure out how you do it."

"Maybe you will," was all that Sammi would say.

"Bottom line is that I wanted to tell you that I admire you a lot. You're quite good."

"Thanks, Amilio, I appreciate that. And I have a question for you?"

"Oh yeah, what's that, Sammi?"

"What inscription do you want on your grave?"

Amilio smiled, thought for a moment and answered in a rather tongue-in-cheek style as he said, "How about "Gone, but still around somewhere."

Sammi laughed. "That seems to say it all. I'll make sure it gets added."

And then they all entered their individual cars and headed for the restaurant. Sammi was somewhat thoughtful on the way. She had Todd Mayfair, Jill's brother, trying to figure out how she knew things, and now she had Amilio wondering, as well as Ben, who'd never totally given up. Luckily they were all on the same side of the law, the right side. And they could have their suspicions, all they wanted. But they didn't know. And they wouldn't. She would see to that. Besides, she enjoyed playing the game with them.

5086433R0

Made in the USA
Charleston, SC
27 April 2010